Shoot The Moon
By Iain Henderson

To my mother Fiona and my partner Sharon for all their love and support, and to my beautiful children Jess and Will; I love you all.

1

Tearing through the dark city streets, Mickey's eyes flicked to his mirror. The chasing pack were miles behind – if only he could get rid of the chopper. Appearing to circle ever lower, its brilliant light continued to flood through his windscreen; blinding him with every revolution.

How on earth had they got above him so quickly? And of all the nights to be chased, why did it have to be tonight! Still, only half a mile to go; he just had to stay focused, they'd soon be home and dry.

The empty road was dead straight ahead, with green lights shining brightly in the distance. He briefly glanced down at the speedo; 110 and climbing. There was no need to slow, he'd just bury the throttle, and feel the horses kick in. Eating up the tarmac, his turbocharged Audi raced towards the intersection, and then suddenly he spotted it...

Right at the edge of peripheral vision, there was movement; rapid movement!

In an instant he reacted. Lifting his foot off the gas, his head spun to face the danger. Blazing headlights on a collision course charged towards him. What the fuck were they doing; *their* lights were on red!

Ignoring the screams rising from his friend's mouths, he yanked on the wheel and plunged his brake pedal down. Instantly, the Audi's bonnet nose-dived towards the tarmac; its stability systems struggling to remain in control.

But the black blur was already upon him.

Almost in slow-motion, it began to cross his path; its alloys disappearing beneath his dipping bonnet, its four terrified occupants twisting in their seats towards him.

Clinging onto his steering wheel, he braced himself for impact...

***

For the Heartlands Hospital staff, it had been a typical weekend nightshift: drunks, drunks and more drunks. But now, with the last of their patients safely patched up and sent away, they'd just about settled down for a well-earned break when the red phone's shrill ring spoilt any thoughts of relaxing.

Reaching across from her chair, the Sister took the call.

"Okay everybody, listen up," she said, taking to her feet. "We've got a major incident coming in; a serious RTC with multiple casualties. Come on, get moving, the first one's almost here!"

***

Inside the ambulance, a cop and a medic struggled to keep Mickey restrained. Fighting for balance, they desperately fought to keep him pinned down; his frantic thrashings having ripped away the last of his stretcher's straps.

"Where the hell's his strength coming from?" the officer shouted above the sirens. "He should be dead after what he's been through!"

"Don't be fooled mate! He might be delirious, but we could lose him any moment. His head's taken a battering, his heart's over-stressed; we've got to sedate him somehow!"

Charging through the streets, the battle inside continued. Thrown one way then the other, Mickey's rescuers were running out of time; their energy draining…their patient about to break free.

Lights blazing, they flew through the hospital gates and raced on up the drive. But even as they screeched to a halt beside the awaiting trauma team, the fight carried on regardless. Shoving the medic aside, Mickey twisted on the stretcher; his pupils fixed on the cop, his fist clenched ready to strike.

His strength ebbing away, the officer's options were running out. Diving on top of his manic patient, he grabbed at the flailing arm…just as the rear doors flung open.

"Quick!" he shouted to the trauma team scrambling on board. "He's goin' mental!"

Calmly, efficiently, they swiftly set to work. Seconds later, extra straps bound Mickey's body like a mummy. Turning his right arm over to reveal a throbbing artery, the doctor prepared a needle.

Vein pierced, Mickey's arched body began to deflate.

"Right, that'll make things a little easier," the doctor reassured. "Now get him inside; let's see if the poor blighter survives!"

***

"This had better be important," J.T. growled into his mobile. "Don't you know it's the middle of the bleedin' night?"

"I'm sorry boss," the voice replied. "But there's an update on the raid tonight…and it's not good news."

Swinging his legs out of bed, J.T. made his way to the bathroom. "What do you mean 'it's not good news'? When I went to sleep, you assured me everything had gone to plan. All they had to do was get back in one piece!"

The other end remained silent.

"Porter – what the hell's been going on?"

"Well it's all a bit sketchy at the moment," his henchman began. "But from what I can make out, they were picked up by the chopper and chased back to Birmingham. Apparently they split up, and returned separately…which is when it happened."

"When what happened? Don't piss me about Porter, what the fuck happened!"

"Erm, well it appears as though…"

"Porter!" J.T. thundered. "Spit it out!"

"Okay, okay," Porter stammered. "Mickey's totalled his motor; the lads are in a bad way."

"I don't give a shit how *they* are! All *I* want to know is, what's happened to my watches? If they've lost as much as one fucking Rolex!"

"I'm afraid it's significantly more than one. Although the third car's returned with a bagful, the rest were in Mickey's motor; we've lost about half."

"Half!" J.T. exploded, hurling his mobile against the tiles. "He needs to pray he doesn't walk out of that hospital," he shouted at the shattered pieces, "'Cos if he does – I'll break *him* in fucking half!"

***

Walking out of hospital was looking increasingly unlikely. While J.T. raged, Mickey's life was ebbing away.

"He need's hooking up; we're losing him!" the doctor demanded, diverting the stretcher to resus.

Like clockwork, the trauma team sliced through Mickey's blood-stained clothing, before attaching the spaghetti like leads.

"Heart rate's dangerously high!" the ECG nurse called out.

"I'm not surprised after what this lad's been through," the doctor replied. "Be ready to 'shock' him; he could arrest any second! I want CAT scans the moment he…"

Suddenly the curtains burst apart; a red-faced nurse rushed in.

"Ambo control are back on the phone. They say the second one'll be here any moment, and there's another one flat-lining at the scene!"

Shaking his head, the doctor looked down at his unconscious patient.

"If what we've heard is true, and this lad's responsible for the carnage, he may not want to survive the night. Still, we're not here to judge; we're here to keep him alive. Keep an eye on his vital signs, make sure he's stabilised, and clear a space for the next two," he instructed, glancing at his watch. "The golden hour's ticking; they need to get here before it's too late!"

***

Transferred to intensive care, Mickey lay unconscious throughout the morning; his organs maintained by machines.

By mid-afternoon, temperature, heart rate and breathing were well under control, and as a medical party shuffled to a halt beside him, the sister read aloud from his clipboard.

"Bed number 6, Michael Wilding, eighteen years. Arrived twelve hours ago, another victim of his own actions," she stated matter-of-factly. "According to the police, he was driving a stolen car involved in a high-speed collision. Currently under sedation, he's critical but stable."

"I see," the consultant nodded. "And tell me, how's he coping?"

"To be honest, it's still too early to tell. But he's made it this far, so he's in with a fighting chance."

Taking hold of the notes, the consultant turned a page. "MRI, CAT scans? Have we had the results yet?"

"Due to the bleeding inside his skull they're not very clear I'm afraid. However, we have identified some swelling to his brain. Should his condition deteriorate, we'll need to consider operating to release the pressure."

"Continue round-the-clock observations," the consultant nodded, handing back the clipboard. "If there *are* any major changes, contact me immediately."

To their side, Mickey's open mouth released a barely audible groan; his disturbed mind rushing from one nightmare to another. But time and again it returned to the carnage he'd been confronted with as he'd sluggishly come round at the scene. Through shattered glass and twisted metal, a haze of blue light had initially blurred his vision. Agonisingly, his head had rolled to the left, focusing on the reason for his nightmare. There, in what remained of his seat, his life-long friend sat facing him; chin resting limply on chest. Staring at the blood-covered face, his mouth began to form the word 'Danny' over and over again.

His voice gaining in volume, the medical team's discussion swiftly broke off.

"Quickly sister, increase the sedation before he comes to!" the consultant ordered.

But Mickey's eyes were already wide open; darting wildly from side-to-side. Muscles tensing, veins bulging, he suddenly sat upright, screaming, "Danny! Danny! Danny!"

"Now Sister! Before he arrests!"

His dose dialled up to the max, drugs rushed into his rigid body, but couldn't reach their target in time.

With his senses shutting down once more, only the medics could hear the high-pitched monotone alarm to his side. Even as they scrambled to attach defib paddles to his bare chest, Mickey's tunnel of light was slowly constricting. For a moment though, it paused, settling on childhood memories with Danny, and then…

And then the light went out.

2

"You goin' to school tomorrow?" Mickey asked.

"Nah, can't be arsed," Danny replied. "Teacher's doin' my head in."

Shivering in the frosty November gloom, the eleven-year-olds hurried towards the Estate's chippy. With shoulders hunched, and hands thrust deep inside his hoody's pockets, Mickey thought about what they'd get up to if he skipped school with his mate.

"How about we make a guy, and go collecting?"

"Can do," Danny shrugged. "There's always mugs on the posh estate who'll cough up some dough."

Darkness gave way to streetlights as they approached The Square. Apart from the pub opposite, 'The Golden Plaice' was the only surviving business; the others boarded up, covered in graffiti.

Entering the chip shop's warm shelter, Mickey wiped the snot from his nose, and standing on tiptoes, placed his order.

"The usual please."

"Coming right up," replied Mr Bambos, whose shop had survived the inner city challenges by virtue of his man mountain physique, quick temper, and meat cleaver beneath the till. "Any news on your dad?"

"Nah, still banged up I think."

Suddenly, the shopfront was ablaze. Powerful headlights flooded through the steamy windows, while screaming tyres sent the boys scrambling to the door. Practically tripping over each other, they dived onto the pavement outside.

"It's an AMG Mercedes!" shrieked Danny.

Screeching away from the boys, the high performance motor charged to the far side of The Square before spinning 180-degrees.

"Wow, did you see that handbrake!" Mickey grinned. "Who do you think's behind the wheel?"

"It's got to be Deano, he's the king!" Danny shouted back, his eyes fixed on the entertainment.

Across the street, older youths began to pour from The Black Horse pub, roaring their encouragement to the performing sports-car. While the front passenger gestured triumphantly from his window, the Mercedes aimed back towards the young boys.

Spellbound, they didn't move an inch; their perilous position perfect to see inside the car.

"It is – it's Deano!" Danny yelled above the noise. "And he's got his posse with him!"

Blasting back towards the rowdy drinkers, the show approached its climax. Turning in with full lock, the driver buried the throttle, his powerful motor laying thick black doughnuts onto the tarmac. Spinning wildly on the spot, it became lost inside the billowing smoke, its headlights burning through with every revolution.

Finally, a continual horn blast signalled the display's end. Without lifting off the power, the driver straightened the motor's nose, and catapulted away into the night.

Show complete, laughter drifted over from the pub regulars as they returned to their evening's drinking.

Mickey and Danny didn't move a muscle. Maybe, just maybe they'd get another glimpse of their heroes?

But it wasn't to be. With no sign of its return, the lads hurried home with their grub; their voices reaching out into the darkness, mimicking the nicked car's display.

Running up the garbage strewn stairwell to his first floor maisonette, Mickey threw open the door. Close behind, Danny followed him into the brown tiled hallway, their trainers squelching on its tacky surface.

"Mom, we're back," Mickey shouted into the darkness.

Shadows flickered down the passageway, their light source the 50-inch screen in the lounge. Fag in one hand, remote in the other, his mother's gaze remained fixed on the telly.

"You took your time," she tutted. "Your little brother's starving."

"Sorry mom, there was a queue at the chippy," he lied, opening up the warm package. "We ran home as fast as we could."

Eating straight from the wrapping, everybody tucked in; the only sounds the background noise from the TV.

And then, barely audible to begin with, a distant siren gradually rose in volume, until eventually blue lights briefly shone through the net curtains.

"Who're the pigs after?" his mum asked casually.

"Deano. He's been blitzing round the estate, he was wicked!" Mickey raved, shooting a glance at his mate.

"Well don't get hanging around with that lot; you'll end up as bad as your father!"

Mickey's cheeky grin said it all. Fortunately his mum was still focused on the soaps.

Danny gave him a wink, crumpled up his empty chip packet, and made towards the door.

"I'd better get back to mum," he said letting himself out. "I'll call for you on the way to school."

"Well just be careful on your way back," Mickey's mum called over her shoulder. "Don't go talking to any strangers; your mum's got enough on her plate as it is."

"Who's gonna get me – the bogeyman?" Danny laughed back. "You can see our flats from your window!"

With his mate gone, and his own grub finished, Mickey cleared the rubbish away. Climbing onto his bare mattress, he pulled his duvet tight. The moment his eyes closed, images of the performing Mercedes filled his mind. What must it be like to be inside the car he wondered? It was exciting enough to watch from the outside: the screeching tyres, the roaring engine, the smell of burning rubber. To be inside the car though, that'd be something else. One day, he promised himself as he slipped into deep sleep, he'd find out; one day…

***

By the time Danny called round the following morning, Mickey had just about managed to haul himself to his mattress's edge; the cartoons on the big screen having stirred him from his slumber.

"Hiya Danny, how's your mum?" Mickey's mother asked, lowering her steaming mug.

"Well she says she's fine," he replied, shrugging his shoulders. "But she's still lying in bed all day. Can I stop and watch telly please?"

"You're as bad as Mickey," she laughed. "No, it's time for school for you pair. Come on son, get your shoes on or you'll be late."

"Oh muuum," Mickey groaned. "Do I have to?"

"Yes you have to. Now get going while I wake your brother up."

With an almost silent tut, Mickey bent down, and forcing his trainers on, joined Danny at the door.

"And don't get up to any mischief!" his mother called after them.

"We won't," they replied in unison, trudging down the steps.

Just in case she was still watching, they walked off down the normal alleyway. Slightly taller than his wiry mate, Mickey glanced over the wall to look up at his window.

"It's okay, she's not there," he confirmed, as they reached the passageway's end. "Let's take a breather."

"So what we gonna do then?" Danny asked, taking a seat on their regular resting-place; a garden wall well out of view.

"Dunno, I suppose we could make the guy we talked about."

Looking down at the pavement Danny swung his legs back and forth, chipping away at the bricks with his heels. Eventually he broke the silence. "C'mon then, let's go to the park and check out the bonfire."

Together they dropped down, but as they crossed the road, Mickey spotted some classmates in a passing car. It was too good an opportunity to miss. Raising the middle finger on both hands, he gestured wildly as they drove by, laughing out loud at their horrified mother's face. Now why would he want to go to school, he grinned, when he could be out having fun with his mate all day!

Making their way onto Woodlands Park, Mickey gave Danny a nudge as they approached the metal fencing protecting the growing pallet stack. He knew full well why the fencing was there; last year he'd been caught attempting to light the bonfire a week before the November 5th celebrations. On spotting him, the 'Parkie' had given chase, but much to Mickey's amusement, the pot-bellied ex-copper had practically keeled over trying to get anywhere near him!

And if he wasn't mistaken, there he was again, barking out orders to the fluorescent jackets building the bonfire mound.

Pressing their faces to the wire fencing, they began to poke fun at the men, until eventually their laughter caught the attention of Parkie.

"Piss off, you little shits," he shouted, picking up the nearest log. "If I catch hold of you, there's gonna be trouble!"

"What you gonna do Grandad," Danny mocked. "Have a heart attack like last year!"

Incensed, the park-keeper launched his missile at the lads. Slamming against the fence, it fell harmlessly to the floor.

"Temper, temper!" Mickey joined in. But as he went to drag the log under the fence, he could see his red-faced opponent bearing down.

"C'mon," he smirked at his mate. "Time to do one!"

Legging it away, their pace was too much for Parkie, whose attempt to give chase quickly ran out of steam. Now at a safe distance, the lads stood and flicked the 'V's, goading him to come after them once more. But he'd had enough, and with a wave of his arm, returned to join his men.

Their fun over, they ambled off to their den; a natural lair hidden inside dense hedges overlooking a rarely used car park. Inaccessible to adults, even Mickey had to wriggle on his belly to avoid the overhead thorns. After crawling ten feet through its clutches, an isolated patch of grass offered just enough space for them to lie side by side. While they could see out, it was impossible to see in; perfect for spying on couples getting friendly in the cars outside!

Mickey led the way in, and opened their stash of fags.

"This is the life," he grinned, lighting up. "Beats going to school any day!"

Sucking in deeply, he passed it on to his mate.

"Aye, aye, what do we have here?" Danny smiled, ignoring the fag as he parted the bush with his fingers. "Looks like somebody's left us a present!"

Mickey quickly squeezed alongside, his eyes immediately spotting Danny's 'present'.

Parked facing their den was a tatty old Fiesta; tailgate up, and nobody in sight.

"It's gotta be a knock off," Mickey whispered. "Let's give it a few minutes, then we'll take a look."

Nobody, not even a dog-walker passed by. The coast clear, Mickey eased his way out, and ducking down, edged around the bushes.

Sidling up to the car, he carefully peeked in through the windows.

Yes! It was empty; now they could have some fun! With a final glance round, he slipped his fingers beneath the door handle, and slowly lifted upwards.

The moment it 'clicked', he threw open the door, and jumped onto the driver's seat. Grasping hold of the bar beneath, he yanked the chair forward, and perching himself on its edge, could just about see over the wheel!

"Come on, get in!" he hissed.

Gleefully, his mate flung himself onto the passenger seat. For a moment, they just sat there, grinning at each other; it was time for their first joyride!

"Let's go!" Danny shrieked, as Mickey slammed the gearstick forward.

Just like he'd seen on 'Fast and Furious', Mickey danced his feet up and down on the pedals. Blasting through the gears, 'nitro-boosting' at every opportunity, he made the engine and braking noises, while Danny delivered a running commentary.

"Red light ahead, we're doing seventy…go for it Mickey, go for it…shit that was close…great driving…lets handbrake it and do it again…watch out, the pigs are behind us…nee-naw, nee-naw, nee-naw…floor it!"

Suddenly, the driver's door was wrenched open…

3

"What the fuck do you think you're doing!" a voice screamed, as strong hands reached in and dragged Mickey from his seat.

Wide-eyed, he looked up, his legs turning instantly to jelly. Standing over him, his attacker's drawn fist left him in no doubt the trouble he was in.

"Well? Are you goin' to talk to me, or do I have to teach you a fucking lesson, you scrawny piece of shit!"

Mickey didn't say a word; what on earth could he say anyway? He'd been caught red-handed, he'd just have to take his punishment. Closing his eyes, he tensed his body, and waited for it to begin.

But as the older youth continued to rant, his threats were cut short by a calmer voice from behind.

"Aren't you Dave Wilding's son?"

Mickey's head turned towards the voice, his eyes daring to squint open a little. It couldn't really be him could it?

Widening by the moment, his eyes definitely weren't tricking him. Two youths were approaching, the taller one unmistakeable; it was Deano!

The bully hauled on Mickey's collars, pulling him up onto tiptoe, their faces almost touching.

"Well...fucking answer him!"

Mickey swallowed hard. "Yes, that's me."

"Okay Hood, put him down," Deano instructed, directly meeting the youth's gaze. "I'll sort this one out."

Slowly releasing his grip, Hood stepped away.

For a moment, Mickey and Deano looked at each other, neither saying a word.

Seventeen years old, with waxed hair and designer gear, Deano looked every inch the leader Mickey knew him to be; he just wished he hadn't met him like this!

"So did you both have some fun?" Deano asked, eventually breaking the silence.

Mickey swallowed hard; he didn't have a clue what to say. Of course they'd enjoyed themselves, but the motor obviously belonged to the posse; they shouldn't have been anywhere near it. He decided to stay quiet.

"C'mon lads, I'm not here to beat you up," Deano smiled. "If you're shitting yourselves, you can leave now if you want; you've already learnt your lesson."

A tug on his sleeve signalled Danny's thoughts. But Mickey hesitated; he might never get the chance to speak to Deano again.

Head stooped, he quietly spoke up. "That was great what you did in the Mercedes last night."

Silence.

All eyes turned towards Deano. His smile had disappeared; in its place a frown.

Mickey kicked himself. Had he gone too far? Had he blown it already?

Slowly, deliberately, Deano looked him up and down.

"You're a cocky one for sure," he nodded. "So how about you do a little work for me. You both got bikes?"

Awestruck, Mickey couldn't answer quickly enough this time. "Yes, yes, we're out on them all the time."

"Good, well listen up 'cos we run ourselves by strict rules. You break the rules; you're history," he said, scribbling down his number. "Ride round the estate keeping your eyes open. If you see anything suspicious, call me. If the info's good, you'll get rewarded. Oh, and one more thing...never get in my cars without permission again. Now fuck off before I change my mind!"

Having pushed his luck once, Mickey didn't need telling again. Pulse racing, he hurried away with a grin on his face. He couldn't quite believe it; not only had they met their hero, they were now going to be part of his gang!

***

Laced with complex alleyways and service drives, the Greet neighbourhood spread out like a web. Only the estate's kids knew it intimately; their curiosity and daily adventures forming a blueprint no sat-nav could ever match – perfect spies for the criminal underworld to exploit.

Now two such children, Mickey and Danny set to work, spending every waking moment scouring the neighbourhood; desperately hoping for something...anything that'd prove their worth. Night after night they returned empty-handed, enduring false call after false call, until one Sunday night, their snooping finally paid off.

With midnight fast approaching, it was time for them to make their way home. Mickey pedalled tiredly along Broad Lane; it had been another quiet night, and only boring school to look forward to in the morning. Trundling alongside, Danny's head suddenly spun to the right.

"Shit, did you clock that?" he said under his breath.

"Clock what?"

"The Insignia back there!"

Mickey shook his head.

"I've never seen it before, and there's a dodgy bloke inside!"

For Mickey, the alarm bells rang loud and clear. Danny's flats overlooked Broad Lane; he knew every single car in the road. Yeah, the bloke could be a visitor, but why was he sitting in his car at this time of night?

In unison they ducked down the next alleyway, and stopped to talk it over.

"I couldn't see much; it was too dark," Danny whispered, huddling close to his mate. "But he definitely didn't look right."

"Well we can't ride past him again."

"So how are we gonna see what he's up to?"

Mickey thought for a moment. "There's only one thing for it; we'll have to creep up behind and hope he doesn't spot us."

No sooner had Danny nodded his agreement than Mickey was off, leading the race through the back alleyways to the closest point he dared. Behind a hedge line, twenty metres from their target, they dismounted in silence and crept along the unkempt lawn to an empty space where the remains of a gate loosely hung. Tip-toeing forward, Mickey peered round the gap.

No wonder he hadn't spotted it; its dark colour blended in perfectly with the older, dirtier cars in front. Well out of the nearest lamppost's reach, the driver sat in virtual darkness; his only giveaway a glowing cigarette end. Mickey watched transfixed, willing him to drive off. But as the driver lit up another fag, he knew he couldn't wait any longer.

"It's no good, we're gonna have to get nearer," Mickey whispered. "You keep watch, I'm going in."

Cautiously, he scanned up and down the road. Nothing moved, it was now or never.

Stooped over, he scampered across the pavement, stepped onto the grass verge, and dropped like a stone to his belly. Raising his head, he checked out his prey.

Good, the man hadn't been spooked...yet. But he had to get closer, he needed to see inside; the posse were depending on him.

Inch-by-inch he advanced through the gloom, slithering slowly across the wet turf. Time and again he paused, his heart pounding as he edged ever closer.

Cautiously, he rose to a crouch. But almost as he did so, the sound of an engine approached, quickly followed by headlights swinging left as the car turned onto Broad Lane...headlights about to light him up like a beacon!

He dropped to the ground again, cushioning the impact as best as he could with his hands. Surely he'd made too much noise, or had the passing car muffled the sound?

He was about to find out.

Pressing himself into the wet surface, he paused as the lights passed over and away. Carefully, he lifted his head again.

Nothing. The driver hadn't moved.

Thank fuck for that, he cursed under his breath. It was time to get out; he'd seen what he needed to see.

Hunched over, he sprinted back to his mate. "He's gotta be a cop!" he whispered excitedly. "He was talking to someone, something about 'them being here in a minute'. It was pretty dark inside the car, the only thing I could see was a black case on the back seats."

"But if he is a cop…where's his mates? They never work alone," Danny replied hesitantly.

"You're right, we've gotta find them," Mickey said jumping back on his bike. "And I reckon I know exactly where they'll be!"

Using The Square as their theatre, the joyriders only routes in and out were along Broad Lane, which ran straight through one of its sides. If Mickey guessed right, and a trap had been set, another unit would be hidden at its other end.

Sure enough, his hunch was spot-on.

Parked between other motors, to the average passer-by, the dark grey Mondeo would have attracted little attention. To Mickey however, it screamed out as if coated in luminous paint. Too clean and practically brand new, it was a complete misfit; as was the lone male in the driver's seat. There was no need for a closer look; the trap had been set…only they could stop it being sprung.

Pedalling furiously to the nearest phone box, Mickey threw his bike to the ground and dived into the booth.

"Shit!" he cried in disbelief, spotting the smashed handset. "We should have checked the phones!"

"There's another couple on The Square," Danny replied breathlessly. "They're definitely working, the smackheads were in 'em earlier."

"No chance, we can't ride past the cop again. C'mon, follow me!"

Riding as if their lives depended on the call, they hurtled through the dark alleys to the next phone box. Mickey dropped his bike on the move, pulled open the heavy red door, and lifted the hand piece…

A dialling tone! He'd got lucky.

Fumbling inside his pocket, he snatched out his treasured piece of paper. Hands trembling, he punched in Deano's number.

It started to ring.

"Hello," the voice answered.

Mickey pushed in his first coin.

"Is that Deano?" he asked hesitantly.

"Who's asking?"

"It's Dave Wilding's son, Mickey."

"Go on, what you got for me?"

Gasping for air, he hurried through what they'd seen, his voice slowly increasing in strength as he continued un-interrupted. Finally, after passing on the cops' exact locations, he paused for breath.

"Anything else, anything suspicious?"

"Well I don't know if it's important, but there was a black box on the rear seat."

"Good work Mickey. Get yourselves to the roundabout, we're gonna have some fun!"

Goosebumps spread across Mickey's body. Had they actually saved their idols? He just prayed they hadn't missed something important; Deano was depending on them – they had to be right, they just had to be.

"Come on, what are you waiting for!" Danny shrieked, frantically pedalling away.

"Just giving you a head-start," Mickey grinned. "Race ya!"

Minutes later, they found an ideal spot. Behind a sparse hedge on a garden's edge, they had a perfect view up Broad Lane's gentle hill; the Mondeo sitting just ahead of the roundabout before them. All was quiet on arrival, no sign of the fireworks to come.

Moving closer to keep warm, the boys sat and waited, their excitement slowly waning as the wintry chill took hold.

"Do you think anything's gonna happen?" Danny shivered. "They could just be testing us."

"Maybe," Mickey shrugged. "But by the way he spoke, I really think he meant it. Let's give it fifteen and see what happens."

Desperate for their heroes to arrive, they continued to gaze towards the crest. Mickey looked down at his watch. Five minutes passed, then ten minutes and still no movement; maybe they were being tested after all.

Then at last, a distinctive noise in the distance. It sounded like an engine being hammered, its high pitched shriek disturbing the quiet night. Forgetting his discomfort in an instant, he parted the hedge as much as he dared; the posse were on their way!

Slowly increasing in volume, the sounds drew ever nearer. Suddenly, the Mondeo's door opened and the driver reached into the rear. Out came another flat box; it was the same as he'd seen in the Insignia!

Eyes widening in horror, he watched helplessly as the man placed it on the floor and flicked the latches.

Still out of sight, the 'knock-off' had to be close; its screaming engine now hard to make out above a wailing siren. And then there they were; blazing headlights flying over the hillcrest towards them.

"Shit," Mickey exclaimed, his attention returning to the Mondeo. "What's he got out of the box?"

4

In the dark night, as the man ducked behind his motor, it was difficult to tell for sure. But what light there was, glinted briefly off the flat object.

Oblivious to his actions, the lead car hurtled towards the roundabout; the Insignia struggling to keep up behind. Suddenly, the man emerged from his cover, and in one fluid movement threw out the object. Metal spikes instantly burst free; their deadly strip reaching out to the opposite kerb.

"He's got nowhere to go!" Danny screamed above the noise.

"He'll have something up his sleeve," Mickey replied hesitantly. "He has to!"

Despite the distance between hunter and hunted, it looked like the police had executed their plan perfectly; their 'stinger' ready to claim its next victim. However, just when it appeared it was about to be 'stung', the lead car's bonnet suddenly drove downwards; its brakes struggling to cope with the driver's demands. Side-to-side the hot-hatch slew, smoke billowing from every corner. But it wasn't enough; it was still carrying too much speed, it was about to drive over the spikes.

Mickey couldn't stay behind his cover any longer; he needed a clearer view! Disregarding the hedge's safety, he jumped to his feet just as the stolen motor turned sharply to the left. Striking the nearside kerb, it bounced up onto the pavement, and with a quick blast of acceleration, flew past the spike-strip; its return to the road accompanied by a two-fingered salute from the driver's window.

Barely managing to haul the stinger in before his colleague careered through, the officer waved his fist at the disappearing car; his abuse drowned out by the passing siren. The diversion to the footpath had made a difference though; the Insignia was back in touch, with hardly a car length between them.

Now on top of the roundabout, the lead car turned sharply to the right, its blinding headlights veering away from the boys for the first time.

"Mini Cooper!" Danny shrieked.

In full view, Mickey remained standing, merely nodding his head in reply. This show was for him – he was going to savour every moment. Three times the hot hatch tore round the island, its passengers pumping fists through their windows, while the chaser struggled to keep up behind.

Finally, the Mini exited at speed, the pursuit heading off into the darkness. Rooted to the spot, Mickey craned his ears, desperately hoping for his hero's return. But the sirens slowly drifted away; their fun for the night was over. With the cold seeping into his tired body once more, he picked up his bike and joined Danny for the short ride home.

Could things have gone any better he grinned? Surely they'd passed their first test...now what was to be their reward?

***

The following morning, Danny was at Mickey's bright and early. Their eagerness to talk over the night's events would have to wait though; Mickey's mum had a chat of her own in mind.

"Hey you pair, don't go rushing off; I've got some questions for you," she began as they headed towards the door. "We'll start with where you were last night, and for that matter, most nights!"

With a sly wink to his mate, Mickey turned to face his mum; his well-rehearsed story slipping easily off his tongue.

"Sorry mum, I thought you knew," he smiled. "You know the tracking game we like playing?"

"Err, I think so," she replied uncertainly. "Where you follow chalk marks on the pavement?"

"That's it," Mickey enthused, rooting out broken chalk from his pocket. "We just got a bit...carried away."

"Don't try and pull the wool over my eyes son; we both know you can't play at night. I mean, how do you see the..."

Before she'd even had chance to finish, a grinning Danny had pulled the answer from his pocket.

"It's way better in the dark Mrs Wilding; my torch searches everywhere!"

"Mmm...I guess so," she frowned. "Just make sure you're back a little earlier in the future, okay?

"Okay," they replied in unison. "We promise."

Interrogation complete, the lads left for school, excitedly talking over the previous night's events. Lessons passed by in a haze; their minds on far more interesting subjects. And by the time they left at the day's end, they were still too wrapped up in their chatter to notice the hooded figure waiting for them outside the gates.

"Mickey Wilding?"

Startled, Mickey spun round.

"Well, lost your voice or something?" he continued.

"Yeah, I'm Mickey."

Reaching inside his top, the youth pulled out a carton of B&H fags. "These are from J.T. He says you did well last night. There's more where they came from if you keep up the good work. Don't sell them on; you're not allowed to yet. Understand?"

The boys nodded.

"You call me Soldier. Next time you give good info, you meet me round the back of The Black Horse after school. Four o' clock on the dot, okay?"

"Sure," Mickey answered. "But how did you know…"

It was pointless finishing his question; Soldier had already walked off.

Stuffing the fags inside his jacket, Mickey turned to face his pal. "So who the hell was he?"

"Well he's gotta be Deano's mate to know what happened last night," Danny replied. "It's strange we've never seen him before though; I thought we knew all the posse."

It was just the first of many questions bouncing around Mickey's mind. Why *couldn't* they sell the fags; they could easily make a few quid from the packets they didn't need. And who the hell was J.T.? He'd always thought Deano was in charge.

But one thing *was* for sure…until they found the answers, they'd do *exactly* as they were told.

***

Christmas came and went without incident, the lads having little chance to prove themselves further. Knowing nods as the posse occasionally cruised by was as much contact as they had, until eventually, on a wintry afternoon, their hard work was to pay off again.

Out on the streets, all was quiet; the freezing conditions keeping residents tucked away indoors. With little to interest them, Mickey and Danny cycled in silence, their hoodies pulled tight to shut out the driving snow. Dropping down yet another kerb, they crossed fresh tyre tracks leading towards a nearby garage block.

That's strange, Mickey thought to himself, nobody had used the garages for years. Completely vandalised, the only doors remaining hung limply on their hinges, while the surviving roof girders had become an aerial playground for the kids. So why would anyone drive up there? With only one set of tracks imprinted on the snow, the answer couldn't be far away.

And sure enough it wasn't. The moment he turned into the garage square, he saw it: a white van bearing 'Council Housing Dept.' markings sat beneath a streetlight, while next to it, perched on a ladder's top ring, a man in overalls reached tentatively into the lamp unit.

What was he thinking, Mickey chuckled. Didn't he know the local kids would immediately spot the new light? They'd fight to see who could smash it first, just as they'd done with all the previous ones. There was nothing to see here; he was cold and hungry, it was time to go home to eat.

With the snow continuing to fall, they recharged their batteries; Pot Noodles on the sofa, followed by a warm in front of the telly. Eventually, Mickey stood up to look out through the window. The roads were deserted, another quiet evening appeared to be in store. But something was niggling away at him, something about the council man just didn't sit right.

"C'mon," he said to Danny, putting his damp coat on. "We're going back to the garages; I wanna see what he's been up to."

Cutting through the snow on their bikes, they made their way to the scene. Despite the snowfall, a second set of tracks was just about visible. It looked like the van had long gone, and yet, as they turned towards the garage block, the whole area was in darkness.

"That's odd," Mickey said bringing his bike to a halt. "It's only been an hour; surely the kids haven't smashed them already!"

"Maybe he couldn't fix 'em? Let's face it, they haven't worked for years."

"Well I don't like it," Mickey grumbled, squinting through the flakes at the light. "Something's not right, we need to get a closer look."

Back pressed against the garage wall, Danny quickly gave him a bunk up. Balancing on his mate's shoulders, Mickey reached up, grabbed the guttering, and hauled himself onto the corrugated roof. Cautiously, he crawled forward, picking his way around the holes, before slowly rising to his feet. Now practically within touching distance, he focused his torch on the target.

In perfect condition, the lamp unit didn't have as much as a scratch on it. Puzzled, he inched round the roofs to examine the others. But they were all still smashed to pieces...why hadn't the man bothered with them? And why was the one he *had* repaired not working? He needed to check it again.

Gripping the metal pole with one arm, he leant out from the roof on tiptoe; his other arm outstretched with his torch. Straining his neck, he attempted to peer in.

What *was* that inside the lamp unit? Adjusting his hold so that his bodyweight slipped further around the lamppost, he strove to get a closer view.

And then he saw it. Now he knew exactly what the man had been doing!

5

It didn't look like any bulb *he'd* seen before; it looked more like a little black box…a little black box with a lens on the end!

Jumping down, he rushed back to Danny. "It's not working 'cos there's no bleedin' light inside! He didn't repair it; he put a fucking camera in!"

"Heh. Why would he put a camera up there? It's just a dump round here!"

"I guess he must know something we don't. You keep watch, I'll take a look in the garages; there must be something inside."

With the few doors remaining taking little force to swing open, it didn't take too long to find. Practically opposite the repaired lamppost, a glance inside confirmed Mickey's suspicions.

"Dan, come over here!" he hissed.

"I don't believe it!" Danny exclaimed as Mickey re-opened the doors. "It's the Mini Cooper Deano was in!"

"Exactly. That's what the camera's after!"

Danny's excitement slowly turned to panic. "So it must be watching us right now then?"

"Shit!" Mickey exclaimed, slamming the doors shut. "Let's get out of here!"

Despite the clogging snow, they pedalled as rapidly as they could manage away, only slowing when they'd reached the safety of Danny's flats.

"I don't get it, why didn't the council just recover the car?" Danny panted.

"'Cos it wasn't the council who put the camera in."

"It was. We saw the man in overalls, the ladders, the van, everything!"

"Yeah, that's what he wanted us to think, so nobody would be suspicious," Mickey smiled, his breath slowly returning. "He's a cop of course; they want to catch Deano having the car away!"

"But they've seen *us* now!"

"Yeah, but we're just kids being nosey; Deano won't be so lucky. If he comes to move the motor, he'll get locked up for sure. We're gonna have to give him the heads up."

"Bollocks," Danny scowled. "What you gonna say? Remember the last time he caught us snooping round his cars? He said he'd kill us if it happened again."

Resting on his handlebars, Mickey chewed it over.

"We've got no choice mate, we're gonna have to tell him everything," he eventually decided. "If we drop in the shit…we drop in the shit!"

This time, he knew the phone box was working; he wouldn't make that mistake again! As before, Deano listened, thanked him, then the line went dead.

Heading home, Mickey remained deep in thought. They'd certainly saved Deano's bacon – but at what cost? Okay, there was a small chance the police could identify him and Danny, but he really didn't give a shit about that; it was Deano he was worried about. Would he reward or punish them? One thing was for sure; they'd find out the following day at the rear of The Black Horse. An uneasy night's sleep lay ahead.

***

The following day, they cycled through dirty slush towards the back of the pub; its dirt track bounded by ramshackle wooden fencing. Arriving five minutes early, Mickey waited nervously, only half listening to Danny's excited chatter.

"...what do you think happened to the Mini...are we gonna be in trouble...who the hell is J.T.!'"

Then, at four o'clock precisely, Soldier stepped out from behind a hole in the fence. Again Mickey kicked himself; why hadn't he checked when they arrived? If Soldier had been there all along, he'd be bound to have overheard Danny's ramblings.

"You two are proving quite useful, even if you are a little nosey," he began. "It's alright, you can rest easy; thanks to you boys the posse wore their balaclavas when they moved the motor this morning."

Mickey shot a glance at his mate; they were in the clear, they'd got it right!

"You're in J.T.'s good books for the moment, so he wants you to expand your operations a little. The Old Bill's getting too on top round here, so we're finding it harder to stash our cars away. Get yourselves onto the posh estates and find us some garages to use, understand?"

"No probs," Mickey nodded. "And our normal stuff? I take it we carry on as usual?"

"Of course," Soldier replied. "And in reply to who J.T. is...I don't have a clue. All *I* know, is that he's the boss, and you don't want to upset him!"

Mickey scowled to himself; so he had overheard Danny's chatter!

"Anyway, here's your money," he said, handing the boys twenty pounds each. "Keep up the good work," and with that, ducked back through the fence and away.

Wow, Mickey grinned. Twenty pounds each, just for doing something they loved. And by the sounds of it, there was plenty more to come!

***

"Right, time to get down to business."

Their banter cut short, soft leather armchairs squelched as the men turned towards their boss. His home lay at the heart of The Greet housing estate; an ex-council 'semi' he'd lived in all his life. In contrast to the dreary properties all around, J.T's boasted a full length glass conservatory, a freshly laid gravel driveway housing a pair of brand new BMW's, and pretentious chandeliers that shook with the passing of every inter-city train.

Before him sat 'The Power Firm'; trusted friends whose loyalty ensured his position remained unchallenged. For fifteen years they'd controlled the local neighbourhoods; fifteen years eliminating rivals, fifteen years ruling by fear. Six foot four, and eighteen stone of muscle that clad him like a suit of armour, J.T. demanded respect, and woe betide anyone who didn't show it.

As the room quietened, he motioned for his brother Johnny to start.

"Erm, well things aren't going too badly," he said, nervously adjusting his glasses. "But we're five per cent behind our projected target for this financial year. With four months remaining, we need an increase in productivity to regain the lost ground."

Second only to his brother, Johnny's accountancy training left him solely in charge of The Power Firm's books. Loyalty to their network was not only commanded through fear, but also bought by rewards. Johnny ensured that every order, every theft, and every payment was meticulously recorded.

In turn, the three remaining members began to deliver their respective reports: the pockmarked Chapman, responsible for employees and recruitment; the immaculately dressed Porter, acquisitions and sales; and the meathead Razor...enforcement.

"My guys are working flat out," Chapman defended. "We're busy recruiting to meet demand; it'll just take a little time to get everybody up and running."

'My guys' meant the likes of Deano, who like middle managers in business, linked the bosses to their workers.

"Well *my* order book is full," Porter replied nonchalantly. "My contacts are screaming out for more business; they can't get enough of it!"

"Good for you," Chapman hissed back. "Perhaps you can open your magic box and conjure up more workers!"

"Okay, settle down gents," J.T. interrupted, slowly rising to his feet. "We **will** hit our end of year target! Chapman, speak to your boys; they **will** meet Porter's demands. And Porter...make sure your contacts live up to their promises, or Razor'll be paying them a visit! Do I make myself clear?"

Almost as one, the two men nodded their agreement.

"Which brings me to the main topic on our agenda. As you all know, the last few years have been good, very good in fact. However, we're not going to rest on our laurels; we're going to seize this opportunity to expand. It'll require us broadening our borders and increasing our workforce. It's all laid out here in Johnny's three year plan," he announced, as his brother handed out paper copies. "As you can see, the key to our expansion is recruiting workers we can trust; *that* will become our priority."

A puzzled look came over Razor's scarred face. "There's a lot of zeros on here boss," he said uncertainly.

"Yes, and a rather large number in front of them," J.T. smiled back. "And if the boys do exactly as they're told, those numbers will soon end up in our bank accounts!"

"Don't worry boss," Razor grinned. "They'll do *exactly* as they're told!"

"I'm sure they will," J.T. replied raising his glass. "So here's to the next three years, and the future success of The Power Firm."

"The Power Firm!" they toasted as one.

6

For Mickey and Danny, the following three years passed quickly; their secret world proving the perfect release from their problems. Danny's life had been turned upside down after his mum had surrendered to her cancer, leaving him orphaned, in the care of Social Services. Having been sent to the local Children's Home, he'd been able to roam the estates with complete freedom; freedom the fourteen-year-old Mickey desperately longed for. Instead, he'd had to come to terms with his own problem; the return of his drunken father. Released on parole, he'd taken over at home, and until he was sent down the steps again, his dad was calling the shots.

With the streets their only escape, they'd become wrapped up in their exciting adventures: spying on cops, finding new hideaways, patrolling the local neighbourhoods. Though Soldier remained their mentor, they'd soon found out he was also running another kid in their year; a kid who'd swiftly become their bitter rival…a kid called Tommy Burns.

Out on a nearby 'posh' estate, Mickey and Danny took a break. Arms resting on handlebars, their eyes followed two girls tottering past in high heels.

"Do you reckon Tommy's boys'll be out tonight?"

"Doubt it. His mommy won't allow him out after eight; it's past that tosser's bedtime!" Mickey joked back. "And anyway, why would we give a shit? As long as he keeps away from our patch, I couldn't give a damn what he gets up to!"

"Yeah, you're right. It's just all that crap he was saying at school today; you know, reckoning he's been out with the posse and stuff."

"Nah, he's full of it," Mickey replied as Danny wolf-whistled the girls. "There's no way Deano'd go to him first; *we've* been working our nuts off for years."

Their amusement at the girls' two fingered reply was cut short by the ringing inside Mickey's pocket.

"Right on cue," he smiled, unzipping his Berghaus. "He must have heard us talking!" Sliding his finger across the screen, he took the phone to his ear.

"Hiya Mickey, you with Danny?" the voice asked.

"Yeah, we're out patrolling the Posh."

"Good lads, now listen up. Get your arses down to the cinema for nine; Soldier'll meet you out the front," Deano instructed. "Oh yeah, and make sure you get there by bus; you won't be needing your bikes on this job!"

Mickey's stomach tightened. Could this be the step-up they'd been waiting for?

"What did he say, what did he say?" Danny asked excitedly as Mickey ended the call.

"He's arranged for us to meet Soldier later – no bikes allowed."

"No bikes? You know what that means!"

"Damn right I do; we're going home in a motor!"

"Yeah, and before that dickhead Tommy! Wait 'til we see him tomorrow; he's gonna be sooo fucking jealous!"

***

Four miles from home, amongst Solihull's wealthy suburbs, the multiplex lay close to the airport. Popular throughout the year, its car parks teemed with luxury cars, and as Mickey found out when he arrived, tonight was no exception.

"Jeez Dan, have you checked out all the Beemers," he marvelled, taking a seat outside the front entrance.

"Yeah, imagine if we have one away tonight?" Danny beamed. "You and me goin' for a blast in a BMW!"

"I guess we're about to find out," Mickey said gesturing with his eyes. "Here comes Soldier and one of his mates."

Rising from their bench, the lads fist-pumped the new arrivals.

"So guys, what do you reckon you're here for?" Soldier asked.

"We're hoping it's got something to do with those beauties," Mickey grinned, nodding towards the packed car park.

"Well don't get your hopes up too much," Soldier laughed. "Most of those bad boys need special tools! You're right though, we're having a motor away. Tonight, you're gonna learn how to hotwire!"

'Yes!' Mickey's inner voice screamed; at last, it was really going to happen!

"Now listen carefully, 'cos I don't want any fuckups," Soldier continued. "We get going at nine-thirty while the films are half-way through. Normally, the only person on the car park is the security geezer, 'old Bert'. But you can set your watch by his patrols; every hour he does one slow lap, before going back to his office to watch CCTV. So our best time to strike is just after he's passed our target. Now tell me, where's the best place to look for your motor?"

Mickey shrugged, and looked to his mate.

"Somewhere round the edge, I guess," Danny offered nervously.

"Go on," Soldier nodded.

"Well the lights are in the middle of the car park, so round the edge it's darker – makes it difficult to spot us. It's also easier to leg it into the bushes if we need to."

"Bang on. Now go and find the right car. Make sure it's an old knacker without an immobiliser."

While Soldier and his mate took to the bench, the lads headed off to the car park.

Sprawling to all sides, the tarmac expanse was surrounded by a low brick wall, beyond which lay shrubbery and trees. Hoods over heads, the lads sauntered around the perimeter, scanning for the perfect target…and there it was, all alone in the corner; a tatty red Vauxhall Astra.

His pulse quickening, Mickey glanced across to his mate. The faintest nod was all the reply he needed; the Astra it was.

Having completed their circuit, they returned to Soldier, who immediately quizzed them on their choice.

"How many doors?"

"Two."

"Think about it, there's four of us here. What happens if we get chased and have to dump it? How do *you* boys get out?"

Mickey cursed to himself. Of course, they should have chosen a four door.

"Don't worry, it'll do for tonight, but think about it for the future, okay? Everybody needs to get out quickly, not just the wheelman," Soldier instructed. "Now, what about an alarm; was there an L.E.D?"

"No, nothing." Danny replied.

"Good," he nodded, looking at his watch. "Now let's get into position; Old Bert'll be out in five minutes dead."

Sure enough, at 9:30 on the dot, the security guard set out on his hourly rounds. Just inside the tree line on the car park's edge, the lads lay in complete darkness, watching his leisurely patrol. Closer and closer he approached, until, only metres away, he fanned his torchlight towards them. As one, they ducked down, the beam briefly flickering across their position…but he was just going through the motions, his eyes barely following the light.

Carefully, Mickey raised his head as the footsteps faded. In the distance, Bert's torch slowly disappeared from view. To his side, Soldier raised his right arm, motioned towards the Astra, and led them to the driver's door.

Heart slamming against his chest, Mickey watched open-mouthed as Soldier set to work. Taking a flat bladed screwdriver from his jacket pocket, he forced the door-skin away from the lock.

"Once you've made the hole, insert the screwdriver, jiggle it around, and hey presto…" Soldier explained as the locks popped up. "You're in!"

Swiftly lifting the handle, he threw the door wide open, triggering the interior light. Straight down to his knees, he reached in, grabbed the plastic cowling beneath the steering column, and ripped it away.

"Next, you remove the black box…" he instructed, prizing off the ignition barrel's end. "And start her up!"

In the seconds it had taken Soldier to fire up the engine, his mate had jumped into the passenger seat, and was now leant over with his hands on the wheel.

"Which just leaves the steering lock!"

Combining their strength, they wrenched the wheel from side to side, until eventually a loud 'crack' signalled its submission.

"Right, get in!" Soldier hissed.

Almost tripping over his mate, Mickey scrambled into the hatchback's rear. He couldn't believe it; from start to finish, less than thirty seconds – as quick as the owner with keys!

"Now don't draw attention to yourselves," Soldier continued, placing the Astra into gear and flicking the lights on. "The last thing you want is the Old Bill after you in a car like this, especially if you're not on your manor!"

Following the one-way system, Soldier drove off the car park, casually passing Old Bert as he approached the end of his round.

This was unlike any journey Mickey had experienced before. Four youths in hoodies in a stolen car? Surely they'd stick out like sore thumbs, and yet...nobody paid them the slightest bit of attention; it was as if they were invisible. Looking through his window at the passing night, his pulse began to ease. And now as they returned to the safety of The Greet, he wondered whether it was about to be his turn. Would Soldier actually let *them* have the car?

He didn't have to wait long for his answer. Having driven onto Woodlands Park, Soldier ended the journey with a deft handbrake turn by their den.

Removing the screwdriver from his pocket, Soldier turned in his seat, and passed it to Mickey.

"Here, get some practice with this; you'll be expected to do it yourselves soon," he said, opening the door to leave. "It's all yours to do what you want, but make sure you don't leave the car park; you'll only get yourselves caught...or killed!"

Mickey watched the older lads walk away before turning to his mate. "Can you believe it?" he grinned.

"It's wicked!" Danny squealed. "So what are we gonna do first!"

"You're gonna try and beat me to the driver's seat!" Mickey beamed, diving between the front seats. "But you're too late, I'm already there!"

Alongside him in an instant, Danny grabbed at his seatbelt as Mickey slammed the car into gear.

Clutch down, Mickey prodded at the accelerator; his grin broadening with every blast.

Pushing more and more each time, he finally drove it into the carpet. "Right, it's time to watch the master in action!"

With the engine screaming for mercy, he dumped the clutch, sending the old car lurching forward a few feet before spluttering to an embarrassing stop.

Howling with laughter, Danny looked across to his mate, who stared at the controls in disbelief.

"What a dickhead!" Mickey sniggered, shaking his head. "C'mon, let's try it again."

Time after time, he attempted to master the basics, leaving thick, black lines in his kangarooing wake. Danny proved just as inept, until the rising stench from beneath the bonnet signalled the clutch's demise. But their fun had only just begun; next up was theft…a skill much easier to perfect. Following Soldier's lead, they took it in turns with the screwdriver; lock, unlock, start and stop, quicker and quicker against the clock.

Undisturbed, time flew by, until with midnight approaching, Danny begrudgingly brought an end to their fun.

"We're gonna have to get back before we drop in the shit," he said pocketing the screwdriver. "There is still one more thing to do though," he smirked.

"Come on," a wide-eyed Mickey nodded. "Let's do it!"

Needing no further encouragement, Danny dived into the den and grabbed their cigarette lighter. With a broad grin, he circled their prize before settling next to the driver's door. Reaching into the doorwell, he pulled out a scrap of paper, raked his thumb down on the lighter, and allowed the flickering flame to take hold. Carefully, he laid it onto the upholstered seat, slowly closed the door, and stepped back to watch the show.

Leisurely at first, the flames licked around the seat, as if searching for more fuel. But as they took hold and the heat intensified, Mickey dropped back. He'd watched spellbound many times before, but this time it was different; this time it was their car – their inferno. Glass shattered, tyres exploded, and then in the distance, the first wail of sirens; it was time to disappear.

It had taken three years, but finally they'd done it; all their hard work had paid off.

***

Less than a mile away, a similar bonfire was ablaze. Beside it, two hooded figures gazed at the licking flames.

"It's a shame Soldier's been helping those pricks out," the taller youth sneered.

"Yeah, they think they're sooo fucking special."

"Don't worry, they won't be around for much longer," Tommy grinned, turning to his mate. "'Cos I'm gonna make damn sure of it!"

7

From the outside, Deano's pad looked just like all the other maisonettes in his street, however the inside was altogether different. Spotless laminate flooring led to the hub of activity; a through lounge whose sofas faced the latest wall-hung TV.

Sprawled on his armchair in front of the big screen, Deano's thumbs moved rapidly to control his rally Impreza. Struggling to keep up in his Evo, Soldier cursed out loud, much to the gathered posse's delight.

In between the banter, they discussed their new boys' progression. It had been a few weeks since Mickey and Danny's baptism, and Soldier, having 'educated' them further, was keen for them to advance.

"I'm not disputing they're good lads; they've certainly done us proud so far," Deano said, deftly flicking his Impreza into a powerslide. "It just seems a bit quick. Are you *sure* they're ready to go out on their own?"

"Look, they're as ready as they'll ever be. They've mastered having cars away, and Mickey's already pretty decent behind the wheel. Yeah, they'll be easy meat for the coppers, but you know what, we all had to start somewhere…oh bollocks!" Soldier replied, dropping his controller to the floor. "Half a bloody second again! Next time, I'll kick your ass!"

"In your dreams slowcoach," Deano chuckled. "Okay, we'll give them some rope. Just make sure you pass them old Jonas's details; they'll soon be in need of his services."

He paused for a moment while he scrolled through to the next circuit. "And what about Tommy Burns and his boys; are *they* ready to go yet?"

"I guess they're not far off. Do you want me to do the same for them?"

"I don't think we've got much choice mate," Deano replied. "J.T.'s ordered us to recruit, and from what Chapman's been telling me, he wants it done yesterday!"

"That's bollocks, there's too many of us already!" Hood interrupted, snatching hold of Soldier's joypad. "What's the point in having more fingers in the pot? We should leave 'em where they are!"

Deano turned to face him, a flush of frustration spreading across his face.

"Look, we're not saying they're coming out on jobs with us; they're just training for the future, alright?"

Hood's gaze didn't move from the television as he selected his motor. "Yeah, whatever…just don't say I didn't warn you."

***

Whilst Deano was fuming over Hood's disrespect, his own bosses were, by contrast, relaxing in a sauna's steamy heat. Head reclined against the upper level, J.T. sat on the lower, his dignity covered by a towel. Similarly clad, Johnny lay on the opposite side and remained perfectly still as he spoke.

"Over the past three years, income's risen as planned, with outgoings remaining proportionate to the rise. Drugs are at saturation point, but we've still got room to develop our other areas of business."

"Okay, call a meeting for Monday morning; we'll discuss things further then," J.T. instructed, rising to leave. "Our boys had better be up for some grafting, 'cos it's time we expanded our boundaries again, and nobody but nobody's gonna stop us!"

Outside their private-members club, the car park was an Aladdin's cave of high quality motors. Off limits to the Power Firm's gangs, it rarely suffered crime, and as such had little security. However, while J.T. and Johnny chilled out in the pool, a crew from the other side of town arrived…and couldn't believe their luck.

Having driven through The Glades unguarded entrance, their scruffy old Ford Focus completed a slow tour before parking up close to the exit. Engine running, the three passengers jumped out and strode over to the club's glass-fronted doors which obligingly slid apart as they approached. While his mates kept watch at the front, the lead youth quickly made his way to the changing rooms.

Designer clothing hung unprotected above individual wooden benches. It was all too easy; a quick rifle through the pockets amassed an impressive hoard of wallets, keys and phones. Still undisturbed, he strolled back out, sifting through his rucksack's booty as he walked.

Re-joining his mates at the glass doors, he ran to the most powerful beast on the car park; a sapphire black M5. Three BMW keyfobs in hand, he pressed them in turn, until the welcoming indicator wink confirmed his choice. Moments later, the only remaining evidence of the high-performance saloon was the thick black tyre marks heading towards the exit.

Back inside the health club, the brother's tranquil swim was soon interrupted by two elderly members hurrying in.

"I'm afraid we've had a break in," the leading man fumed. "Some rotten scum have been into the changing rooms and stolen our wallets!"

J.T. was out in a flash. A quick check inside his jacket confirmed his fears; his wallet and keys were missing.

"If my baby's not outside…" he raged, making towards the exit, "…there's going to be fucking trouble!"

Practically naked, he rushed through the sliding doors and onto the car park outside.

Glaring at the tyre marks, he turned towards his breathless brother. "On second thoughts, call that meeting for tonight…and don't accept any excuses!"
∗∗∗

"As you all know, some dickheads had my Beemer away this morning. Our own boys wouldn't dare, so it must be a crew from outside," J.T. smouldered as he paced round his lounge. "Chapman, you've got until Friday to find out who. Razor, we'll decide what's gonna happen to them on Saturday. Porter, when the car's found, make sure it's back on my drive in perfect condition. If the tossers have torched it, they're dead. Do we all understand?"

Heads nodded in unison. With the news of the theft soon to hit the streets, revenge needed to be swift and brutal; J.T.'s reputation depended on it.

"Leave it with me," Chapman grovelled. "My boys'll drop everything; they'll have the answer by Friday at the latest. However, I might have to call in a few favours…if you catch my drift. And I guess that'll take some sweeteners?"

Reaching down from his armchair, J.T. picked up a brown briefcase, and flicked the latches open.

"There's a couple of grand," he said, removing two bundles. "If they need any more, we'll let Razor speak to them nicely!"

A grin spread across Razor's battle scarred face – violence was his speciality. Wide as he was tall, his shaved head exposed his proudest asset; a six inch reminder of a failed axe attack.

The henchman stooped his head as he replied. "Okay Boss, I'll get the boys ready for Saturday; we'll all take a trip in the Transit."

"Good, I want that problem sorted before we get down to our real business," J.T. nodded. "Listen up. We need to make some important decisions regarding our future plans. Chapman, Porter; by our next meeting, I want accurate projections for the next twelve months. What I decide to do is gonna be based on what you say, so don't disappoint me, understand! In the meantime, find those little wankers and break their fucking legs!"
∗∗∗

Chapman soon set to work. From school playgrounds to youth centres to back street pubs, his citywide cobweb listened in. But with two days passing without as much as a whisper, he was beginning to get nervous. He needed a break, and quick…or J.T. was going to go ballistic!
∗∗∗

Straight after school, Mickey and Danny jumped on a bus, heading to their instructor's latest meeting. Trusted screwdrivers tucked inside jacket pockets, they hopped off outside the railway station and hurried towards Soldier's car.

Approaching the dark coloured VW, Mickey's pace slowed; his attention drawn to its rear seats.

"I don't fucking believe it!" he said.

"What's the matter?"

"Tommy and his bleedin' mates, that's what!"

"Bollocks, what are *they* doin' here?" Danny scowled at the grinning faces, who by now were welcoming their arrival with middle fingers raised.

Remaining in the driver's seat, Soldier leant across Tommy, and handed Mickey a business card.

"You're on your own now lads; you've been given the nod to take to the streets. When you drop in the shit, ring this number; he'll look after you. Now I suggest you get some practice in, 'cos these boys reckon they're way better than you!"

Slightly taken aback, Mickey hesitated in his response...unlike Tommy's boys, who immediately ripped into him; their taunts changing to hand signals as the VW moved out into traffic.

"Wankers!" Mickey cursed half-heartedly; his mind more focused on Soldier's bombshell. Yeah, he was pissed off with Tommy's involvement; he'd hoped they'd stay one step ahead of their enemy...but way more importantly, they'd been given the green light to go solo!

"What's on the card mate?"

His thoughts interrupted, Mickey looked down at Soldier's gift. "Algernon Jonas; solicitor with Parker, Jonas and Co." he read aloud. "We don't need this; we're too good to get caught!"

"Yeah, the pigs'll never get near *us*," Danny laughed back. "*We're* freakin' awesome!"

"Too right. Anyway, we'd better hang onto it; we can pass it to Tommy when *he* gets banged up!"

Laughing as they crossed the road, they walked onto the station's car park. Jam-packed with commuter's motors, there was still an hour before their owner's return...ample time to create a new space!

Wire fencing prevented access to the railway lines behind, while on the other side, a low brick wall offered a perfect place to rest while they eyed up the selection before them.

"Fancy the blue Mazda?" Danny suggested. "It's got nice alloys."

"Nah, it's massive; we're only used to the smaller ones."

"How about the GTI?"

"Don't be daft; it's far too quick! Imagine if we smashed it first go – Tommy'd wet himself!"

Mickey scanned the 'showroom'. Hatchbacks, estates, saloons or coupes...and without a salesman in sight! In fact, there was nobody; no witnesses and no CCTV, just the occasional *'vehicles left at owner's risk'* notice hanging loosely from the fence.

"Nope, that's *our* little beauty down there," he pointed out, dropping to the ground. "Nobody'll notice us in a crummy old Corsa; it's perfect!"

Tightly packed in amongst the other cars, their target proved all too easy; Danny's well practiced screwdriver skills entering and starting the car within seconds.

Jamming the car into reverse, Mickey glanced over his shoulder. It was all clear; the car park was empty. Eager to get going, he lifted the clutch a little too sharply.

"Whoa! Easy tiger!" Danny chuckled. "Let's get it out in one piece!"

Come on, relax, Mickey scolded himself – just act normal and no-one'll bat an eyelid. Swinging out, he headed to the exit…and onto the public road! Danny's grin matched his own. Here they were, fourteen years old, and driving their very own 'knock-off'!

The only problem was, they were still a few miles from home, and being in and around the other drivers wasn't quite as easy as he'd thought. Fun though it was, his pulse was beginning to quicken; the sooner he could reach their dumping ground's safety the better.

Hoody pulled up, he focused on the road ahead; cursing at the slow-moving traffic.

Fifteen minutes passed before the Greet signs finally came into view. Unfortunately, so did the very thing he dreaded the most…and there was no possible way to escape it!

8

A police Panda was approaching, they'd have to pass it side-by-side. The officers couldn't fail to see them; they were the only other car on the road!

"Watch 'em when they pass," Mickey called out. "If their brake lights come on and they start to turn, we'll have to dump it and run!"

Although he'd had plenty of practice off-road, he knew he had no chance in a chase. Their only hope was on foot; they were quick, and knew every escape route around. He glanced down at the speedo. Good, he was doing a steady thirty; that shouldn't catch the copper's attention.

Keeping his gaze dead ahead, the Panda car trundled past to his side.

Danny peeked round his headrest. "They're not braking, they're going straight ahead. I don't believe it, they didn't even clock us!"

"C'mon, let's just drop it on the waste ground," Mickey's relieved voice replied. "We can always come back to it later."

Bounded by dense brambles, a rutted track led to their favourite playground; an open grassy area far from spying eyes. The only other vehicles brave enough to battle through, were the recovery wagons sent to remove their abandoned toys on an all too regular basis.

Dumping it the moment they arrived, they scurried off to the safety of home. Not daring to return until nightfall, they found the car exactly as they'd left it, and Mickey was first to the wheel. With little grip on the muddy surface, he slid and slew from one bush to another; each collision generating a louder and louder cheer, until an impact with an angled tree stump proved one too many for the battered Corsa.

Their fun ended, the lads reclined their seats and lit up. After reliving the day's events, conversation turned to Danny's problems.

"I can't wait to get out of the Home; they're all a bunch of pricks," he complained.

"Yeah, shame you can't live with us."

"Well my brother's gonna get his own place in Ottawa Tower next month. He says I can move in with him if I do the cleaning."

"Will they let you?"

"Dunno, the head carer says they'd have to look at the flat, and check out Jack's background. Trouble is, he's been cautioned twice for petty shit."

"Fingers crossed then heh. Just need my Dad to piss off again, and we'll get all the freedom we need," Mickey replied, sucking the last life from his cigarette. "Come on, time to call it a day."

Leaving the hatchback stranded, the lads headed back up the track.

"Hey, what do you think about J.T.'s Beemer?" Mickey asked.

"If everything we've heard about J.T. is true; I think somebody's in the shit!"

"Too right. Those dickheads are sure gonna pay."

"So who do you reckon it was?"

"Nobody off our estate that's for sure! It's either someone who doesn't know him, or there's an idiot out there who wants to take him on," Mickey replied, laughing quietly to himself. "Well fucking good luck with that!"

***

The following morning, Danny sat in the Home's dining room finishing breakfast. Normally, he'd have wolfed it down and rushed over to Mickey's, but today, the older boy's chatter on the table behind was proving far too interesting.

"Not only did they make a hundred quid each," one lad whispered. "But the motor they had away was fully fucking loaded!"

"Which Beemer was it?" another asked.

"Only the best. An M5 by all accounts, *and* he reckons it's been chipped!"

Pausing for a moment, they waited for a carer to squeeze through before continuing. Danny leant as close as he dared.

"How new was it?"

"Brand spanking; apparently it's the absolute bollocks!"

But before they could say anymore, the care worker was back...the cue for the lads to leave. Not wanting to miss out, Danny left what remained of his food, and quickly followed them into the T.V room.

Spread out on sofas, the older lads chat had finished, their attention now turned to the big screen.

But if it *was* J.T.'s motor they'd been talking about, Danny just had to find out more. He needed to be careful how he probed though; he couldn't risk making them suspicious. Taking his seat next to the sofas, he subtly kicked off the conversation.

"You know you told me how to get into a Honda – I did one at College yesterday."

"Good lad, how long did it take?"

"About a minute; it was a piece of cake."

"Sorted."

"The car on the other side was a bastard though. No matter what I tried, I couldn't get in."

The four older boys looked up from the telly.

"What was it?"

"A fairly new Beemer."

"Hmm, the new ones are double deadlocked; they're quite tricky," the nearest youth replied. "Which model was it?"

"Five series I think."

"Forget it, unless you want to put a window in. You need the keys; it's all done off the fob."

One after the other, the lads chipped in with their BMW stories, but with J.T.'s car not getting a mention, Danny needed to shift the talk once more.

"So have you boys had any five series recently?"

"Nah, you'll not see many round here. They're too big for us anyway, the three series are far better."

"One of my schoolmates saw a black one being blitzed through his area last night," Danny lied. "Said it was going like shit off a shovel!"

"That'll be Kenny Griffiths. His crew had an M5 from The Glades the other day. Kenny's been blasting round Northfield in it for the past couple of nights. Is that where your mate lives?"

"Yeah – I think so."

"The cops won't get near him in an M5! I did some time with him last year; he knows *exactly* what he's doin'!"

Not this time, Danny smiled to himself. This time the cops would be the least of his worries.

With the chatter moving on to other subjects, Danny made his excuses and left. Heading straight over to Mickey's, he couldn't wait to blurt out what he'd heard.

"And how sure are you that they've got the right car and the right kid?" Mickey asked once he'd finished.

"Well I can't be a hundred percent, but everything seems to fit."

"Okay, I'll give Deano a call," Mickey said pulling out his mobile. "I just hope we've got it right mate...'cos poor Kenny's gonna be well in the shit!"

And sure enough he was, but even Mickey couldn't have imagined what his info was about to unleash...

9

By Friday lunchtime, a relieved Chapman sat at The Black Horse's bar, chewing the fat with Porter.

"The info's all down to one of Deano's workers," Chapman said quietly, his mouth practically covered by his rising pint glass. "To be honest I was starting to get a little concerned; nobody seemed to have heard a thing."

"One of Deano's boys heh?" Porter nodded. "Do you know his name?"

"A lad called Mickey; apparently he's Derek Wilding's son."

"Derek Wilding? That waste-of-fucking-space. I hope his lad's got a bit more sense!"

"Well it certainly sounds like it," Chapman replied, raising a finger as his phone's ringtone cut the conversation short.

It didn't take long for a broad grin to spread across his face. "And that just about seals it. Looks like Razor's got some business to attend to!"

"I take it your contact's located this Kenny kid then?"

"Yep, the little shit's days are numbered!"

"And what about the Beemer?" Porter enquired, quaffing his pint's final dregs. "Has he said where it is, or the condition it's in? My boys are ready and waiting to give it the TLC treatment; they'll have it back on his drive in no-time."

"Not sure yet. All he knows, is that it's in a lock up near the shopping centre. Still, I'm sure Razor'll find a way to locate it," Chapman smiled.

"Okay, I'll go with him Saturday to pick it up. Come on, finish your drink, we've got some calls to make."

Driving over to J.T.'s in Porter's ringed Lexus, the men mulled over the following day's plans. Would Kenny be at home, would the car be in one piece, and if they did find Kenny…would Razor know when to stop?

Tactics agreed, they rolled onto J.T.'s drive. But before they'd even reached his doorstep, their boss was out to greet them. "Afternoon gents, I take it you've come bearing good news?"

"Of course," Chapman replied, shaking the outstretched hand. "I've never failed you before and I'm not going to now."

"Good, good. Now come in and grab yourselves a drink."

Picking up a crystal decanter, J.T. poured out two whiskies, and handed them to his men. "So what have you got for me?"

"First off, it's a bunch of kids from Northfield. They don't work for our rivals, so it's definitely not personal," Chapman began.

"Good, what else?"

"The one who had it away is called Kenny Griffiths; he's their leader."

"Do you know where he lives?"

"We do, but we're just waiting to find out where the car is."

"Okay, he'll soon give that up," J.T. nodded. "And when are you looking to sort him?"

"Well we did think about tonight, but Razor's men are out working the doors."

"Alright, give Razor a bell. He can arrange it for tomorrow as planned. Tell him to teach the kid a lesson; hospital not graveyard, okay!"

"No problem," Chapman nodded. "And what about his mates, are we gonna let them walk free?"

"You're fucking joking aren't you! No, one of his pals can have it as well; that should keep the others on their toes. We need to make a statement; **no fucker** messes with me!"

Drink in hand, Porter leant forward. "Once I've recovered the car, I'll let you know how quick I can get it sorted. What we do know, is it's still driveable, so it shouldn't take too long."

J.T.'s calloused fingers tightened their grip on his tumbler. "Well they'd better not smash it tonight, or it might be the graveyard after all!"

***

Packed into Deano's normally spacious lounge, the posse's gaze may well have been towards the telly, but Friday night was job night, and the team was getting ready to work.

"Okay Shags, turn the footie off," Deano instructed. "It's time for us to get started."

Blank sheet in hand, he knelt on the floor and took out a marker pen. "We're off to the city centre – our target's a designer shop in Piccadilly Arcade," he explained, sketching out a crude plan on the paper.

Huddled together, the lads pored over the drawing.

"There's an entrance at either end of the arcade," Deano continued, showing their positions with his pen tip. "While inside, there's a wide pedestrian area between the shops. Our target's called 'Viva'; just here!"

The thick black 'X' left little doubt.

"Roller-shutters cover both entrances, but there's nothing on the shop front itself. Our plan is to reverse through the shutters, run in on foot, then sledgehammer our way through the glass. We're after the stacks of folded jeans; they're piled high on shelving against the left hand wall. The alarms'll trigger the moment we get into the Arcade, so there's only time for one trip. Grab as many as you can, leg it back through the shutters, and dive into the waiting motors. Any questions so far?"

"What about security?" Shags piped up. "There's normally guards looking after those places."

"You're right, there's a couple on all night. The good news, is that they also cover the main Waterfalls Shopping Centre. My contact informs me that they'll check on the Arcade around three, then return to Waterfalls for at least half an hour. Dexy'll have an eyeball throughout; he'll call us the moment they've gone…so we're aiming to strike about 3:15, okay?" Deano continued, briefly glancing up from the map.

"We've already sourced our getaway cars and they're perfect for the job; a Mitsubishi Evo and a Subaru Impreza. I'll take the Evo, Shags'll take the Scooby. Hood, I want you to get hold of the ramming car; just make sure it's got enough power and weight to get through the shutters. We'll all meet up at…"

"Why can't *I* drive the Scooby?" Hood interrupted.

"For fuck's sake Hood!" Ronnie reacted angrily. "Why do you always have to cause problems? You've been told what to do; just get on with it!"

"'Cos unlike you, I can think for myself! Just 'cos you've been on the team longer, it doesn't mean you're any better than me."

"My decision is final," Deano growled. "Shags is a better driver than you. If we get chased, we want to get away, okay?"

"So how do you know he's better; you've never given me a chance!"

Rising to his feet, Shags had had enough. "Shut the fuck up Hood, we all know I'd cabbage you!"

"You reckon? Well how come you smashed the TT last week?"

"And of course, you've never had a crash, have you?" Shags scowled, squaring up to his rival.

"Not on a straight piece of road, no!"

Fists clenched, Shags butted forward. "You got a fucking problem?"

"For fucks sake you pair, cut it out!" Deano stepped in. "Hood, we're doing it exactly how I told you, and if you don't like it, you can fuck off and we'll use someone else, okay?"

Slowly taking his eyes off Shags, Hood turned to face Deano. Jaw as rigid as his stare, he stood facing his leader, neither moving a muscle.

"What's it to be then Hood?" Deano uttered, his glare unflinching. "Are you with us, or are you on your own?"

Silence filled the room; all eyes on the stand-off.

Finally, though his stare remained defiant, Hood's head slowly nodded.

"Good, now let's sit down and get back to business," Deano said returning to his seat. "The sledgehammer's in the back of the Evo; Ronnie, you'll do the job on the window. Mickey's given our garages the all clear, so we'll collect the cars at 2:30. Shags do you know where the Impreza is?"

"Back of Bridge Street, isn't it?"

"You got it. Don't forget to check for Mickey's pebbles before you go in. One more thing; there's a camera outside the Arcade, so make sure you're wearing your balaclavas. If there's no further questions, we'll meet back here at two…okay?" he concluded, shooting a glance over at Hood.

This time, a glower was his only reply.

Meeting over, Deano pulled Shags to one side as the posse began to leave.

"Listen, I know Hood's a pain in the arse, but Chapman insists I keep him on. We both know he's a liability, so maybe we should bring him down a peg or two; you know, teach him a little lesson?"

"Sounds good to me, what did you have in mind?"

"Well, he thinks he's the daddy behind the wheel, so let's give him the chance to prove it. Take him on at 'Tag' and fucking humiliate him!"

"Damn right I will," Shags grinned. "He won't see my ass for dust."

***

Rested, refreshed and changed, they were all back by two o' clock.

Red Bull in hand, Deano walked in from the kitchen. "Everybody got their face coverings?" he asked, looking from one nodding head to another.

"And Hood, have you brought your kit?"

"Of course," Hood tutted, tapping the rucksack at his feet.

"Good. In that case," Deano said, slugging back his caffeine hit. "Let's go get some action!"

As one they stood up and filed out, silently making their way to the garages. On arrival, each team checked out Mickey's simple security system; small pebbles lined up with carefully scratched marks on the base of the doors. Happy they were all in place, the lads entered and fired up their rides.

Undisturbed during their journey, the Evo's speakers beat softly in the background as Deano rolled onto the car park. Hiding up in a building's shadows near the entrance, he waited for the others to arrive.

But inside the Impreza, the atmosphere was altogether different. Supposedly searching for a ramming car, they'd cruised side-street after side-street in practical silence, with Hood turning down every suggestion put forward.

"Just pick one out will you!" Shags snapped, turning into yet another back-road. "Or you'll make us fucking late!"

"Hey, don't try to rush me; it's gotta be just right, okay!"

"You're such a prick! Just choose one, and get on with the job."

Turning towards his passenger window, Hood smirked, his mouth forming the words 'Fuck you' in reply.

Shags continued the low speed tour, but as another five minutes passed, his patience finally broke. Suddenly bringing the car to a halt next to a dark coloured Land Rover, he turned to face his rival.

"Listen, I've had enough of you and your attitude," he erupted. "We're here to do the job as a team, so you either do as you're fucking told, or you can piss off and Wesbo'll do it for you!"

Silence.

Nobody spoke or moved; least of all Hood, who stared defiantly into the empty street outside.

Thirty seconds passed, and still the stand-off remained.

Shags couldn't take it any longer. "Right, get out you fucking prick," he yelled. "You can make your own way home! But you'd better enjoy hospital food, 'cos when Razor finds out, you'll..."

"Fuck you!" Hood interrupted, throwing his door open, and grabbing his bag from the footwell.

Slamming his door shut, he entered the Land Rover within seconds. Moments later, he'd started it up, and despite the heavy 4x4's weight, screeched smartly out of its parking space.

Although they travelled swiftly into the city, by the time they'd reached the car park's shadows, they were running late, and Deano wasn't impressed.

"What took you? You were supposed to be here ten minutes ago!"

"Ask him," Shags scowled, shooting a glare in Hood's direction. "Trouble making his mind up apparently!"

"Well it's a good job Dexy hasn't rung yet," Deano glowered, looking down at his watch.

3:15, the call was late – was there a problem?

Arms folded, he sat on the Evo's bonnet as Hood slowly sauntered over.

"After tonight's job, you and me are gonna have a chat."

"What about?"

"You know what," Deano answered, his eyes distracted by his mobile's screen lighting up. "Just make sure you do your job tonight!"

Ignoring Hood's shrugged reply, Deano took the call. "Good, they patrolled on time," he confirmed. "Okay, we're on our way, bell me if anything changes. When you see us, make yourself scarce."

Call ended, he stood up and pulled down his balaclava. The raid was on, it was time to roll.

One behind the other they moved out; Deano at the front, Shags providing cover at the rear. With only a short distance to their target, not even the CCTV cobweb caught sight of their approach. And so, as Deano slid to a halt outside the Arcade, the team moved into attack.

Roller shutters filled the Victorian stone archway; a modern solution to an age old problem. Inside, a marble effect walkway ran the Arcade's length, while rising from the ground every 20 metres, tall trees reached ever higher to the pitched glass ceiling above.

As the posse jumped out, Deano flung open his boot. Pausing for a moment, he scanned up and down, searching for the slightest movement.

But nothing stirred; the only noise a deep rumble from the powerful engines.

Inside the Land Rover, Hood placed the gear into reverse. Eyes locked on Deano, his foot built pressure on the gas.

Holding up his right arm, Deano took a final glance around…and then Hood's patience snapped.

Clutch dumped, his tyres shrieked as they bit into the block-paving, propelling him towards the metal barricade.

The impact was deafening; metal, sparks and stone exploding far and wide.

Keeping his foot planted, Hood rammed the shutters inwards, but their sides extended deep into the stone recess. As his momentum continued, the metal wall wrapped itself around the car, until, with all rear traction lost, its tail rose sharply into the air. Finally coming to a halt at 45-degrees, only the stricken car's nose remained in contact with the ground.

Critically though, beneath the rear axle, a small opening was visible…but would its precarious position hold?

Everybody looked towards the twisted metal; its groaning audible, even above the sirens. But crucially the car didn't move; it appeared to be wedged in place.

Ronnie was the first to react. Sprinting forward, sledgehammer in hand, he dived beneath the damaged motor; the others following quickly behind.

Through the Arcade Ronnie raced, his trainers struggling to find grip on its polished surface. Sliding to a stop outside the target, he swung his heavy tool forward and crashed it through the plate glass window. Ignoring the splinters raining down, he punched the iron head through the remaining glass, and having cleared enough room, clambered through into the shop.

The posse were right on his tail. In through 'Viva's' breached window they poured, rushing to the stacks of jeans. One after the other, they grabbed their loot, and raced back to the misshapen shutters.

Arms full, Ronnie was the first to appear from beneath the wrecked car, but behind him, the blockage was haemorrhaging time. And as they were about to find out…there was precious little left.

Less than a hundred metres away, two security men suddenly burst out of The Waterfall's fire doors. Stood in the Evo's door-well, Deano had the perfect view, his hand repeatedly sounding the horn. One-by-one his posse emerged, but with the guards closing in, two remained trapped inside.

Despite being locked and loaded, Deano's Evo didn't move an inch; as engine growling, Shags' Scooby waited for its final pair to appear. Next out was Wesbo, scrambling through the tight space before dumping his haul in the Impreza. Now only Hood remained.

Racing towards them, the guards were approaching the tangled mess.

"Hurry up, hurry up!" Deano yelled, slamming his fist on the horn.

Finally, from beneath the car, Hood's upper body wriggled clear, desperately pushing his loot out in front.

But the guards were almost on top of him; he had no way out, he was trapped!

And then a sound more threatening began to rise above the din...a metallic groan overhead.

Struggling to contain the wedged Land Rover's weight, the shutters were about to let go.

"Watch out!" Deano yelled, but his warning was futile. All he could do was look on as the twisted metal released its grip.

Spinning onto his back, Hood looked up in horror...

10

Reacting in an instant, Hood threw himself to one side.

Almost as he did so, the two tonne mass slammed down…its rear wheels missing his head by a fraction. Abandoning his swag on the floor, he jumped to his feet and sprinted towards the getaway cars; his pursuers practically touching behind.

Eyes glued on their mirrors, Deano and Shags began to roll forward.

Only the Scooby's rear door was open. Clinging onto it, Wesbo yelled his instructions, his other arm beckoning Hood towards him.

But now, almost on top of the cars, the lead guard lunged at Hood…just as he dived towards the outstretched arm.

In one fluid movement, Wesbo grabbed hold, and with a scream of, "Fucking go!" yanked Hood headfirst inside. Instantly flooring the accelerator, Shags left the security guard grasping nothing but thin air as he tumbled in the escaping car's wake.

Across brick paving the two cars powered away; their smoking tyres shrouding the guard's angry gestures. Throttles planted, they slid wide onto the main road, and disappeared off into the night.

Cranking drum and bass up to full volume, they raced back through the city streets. Undisturbed by the police response, their bee-line back to The Greet was over within minutes. Straight into garages, loot left in cars, they instantly split up and returned to their homes. Job done, it was time to lie low for now. Porter's men would finish the job off; shifting the jeans on to greedy clients while the posse caught up on their sleep.

***

The following morning, Razor was up bright and early in his battered white Transit. To his rear, having picked up an exhausted Deano, Porter's Lexus followed a few car lengths behind.

Turning into Kenny's road, Razor quickly found a parking space between resident's cars. Across the street Kenny's tired looking terraced property stood amongst a line of fifty similar homes. Curtains covered the windows, while the morning's free newspaper hung loosely in the door.

"Looks like the little bleeder's havin' a lie in," Razor grinned, checking his watch. "We'll let him make the most of his beauty sleep, but if he's not out by twelve, we're goin' in. Pass me a sarnie, will you."

Obediently, the meathead to his side handed out the bacon sandwiches. Sat amongst rubbish in the rear cabin, two more heavies gratefully accepted their grub. A single bulb lit up their dark space; the windows long since replaced by metal plates.

Time passed slowly as they watched and waited, but there was definitely someone at home. The newspaper vanished, curtains opened, a figure looked out of the window. And with the clock approaching Razor's midday deadline, a youth emerged from inside.

"Here we go," the front passenger said. "Is this the one?"

"He's supposed to be a tall skinny kid with ginger hair," Razor replied.

"Looks like he's our lad then. Let's go and find out."

Before starting his engine, Razor allowed the youth to walk a short distance away. With Porter in tow, he drove slowly up the quiet street, until, drawing level with their suspect, Razor's passenger opened his window.

"Alright mate. You Kenny Griffiths?"

"Yeah, who wants to know?" the youth replied curtly.

Keeping pace alongside, the front passenger kept the lad's attention, while his two mates quietly opened the rear doors, and dropped silently to the road.

"We just wanted to have a chat with you, that's all."

"Who's we?" Kenny asked indignantly.

His question was answered by a sudden vice-like grip on his arms.

Way too late, he thrashed out in a desperate attempt to break free, but a powerful punch to his stomach instantly ended any resistance. Doubled up, the men hauled him off his feet, and threw him into the rear; quickly pulling the doors shut behind.

Though struggling to breathe let alone speak, the interrogation started regardless.

"So Kenny, do you know why we're here?"

Gathering what little breath he had, Kenny remained defiant. "Fuck off you tossers!"

"Now that's not very polite, is it? Perhaps we'd better teach you some manners."

Pinned down, face up, the men pulled out his left arm and rotated it, leaving his elbow facing the roof. While one sat on his chest, the other stood on his wrist; his metal baseball bat raised high.

Kenny looked up, his face grimacing in fear. But before he could even plead for mercy, the weapon crashed down, shattering his elbow on impact. The terrified scream from his mouth wasn't his only release; his darkening jeans swiftly revealing the other.

"I'll ask you again, do you know why we're here?"

Arrogance gone, his face contorted in pain, their victim couldn't blurt his reply out quick enough.

"No, no, I'm sorry, I'm sorry," he whimpered.

"Ah yes; that's more like it," the bruiser smiled. "Now then, there's a certain BMW you've been running around in that's of interest to us…it belongs to our boss you see. Be a sensible boy; tell me all about it."

"Beemer? What Beemer? I don't know anything about it," he spluttered. "You've got to believe me."

"Ahh, now that is a shame. Well let me refresh your memory."

Shuffling Kenny's body across the floor, the men repeated their previous preparation; this time holding out the right arm.

His eyes widening in terror, Kenny stared helplessly as the baseball bat prepared to strike again.

"Alright, alright, I'll tell you what you want!" he squealed.

"Good lad, my boss *will* be pleased. 'Cos you know what, he's rather fond of his little motor, and he's keen to have it back. So, your first job is to take us to it, and I don't expect any fucking about," the heavy ordered, brushing the weapon's shaft against Kenny's cheek. "Now which way do we go?"

His resolve broken, Kenny did exactly as he was told. Carefully following the blurted directions, Razor soon pulled up outside a line of garages.

"It's the one with the red door; there's no lock on it," Kenny croaked.

Engine running, Razor left his Transit and lifted the up-and-over door.

Sure enough, a BMW's front grille stared back. Deano quickly peered inside.

"Can you find out where the keys are," he asked. "The less damage we cause the better."

Seconds later, Razor returned with the answer. Dropping to his knees, Deano felt beneath the front wheel. Sure enough, the keys were there.

It was a tight squeeze, the car's flared arches barely wide enough to fit through the gap. Once out into the open, the state of J.T.'s pride and joy was plain for all to see. As expected, it was plastered in filth, but bodywork wise, other than a smashed wing mirror, all appeared to be in good condition.

Turning to Razor, Porter nodded. "Okay, leave the motor with us, it shouldn't take too long to sort. I take it your work still needs…completing?"

Razor grinned his reply, and returning to his Transit, began to drive back to The Greet. The sedate journey, however, belied the activities inside. Using a heavy metal hammer to systematically shatter Kenny's fingers, Razor's men soon extracted his accomplice's details. Item-by-item, they pilfered his pockets, ripped the clothes from his body, and left him face down on the floor.

Once back on his manor, Razor turned off the main drag and picked his way across a wasteland. Free from prying eyes, he eventually came to a halt.

Opening up the rear doors, bright light flooded into the cabin. Bound and gagged, Kenny's limp body lay at the meathead's feet. With an unsympathetic shove, they rolled him off the edge, sending him sprawling in a heap on the ground.

Shocked back to consciousness, Kenny's eyes opened…just in time to see the horrific conclusion.

Doors slammed shut, reverse lights came on, Razor stared deep into his mirror.

With Kenny's body lying in full view, he pressed the gas, lifted the clutch, and rolled back along the hard track.

In desperation, his victim attempted to roll clear, but it was too little, too late; the Transit's rear axle kicking up as it snapped his legs like a pair of twigs.

But the only ears that could hear Kenny's muffled screams were travelling slowly away; their task now practically complete. All that was left was an anonymous call to the emergency services. As long as they met their response times, Kenny had a chance to survive.

**

By six in the evening, the posse were gathered back at Deano's, ready for debrief and payments.

Drink in hand, legs sprawled over the side, Deano chilled out in his armchair. "Good result last night guys; Porter's well chuffed. All a bit close for comfort in the end though."

"Only because some prick messed up with the shutters!" Shags grumbled, shooting off the now familiar scowl.

"Like you'd have done any better," Hood bristled. "Anyway, you're the one who chose the car; it wouldn't have happened if you'd picked something with a bit more poke."

"Fuck off, you had plenty of time to choose. You're a liability Hood; you nearly made us late, you went before the signal, and you never even got your jeans out. You know what…we should have just left you there!"

"Oh I'm fucking sorry! I'll let the car fall on me next time shall I?" Hood replied, rising to his feet.

Shags shrugged his shoulders. "You'd be no loss to us."

Hood took a pace forward. Shags rose to meet him.

"Don't be a pair of dickheads," Deano intervened, pushing the rivals apart. "If you really want to sort things out, we'll do it our normal way, okay?"

"Any time, any place; I'll piss all over him," Shags goaded, his stare unflinching.

"You're full of shit," Hood scowled back. "Hope you're used to hospital food."

"Enough!" Deano yelled. "Nobody's gonna get hurt, it's just a game of 'Tag', okay?"

He waited, looking from one to the other, until begrudgingly, they each nodded their heads.

"Good. Tomorrow night at eight it is then. I'll let you decide what to bring."

Again, the two opponents nodded.

"Right, now sit down and shut up unless you've got something useful to say."

Squabble over, Deano concluded the de-brief, and shared out Porter's payment. Cash-in-hand, the posse left one-by-one until only Shags was left.

"Be careful mate," Deano warned as Shags made towards the door. "Hood's an evil piece of shit. He'll do *anything* to take your place."

***

The following evening, phosphorous lights lit up the Greet streets with their yellow glow. Lined up next to each other on dry tarmac, the two rivals revved their powerful engines, goading with every prod.

Windows down, Shags sat in a gunmetal-grey Honda Type-R, exchanging insults with his opponent.

"You're gonna be eating my dirt you cocky twat!"

"Yeah, yeah, I'm really scared," Hood replied, his eyes staring through the Clio Sport's windscreen. "It's you who needs to watch your ass, 'cos believe me, I'm coming to take you out!"

"Yeah right. Don't forget; when the flag drops, the bullshit stops," Shags sneered back, his words drowned out by another blast from Hood's exhaust.

The 'tag' match was about to begin. Used for years to settle differences, the idea was simple: having been given a three second start, the lead car's objective was to shake off its pursuer. However, the challenger's task made the contest altogether more dangerous; not only did they have to catch the lead car, they also had to 'tag' it, with evidence to be seen on their bumpers.

Stepping between the cars, Deano raised two arms aloft.

Roaring their encouragement, the posse's volume rose as their leader counted down.

Revs bouncing off its limiter, the moment his arm dropped, the Type-R suddenly launched forward; its fat tyres instantly finding traction.

No sooner had it raced away, than the posse's attention turned to the Clio.

Hood hadn't move a muscle. Engine screaming, he waited to unleash the power.

"Go!" Deano shouted, his left arm plunging to its side.

Handbrake released, tyres billowing smoke, the Clio charged after its prey.

Left huddled on the pavement as the racing engines disappeared into the night, the posse chatted amongst themselves: who was going to win, how long would it take…would they both return in one piece?

11

In the darkness, Danny's bike cruised beside Mickey's.

"You heard anything off Deano yet?" Danny asked. "He's normally pretty quick getting back to us. What if I got it wrong, and it wasn't Kenny?"

"Nah, don't worry mate, your info was bang on. He's probably just busy or something; he'll soon give us a call," Mickey replied. "And you know what, he's gonna be chuffed as fuck when he does!"

Confident words, but not matched by his feelings inside. Why *hadn't* Deano been in touch? Surely Kenny would have been visited by now? Had Danny made a mistake after all…shit, that wasn't even worth thinking about! Riding in silence, he ran through the possibilities over and over again. He could call Deano and ask him direct – but that wasn't how things were done; he was supposed to call with info, not questions. No, it'd have to wait; they'd just have to sweat it out.

Faraway, a noise filtered into his brain, disrupting his thoughts. Faint sounds to begin with, but they were definitely engines, and thrashed engines at that. Bringing his bike to a halt, he cocked his head to one side; craning to make out where they were coming from.

"Can you hear them?" he asked, as Danny pulled alongside.

"Yeah, sounds like they're having some fun."

"By the sounds of it, there's two of them – maybe it's a chase!" Mickey said excitedly.

"Wicked! Hope they come this way; I can't wait to see the pigs getting blitzed."

Stood over their bikes, they waited at the deserted roadside, mesmerised by the sound's ebb and flow as time-and-again the cars appeared to draw ever closer, before disappearing into the distance once more.

Again the engine noise started to rise.

"They're definitely coming towards us this time!" Danny squealed.

Mickey gazed up the long straight, shielding his eyes as headlights burned into his retinas. He was right, there *were* two cars, and they were definitely chasing each other. But where were the lights and sirens? This was no ordinary chase; these were hot-hatches…and they were flying.

Within seconds, less than a car length apart, the motors were almost upon him; their high-pitched screams filling his ears.

"The Type-R's going V-Tec!" Danny yelled above the din.

Ignoring his friend, Mickey's focus remained fixed on the racers. Well in excess of 90mph, the lead car turned into the downhill corner, its brake lights briefly flickering as it started to drift wide. Although the minor adjustment brought the Honda back in line, it allowed its chaser to close the remaining gap.

Accelerator floored, the Clio was instantly on top of its prey, striking the rear with its bumper. Already at its grip's limit, the Type-R's back-end gave way. Out of control, it spun wildly, mounted the kerb, and slammed into a low garden wall.

Braking heavily, the Clio stopped next to the smoking wreckage; the driver watching, waiting.

But nothing moved.

And then house lights came on, doors opened, people began to pour out. Slowly at first, the Clio started to roll away, and then, as the first group reached the Honda, it extinguished its lights and raced off into the night.

Mickey shuffled closer to the damaged car. Hot brakes, rubber and oil filled the air; while the settling dust began to reveal a motionless figure at the wheel. Rushing to help him, the residents frantically tried to get in – but it was hopeless; the door was jammed shut.

Shifting position for a better look, Mickey craned his neck around the ever growing crowd. The driver had to be in a bad way, maybe even dead; but no matter where he moved, he could only get fleeting glimpses inside.

Within minutes, emergency services started to arrive. Medics rushed to the trapped victim, while firefighters made ready their jaws-of-life, and flooded the scene with their lighting.

"And what about you two, did you see anything?" a voice suddenly disturbed Mickey's concentration.

His attention completely focused on the wrecked Type-R, Mickey hadn't noticed the police's activities. Looking up, he saw a Traffic Officer's white cap and fluorescent jacket.

Pen and paper in hand, he stared directly at Mickey.

"Well, cat got your tongue?" he frowned.

"Erm, no, no, sorry," Mickey stammered. "We were riding past when we saw everyone around the car. We just thought we'd come over and see what'd happened."

"And what about you?" the policeman said, turning to Danny. "Are you just here for a nose, or did you see more than your mate's letting on?"

"No, no," he replied nervously. "We just came across it, honest."

"Hmm, well if something does jog your memory, you know where we are. Anyway, there's nothing to see here, so it's time for you pair to clear off, understand?"

"Okay," they replied in unison, remounting their bikes. However, as the officer turned his attention to the next witness, they quickly ducked out of sight, re-emerging amongst the crowd on the other side – this was far too interesting to leave just yet!

Shadows flickered beneath the floodlights as firefighters moved to and fro across the gruesome scene. Calmly attempting to release the driver's trapped leg, their jaws-of-life attacked the 'A' pillar; slicing and carving its way into the crushed footwell.

Neck-brace in hand, a medic immobilised the youth's spine, and fleetingly stepping back, provided Mickey with his first real glimpse of the victim. Hardly recognisable as a human face, a bloody pulp groaned towards him. His stomach turning, Mickey swiftly took a step back.

"I thought I'd told you two to piss off!"

The traffic cop was back, and in no mood to be ignored twice.

"Sorry sir, we'll get going," Mickey answered hastily, his feet jumping back onto the pedals.

"Too right you are, now get out of my sight!"

Riding a little further away, they stopped again and continued to watch the spectacle. Paramedics came and went, fire-fighters threw sand on the road, police specialists began taking photos.

But eventually, once the crowd had drifted away, a lone recon team measuring skid-marks were all that remained.

"Come on," Mickey said, turning away from the scene. "The fun's over, it's time we were getting back."

"So do you reckon the Clio hit him on purpose?"

"Definitely," Mickey nodded. "And if it's got anything to do with the posse…there's gonna be fucking trouble!"

***

Having waited patiently for half an hour, the faraway drone of a racing engine finally reached the posse. As one, they rose to their feet and looked towards the horizon. Headlights swung towards them, the glow growing ever brighter as the motor accelerated hard. With a final flourish, the car's nose hunkered down under heavy braking, spun 180 degrees on the handbrake, and slid to a halt alongside.

A broad grin straddling his face, Hood jumped out and strolled to the front of his car. Sure enough, clearly visible on the bumper's offside was a dent bearing the tell-tale gunmetal grey paint.

"Well done," Deano acknowledged, examining the damage. "But how come Shags hasn't followed you?"

"How am I supposed to know," Hood shrugged. "After I nudged him, I came straight back. Those are the rules aren't they?"

"I think I'll give him a shout," Deano replied sceptically, walking off to make the call. "He can tell me for himself what's happened."

It didn't take long to find out; a medic answered the phone.

"Who's speaking please?" she asked.

"Er – just a friend," Deano answered, the colour draining from his face. "Can I talk to him please?"

"I'm afraid that's not possible at the moment. Perhaps *you* could assist us though; we really need to identify your friend. Can you help us out?"

Deano paused for a moment. "Look, I'm really sorry, I just know him by his nickname. I'll get his mom to call you straightaway; she'll fill you in. Is he…is he okay?"

"I can't discuss his condition over the phone. What I can tell you, is that we're taking him to Heartlands Hospital. It's probably best for his mom to speak to us there."

Call ended, Deano marched back to confront the victor.

"He's on his way to the fucking hospital! What the hell really happened?" he seethed. "And don't give me any bullshit!"

"I told you, all I did was give him a nudge. After that, he just pissed off at speed – he's probably had a head-loss and cabbaged it somewhere!"

"Well if I find out any different, you're fucking dead!" Deano spat back. "Now I suggest you torch the motor and make yourself scarce, 'cos if Shags doesn't manage to pull through…I'll be the least of your fucking worries!"

12

"And then the poor kid fell out of my van, which was very careless, 'cos I was reversing at the time. How was I to know his legs were underneath?" Razor sniggered, finishing the story of Kenny's demise.

"And what about the others," J.T. asked, languishing in his armchair.

"Well as luck would have it, young Kenny squealed like a pig; gave up his mates' names with very little persuasion. So we went round to the one lad's place and knocked on his door. The little toe-rag only went and told me to 'Piss off'!"

"Tut, tut," J.T. frowned, gesturing for his henchman to continue.

"As you can imagine, I was right taken aback. There I was, with a couple of my bigger mates, and a five-foot streak of piss thinks he can take the mick! Well, *he* thought that'd be the end of it and went to shut the door, but when he found my size twelves in the way, he did no more than kick me in the bleedin' shin! Now you know me J.T., I'm normally quite a forgiving chap, but this kid had really pissed me off, so he quickly found that my hand fits nicely round his throat. He was a right cocky bleeder though, kicking and punching for all his worth…so I kept hold of his scrawny neck and held him over the balcony. I told him he shouldn't have nicked your Beemer, and to be fair to him, that did shut him up for a few seconds. He soon found his lungs though, 'cos my hand was a bit sweaty and he just…fell out of my grasp!" Razor chuckled. "Only trouble was, his flat's three floors up and the concrete he landed on could have been a bit softer. Oh well, at least Kenny's got someone to talk to in hospital now!"

Raising his glass, J.T. began to congratulate his heavy, but was almost immediately disturbed by the sound of heavy tyres rolling onto the gravel outside.

"My baby!" he beamed, glancing out through his window. "She's back!"

Razor jumped quickly to his feet, holding the doors open as his boss made his way to the car.

"As good as new," Porter greeted him, handing over the keys.

Meticulously, J.T. inspected every inch of the gleaming bodywork. Once inside, his seat's memory setting silently adjusted position, Vivaldi's woodwind piped softly through the speakers, and on pressing the starter; the big V8 roared into life.

"Thank goodness for that," Johnny said, looking at J.T.'s grinning face. "He's been like a bear with a sore head since it was taken; you know what he's like if somebody upsets him. Is his car really as good as before?"

"If not better," Porter smiled. "I've even knocked the mileage back to where it was."

While their leader went off for a cruise, The Power Firm returned to the lounge, helping themselves to his drinks bar. Several whiskies later, J.T. was back, his beam as wide as before.

"It's bang-on Porter, you've done a grand job; in fact you've all done a grand job. So tell me Chapman, how *did* you find out who nicked it?"

"Trade secrets boss," he joked. "What I can tell you is that Mickey Wilding's buddy got the ball rolling. We might have been struggling without him."

"Good lad, good lad," J.T. mused. "Those two are working out pretty well. Make sure you reward them properly; they could be useful to us in the future – which brings me to the real reason why we're here. Our little operation may well have expanded nicely over the past few years, but we need to get greedy; it's time to ramp things up a notch," he said, knocking back his scotch. "Now, I asked you to bring in your projections for the coming year. Porter, we'll start with you."

Taking a final drag, Porter casually stubbed his nub-end into the ashtray at his side. Instrumental in the Firm's expansion, his wily negotiation skills had made him irreplaceable to J.T. and customers alike. Future trade relied solely on his enterprise, and so, with the diversion of finishing his cigarette complete, the group's attention was fixed firmly on him.

"Gentlemen," he began. "I concluded an interesting meeting with a counterpart from London last week. His contacts are desperate for our merchandise; we're talking fifty-grand's worth, every…single…week!"

Allowing the figures to be digested, he pulled the next fag from his packet.

"Effectively, this requires us doubling current production levels. And he assures me, that if we honour this initial commitment, there will be substantial increases in the future."

"And what about motors? How much room do we have for expansion?" J.T. enquired.

"To be fair, the problem doesn't lie with getting rid of them; I can handle as many as we can get hold of. But gone are the days when our boys could walk onto a car park armed only with a screwdriver; today's decent motors are crammed so full of security, immobilisers and Trackers, you'd need a bleedin' electronics degree to have 'em away! Of course, as we know all too well, nothing's impossible; if you nick the keys, you nick the car. The trouble is, it's riskier, takes extra planning, and is far more time consuming."

"Thank you Porter, food for thought indeed," J.T replied, drawing deeply from his cigar. "Well gentlemen, to me the way forward seems pretty damn obvious! We have the opportunity to expand in all areas, and the only thing stopping us is a lack of workers! The equation needs correcting. We *will* meet the demand, we *will* increase our workforce! Chapman, are you hearing me loud and clear?"

Chapman swallowed hard; his updates weren't going to go down so well.

"I'll certainly do my best, however as it stands, we only have one established crew we can trust to do the jobs. And yes, up to now Deano's posse have been very successful – they've been running two cars on every job to maximise returns. Unfortunately, things haven't been helped by last night's incident."

J.T. shifted in his chair, a frown beginning to form. "What do you mean 'last night's incident'? Is there something I'm not aware of?"

"I'm afraid so boss, I guessed this meeting would be the best time to bring it up."

"Get on with it Chapman, spit it out!"

"Okay, okay," he stuttered. "Apparently there were some issues within the group. Rather than coming to me to sort them, they decided to play tag; it's where two cars..."

"I know what fucking 'tag' is," J.T. exploded. "Just tell me what fucking happened!"

"Well from what I can gather, it ended in one of the lads having a smash; Deano reckons he's lucky to have only lost his foot. And what with a few court cases coming up, we could end up losing some more."

"What the fuck are they playing tag for!" J.T. raged, jumping up from his seat. "Lost his fucking foot...serves the tosser right! And you can tell Deano from me, *he's* on borrowed time as well!"

Unmoving, Chapman waited for J.T. to return to his armchair before continuing. "However, I've anticipated our future demand for loyal workers, and recruited carefully. We've got a large feeder group already helping to prepare jobs, while beneath them, our younger teams can't wait to get involved in the juicy stuff. Rest assured, we'll handle any extra work in the short term, and as we expand over the next few years, the younger lads will be coming through nicely. I just need your approval to allow the tiers to rise, so to speak."

"Looks like it's decided then," J.T. nodded. "Any questions gents?"

Razor's hand shot up; confusion spread across his furrowed brow.

"Yes?"

"So who do you want me to do over next, boss?"

"You've not quite kept up with this morning's meeting have you buddy," J.T. sighed, shaking his head despairingly. "I think we'll let the others run scared for the moment. But don't worry, I'm sure we'll be needing your talents again...and next time we won't be so kind!"

***

Heartland's trauma unit were used to caring for teenage victims; their latest two little different to the many treated before.

Curtains drawn around his bed, Kenny's motionless body lay beneath the white sheets. Legs in traction, elbow shattered, he winced as he croaked out his woeful tale.

"Lads, I'm telling you, they didn't give a shit. They just left me there to die!"

"Well they won't get away with it," his mate replied angrily. "We'll soon sort the fuckers out!"

"Have you not been listening to me? These blokes don't mess about; they're absolute nutters!" Kenny grimaced. "They'd kill you without a second thought."

The two mates shot each other a look.

"Well who the hell are they?"

"Yeah, and why did they go for you in the first place?"

"It's that bloody Beemer we had away from the posh Health Club; it belongs to one of their mates. Somehow they found out I nicked it, and you can see what happened next. If they found me, they might..." Kenny paused, slowly rolling his head to look his friends in the eye, "...be able to find you. Watch your backs lads, they're evil bastards."

Colour draining from their faces, they replied almost as one. "You didn't give them our names did you?"

"Of course not, what do you take me for?"

"'Cos Jimmy's lying in another hospital with his legs broken. His mum won't let us near him, says it was an accident...that he fell off his balcony. But we all know that's a load of bollocks; Jimmy's proper streetwise. How the hell did they find out where he lived? Are you sure you didn't give us up, 'cos we're in deep shit if you did?"

"Of course not," Kenny muttered, turning his head back. "The only thing I told them was where the car was, and that was only after they'd smashed my fingers!"

Before they could press him further, the curtains suddenly pulled to one side. Two uniformed officers walked in.

"Oh dear, if it isn't our old friend Kenny Griffiths," the WPC smiled. "Unless I'm mistaken, I'd say someone's taken a serious dislike to you!"

"Very fucking funny," Kenny groaned. "Now piss off, I've got nothing to say!"

"Come now Kenny, for once in your life you're a victim. We're here to help victims," the officer said sarcastically.

"Fuck off, you don't give a shit!"

"Now, now, let's not get abusive, we're just having some banter with you," the cop smiled, pulling up a chair. "We really *have* come to take details of the attack. What can you tell us about it?"

"Listen, I can't remember a thing. One minute I was leaving home, the next I was waking up in hospital, okay!"

"Alright, alright, I understand you're upset," the officer said sitting back. "But what about the people who did this to you; surely you must know who they are?"

"No, why should I?"

"Well in your short stay on this planet, you've managed to upset quite a few people. Perhaps you upset the wrong ones this time?"

The policewoman's accurate guess hit a nerve.

"Just piss off will you!" Kenny replied, turning his head away.

"Suit yourself. I just hope your friends don't end up in a similar condition," the officer said, rising from her seat. "That would be a terrible shame!"

Leaving the lads to mull over her parting words, she and her colleague strolled off the ward, but not before they passed two traffic cops on their way in.

"Crikey, it's busy in here today!" she smiled. "You're not here to see Kenny Griffiths as well are you?"

"Thankfully not, what's he been up to this time?"

"Would you believe *he's* the victim for once? Somebody's done him over good and proper – looks like a professional job. He's not going to be troubling us for a while, that's for sure! So, what *are* you guys here for?"

"Oh, just another joyrider whose thieving days are numbered. Survived the accident, but lost his foot."

"Aaah, what a pity. At this rate we'll soon be out of a job!"

"If only that were the case," the traffic cop replied, shaking his head. "Unfortunately, we all know that as one departs, another one takes their place, and so the cycle continues."

"Ain't that the truth! Still, it's nice to see them get their karma occasionally; just like Kenny's mate we're off to see next. He's nursing two broken legs and a shattered pelvis. Our anonymous witness tells us he was hung over a balcony and dropped, but what's the betting his memory's as bad as Kenny's! Oh well, we'd better get off to see him, catch you guys later."

"Later," the traffic cops replied, and headed towards their own victim's bedside.

Although conscious, Shags' breathing was deep and laboured. Grief stricken, his mother sat at his bedside clasping his hand, her eyes fixed on the empty space beneath the sheet where her son's right foot should have been.

"Hello Mrs Nash, I'm PC Draycott and this is PC Wilson. We're investigating the collision your son was involved in. Do you mind if we join you?"

"Yes, yes, please sit down; I've been waiting for some answers all day. The staff here won't tell me a thing, my lad's too out of it to help, and my calls to the cop shop never get answered! So tell me, what the hell happened?"

Taking a seat, PC Draycott began to explain; giving away little more than had already been released to the Press.

"I've told him 'til I'm blue in the face about those damn cars. He promised me he'd stopped, but how am I supposed to keep my eye on him? Since his Dad left us, I have to work every hour God sends!" she said angrily, pulling a tissue from her pocket. "And now look at him, his future's ruined!"

Hunched over, she buried her head in her hands.

"Don't blame yourself Mrs Nash, it really isn't your fault. Fast cars are like a drug to kids everywhere; it gives them relief from the boredom of life. You're not alone, parents all across the country feel just as powerless to stop them."

He waited for her to dry her eyes before continuing. "If it's okay with you, I'd like to have a few words with your son; see if he can shed some light on a few issues still puzzling us."

"You carry on, although I wouldn't hold your breath; he won't tell me anything."

Having turned towards the conversation at his side, Shags stared wearily at the officer.

"I know you probably don't want to talk to us right now, so I promise I'll keep it brief, okay?"

Shags head slowly nodded.

"Thank you, we're hoping you can fill in a few blanks. Can we start with what you can remember about the bump?"

Shags swallowed hard. "It's all a bit fuzzy I'm afraid…I just remember losing it on the bend," he croaked slowly. "Did anyone else get hurt?"

"No, you just left the road and hit a wall. However, we *are* concerned by the scrape to your car's rear bumper. It's bright red, and our recon boys tell us it's fresh. Do you know anything about it?"

Visibly wincing, Shags turned his head away.

"I'm sorry, I didn't quite catch your answer?"

"No," he muttered, staring at the ceiling above. "I don't know."

"Ok officer, I think my son's starting to tire, do you mind…"

"No, not at all, we understand," Draycott smiled, passing her his business card. "If anything changes, or if you have any other questions, don't hesitate to call me. In any case, we'll pop back in a couple of days; it's quite normal for memories to slowly return after heavy impacts like this. And you never know, he might remember something that could assist us all!"

Rising, the officers bid their goodbyes and left.

"So what do you think?" Wilson asked his colleague as they made their way to the front entrance.

"Maybe he can remember the bump, maybe he can't. But one thing *is* for certain, he knows more than he's letting on."

"Yeah, you're not wrong there; shame he'll never share it with us."

"Perhaps *he* won't, but I spy someone who might be a little more forthcoming."

His head down, a well-dressed youth wearing sunglasses was approaching.

"Afternoon Deano," Draycott greeted him. "You come to visit your friend?"

"Yeah, I take it you guys have just been to see him. How is he?"

"Well he's certainly going to live, but as you know, he's got a tough road ahead. And just to give you a heads up; his mum's with him at the moment, so you might be in for a frosty reception."

"Can't really blame her," Deano nodded. "I guess I'll just have to face the bollocking; I know he'd do the same for me."

"Listen," Draycott said, his voice quietening. "You and I go back a long way. I know you don't grass and I wouldn't expect you to, but I also know you don't stand for any violence. Tell me, and this is strictly off the record; we've got a cherry red dent on Shags' bumper, and just before the collision we had a report of two cars racing each other in the area. If I put two and two together, would I come up with 'tag'?"

"Off the record?"

"Off the record," the officer confirmed.

The faintest of nods was all the reply he needed.

"You know I can't tell you who else was involved," Deano said under his breath. "But I would be interested to know whether it was the tag that sent Shags off the road?"

"To be honest, recon can't prove one way or the other, and so far no witnesses have come forward. We're going to have to rely on what Shags tells us, which let's face it, will be very little; *you* might get more joy of course. Well, you know where I am if we can help each other any further."

"Okay, thanks for that. Look I'd better get off," Deano replied, glancing around. "No disrespect, but I can't be seen chatting to you guys!"

Head back down, he headed off into the hospital.

"Hmm, I sense all is not well in Deano's little posse," Draycott frowned. "Mark my words, there's trouble ahead, and next time they won't be so lucky!"

13

For Mickey and Danny the following three years passed by in a blur. Having dropped out of school without a qualification to their names, they'd been able to devote their lives to what excited them most. Entrusted with keeping a watchful eye on the new kids below, they'd handed over their old tasks; leaving them free to focus on the wholesale theft of motors.

While Danny had developed a reputation for his light-fingered expertise, Mickey's growing confidence behind the wheel had led to many a close shave; his intimate local knowledge time and again frustrating his pursuers. Permitted to steal cars at their leisure, their daily blasts through the city streets could only mean one thing…their luck would eventually run out.

Inside another hot hatch, Danny's head nodded in time to the cranked up beat. The theft had once again proved all too easy; the keys removed from a jacket while their owner went up to the bar.

"Not as quick as last night's Focus," Mickey shouted above the music, his right foot pressed deep into the carpet.

"Yeah, but the stereo's decent, let's see how loud it'll go," Danny bawled back, turning up the bass.

Windows down, fists pumping, they belted out the song…but their makeshift karaoke was about to be brought to an end.

Seeing a roundabout approaching, Mickey lifted off the gas and glanced down at the speedo – 120mph, not bad, not bad, but still ten less than the Focus he grinned.

Suddenly, Danny stopped singing. "Shit, traffic cops ahead!" he yelled.

Now onto the brakes, Mickey glanced to his right; the hairs on his neck instantly standing to attention. Sure enough, a liveried BMW sat waiting; side window down, its passenger staring directly at them.

Despite his path towards the junction being clear, Mickey continued to cut his pace. Maybe, just maybe, they were after somebody else. After all, they'd only just nicked the car; it couldn't have been circulated yet…could it? A quick glimpse in the mirror gave him the answer.

"Bollocks!" he groaned. "They've dropped in behind; I think we've been rumbled."

"Who gives a shit!" Danny grinned, flicking the 'V's out of his window. "C'mon, it's time for us to play; let's kick those coppers' arses!"

Needing no further invitation, Mickey floored it; his tyres screeching as they slew across the road surface. Adrenaline firing, he focused on the road ahead. He'd done this so many times before; he just needed to stay calm, get back to the Greet, and take them into the alleyways – it should be a piece of piss.

Two minutes passed, and all was going to plan. But pulling out to overtake the next motor, a brief mirror check revealed a second car tucking in behind.

"Looks like we've got company; you spotted the unmarked Audi?"

"Good, more for us to blow then!" Danny enthused. "C'mon, let's see what this thing'll do!"

Increasing the pace, Mickey hurtled towards the Greet's relative safety. This was what he lived for he smiled; fast cars and the thrill of the chase! And to his side, his best mate clowning around as usual; stood up through the open sunroof, goading the pursuers behind!

But his enjoyment was short lived. Waiting at the next junction, more battenburg sat ready to pounce.

"Something's not right," Mickey said anxiously, racing past its nose. "We've only done four miles and we've already got three cops on our tail!"

"Bollocks," Danny scowled. "Somebody at the pub must have spotted us!"

"Oh well, they'll soon disappear when we do *our* vanishing trick!"

Danny's face lit up. "Are you thinking what I'm thinking?"

"Damn right mate," Mickey smirked. "Our old favourite…the Alwold Road jump. They'll never see us again after that!"

But with two miles still to go, he still needed to be on his guard; what might the police be planning for him? He'd managed to evade their stingers before, he'd even driven around makeshift roadblocks; but there was nothing he could do about their ultimate weapon. In car or on foot, there was no way to outrun the helicopter, and by now it couldn't be too far away.

Through the streets he blasted, driving as fast as he dared. Eyes constantly flicking up through the sunroof, he scanned the heavens above – still no sign of the chopper, and only one mile to go.

"Nearly home and dry mate," Danny confirmed. "They're all about to be history!"

To the rear of the houses in Alwold Road, a service track ran its entire length. Finally ending in a raised earth mound known as 'The Jump', joyriders regularly raced up its steep sides, launching their cars into the air…before crashing back down onto the dirt track behind.

He'd been over it so many times before; he knew the speed, he knew the angle for 'take-off', and most importantly, he knew the police wouldn't follow; he just had to get there in time. Pushing the Golf to its limits, he scanned the road ahead. Still no sign of cops or stingers; nothing could stop him now.

Onto the final roundabout, he deftly slid the GTi towards its exit, before flicking the wheel to the left, and launching it straight onto the service track. Flooring the accelerator along its uneven surface, he looked in his mirror for the final time…like lemmings into my trap, he smiled.

Eyes returning to the path ahead, his smug grin instantly disappeared. There in front of him, just prior to the jump, blue strobes greeted his arrival. Behind the Panda car, two officers stood cross-armed, staring straight at his rapid approach.

There was no way out. Barely the width of his car, the track was hemmed in by dense bushes either side – *he'd* fallen into *their* trap.

"Shit!" Danny shouted. "What the fuck are we gonna do?"

Mickey instinctively knew the answer; they had to dump it and run. Okay, the cops had them cornered, but only he and Danny knew every inch of the neighbourhood. All they needed to do was split up, divide their pursuers, and leg it home before the chopper arrived.

"I'll drop it by the fencing!" he yelled, jumping straight onto the brakes. "You aim for the track, I'll go over the gardens. When you get home, lie low and I'll call you later!"

Before the final word had even left his lips, his mate was out and running.

Mickey was only moments behind; his trainers biting briefly into the dirt before he leapt at a six-foot wooden fence. Clambering over the top, he landed in bushes, before sprinting off through the rear garden; his eyes fixed on the gate at its end. Over that and he'd be onto Alwold Road. Twenty more metres and he'd duck into the alleyways. After that…he'd be home and dry.

Wide-eyed, pulse pounding, he sprung upwards, hauling himself to the top of the gate.

But suddenly, a squad car skidded to a halt outside. Doors bursting open, its officers were out in a flash.

Surrounded; he had to think quickly.

Cut off at the front, hemmed in to the side…only one option remained.

Retracing his steps, he rushed towards the oncoming cops. A deft sidestep avoided the first officer's lunge, and gave him enough momentum to leap at the fence alongside. Headfirst, he attempted to throw his lithe frame over, only to become stranded at its peak; his body one side, his ankles clamped by strong hands the other. Thrashing out with his legs, he felt the grip slacken, until with one final kick…he managed to break free; his body tumbling onto the flowerbed below.

Onto his feet and away, he attacked the garden boundaries like a steeplechase. Over walls and bushes, hedges and fences, he attempted to outrun the pack. But the makeshift assault course was sapping his energy. Lungs bursting, his strength began to fade.

He glanced back over his shoulder. The nearest cop was stumbling through a hedge, and still two gardens behind. They were just as knackered as he was; maybe he had a chance after all!

Clambering over a tall wooden fence, he angled right, his movement hidden from view. Up past the side of a house, he leapt onto a dustbin, hauled himself over the gate, and landed feet first on the drive.

"Well, well, it must be the Olympics hurdling champion!"

Startled, he spun round to face the voice...

14

Two sturdy hands seized hold of his arm. With what energy remained, Mickey attempted to jerk away, but it was useless; he was shattered…he'd been caught.

"Don't be silly son, your fun's over for today," the officer warned, slipping the first handcuff on. "Tango Charlie One Five to control. I have the driver in custody, show me en-route to Stechford."

"Yes received," the radio crackled back. "Driver in custody, passenger still outstanding."

Mickey's ears pricked up. Was that a glimmer of hope? Had the cops been too focused on him…had Danny managed to escape?

"So young man, you gonna tell us who your mate is?"

Still struggling for breath, Mickey panted his reply. "I don't know…what you're…talking about."

"Oh you will. And if you haven't realised yet, you're under arrest for stealing the Golf, okay?"

He couldn't be bothered to make a reply; he'd messed up, and now he'd have to pay the price. Head stooped, he was led away to the police car.

Driving off, the officer tried to spark up a conversation. "I'm PC Draycott, I don't think we've met before. Are you new to this game?"

Mickey's thousand-yard-stare didn't waver.

"You don't have to talk to us if you don't want to, but remember this; we're just here to do a job and it's not meant to be personal. If it's any consolation…you put up a good chase in that GTi; you're a pretty decent driver."

The compliment passed him by; his mind far away, thinking over the consequences. His mum would go mad if she found out; she still didn't have a clue what he was up to. And what about the posse? It might well be the first time he'd been arrested, but would Deano still trust him to keep up his work? More importantly, what about Danny; had he managed to escape, or was he following in a cop car behind? Over and over, the questions ran through his mind, his focus only shifting as his car slowed for the barrier ahead. This was reality; this was Stechford nick.

Inside the detention bay, roller-shutters rattled closed behind, as handcuffed to the rear, Mickey stooped forward to exit the car. Escorted to the metal door in the corner, he took one last look around…before entering inside the slammer.

Drab grey walls gave way to a small caged area, beyond which a counter sat above a four-foot solid wall.

Led to a wooden bench inside the cage, he was left handcuffed and alone. Staring blankly through the bars at the officers laughing amongst themselves, his mood couldn't have been any more different. Why had he thought he was so invincible; he should have known he'd get caught in the end. Maybe if he hadn't been so cocky, they might just have got away? If he hadn't raced towards the first cop car, if he'd dumped it somewhere different, if he'd just…

The metal door opened once more; a familiar voice broke his train of thought.

Looking up, his heart sank. Hunched over between two burly officers, the crestfallen figure was unmistakable.

Mickey shuffled along the bench, his mate taking a seat alongside.

"And don't even think about speaking to each other," the officer ordered, slamming the cage door behind. "Everything's recorded, so you'll just drop yourselves in the shit!"

Heads stooped, the lads sat in silence enduring the banter outside their cell; banter just audible enough for them to hear.

"Reckons he was out playing tracking!" the officer laughed. "Unfortunately for him, the camera in our car says different; particularly the bit where he's hanging out of the sunroof giving us the 'come on'!"

A scowl spread across Danny's face.

Ignoring the cops, Mickey gave his mate a nudge.

"You okay?" he said in a low voice.

"Yeah, just pissed off. You?"

Before he could reply, the bars swung open again.

"Come on mate," PC Draycott instructed. "Time to speak to the custody sergeant."

Slowly rising to his feet, Mickey trudged his way towards the man-mountain.

One at a time Draycott removed the handcuffs. Mickey rubbed his wrists; the red imprints fresh and sore.

Eyes narrowing, the Scottish sergeant was quick to pass on his advice. "Don't be worrying yourself with those teeny marks son, you've got far more important things to think about. Now then officer, why is this lad before me?"

Leaving little out, Draycott began to run through the afternoon's events; from the theft, to the car chase, to the arrest.

"So laddie, do you understand why you're here?"

Mickey nodded his head forlornly, his eyes remaining rooted to the floor.

Without warning, the sergeant's hand slammed down on the counter beside him.

"Look at me when I'm talking to you sonny!" he shouted. "You're in big trouble, so you'd better change that attitude of yours. Do I make myself clear!"

Mickey swallowed hard. Shit this was different from his old school's softly, softly approach.

"Yes, yes…I understand," he stumbled, looking up to face the irate sergeant.

"Good, that's more like it," the officer nodded, sitting back down. "Now then, let's start with your name."

Mickey couldn't blurt his replies out quick enough; instantly complying with every instruction given. Details passed, search completed, the sergeant reached the procedure's conclusion.

"Now listen carefully, the final thing I need to do is to give you your rights. You can have someone informed of your arrest, you can speak to a solicitor either in person or by phone, and you can consult with the codes of practice."

"I'd like a solicitor please."

The sergeant shot a glance at Draycott.

"Very well," he said. "Do you have one in mind, or would you like us to call you the duty solicitor?"

Opening his wallet, Mickey selected the card handed to him three years previously. "Algernon Jonas, solicitor with Parker, Jonas and Co." he read aloud.

"I see," the burly sergeant frowned. "You're not quite the small fry you've led us to believe, are you laddie? Never mind, Mr Jonas it will be."

Formalities over, Mickey was led away. Home for the coming hours was a dingy eight-foot square; its only furnishings a wooden bench with thin plastic mattress on top. Dejected, he sat and cupped his head in his hands – how the hell was he going to get out of this?

Hours passed slowly; the only interruptions the custody staff's regular welfare checks. But after what seemed like an eternity, the cell door finally opened.

"Come on, time for you to get up; your solicitor's here."

Slipping his trainers back on, Mickey was led to a tiny consultation room. Bent over a pile of papers, seemingly oblivious to his entry, a hunched figure sat writing at the desk.

"Mr Jonas," the custody assistant piped up. "Your client?"

Without bothering to look up, the grey-suited man beckoned for Mickey to sit down.

"Algernon Jonas is the name…you call me Mr Jonas," the solicitor instructed, extending his right hand across the table.

Hesitantly, Mickey took up the invite. "Mickey Wilding."

Jonas wasn't quite what he was expecting. Paper-thin skin covered his skeletal frame, unkempt grey strands sparsely covered his head, and the dull grey suit he wore had seen better days; its grease marks matching those on his tie. He looked frail, and yet his handshake was surprisingly strong.

"Well, well, Mickey, we haven't met before but I'll tell you this much; if you know what's good for you, you'll take my advice when I give it. I've been expecting your call for a number of years now; you've done well to avoid getting caught. But today your luck's finally run out, and it's my job to minimise the damage. Now before we start, do you want a fag?"

Taken a little aback, Mickey stuttered out his reply. "Yes, yes please. But what do you mean by…"

"Like all the others before you, you're probably wondering how I know so much," Jonas cut him short. "It's quite simple really. I look after all your crowd; from J.T. at the top, to the waifs like you at the bottom. If I'm going to extricate you from the trouble you invariably find yourselves in, then it pays for me to keep myself in the know. Still, you've lasted longer on the streets than your Dad ever did."

"You looked after my dad?" Mickey asked in amazement, leaning forward to grab a light.

"Oh yes, I've certainly had that displeasure," Jonas answered slowly. "I just hope you're a little more switched on. But enough of that, let's get down to business."

Still reeling from Jonas's revelations, Mickey sat back and exhaled the smoke.

"Right, I've had opportunity to examine the evidence, and to put it bluntly…you've been caught red handed. There are witnesses to the theft, videos from the pursuit, and the arresting officer's identification is watertight. As it's your first offence, if you make a full admission they'll have to caution you. Do you understand?"

Was his brief *really* telling him to admit the crime? Surely he was supposed to get him off the offences?

Jonas's fixed stare made things pretty damn clear.

"Err, I guess so," Mickey stammered.

With little to discuss, the consultation was soon over. Moving next door to the cramped interview room, two officers sat side-by-side facing Mickey across a wooden table. Devoid of natural light, he was surrounded by dull-grey soundproofed walls; the cold air pumped in from the ventilation above.

Introductions over, Draycott opened the questioning. "Right then Mickey, tell me in your own words exactly why you're here?"

Taking in a deep breath, Mickey glanced at his brief and began. Only telling the cops as much as they already knew, he ran through the afternoon's events, before finally relaxing back in his chair.

To begin with, neither side said a word.

Mickey crossed his arms. He'd said his piece – they could keep up the silent treatment as long as they wanted!

"Well, I'm grateful for your honesty in this matter," the officer eventually relented. "However, one thing still troubles me. You're seventeen, you tell me you've never driven before, and you've certainly not passed your driving test. So how is it that you can control a car with all the skills of an experienced driver? It just doesn't add up! Tell me Mickey, where did you really learn to drive like that?"

Mickey's stomach tightened.

"Officer, I object to your line of questioning," Jonas interrupted angrily. "My client has fully answered your questions in relation to the alleged crime, so I do not appreciate you alluding to other offences for which he has not been arrested. I will advise my client to make no further comment."

Perhaps old Jonas wasn't such a bad solicitor after all, Mickey smiled.

"Your comments are noted Mr Jonas. However, the question is for your client, and I would be grateful for an answer," the officer said turning to Mickey.

Arms still crossed, smile still broad, Mickey made his reply.

"No comment!"

Round in circles the discussion continued: officer's questions, Jonas's advice, Mickey's 'no comments'. All avenues explored, the interview eventually wound up, and Mickey returned to his cell.

Left to mull over the day's events, he felt strangely elated. Was that it? A few hours in a cell, a breeze of an interview, and a slap on the wrist! The cops were powerless to stop him, he'd be free in a matter of hours; free to carry on regardless.

All that was left was the formality of his caution. Returning to the interview room, he was left alone with the duty Inspector.

"My name is Inspector Gladstone, I'm here to finalise today's events," the senior officer began. "I've read through the officer's evidence, and I'm told that you've fully admitted the offence of taking a motor vehicle without the owner's consent. Is there anything you wish to say?"

Immaculately turned out, the silver-haired Inspector leant forward, staring him straight in the eye.

"Erm," he began to reply, suddenly feeling very lonely.

"Spit it out!"

"Erm…only that I'm sorry for what I did, and it won't happen again," he recited.

"That's right, young man, because if *I* find you in my custody suite again, I'll make damn sure you're put straight before the courts!" the Inspector bellowed, his face reddening by the second. "And just because you're getting cautioned, don't think for one minute you've got away with it; this is a conviction and will sit on your records forever! If you go before the courts in the future, they'll look at your past history and sentence you accordingly, understand?"

Mickey nodded his head feebly.

"And I certainly don't believe this is your first offence," the Inspector continued, rising from his chair. "I've seen the video sunshine; nobody drives a car like that their first time, so don't think we've fallen for any of your bullshit!"

Where was Jonas now, Mickey thought as the six-foot three gaffer stepped around the table. Rocking back in his chair, he prepared himself for some summary justice.

Butting forward, his face now practically against Mickey's, Gladstone bellowed in his ear. "So make damn sure you stop your silly games, and *never* darken my doors again. Now sign this card and get out of my sight!"

Mickey couldn't leave the room quick enough, instinctively ducking as he hurried to the door. Caution completed, he retrieved his property, and together with Jonas was led out into the cool night air.

"Let me guess. From the look on your face, old Gladstone tore a strip off you?"

"You could've warned me; I thought he was going to batter me!"

"Don't worry, he's reduced many to tears in his time," Jonas smiled. "He's just doing his job; his bark's much worse than his bite. Right, I'm off, you know where to get me the next time you're in trouble."

"Err, I'm not planning on there being a next time," Mickey called after him.

"Oh there will be," Jonas replied inaudibly. "There will be."

15

Nestled in the English countryside, The Red Lion's gardens stretched out alongside a peaceful canal. Relaxing in the afternoon sunshine, the only group remaining at the water's edge were spread out around a large wooden table, tucking into the food laid before them.

First to finish, J.T. was keen to start, banging his glass on the table.

"Porter, you might as well lead off."

Still halfway through his own meal, Porter chewed quickly and swallowed.

"Look, I'm going to have to repeat the same story I repeat every month I'm afraid. Orders are flying in from every direction and we're simply not meeting them all. It's criminal – we're missing out on good business. How can I make this any clearer; either our teams need to work harder, or…"

"Don't talk bollocks!" Chapman interrupted. "The lads are at breaking point as it is!"

"If you'd let me finish…or we need to recruit extra staff to spread the load."

"And as I've told you before, there *is* no magic box you can just pull them out of!"

"Well I'm not being funny, but that's not my concern. *I'm* bringing the work in, it's down to *you* to get it done!"

"Do you have any idea what I have to contend with? Well let me simplify it for you," Chapman replied, his voice rising in volume. "The more you demand, the more they work. The more they work, the more they get caught. And I take it even *you* can see where that equation is heading!"

"Of course I can, but it doesn't change the fact that you need more recruits does it?"

With the two men leaning ever closer across the table, J.T. finally stepped in.

"Ok, thank you gents; I think we all understand the challenges. Nevertheless, we're here to find solutions, and if that means helping each other out, then so be it. Chapman, what recruitment options *do* we have?"

Taking his opportunity with both hands, Chapman started by reminding the group how the rift between Deano and Hood had widened so much that the posse had split into two teams. While Deano continued to lead the majority of his original posse, Hood had taken over a second group; the bitter rivalry resulting in a significant increase in productivity. Now directly responsible for their own feeder groups, Deano had taken the likes of Mickey and Danny under his wings, while Hood had welcomed Tommy Burns's boys under his own.

"Despite us doubling our numbers, we're forever taking hits from the law," Chapman continued. "Deano's lad is about to get two years, while from what Jonas tells me, Hood's worker will be lucky if he only gets five!"

"Five years? What did he do – rob the crown jewels?" Razor sniggered.

"Not quite, he took a lady's Aston Martin at knifepoint; the judges don't take too kindly to that sort of thing."

"Bloody hell Chapman, there's some nasty buggers in that team," Razor grinned.

"Mmm," Chapman nodded. "I can't say I agree with all of their methods…"

"Well you're getting too fucking soft then, aren't you?" J.T. bellowed, his calmness broken. "Are their methods working? That's the question you should be asking. Or is the more appropriate question, whether *your* methods are working anymore?"

All eyes turned to the squirming Chapman.

"With respect, that's not what I meant. Yes, Hood's crew are able to supply us with plenty of cars, but as I've already evidenced, when they do get arrested they get hammered at court," Chapman replied falteringly. "And if that continues, we'll have short term gains for long term losses."

For a few moments, nobody spoke.

"Well if that's the case," Razor piped up, breaking the silence. "Tell the buggers not to get caught!"

Ignoring the comment, J.T. continued. "I don't give a shit about the ones who've been caught; they should have been more careful. What I do give a shit about is results; by whatever means necessary! If that means you need to increase your numbers, then so be it. Do I make myself clear?"

"Of course J.T."

"Good. So tell me, how *are* you going to do it?"

"Well, the only real answer is to bring the next tier up. Both crews have a few lads who are nearly ready; I just hadn't anticipated moving them up just yet. But, if that's what you want, then I'll move them straight away."

"Do it," J.T. replied calmly, slowly lifting his pint glass to his lips. "Anyway Porter, before we became a little…side-tracked, you were presenting your findings; carry on."

"Thank you. As I was saying, demand outstrips supply, particularly in the luxury car market; so when your lads do have a little downtime," Porter glared at Chapman. "Tell them to find me some motors."

Chapman's disconsolate head shake wasn't lost on J.T.

"Do you have a problem with that Chapman?"

"No," he replied tiredly. "I don't have a problem, but as has been pointed out many times before; stealing keys is a risky business."

"That's not our problem," Porter responded. "They're here to do as we say!"

Shooting him another scowl, Chapman returned to his pint.

"Perhaps it's time to increase the rivalry then," J.T. suggested. "How about changing their reward structure? Instead of each crew receiving their normal cut, we could pool their money together every month. The team who makes the most cash…takes away the whole of the pot!"

"Err, that could be fraught with danger," Chapman replied nervously. "They might take too many chances…"

"I'm sorry, did I say this was up for discussion? No, I fucking did not!" J.T. raged. "I've told you before – I don't care about the risks they take, just give me the fucking results!"

"Okay, okay," Chapman quickly backtracked. "Leave it with me, I'll get on to it straight away."

"Good, now let's move on. Porter, tell me what's happening with The Bulawayo Boys."

Slowly, Porter downed his remaining dregs before continuing.

"As you all know, since striking the deal to allow our drug dealing friends unlimited access to our territory, things have been progressing nicely. While they take all the risks, we continue to receive a very healthy cut."

"What do you think Johnny," J.T. said, turning to his brother. "Are they paying us our agreed share?"

"It's impossible to tell for sure; but their payments increase every month, they always cough up on time, and their accounts haven't raised my suspicions so far."

"So do you think we should push them for a bigger slice?"

"To be honest, it's probably more trouble than it's worth," Johnny replied adjusting his specs. "They've proved trustworthy so far, and while that situation remains, I suggest we keep the status quo."

"Yep, they're definitely nasty bastards," Razor said, shaking his head. "They're good to have on *our* side; they'd be a bleedin' handful if we had a fallout."

"Okay, we'll leave it as it is for the moment. Johnny, let me know if anything changes, 'cos believe me, I don't care how fucking handy they are…we set the rules round here, *we're* the ones in charge!"

***

Chapman quickly spread the word. As evening fell, Mickey's iPhone lit up with Deano's name.

"Hiya," Mickey answered, flicking it to speakerphone. "I wasn't expecting to hear from you tonight. Everything okay?"

"Yeah, all's good mate. You busy later?"

"Nothing we can't change," he replied, glancing at Danny. "You got another job for us?"

"You could say that," Deano laughed quietly. "Except this one's a bit more interesting. Get yourselves over to my place for eight and I'll fill you in, okay?"

"Yeah – no probs," Mickey replied slightly puzzled. They'd never been to Deano's pad before, something was going on.

"What do you reckon that's all about?" Danny asked, as Mickey finished the call.

"Dunno, but I can't wait to find out, can you?"

"Dumb question mate," Danny beamed. "Maybe it's time for us to get some real action!"

Eight o' clock couldn't come quickly enough. Having spent the afternoon chatting excitedly over the possibilities, the lads wolfed down their grub and hurried round to Deano's.

Approaching his door, Danny sniffed the air. "What's that stench?"

"Dunno, smells like shit! You trodden in something?" Mickey replied, leaning against the wall to examine his trainers.

Danny made no reply, the cake on his sole said it all.

"Geeez Dan, you could've picked a better time to tread in that," Mickey grimaced. "Come on, let's get it cleaned up before anybody sees us."

While Mickey found a small pointed twig, Danny scraped his filthy trainer on the garden's long grass. Having prized out the stubborn muck from its tread, Danny gave his shoe a final wipe down, and slipped it back onto his foot.

Finally ready, Mickey banged on the door; his knock immediately answered by footsteps rushing down the stairs.

"Come on in boys," Dougie grinned. "We've been expecting you."

Stepping into the first floor lounge, Mickey quickly looked round the room. On the opposite wall hung the biggest TV screen he'd ever seen, beneath which, glass shelves supported a series of games consoles. Sat facing the entertainment systems, the posse sprawled out on soft leather sofas, while from his armchair opposite the door, Deano beckoned them inside.

"Come in, come in. You'll have to sit on the floor I'm afraid; this lazy lot won't move for anyone!"

Mickey took a seat opposite the big screen, but something wasn't right. He'd hoped the posse would be pleased to see them, but the grins on their faces went further than that. Even Deano looked like he was ready to burst. What was going on? This wasn't what he'd expected.

He didn't have to wait long for the answer.

16

"Are you pair wondering why we're ready to piss ourselves?"

"I guess so," Mickey mumbled, shrugging his shoulders.

"Well I'll give you a clue. Take a look at the telly."

As Deano clicked the remote, Mickey watched a small window in the TV's top corner enlarge to fill the screen. It looked like a pathway outside a house.

Shit, it suddenly hit him, it was *this* house!

"Let's rewind," Deano jibed.

Head in hands, Mickey groaned as 'the scraping of the shoe' played out in cinematic widescreen, the acoustic surround sound only serving to heighten his embarrassment.

The room erupted in laughter.

"What a pair of muppets," Mickey chuckled.

"Gentlemen," Deano announced, lifting his glass. "I give you Mickey and Danny; a right pair of muppets!"

With the posse cheering around him, all Mickey could do was just sit and shake his head.

Once the merriment died down, Deano continued. "So you're probably wondering what you're doing here tonight?"

They'd chatted it over all afternoon; he knew exactly what he hoped it would be! Was all their hard work about to be rewarded?

"I won't beat about the bush lads; we want you to join the posse...that is, if you want to?"

"Fucking right!" they replied together.

"Good, that's exactly what I thought. Being honest with you, you *are* less experienced than I'd normally accept, and you've got some pretty big boots to fill. You're gonna have to be at the top of your game guys, but I'm sure you won't let us down."

"We won't," Mickey confirmed. "I swear you can rely on us."

"To start with, you'll come out on jobs and do exactly what you're told. When you prove yourselves worthy, I'll give you more to do, okay?"

"Fair enough," Mickey nodded.

"Right, before we go onto tonight's job, I've got some news I need to pass on," Deano continued, his focus turning to the posse. "I had a tough meeting with Chapman this morning and the upshot is, we've got to stomach some big changes in how we get paid. J.T.'s decided that from now on, we're in direct competition with Hood's boys. Both crew's monthly payments are going into one pot; whoever makes the most cash...gets to take the pot!"

In an instant, the atmosphere changed. Ronnie's backlash was immediate.

"That's fucking bollocks, they know we haven't got a prayer! Hood's dodgy methods will always bring in more dough!"

"Yeah, you're right," Wesbo nodded. "And let's face it, unless we do the same, we'll never get near them."

"No, we've spoken about this before," Deano replied calmly. "We agreed that we're going to stick to what we know. Don't forget, we've been running short for a while now, but with Mickey and Danny joining us, we're gonna have the numbers to beat them. We've just gotta work harder."

"Harder?" Wesbo reacted. "We're already out every night; we've got to sleep sometime you know!"

"Alright, alright, don't shoot the messenger. I hear what you're saying, and let me be quite clear; I don't like it any more than you do. I even gave Chapman an earful this afternoon, but he wasn't interested. The decision's been made, and that's that. We've just got to accept it, and work out how we're gonna beat Hood's boys."

Pausing for a moment, Deano allowed his words to settle before continuing.

"To be fair to Chapman, he's promised to hand the jobs out evenly, so it'll just come down to the cars we can supply. From what he says, Porter's crying out for quality motors…"

"And as everybody knows," Wesbo interrupted. "You need keys to have decent wheels away, which brings us back to the fact that Hood's ways are the most effective!"

"No!" Deano retorted. "We're not going to put people in hospital just to line our own pockets. If anybody wants to go down that road, you can leave now; I'm sure Hood will welcome you with open arms!"

Nobody, least of all Mickey, made a movement.

Opening a can, Deano took a swig before continuing.

"Let's work our nuts off this month and see where we stand. If results don't go our way, we'll sit down and re-assess the situation, agreed?"

Mickey looked around the room. Yes, the posse were behind their leader, but if they found themselves working month after month for nothing, how long would their loyalty last? He knew *he'd* follow Deano to the end of the earth, but what about the others – how would they react? He hoped he wouldn't have to find out; they *had* to win the contest.

"Right, let's get onto the plans for tonight then. Porter's given us two phone shops to strike. We'll hit the city centre one first, then return here to lie low for a few hours. Once the heat dies down, we'll change the plates, and head over to the second one in Solihull."

Secretly Mickey nudged his mate in the side; they were going on their first ram-raid!

"We're using two vehicles. I'll drive the Mercedes Mickey delivered this afternoon, Wesbo'll take the Jag. Mickey, Danny and Ronnie are with me; the rest are with Wesbo. Guys, you need to be on your guard tonight; the boys preparing the shops are new to the business, so they might have made mistakes. Just as Mickey and Danny have moved up to join us, the new boys have taken their place."

"They're good lads," Mickey confirmed. "They won't let you down."

"I'm sure they won't, but it'll do us no harm to be ready for anything," Deano replied. "Wesbo, make sure you've got the right tools in your car, and let's be careful not to prang them; they'll be part of this month's quota. Any questions so far?"

"What times are we looking at?"

"Meet here at one. The first job goes down at two, the second one at five."

Absorbing every word as Deano went into detail, everything was as Mickey expected; face coverings to avoid identification, thick jackets for glass protection, and gloves to avoid leaving prints. Having prepared the Merc earlier in the day himself, he knew it was ready to go…and now he knew why he'd had to put a spare set of plates in the boot!

Briefing wrapped up, Deano pressed his remote; the screen instantly flicking to Gran Turismo's opening credits. A mad scramble for gamepads ensued, with Wesbo and Ronnie split seconds ahead of the pack.

"They're always the same when it comes to games time – like a bunch of bloody kids," Deano joked to Mickey. "You can stop here and play if you want, or sort yourselves out and meet back at one."

"Are you kidding? Of course we're stopping. I'll just give mum a bell and let her know I'm out for the…" Mickey's voice trailed off as he realised his mistake.

"Ah, poor little Mickey," Wesbo mocked. "Needs to phone his mummy-wummy!"

Head shaking in disbelief as the lads descended into laughter, he couldn't believe he'd done it again.

"Don't worry mate, you'll soon get your chance to get your own back," Ronnie chuckled, handing over the controller. "Here have a go at this, I've heard you're a bit of a driver."

Gratefully, he accepted the gift; anything to get out of the spotlight! As the flag dropped and his racer sped away, he smiled quietly to himself. They'd done it, they were part of the posse at last; tonight was going to be a night to remember.

***

With midnight fast approaching, it was time to get ready. Having spent the evening at Deano's, Mickey and Danny headed to their changing room-cum-storage HQ. Padlocked on the outside, power supply inside, they'd turned the disused garage into a well-stocked hideaway. Around the sides: clothing, tools, food and drink sat neatly stacked on shelving, while on the concrete floor a custom-made number plate builder sat surrounded by blank plates.

"How you feeling?" Mickey asked, changing into his 'job' clothes.

"Shitting myself! You?"

"I'm cool, should be a walk in the park."

"What's that smell?" Danny asked sniffing the air. "Is it eau-de-bullshit!"

"Yeah yeah, very funny!" Mickey smiled. "Okay, maybe just a few nerves then."

The truth was, he was just as nervous as his mate. Before tonight, it had only ever been the pair of them; if they messed up, they were the only witnesses. But this was different; tonight they were being watched – tonight they just *had* to get it right.

Without another word, they hurried back to Deano's. On the surface, everything appeared the same as before; Wesbo and Dougie on the Playstation, the others still lounging around. But to Mickey, the atmosphere was altogether different. Gone were the winks and smiles, gone was the playful banter.

At one o' clock precisely, Deano brought the group to attention.

"Okay boys, it's time to rumble. Before we go, are there any final questions?"

Nobody said a word.

"Good. Everybody got their face coverings?"

Checking his pockets for the umpteenth time, Mickey followed the others to the door.

In silence, they hurried to the garage, where dropping to his knees, Mickey focused his mobile's torch on the pebbles. With everything in order, he swung the doors open, while Deano jumped into the Merc. V8 growling, it rolled out into the open.

"So guys, just to keep you in the loop," Deano began, as they all took their seats inside. "Right about now, the new boys will be removing the padlocks off our target's shutters; they'll give me a bell once everything's ready. We're meeting the other crew in a side street half a mile from the shop; we used to get closer, but CCTV's moving further and further out, so *we* have to do the same. We'll get another call about five to two, to give us the all clear…and then the action begins!"

The journey into the city continued sedately; Deano explaining exactly what was expected, the lads hanging onto every word. By the time the first call came in, every eventuality had been covered; nothing was being left to chance.

Bang on time, they rolled into their meeting point's shadows, followed seconds behind by the sleek white Jag. Deano and Ronnie alighted.

Alone in the Merc, Danny turned to his mate. "He's shit hot with his planning, isn't he?"

"That's why he's still out there doing it," Mickey replied, leaning back in his sports seat. "He's gotta be the best in the business."

Eyes closed, he tried to chill, but it was impossible; his mind refusing to focus on anything other than the raid ahead.

"Ten minute warning guys," Deano announced, returning to the car. "We're just waiting for the final call, then we're going in, okay?"

Stereo off, all lights extinguished; they sat quietly in the darkness.

Time crept slowly by, and then...Deano's mobile broke the silence.

It was a short one-way conversation; Deano's head merely nodding as they spoke.

"Cheers guys, make yourselves scarce," he said ending the call.

Tucking his phone away, Deano turned to the lads. "That's it, we've got the green light."

Starter button pressed, six litres growled into life. Rolling forward, Deano disengaged traction control, flicked to dipped beam, and pulled out his balaclava.

Scarf wrapped around his face, Mickey pulled his hoodie tight. Stay calm, he tried to assure himself; you've got a job to do...do it!

Having picked their way through the outer streets, the Merc suddenly launched forward, its blazing headlights lighting up their target.

Mickey flung his door open as they slid to a stop. Out in a flash, he rushed towards the shutters.

Everything was going to plan...so far.

17

The mood inside Hood's high-rise flat was altogether different. Stood at his top floor window, Hood looked out towards the far horizon, the city centre's office blocks silhouetted against the night sky. Slowly at first, they started to sway…one way, then the other; his drug and alcohol cocktail beginning to take its effect.

Turning to face the room, he grinned at his mates.

"Did you see her face when I slashed her? Cheeky cow, she'll be quicker to hand them over next time."

While most of his crew lounged on his threadbare furniture, a couple lay spaced out on the floor.

"Yeah, and I bet Deano's poxy crowd can't do better than a fifty grand Lexus," Soldier boasted from his ripped leather sofa.

"They won't nick fifty grand's worth in a whole week; fucking amateurs!" Hood replied, managing to just about place himself in a chair.

Taking another drag from his spliff, Soldier passed it to Tommy Burns at his side.

"And how's our new boy getting along then?" Hood asked.

Inhaling deeply on the reefer, Tommy nodded his head. "No problems, no problems."

"And you're happy to be with the 'A' team?"

"Fucking right I am; I don't want to be with those wankers. Especially now *'Mickey and Danny'* are with them," he mocked.

"Good, that's what I like to hear. You boys have joined at just the right time. You're gonna see the end of Deano, and every one of his fuckin' posse – including your old school chums."

"Thank fuck for that," Tommy replied, slowly exhaling the smoke from his lungs. "They're gonna get exactly what they deserve!"

***

The moments that followed were like scenes from a movie. Stood to one side, Mickey watched his team heave the shutters up, smash through the window, and swiftly clamber inside.

Adrenaline pumping, he scrambled through the jagged glass after them. Sirens blaring in his ears, he jumped over the window display and ran toward the shop's rear, where Wesbo's sledgehammer was already attacking the storeroom door. Lined up behind, the posse waited for it to give way. Each strike buckled it steadily inwards, until a final blow took it clean off its hinges. Piling in, the first raiders grabbed everything they could find. Binbags crammed to bursting, they were quickly out, sprinting past Mickey while he waited his turn.

Looking over his shoulder, half expecting to see blue flashing lights, he tried to stay calm. Come on…come on…hurry up…hurry up, he murmured under his breath, as one after another, his mates raced away. Finally, only he and Danny were left. In a flash, Danny dived into the storeroom, his hands a flurry as he scooped up the shelves' remaining stock. Bag full, he was out, almost colliding with Mickey as they passed.

By now the room was in disarray, the remaining phone boxes strewn far and wide. On hands and knees he frantically grabbed whatever he could find. With the alarm screaming and the showroom completely empty, he suddenly felt very alone; the icy fingers of fear beginning to crawl down his bent back. He had to get out; the desire to run overwhelming.

No! He couldn't return half-empty, he had to finish the job.

Like a man possessed, he flung carton after carton into his bag, until, barely able to close it, he was back on his feet and away.

Booty slung over shoulder, he raced out of the stockroom, and leaping onto the display, launched himself through the window.

Both cars were waiting. Perched half in the passenger doorwell, he could see Ronnie beckoning towards him. But he didn't need any advice; this part came naturally. Without breaking stride, he slung his sack in the boot, and joined his mate in the rear.

The moment he landed, Deano floored the accelerator.

As the car launched away, Mickey adjusted his position to get a better view. Wedging himself between the front seats, there was no way he was going to miss out on his hero's high-speed escape!

And he wasn't disappointed; the insane pace expertly controlled…until the Greet's outskirts raced into view. Then, without warning, Deano suddenly slowed down.

Mickey checked over his shoulder. "What's wrong, have we been spotted?"

"Well if we have, they're a long way behind!" Deano laughed quietly. "No, now we're back on our manor, we don't want to bring attention to ourselves. The last thing we need is some nosey neighbour spotting us putting the car away."

"Sorry," Mickey replied, sitting back in his seat. "Dumb question."

"Not at all mate, my fault for not covering it earlier. Oh, and something else I forgot to tell you; you've only got ten minutes to swap the plates. Porter follows my iPhone; his men'll be despatched to empty the car as soon as we return, and believe me, they won't want anybody there when they do!"

The moment they landed, Mickey and Danny set to work. By torchlight, they changed the plates, secured the garage, and hurried back towards Deano's.

"That was just the bollocks!" Danny whispered excitedly.

"Can you believe it! *And* we get to do it all again in a couple of hours!"

Falling silent as they pushed open the front door, they made their way upstairs.

"Grab yourselves a Red Bull," Ronnie grinned, opening his own. "And tell me, what did you think of your first job?"

"Fucking amazing!" Mickey beamed. "Can't wait for the next one."

"Good, well now you've had your first taster, be warned; it doesn't always go so smoothly. Now make sure you grab a seat before the others turn up; Wesbo's just called, they'll be back any moment."

Lying low, time swiftly passed by as they re-lived the fruitful raid. But as quarter past four approached, Deano called them to order; it was time to get serious once more.

"Okay, as we discussed earlier, our plan's the same as before. The shop belongs to the same company and I'm assured it's laid out identically. But listen up, we need to be on our guard guys; the plate changes may fool ANPR, but they won't kid the boys in blue. Our cars will be easily spotted; we need to be in and out as quickly as possible."

Briefing completed, they were soon back out on the streets. Keeping to the back roads, they ducked and dived through the city, reaching the rendezvous with only seconds to spare.

No time for nerves this time, Mickey pulled up his scarf, and prepared for action. Onto the high street they screeched; their target in a prime location for the passing public...in a prime location for CCTV. Like an action replay, the team replicated their moves; shutters, window, storeroom door.

Pulse racing, Mickey soon found himself alone again. Scrabbling around the floor, he filled his bag and rushed back to the shattered glass.

But something was wrong. Why was the Jag starting to move?

The knot in his stomach tightened.

Not only was it moving, the rear tyres were lighting up! That could only mean one thing...

18

Panic setting in, Mickey flung himself through the jagged window, his jacket tugging on a shard as he fell to the ground. Picking himself up, he could see exactly what the problem was.

Lights blazing, a squad car was almost on top of him.

For a split second, he froze.

Skidding towards him on the uneven surface, it had nowhere to go…it was about to smash into him.

Suddenly coming to his senses, he dived forward and curled himself into a ball. His back cushioning the impact, he bounced off the bonnet, rolled over the wing, and dropped to the cobbles below. Adrenaline firing through his veins, he was back on his toes the moment he hit the ground. Bag still in hand, he fled towards the Merc, an officer only paces behind.

Just ahead of him, his getaway was rolling forward. Its boot already secure, Danny hung from an open rear door, desperately urging him on. Headfirst, Mickey hurled himself through it, his legs barely gathered in before Deano hit the gas.

Exhausted, but relieved to be back in the car's relative safety, he picked himself out of the footwell. His eyes flicked to the rear window; it was filled with blue lights – the Insignia was right on their tail.

Deano kept the throttle floored; his Merc's rear wheels spinning wildly as they fought to find grip on the cobbles. Despite all their extra horsepower, they were struggling to pull away.

Approaching the High Street's end, Deano flicked the wheel to the left, before briefly tugging the handbrake. Expertly controlling the slide with opposite-lock and more gas, he slid the big Merc from cobbles to tarmac. The rest was simple; tyres delivered traction, 500 horsepower hit the road…the Insignia was about to be history.

V8 reverberating off tall glass buildings, the chasing sirens dwindled further and further away until, as the town centre disappeared in the rear view mirror, so did their pursuers.

Half a mile later, Deano dived off the main road, his breakneck pace unrelenting.

"Keep your eyes open for any others," he called out, blasting through yet another junction. "We're not out of danger yet."

Mickey's eyes couldn't be more open. Frantically scouring the streets, he knew they couldn't afford to slow; the helicopter was bound to have been scrambled. By Deano's calculations, they needed to be tucked away within twelve minutes…or they'd be easy meat for the chopper.

Eleven minutes had passed; the Greet's safety still a few miles away. Having abandoned the main roads to avoid detection, the extra time now threatened to expose them.

"Twelve minutes up!" Ronnie announced, leaning forward to look up through the windscreen.

Instinctively, Mickey followed his lead, scanning the sky all around. He knew they'd be easy to identify; they were practically the only car on the road, they were travelling at high speed, and their white hot engine would be like a beacon for the chopper's thermal camera.

Fifteen minutes. Was that a traffic car approaching?

Deano ducked down another side street. More time lost, and if that *was* a squad car, the helicopter wouldn't be too far away. Mickey felt the tension rising; Deano was good, but even he was under pressure.

At last, their estate came into view. There was no losing speed on the outskirts this time. Keeping the pedal jammed to the floor, Deano raced straight back to the garage. With their motor tucked safely away, by the time Mickey had replaced the pebbles, Deano and Ronnie were gone. And with the faraway hum of rotors drawing ever closer, so were he and Danny.

***

By the time they arrived at Deano's the following afternoon, the de-brief was well underway.

"Look, when we're doing jobs in town centres, it's obvious we're gonna get rumbled," Deano explained as the lads took their place on the floor. "CCTV's everywhere; they'd have been on to us the moment we drove along the High Street. As long as the bloke behind the screen was awake, they'd have spotted us straight away."

Dougie sat shaking his head. "Well let's just hope Porter's targets are out in the sticks next time."

"Yeah, he can give Hood's wankers the next city centre job," Ronnie replied. "They're welcome to it after last night!"

"Well by my reckoning, we were in and out in two minutes flat; that's pretty much a record. Even then we were within a gnat's knacker of getting caught," Deano frowned. "There's no way Hood could do any better than that."

"You pair not joining in?" he added, looking over at Mickey and Danny.

"Can't get a word in edgeways with you boys," Mickey chuckled.

"Listen to him!" Ronnie teased. "Gets all cocky now he's been out on a couple of jobs. He should think himself lucky; we don't normally hang around for the new boys!"

"Gee thanks Ronnie, you're my hero," Mickey replied, ducking to avoid a flying cushion.

"Seriously lads, you all did a good job last night. If we hadn't been so slick, we wouldn't be sitting *here* right now," Deano continued. "Mickey, Danny, you needed to be switched on, and you didn't let us down. Fuck me though Mickey, I honestly thought you were a gonna! That cop car looked like it gave you a right pisser…you got any knocks?"

"Nah, of course not! Didn't you see my stunt training kick in? Up over the bonnet, and away," Mickey joked. "I did more damage coming out of the window; my jacket is ripped to shreds!"

Deano's face changed in an instant. "I hope you're kidding mate. Have you checked your arm for any cuts?"

"No, no, I didn't feel a thing. More than can be said for my jacket!"

"Show me," Deano demanded, moving closer. "If you've left even the smallest speck of blood, you're screwed. Lew went down the steps for two years 'cos of a DNA hit. I fucking hope you haven't done the same!"

Mickey could see Deano wasn't joking, and looking round the room, neither was anyone else. All eyes were on *him*.

Rolling up his sleeve, he turned his arm over…

19

"Right then, the first month's over, give me the results," J.T. instructed, leaning back in his leather chair. "Oh, and make sure it's good news, 'cos I'm in no mood to put up with any shit!"

"I'm sure you won't be disappointed, it's certainly been a lucrative month," Porter grovelled. "The lads appear to be rising to the challenge alright. On top of our anticipated burglary returns, they've managed to double the vehicles supplied; a number I'm sure will be reflected in Johnny's figures."

All eyes turned to J.T.'s brother who sat impassively behind his desk in the corner.

"Yes, yes. It is without doubt the most profitable month to date," Johnny replied, adjusting his glasses. "I do have a few more transactions to record, but it's all looking very positive."

"Do you hear that Chapman, the most profitable month to date!" J.T. mocked. "So much for your poxy concerns!"

Chapman squirmed on the sofa. "Yes, yes, the results are of course good news," his voice trailed off.

J.T.'s brow furrowed, his eyes narrowing.

"Go on, you've obviously got something more to say."

Chapman paused before replying. "I presume you'll be enforcing the payment structure we discussed?"

"Of course I will!" J.T. roared, slamming his fist down. "And for your information, the payment structure wasn't 'discussed', it was fucking 'agreed'!"

His fist remaining clenched, J.T.'s stare drilled straight through Chapman's eyes. Everybody remained quiet, the only sounds the passing traffic outside.

Slowly, his fingers uncurled, and grasping the tumbler from next to his seat, he took a deep swig before continuing.

"I know you mean well Chapman, but these are challenging times. We have to make changes to stay in control, that's all. The loyalty to your lads is admirable; it's what I'd expect – it's what makes you good at your job. However, don't lose your perspective. Ultimately, it's the men in this room who deserve your allegiance; those beneath us are completely expendable – it's called survival of the fittest. If they get caught or fall by the wayside, it's their own stupid fault, and don't forget it. Your job's to make sure that there's always more to replace them, okay?"

Chapman nodded his stooped head.

"Good, I'm glad we're all in agreement," J.T. continued. "Now it's time we had the results; the winners deserve their rewards. Johnny, you sorted the figures out yet?"

"Two minutes," he replied, his fingers typing away.

"Okay, we'll come back to you in a moment. While we're waiting, does anybody else have anything we need to discuss?"

"Well, I could do with your permission to make a small…donation, to a mutual friend of ours." Porter asked.

"Go on."

"The yearly bonus to our contact at the cop shop?"

"You tell me. Is he still coming up with the goods?"

"Well he's tipped us off several times when our lads were due to be raided. And to be fair to him, he's handed us a couple of decent jobs." Porter paused to chuckle. "That electrical warehouse must still be wondering how unlucky they were to get hit on the only night their alarm system wasn't working. Apparently, they think it was an inside job; if only they knew the loose lips belonged to the copper they told in the first place. Suckers!"

"In that case, we'll keep him on the payroll. I'm sure he'll be happy with his usual ten grand."

Calculations complete, Johnny cleared his throat.

Turning to his brother, J.T. gestured for him to continue.

"As Porter has already alluded, the figures show a significant improvement," he began. "Vehicle supply has indeed doubled, while all other merchandise is up twenty percent."

"What did he say?" Razor asked, confusion etched across his face.

J.T. sighed. "He's telling us the boys have done well, you half-wit."

"Cheers boss, I wish he wouldn't talk so…" Razor started, his reply cut short by Johnny's raised voice.

"On the burglary front, our teams have returned almost identical figures. However, Hood's crew have supplied almost two vehicles for every one of Deano's. Hood is therefore declared the winner."

"Thank you Johnny, I'm sure Chapman will be happy to deliver the news."

"Leave it with me," Chapman replied wearily. "I'll call them straight away."

"Good," J.T. smiled. "And make sure they understand we expect even better next month!"

***

After taking Chapman's call, Hood rushed out to meet him, and happily pocketed the sixty grand reward. By the time he returned home, his crew were gathered in his lounge, eager to hear the result.

"I won't keep you in suspense lads…we fucking walked it, just as I said we would!"

As the cheer went up, he shook his beer can violently, spraying its contents far and wide. Screams of joy accompanied the soaking, the bare floor left even tackier than normal.

"And for the winners come the spoils," Hood grinned, taking the wad from his pocket. "Fifty fucking grand!"

Tommy Burns whistled in awe.

"Everybody gets their normal cut; you boys'll get five each," Hood continued, counting out the first payment. "We'll split five between the lads beneath us, and I'll have the remaining ten. Agreed?"

Seven pairs of outstretched hands made their conclusive response.

***

The contrast in Deano's house couldn't have been greater. Sat in his lounge, the posse stared blankly at the widescreen TV.

Mickey was as hacked off as the rest. Yes, the cash reward would have been nice, especially after all the work they'd put in over the past few weeks. But what really hurt, was the thought of Tommy Burns's gloating face wallowing in his victory, and no matter how hard he tried, he couldn't get rid of the image.

"Snap out of it lads!" Deano said, finally breaking the silence. "We need to come up with some answers, not mope around like a bunch of losers!"

"Well we could start by getting rid of this ridiculous system. It's a load of bollocks!" Ronnie retorted angrily. "We've spent the last month working our arses off…for what? Fuck all!"

"Fat chance of that happening," Deano replied. "We all know the system's here to stay. And let's face it, as far as they're concerned, it's working isn't it? They're raking it in."

"Yeah, but it's all at *our* expense. We're working harder, for longer, for less!" Ronnie continued. "Look at the risks we're taking; how close were we to losing Mickey on the phone job? At this rate it's only a matter of time before we're all banged up. Why should *we* take extra risks when there's no fucking reward!"

Mickey kept quiet. He didn't need reminding of the phone shop shambles. Even now, weeks after, he didn't know whether the law was going to catch up with him. Having narrowly escaped on the night, his snag on the glass was never far from his mind. The leather sleeve may well have prevented serious injury, but the shards had penetrated deeply, delivering him the faintest of scratches – only time would tell whether he'd left enough for a DNA hit. With his sample already on record after the Golf chase, it would be a simple enough match-up for the cops. So now he lay awake at night, twitching the curtains with every passing noise…half-expecting his door to fly off its hinges at any given moment.

"We haven't got a choice mate, I can hardly ask Chapman to change back to the old system," Deano replied angrily. "We'd look like a right bunch of losers wouldn't we? No, we've got to stop feeling sorry for ourselves, and remember what we've achieved over the past few years. Look me in the eyes and tell me you haven't enjoyed every minute?"

Ronnie hesitated for a moment, before nodding slowly. "Yeah, you're right. But we need to sort something for the future...or we're gonna be left without one."

"I agree. We need fresh ideas if we're going to beat them," Deano said, the harshness disappearing from his voice. "And I'm open to what anybody's got to say on the matter."

Mickey looked around the room, waiting for someone to start the ball rolling. They had to find an answer, they just had to; there was no way he was going to allow Tommy to triumph every month.

Eventually Wesbo stood up and walked towards the window. "We *all* know what the answer is," he said, looking out across the estate. "I might be the first to have the balls to say it, but the *only* answer is exactly what we discussed last time."

"And as I said before; I will **never** resort to using those tactics. Hood and his crew should be ashamed of themselves. You saw the woman in the paper last week; eighty years old, beaten black and blue 'cos she wouldn't hand over her keys. For fucks sake, they nearly killed the old dear!"

"I'm not saying we need to go to those lengths, it's just that we need to be more..." Wesbo chose his words carefully as he turned to face his audience, "...practical."

"By which you mean violent, I presume," Deano replied scathingly.

"I don't know. I just think we need to do something different or we're finished. We know Hood's methods work, and ours don't work as...effectively. There must be some middle ground we can use that'll give us a fighting chance."

"Ask yourself this," Deano said, taking a sip from his energy drink. "We've done hundreds of jobs, and nicked millions of pounds worth of gear. But when have you ever felt guilty?"

Wesbo stood motionless for a few moments before replying.

"Never. As we've always said, they're wealthy and bound to be insured."

"Exactly, and the first time you put a knife to someone's throat, or whack an old granny over the head; how're you gonna feel then? We'll be exactly the sort of scum we've always despised; won't we?"

"I'm not saying you're wrong, but the time's coming when we have to make difficult decisions. You tell me another way that'll work?"

Just like the others, Mickey watched and waited.

Deano shifted back in his chair. He was under pressure – they were all under pressure.

But there *was* something Mickey had in mind. He and Danny had been talking about it for a while now, but that's all it was, talk. Maybe this was the right time to share it; nobody else seemed to have a clue.

"Danny, why don't you tell the guys about your latest brainwave," he said, nudging his mate.

"Well I'm not really sure. I was hoping to try it out first."

"Don't worry, feel free to share your thoughts," Deano encouraged. "I can't hear anyone else shouting up."

"Err – okay," he replied nervously. "I just think we've got too hung up on nicking keys. When you guys first started, you could nick any car, anywhere, just by using a screwdriver. Nowadays, the immobilisers are built into the brains of the car, so we *have to* steal the keys to get around the problem."

Danny paused.

Mickey read his mind. "Go on mate, everybody's listening."

"Well…we need to get back to stealing any car anywhere again, and just like before, we don't want to clash with the owners."

"Agreed, but I don't think they've invented a magic screwdriver yet!" Wesbo jibed.

"Let him finish!" Deano said, cutting the sniggering dead. "So what's the solution then?"

"I've done some research on the internet, and I think it's pretty simple. All modern cars have an on-board-diagnostics computer or OBD for short. To make access easy, the manufacturers normally install its connector in the footwell."

"Fuck me, since when did *you* become a boffin?" Wesbo joked again.

This time there was no supporting laughter; Danny had the posse's full attention.

"We can buy an OBD reader, connect it to the port, and effectively suck the key-code out."

"Okay, I'm with you so far," Deano frowned. "But what good's the code? How's that going to help us to steal the car?"

"The OBD reader is a clever piece of kit. It's normally used to diagnose the car's problems, but importantly for us, it comes with an inbuilt electronic pad that re-programs your key…."

"…and all we need to do," Deano interrupted, grasping Danny's train of thought. "Is bring our own key, place it on the pad, and re-program it using the car's own code! That's brilliant!"

"Fuck me," Wesbo grinned wide-eyed. "It *is* a magic screwdriver!"

"So this OBD reader; how do we get hold of it?" Deano continued. "Do we need to steal it from a dealer?"

"Pass me the remote control," Danny laughed.

Looking slightly perplexed, Deano handed it over.

Danny pressed 'talk' and brought it up to his mouth.

"Internet. Amazon UK," he stated clearly.

All eyes moved to the widescreen, where the familiar website quickly popped up.

Danny clicked on the search box. "OBD key programmer," he commanded.

As a wide selection appeared before them, the posse almost took in their breath as one.

"I don't fucking believe it," Deano said shaking his head. "It surely can't be that easy, can it?"

"I've watched the technician's training videos on YouTube; it looks like a piece of piss!" Danny continued. "There's different devices for each manufacturer, so we'll need to choose which one to go for first?"

"I'm easy mate. You seem to have all the answers; what do you suggest?"

"Well…" Danny hesitated for a moment. "I think I've spotted a weakness in the BMW alarm system. I reckon we can smash the driver's window, access the OBD port, and the alarm won't even detect we're in."

"Sounds a bit unlikely mate, those systems are really sensitive," Ronnie queried.

"They are, but they're controlled by a sensor in the roof's headlining. We've tested everywhere in the car, and it just *can't* detect movement by the front doors; I guess the seats get in the way of its beams."

"Geez, you boys have been working hard. Beemers it is then," Deano replied, taking the remote back. "There's no time like the present – let's click and pay," he added, sending a BMW OBD reader to the checkout.

"Guys, thanks to Danny, it looks like we've found a secret weapon against Hood and his cronies. Now make sure we keep it that way; it stays secret, no boasting, okay?"

Transfixed, the posse spent the following hours watching Danny's videos, stunned by the simplicity of hacking security systems that had cost manufacturers so many millions to develop. Being brand new territory, and with no experience to call upon, everybody joined in, so that slowly but surely, their plans took shape.

By the time the meeting ended, despite the first month's loss to Hood and his cronies, Mickey walked out on a high.

"Nice work mate," he said, oblivious to the pouring rain. "I think you've turned yourself into a hero!"

"Pressure's on though. What if it doesn't work? I'll be hero to zero in an instant!" Danny replied.

Hands shoved deep inside his trouser pockets, Danny kicked at a pebble on the pavement.

"No chance. We've done the research, it's definitely going to work," Mickey said, side-footing the stone a few paces forward. "Hood's boys won't know what's hit them next month."

"I fucking hope so; Tommy's face'll be a picture!" Danny grinned, booting the pebble so hard that it skidded across the drenched road surface.

Though still daylight, visibility in the early winter rain was poor. Mickey followed the pebble's path as it skipped over the road, directly in front of an approaching dark car.

Without warning, it suddenly swerved towards them, diving towards a deep puddle in the gutter. With little time to react, Mickey jumped to the side...too late.

Fat tyres ploughed into the flood, the huge wave instantly drenching the lads.

"You fucking wanker!" Mickey screamed at the disappearing car; his abuse provoking an immediate reaction.

Red lights shone through the gloom. The motor was braking – and hard.

With a deft tug on the handbrake, the car span round to face him once more. Like a bull waiting to charge, it paused; its engine note steadily rising and falling...until suddenly, its headlamps changed to full beam, and under maximum acceleration, launched towards him again.

Danny edged towards the wall at their side, but like a matador, Mickey stood firm – glaring at the approaching lights. His instincts told him who was in the car; there was no way he was going to back down.

"Stand firm, Danny. Don't let them see you're scared!" he stated calmly, waiting for the car's next move.

But its path didn't alter; *this* time it was aiming straight for him.

20

Mickey didn't move a muscle.

Rushing headlong at him, the RS Focus continued to pick up speed…until at the very last moment, it turned sharply away, ploughing back through the water, soaking them to the bone again. Continuing for a short distance, it turned and came to a halt. Engine revving, it waited to charge once more.

"Who the fuck is it?" Danny asked, starting to make towards the car.

"Can't say for sure, its lights were blinding me," Mickey replied, increasing his pace. "But it's bound to be that little tosser."

Grabbing hold of his mate's arm, Danny pulled him back. "Even if it is Tommy, what are you going to do?"

"Well if he's got the bottle to get out, I'm gonna fucking batter him!"

But before they could move any closer, the driver was off again. Dumping the clutch, he initially wheelspun towards them, until, shifting up to second, he lifted off the accelerator, slowing the car to a cruise.

His window wound down, sure enough Tommy Burns's gloating face sat mocking them from the driver's seat. Wafting a wad of notes from his window, his abuse was muffled by his stereo's deafening music.

Doing his best to ignore him, Mickey carried on walking, as with a final horn blast their enemy bolted away.

"His time will come mate, I'm gonna see to that," Mickey raged. "In the meantime, we're gonna use your little tricks to trash him next month; that'll wipe the smile off his face!"

"But what if they *don't* work…" Danny mumbled, his words drowned out by the pouring rain, "…it could be the end of the posse as we know it!"

***

Two days later, Mickey and Danny were summoned to Deano's pad with the simple text, '*It's arrived, get your asses to my place!*'.

The posse were already there; their excited faces focused on the small Amazon package lying unopened on the table.

"I thought we'd wait for you boys; it's only fair you get to open it," Deano smiled.

Danny glanced at Mickey.

"Go on mate, it's all yours," Mickey said, pushing the parcel towards him. "You're the brains behind it."

Danny needed no encouragement. Kneeling down, he took hold of the Jiffy bag, and carefully sliced through the Sellotape before sliding his hand inside.

Closing in tight around him, the posse watched on as he pulled out the object, and placed it on the table. It looked exactly as it had on the internet; a blue and white plastic box, similar in size to a remote control. Below the digital display at the top were arrows to scroll through the menus, beneath which was a pad to place the key against.

"Nice bit of kit," Wesbo nodded. "But what I can't get my head around, is why the manufacturers are making it so easy for us?"

"Well officially it's so that back street garages can also work on their cars," Danny replied. "Of course, if you were a little suspicious, you might think they actually *want* their cars to get stolen; it's probably good business replacing them!"

"Whatever the reason, if this thing works, it's gonna make things simple for us," Deano said picking up the unit. "Are you boys ready to try it out?"

Grinning broadly, Mickey pulled a keyfob from his pocket. "Fucking right we are. The old 'fishing rod through the letter box' trick hooked this little baby last night. With a bit of luck, it could be the first time anyone's nicked two cars with one key!"

"Nice one," Deano nodded, handing Danny the OBD reader. "In that case, we'll let you boys go first. Let me know what happens, and we'll have a full debrief tomorrow. Good luck guys, we're depending on you."

***

In a quiet cul-de-sac on a new housing development, Mickey and Danny lingered in the shadows. Midnight had long since disappeared; as had the moon, behind ominous clouds that threatened to release their torrent.

In complete darkness, their target was sat on a detached house's driveway.

Danny glanced round for a final time. "You ready?"

"Let's do it," Mickey whispered back, leading the way towards the 3 series BMW.

With Danny standing guard, he tapped the driver's glass with his window hammer; instantly shattering it into a thousand pieces. Hands protected by gloves, he cleared the splintered glass, and quickly stepped out of the way. All was going to plan; the alarm hadn't been tripped, he hadn't made a noise…and now it was over to Danny.

Leaning carefully through the open window, his mate reached deep into the footwell. Torch in mouth, he held the lead with one hand, and searched for the OBD port with the other.

Mickey remained close; his eyes flicking from the kit, to the house, to the road. Suddenly, the display screen lit up; their lead had found its source!

Scrolling rapidly through the menu, Danny selected 'key download', placed his fob onto the pad and 'entered'. Seconds later, the reader 'beeped' twice.

"In theory…that's it – it's done," Danny whispered excitedly, handing his mate the fob.

Mickey took in a deep breath. Were a couple of kids from a council estate in Birmingham really going to beat a multi-million pound security system?

"Well now's the moment of truth," he smiled, and pressed his thumb down on the fob.

21

Instantly, a brief 'chirrup' accompanied the indicator's wink. They were in; Danny's magic screwdriver had worked!

But they still needed to finish the job. Without a word, Mickey jumped into the driver's seat, disconnected the lead and started the engine. By the time Danny had joined him, the car was in reverse and rolling off the drive; the whole operation having taken under two minutes.

"I don't believe it!" Mickey beamed as he drove off. "You're a fucking genius mate. How easy was that!"

"Makes you wonder what we've been pissing about at for the past couple of years!" Danny laughed, settling back in the leather seat. "That's got to be the simplest theft yet. I can't wait to tell the posse; they're gonna go ballistic!"

He paused for a moment before continuing. "You do know the best way to convince them it's not a one-off don't you?"

"Sure. We could do another one, but I don't...."

"It's just that I've got another idea I want to try out," Danny interrupted.

Mickey shook his head in disbelief. "Go on Einstein, what have you come up with this time?"

"Well, you know how we had to smash the window to get in?"

"Yeah, it's not ideal, but screwdrivers just don't work on those locks."

"That's what I thought, so I've ordered something on the internet called a 'turbo-decoder'; it's basically a modern day lock-picking device. It'll be with us in the morning."

"Why didn't you say something before? I'm sure the boys would have been interested."

"Let's face it, we didn't really know whether our OBD kit was going to work did we? Imagine if we'd tried the ideas out and they'd both failed? We'd have looked a right pair of prats, wouldn't we? Now we know the key programmer works, at least we can try out our next trick. It can be our own little secret. If it doesn't work, nobody's any the wiser."

"Okay, I get where you're coming from, but what exactly is it?"

"Mate, you're not going to believe it; it's even simpler than the other gear. It's just a key with rotating tumblers; they spin round to fit the lock."

"Bloody hell, sounds too good to be true! Tell you what, as soon as it arrives, we'll try it out on this little baby," Mickey grinned, patting the 'M-sport' embossed steering wheel. "If you can get it to work, we'll go and get another motor," he smiled. "You know what mate, we're gonna be fucking heroes!"

***

Up early, the lads were eager to try out their new kit. Inside their garage, Danny set to work on the BMW's locks. Following the instructions on YouTube, he twisted, he turned, but time-after-time the deadlock refused to budge.

Watching at his side, Mickey wondered whether it was just another internet scam. Half an hour passed without success, when suddenly 'pop', up came the locks, as did the grin on their faces.

"You're a bloody genius mate!" Mickey laughed, patting Danny on his back. "See if you can do it again?"

Danny was up for the challenge. Again and again he practiced against the clock, steadily perfecting the art; until by lunchtime they were ready to go.

Sat in a side street with little passing traffic, the 530 was all too easy. Entered without damage, keyfob re-programmed, they were off and away in less than a minute. Having not had to venture far, they were soon back on familiar territory; a private estate on the Greet borders, known locally as The Firs.

Parking up outside a luxury apartment block, Mickey stepped out, and stood back to admire his trophy.

"Nice car. You made of money?" a voice from behind surprised him.

Spinning round, there was no doubting where it had come from. Frozen to the spot, his eyes followed her path towards him.

"Well – is it yours?" the blonde girl in pale blue uniform smiled. "Or are you taking your dad's out for a pose?"

"Err, yeah," Mickey replied nervously, pressing the fob. "Yeah, it's my Dad's."

"Very nice," she purred, her fingers lightly brushing the gleaming paintwork.

For once, Mickey didn't have a clue what to do; and looking across at Danny, neither did he. Should he just walk off, or would that simply make her suspicious? Maybe, just maybe, he should keep the pretence up; after all, she *was* very attractive, and it felt damn good to show off such an impressive motor.

"Strange," the girl said, circling the BMW. "I haven't seen this car round here before, and I *certainly* haven't seen *you* before."

She may have been wearing school uniform, but she wasn't like any schoolgirl Mickey had seen in the past. Tall and slim, she looked way more grown-up than the girls at his old school.

"What's the matter, cat got your tongue?" she teased.

"I'm sorry?" Mickey replied, regaining his composure.

"I said, 'I haven't seen this car around here before'."

"No – no you wouldn't," Mickey stammered. "My dad's in the err....trade, and he's always changing cars."

"And does he often have nice motors like this?" she asked, peering through the smoked glass.

"Sometimes; it depends what he can get his hands on."

Raising her head from the window, she looked deep into Mickey's eyes.

"So what's the chance of you giving me a ride in one?"

Was she *really* flirting with him? His pulse began to race.

"Yeah, yeah…of course I can," he replied hesitantly.

"Great. Next time you've got something tasty, bring it to the Old Varsity on a Friday night. My mates and I are always there. Don't disappoint us!" she grinned, turning to go.

"Okay – we won't," Mickey mumbled.

"It's Lara by the way," the girl said, flicking her hair to one side as she walked away.

Still dumbstruck, it wasn't until she'd turned the corner that he called, "It…it's Mickey," after her. But too late, she'd gone.

"Fuck me, you've pulled!" Danny sniggered.

"Don't sound so surprised you cheeky git. You've either got it or you haven't!"

"Fair play mate, she's a stunner. So you gonna take her up on the 'date'?"

"Not sure about that," Mickey replied. "She *looks* the same age as us, but she's still at school. How old do you think she really is?"

"Well if you hadn't been so smitten, you'd have seen she's at the posh high school. She's a sixth former; seventeen or eighteen at least."

"In that case," Mickey smiled, pocketing the keyfob. "You and me will definitely be going to the Varsity. I think we've earned some downtime, don't you?"

***

Mickey couldn't wait for the afternoon meeting to begin. Bursting with pride, he and Danny strode into the lounge; a sea of ecstatic faces rising to meet them. Handshakes and man-hugs later, Ronnie guided them to empty spaces on a sofa.

"Fantastic news guys," he raved. "Deano's only given us the bare bones, so tell us everything, and don't miss anything out!"

Between them, they ran through the night's events; the posse hanging on to their every word.

"But it doesn't end there," Mickey smiled. "And this bit, even Deano doesn't know yet!"

"Go on," Deano said, shaking his head. "What have you pair been up to?"

"Well, we hadn't even dropped the Beemer off when Danny started telling me about his latest brainwave; another purchase from the internet. Go on mate, you take it from there."

With a grin like a Cheshire cat, Danny uncurled his hand.

"This little beauty is called a 'turbo-decoder'," he said, passing it round the group. "There's no need to smash windows anymore; this'll get you in in five seconds flat – no noise, no damage, no alarm."

"Looks good mate," Deano frowned, working it over in his hand. "But does it work?"

Danny couldn't blurt the answer out quick enough. "The 5 series we had at lunchtime says it does!"

"Fuck me boys!" Ronnie stared in amazement. "You've had another one away?"

"Yep," Mickey smirked. "With Danny's kit, it's like taking candy from a baby. Just wait for next month's results; Hood's muppets aren't going to know what's hit them!"

22

Following the gadgets' initial success, Deano wasted no time in ordering more. Turbo-decoders, blank keyfobs and OBD readers soon arrived 'express' delivery. Split into two teams, they travelled far and wide; taking more cars, in less time, with little risk. By the month's end, they'd trebled their previous tally – blitzing their rivals in the process.

Perplexed and angry, Hood's crew struggled to work out how they could've been beaten. Their only answer was to turn their venom on the unsuspecting public. Fuelled by drugs, their attacks turned increasingly violent in their frenzy to acquire more motors.

But as their crime's intensity heightened, so did the media's interest. Day after day, the pages were bursting with victim's horrific accounts; the community was running scared – the press called out for justice.

Posted through Hood's front door, the freebie paper proclaimed their latest crime.

'**CARJACKERS STRIKE IN VICIOUS ATTACK**!' the headline read, and went on to describe how a middle aged businesswoman had been accosted at red lights. Punched repeatedly in the face, the terrified lady had been forced to hand over her keys at knifepoint, before being callously dumped at the roadside. Accompanied by the battered victim's photo, the article went on to criticise the pitiful police response.

Picking the paper out from junk mail strewn across his brown tiles, Hood returned to the lounge. Blankets acting as curtains hung across the windows; the room in gloomy darkness despite it being two in the afternoon. Stretching his arms out to yawn, he ambled towards the windows, practically tripping over Soldier's sleeping body. Sluggishly, he lifted the window covering, and tucked it into the curtain rail above. Daylight flooded in, sending the waking crew's heads disappearing beneath their covers.

Returning to his sofa-cum-bed, Hood picked up the paper.

"Looks like we've made the *front* page this time," he said reading out the bold headline.

Soldier sat up and rubbed his eyes. "What else does it say?"

While Hood stumbled through the article, the weary lads slowly shuffled closer, their covers still wrapped around them. Lowering his paper to the floor, the victim's battered face stared out.

"Daft cow. She got what she deserved," Decca said flippantly. "She shouldn't have left her doors unlocked should she!"

"Jeez, looks like you got a good punch in!" Tommy Burns grinned. "Have you seen the state of her face?"

"Yeah, decent job," Hood nodded. "The Audi's worth a fair few quid; it'll add nicely to this month's tally."

Snatching the paper from Tommy's clutches, Hood ripped off the front page, grabbed the sellotape and walked over to the lounge wall. Already partially decorated with similar articles, this one was going to take pride of place. Moving smaller pieces to one side, he stuck it down and stood back to admire his work.

"We're gonna need to get a bigger place soon," Soldier joked at the display.

"And with success will come the rewards," Hood nodded. "There's no way those tossers are ever gonna beat us again. We'll do whatever we need to do, agreed?"

There wasn't a murmur of dissent from his crew…drug addictions cost serious dough.

***

As if severe budgetary cuts and the slashing of officer's numbers wasn't bad enough, the dramatic rise in street crime was proving just as challenging for the Midlands Chief Constable. With pressure growing for action, she'd called an emergency conference at her force's headquarters. Tearing into her Chief Superintendents, she made it crystal clear that decisive action was needed. Precious funding would be diverted, but she wanted results, and quickly, or woe betide the consequences.

With his boss's words still ringing in his ears, Chief Supt Moore returned to Stechford nick, and quickly arranged a meeting with his section heads. Inside the conference room, taking advantage of the free coffee and biscuits, they sat idly chit-chatting while they waited for him to arrive.

Eventually, the door opened and Mr Moore strolled in, his secretary scuttling closely behind. Taking his seat at the table's head, he cleared his throat, and turned to face his staff. The chatter died down.

"You're probably wondering why you're gathered here today, so I'll get straight to the point, as I know you all have plenty to do," he began, staring at each Inspector in turn.

"Earlier this morning, my fellow commanders and I were summoned to the Chief's office. It seems that she has suddenly become aware of the escalation in violent carjacking," he continued with more than a hint of sarcasm. "And she's none too pleased with press criticism of our perceived inaction. With our community's trust and confidence being eroded, she's willing to squeeze the budget to provide extra funding. Now, having spoken to our intelligence staff, we are comfortable that our patch has been relatively unscathed by this mini-crimewave, which means that we have an ideal opportunity to divert the extra money and resources into …alternative community projects. In order to pacify the Chief, we will of course set up a squad whose remit includes street crime analysis, but their main responsibility will be to assist with the community issues directly affecting my division."

Shaking his head, Inspector Gladstone looked deep into his coffee cup. With retirement looming, he'd long since given up hope of further promotion, and as such didn't suffer fools gladly; irrespective of rank or position.

"Our youth offending team have presented a strong case for extra funding," Mr Moore continued. "Their community projects have been a resounding success, so this is an ideal opportunity to expand further."

"And what reduction in crime have we seen as a result of these projects?" Gladstone demanded, unable to control his frustration any longer.

"I'm sorry Paul, do you have something you wish to share with the team," his boss replied coldly.

"Only a degree of sanity," he began defiantly. "We're already tying up valuable resources pandering to our persistent young offenders, but I've yet to see any proof of rehabilitation! And now you'd like to waste more money on them instead of sending them where they really belong…behind bars!"

"That's a very narrow minded view Paul," the senior officer frowned. "It's way too early in the project to assess the positive impact these interactive courses are having on young people's lives. We need to intervene early, provide support and guidance; divert them away from a life of crime. This important project is far more worthwhile than wasting money on a problem that does not affect *my* division."

The group remained perfectly still, awaiting his challenger's response. Gladstone didn't let them down.

"By not affecting *your* division, I presume you're referring to your earlier statement that we've been 'relatively unscathed by this mini-crimewave'?"

He paused, and glowered at his boss. Mr Moore's jaw muscles tightened as he nodded his confirmation.

"I presume then, that you are blissfully unaware where these cars have been turning up? Well let me enlighten you; all the cars we *have* been able to find…have been found on *our* patch!"

Again he paused, his words allowed to settle. His boss's fiery red face appeared ready to blow.

"Therefore, my assumption is that the perpetrators are living somewhere on our area. The Chief Constable's initiative gives us an ideal opportunity to solve the problem. Can you imagine how impressed she and the press would be if we smashed this criminal ring?"

"Like you say Paul, your *assumption* is that they live on my area, and that is all it is; an assumption. There's no place in a modern day police service for 'assumptions' or an officer's sixth sense. We live in a computer age of high-tech offender profiling, and as I've already stated, the crime pattern on my division clearly indicates that we do not have a problem with these so called car-jackers. We do not need to address a problem that doesn't exist; is that understood!" he bellowed, his stare daring Gladstone to continue his defiance.

"That's fine Clive," he replied dismissively. "You keep putting your faith in silicon chips, I'll keep mine in the real world!"

"I suppose you know better than a multi-million pound intelligence system?" the commanding officer seethed through gritted teeth.

"I'd prefer to call it common sense," Gladstone replied calmly. "As we all know, the information we get from the system is only as good as the information we put in, and just as importantly; the questions we ask of it. Because these crimes have been spread randomly across a wide geographical area, nobody has taken overall control and interrogated our intelligence systems appropriately. For instance, if they had, maybe they'd have found the concentration of recovered vehicles on our patch. The only reason I'm ahead of the curve is because our response officers are so switched on. They're the ones who spotted the pattern; they're the ones who have identified suspects."

The silver-haired Inspector hesitated for a moment, his focus turning to his colleagues. "The answer is simple. We need to pool our resources together; dedicate a crack team to eradicate this scourge. Traffic, CID, obs teams…"

"Inspector Gladstone, you were obviously not listening to me," Mr Moore cut in furiously, slamming his clenched fist down. "We do *not* suffer the problem, so we do *not* need to cure it. It seems to have escaped your attention that *I* am in charge round here and my decision is final. The extra money and resources *will* go into the community department's budget who will deliver the results I outlined earlier. Now unless there are any further issues, I suggest we move on!"

All eyes turned to Gladstone, who slammed his notebook shut.

Replacing pen in jacket pocket, he sighed, and sat back.

"Oh well, I'm sure our community will sleep easier tonight. I just hope the robberies don't start to encroach onto *your* patch. Still, as you say, you're in charge…the buck stops with you!"

***

Located in the heart of Birmingham's student quarter, the 'Old Varsity's' Victorian facade stood out amongst the brash, modern bars lining the bustling high street. Tonight was no different to any other; while the bar was packed to the rafters with binge drinking youngsters, the car park to its rear was relatively empty. What *was* unusual was the car reversing into its darkest corner; it certainly wasn't the typical student banger.

Inside the sleek cabriolet, Mickey's nerves refused to budge; if only he'd made more of an effort with girls before!

"Jeez mate, I'm bricking it!" he said, bringing the car to a stop. "What if I make a dick of myself?"

"What, any more than normal?" Danny joked.

"Yeah, yeah, very funny. It's alright for you, you've been out with girls at the Children's Home. At least you know what you're doing."

"Now you're the one who's joking. You know they dumped me for exactly that reason – I didn't have a clue what I was doing!"

Laughing together, Mickey checked out his reflection. All was looking good: clean shaven, hair gelled neatly in place, and no fresh zits to frighten Lara off!

"Best of luck then mate," Mickey said turning the engine off. "It's now or never!"

"Hey, good looking dudes like us don't need luck; the babes aren't going to know what's hit them," Danny grinned. "Come on, let's get some action!"

Approaching the rear entrance, an unexpected obstacle stood in their way. Arms crossed, dressed all in black, two burly bouncers filled the doors. The taller doorman looked them up and down as they approached.

"Show us your ID," he demanded, holding out his hand.

Shit! It hadn't even crossed Mickey's mind to bring identification. Opening his wallet, he fumbled around, desperately stalling for time.

"Come on guys," Danny pleaded. "We've arranged to meet some friends inside."

"Unless you've got proof of age, you pair are going nowhere!"

"Hey, that driving licence will do," his colleague stated, spotting the card in Mickey's wallet. "Hand it over."

Mickey's heart sank. Yes, his date of birth was clearly displayed on his provisional licence, but with a month to go until his eighteenth birthday, his evening had ended before it had even started. Passing it over, he awaited the inevitable reaction.

23

The first bouncer laughed and handed it to his colleague. "Huh, more tossers trying to pull the wool over our eyes. This one's underage."

The taller man stared closely at the licence, then back at Mickey.

"Mickey Wilding?" he frowned. "You're one of Chapman's boys aren't you?"

Completely taken aback, all Mickey could do was stammer. "Ye – yes."

"They were talking about you the other day; doing a good job I heard," he nodded. "Guess that explains why you turned up in a brand new Beemer tonight, doesn't it!"

Mickey glanced across to his mate.

"Don't worry, we're all on the same side," he smiled, opening the door. "Have a good night lads."

Not needing to be told twice, Mickey stepped inside; the waves of heat and noise instantly crashing over him. Engulfed by the pulsating throng moving as one to the pounding beat, he jostled his way through. Students queued three deep at the bar, while beyond the overcrowded ground floor, a packed galleried area encircled the room. This was unlike any experience before; the deafening music and laughter intoxicating, but he was soon brought back to reality by Danny's deft tug on his arm.

"What the fuck was all that about with the bouncers?" he shouted into Mickey's ear.

"Mate, I'm as gobsmacked as you are. Still, we're in now, let's grab a drink and go hunting!" Mickey yelled back, making his way to the crowded bar.

Stood waiting his turn, he scanned the room. Face piercings, vivid coloured hair and ripped clothing seemed all the rage here, but as yet no sign of Lara.

Taking a bottle in each hand, they gradually pushed through the bodies, and up onto the elevated gallery. The commanding view was perfect. Roaring at the freaks, whistling at the fit girls, their confidence grew with every swig.

"C'mon, let's get another one; it's time to find our girls!" Mickey shouted, beckoning to his mate.

Danny gave him the thumbs-up and followed through the crowd once more. Having seen no trace of her in the main room, they grabbed more bottles, and jostled their way through to the room at the rear. More of a games room, the 'bar' was only half full, the music less deafening, and the customers less…weird!

Sidling over to the bar, Mickey leant on the counter, and scanned the room.

Instantly, his eyes were drawn to the nearest pool table. Leaning over, preparing to play a shot were tight blue jeans clinging to a girl's slender thighs.

Slowly, her right arm swung forward, calmly rolling the cue ball into the black; the kiss just enough to drop it into the pocket. Flicking her head to one side, she casually strode over to a group of girls stood opposite, and 'high-fived' the first in line. While her beaten opponent trudged back to his own group, another stepped forward, placing his money straight onto the table.

Mickey's gaze remained with the girl, who having taken a drink, turned and beamed at her new opponent. Just as he thought, it was Lara; but God, she was even more stunning than he'd remembered. A dig in the ribs from Danny soon broke his concentration.

"Bloody hell mate, don't make it so obvious. You don't want her seeing your tongue hanging out!"

"I can't help it; have you seen how fit she is!"

"Yeah – well out of your league!" Danny teased.

"Cheeky bastard. Well in that case her friends over there are definitely out of yours!"

"Hey, there's no totty out of Danny's league! But don't worry mate, I'll help you get promoted!"

While their banter continued, Mickey's eyes didn't move from the table. Lara's opponent was making small talk, exchanging subtle smiles between shots; he clearly fancied his chances. His attitude was just beginning to wind Mickey up, when shrieking with joy, Lara suddenly held her cue aloft again. With a broad grin, her challenger opened his arms, inviting a congratulatory hug.

Completely ignoring him, she strutted back to her friends, celebrating with another swig from her bottle. Dejected, the lad returned to his piss-taking mates, whose next nomination stepped forward.

Mickey had seen enough. Without a word to Danny, he pushed his way through to the pool table, and taking a pound from his pocket, thrust it onto the baize, just as the next challenger arrived.

"Too late mate," Mickey declared, taking hold of the cue. "You'll have to go after me!"

"Yeah, okay mate, keep your hair on," the youth replied. "You won't be on for long anyway, she's on fire tonight."

Ignoring him, Mickey bent down to insert the coin. Heart racing, he racked the balls, filled the triangle and waited for Lara to join. Would she even recognise him, he wondered? After all, it had been a few weeks since their last meeting.

Still chatting over her shoulder to her friends, Lara approached the table. Mickey waited at the head; his cue's base between his feet, its tip beneath his chin.

"Do you want to break, or shall we flick to see who starts?" she asked, her eyes rising from the table to his face.

"I'll fire away if it's okay with you."

"Well, well, well; if it isn't Mickey the BMW man," she said, a broad smile forming. "I didn't think you were ever coming!"

So she *had* heard him call out his name.

"You know how it is; we were just passing through – thought we'd pop in for some quiet drinks," he smiled back.

Lara held his eye. Mickey waited for her next move.

"Well come on then blue-eyes, what are you waiting for?" she winked. "Let's see if you can shoot pool."

The frame passed by in a blur, his focus more on his opponent than the game itself. Lara soon potted the black, but instead of her characteristic celebration, she placed her cue down and walked round the table to join him.

"You come on your own, or you brought your friends with you?"

He nodded in Danny's direction. "Just my best mate."

"You gonna join us for a drink then, I promise we won't bite?"

"After that thrashing, I guess I owe *you* one. Another WKD?"

Lara grinned. "You don't miss much do you? Katie'll have one as well ta," and with that returned to her friends.

Over at the bar, Danny was beaming.

"Well played mate, and I don't mean the pool!"

"Yep, done my bit. Now it's time for you to get your hand in your pocket, 'cos she's set *you* up with one of her mates! Come on, they're waiting for us to take the drinks over!"

It was like walking into the lion's den. Drinks in hand, they ambled towards Lara's group, their every step under the girls' constant gaze. Despite the 'dutch courage' he'd already consumed, Mickey's pulse refused to slow. What on earth was he supposed to talk about; he was bound to make a prat of himself.

He needn't have worried though; Lara's friends were well-oiled and flirted shamelessly. But as the night wore on, the two pairings moved closer and closer, laughing and joking together.

"So tell me," Lara said, pulling Mickey towards her. "What wheels are you driving at the moment?"

He'd been waiting for the question all night, and wasn't going to give the answer up easily.

"Oh, a little sporty one," he said, raising a bottle to his lips.

"What sort of sporty one?"

Mickey finished his swig. "Just a soft top Beemer," he replied casually.

Lara's eyes lit up. "Well I hope you've brought it with you, 'cos Katie and I could do with a lift home."

His subtle wink gave Lara the reply she was looking for. With a shriek, she tugged at Katie's shirt and whispered excitedly in her ear.

"So, do you girls fancy another drink," Mickey asked, shaking his empty bottle.

"When you've got a Beemer outside – are you kidding?" Lara answered impishly, grabbing her coat from the bench.

Seizing hold of Mickey's hand, she practically dragged him outside. Despite its dark surroundings, Lara soon spotted the low-slung nose. With a whoop of delight, she released his hand, and rushed over as swiftly as her high heels allowed.

"How long you got this beauty for?" she grinned, stroking the BMW emblem.

Until Deano or the police take it from me, Mickey thought to himself.

"Just for the weekend," he winked at Danny. "But don't worry, I'll have something just as good next week!"

Casually strolling around the car, Lara's hand drifted along its curves, until, as she reached the handle, Mickey blipped the fob. With a squeal, she threw open the door, and ushered Danny and Katie into the rear.

"Do you want to fire her up?" Mickey grinned, climbing into the driver's seat.

"What do you think!"

Leaning across his lap, she pressed the starter, her finger lingering as the engine roared into life. Turning towards him, she pulled him close.

His eyes closing, the world receded away. Deeper and deeper he drifted, time passing without consequence, until eventually, deliberate coughing from the rear interrupted his pleasure.

"Any chance of you pair coming up for air?" Katie giggled.

"Killjoy!" Lara laughed back, sweeping her blonde locks away.

It was time to go; they needed to get off the car park before attracting too much attention. Picking his way between drunken students, he drove carefully to its edge. The main road was clear both ways; time to show off to the girls!

Flooring the loud pedal, he wheelspun away; plumes of smoke left billowing in his wake. Delighted, the girls screamed their encouragement, egging him on as he blasted through the gears.

Top down, music pumping, they cruised around the city centre's nightlife, until eventually, it was time to head back to her parents. Its hood back on and stereo turned down, Mickey leisurely turned into her lane.

The detached pad was impressive; it was just like the homes he so often targeted. As he pulled up outside, he wondered what her father would think if he knew his beautiful daughter was outside in a stolen car!

Lara caught sight of his wistful smile. "What are you grinning at?" she asked.

"Oh, just thinking about you."

"Don't start getting all romantic on me, it doesn't suit you," she grinned, undoing her seat belt. "Now come here handsome!"

A shorter kiss this time, she smiled as she released their embrace. "Thanks for the ride home blue-eyes; we going to see you again next week?"

"I'm not sure," Mickey teased. "We've got a pretty full week ahead."

"Oh well, your loss then," she replied casually, making to push him away.

He wasn't going to let her go that easily. Pulling her back, he closed his eyes.

"Ah, ah…time's up," she chuckled, pecking him on the lips. "I might have turned eighteen, but I'm still daddy's little girl; he's bound to be twitching the curtains."

Instinctively, Mickey glanced towards the house.

"Don't worry, he doesn't bite! You've got my number, give me a bell," she said, climbing out. "I can't wait to see what you've got for us next week; just make sure it's something hot!"

"Oh it'll be hot alright," Mickey called after her.

Closing the door behind, Danny jumped into the front. "Yeah, if only she knew just how 'hot' the cars really are!"

"Fuck me mate, imagine if they did…we'd be right in the shit!"

"Well let's hope they never do then," Danny replied, watching the front door open. "Let's hope they never do."

24

Still buzzing from the night before, the lads turned up at Deano's ready for another action packed day. But something wasn't right. Where were the energised faces; everybody looked hacked off. Even Deano's customary grin was gone.

"Bloody hell you lot," Mickey said, taking a seat. "You look like someone's died! You do know we're on a roll, don't you?"

"Sorry mate," Deano replied dejectedly. "You might have noticed we're one short at the moment?"

Mickey quickly scanned the room. "Where's Wesbo?"

"Remember the nice new Jag we had off the business park? Well unfortunately Wesbo's scarf fell down before he got in. He had the car away all right, but the CCTV was crystal clear, and as luck would have it, the cop who turned up knew him of old. Well you can guess the rest. Let's just say, he's been kept in custody and Jonas reckons he'll get twelve months minimum!"

Mickey didn't say a word, his eyes turning to the big screen. What would be the consequences? To lose Wesbo was a heavy blow; the monthly competitions were tough enough, even with a full crew. He was always the second car's wheelman; so who was gonna take his place – somebody had to?

As he sat there in the quiet, he reflected on the situation. Could Wesbo's departure actually present an opportunity? Who *would* Deano choose to replace him? Mickey reckoned he was as good a driver as any of the others, but did Deano? Maybe this wasn't the right time to discuss it; but when the time came, he'd make sure Deano knew he was up for it. He wanted that seat, and was more than prepared to fight for it!

***

He didn't have to wait long for his answer. The following Sunday they were all summoned to Deano's, and were met by their nervous leader pacing around the room.

"Come in, come in," he said hurriedly. "Grab a drink and sit down; we need to talk."

By the time everybody had turned up, Deano was ready to burst.

"Listen up, Porter's been on the blower," he began. "He's had a massive order for kiddie's designer gear which he needs by next weekend. I told him we're running short, and that we need to sort a new driver, but he wasn't having any of it. He just told me that if we wanted to earn any money this month, it'd be in our interests to do the job. If we can't do it, he'll pass it to Hood."

"It's no big deal mate; I'm sure the seven of us can cope," Ronnie shrugged.

"And if it was a straight forward job, I'd agree. Problem is, the target's in Nottingham!"

Now Mickey could see why Deano was so anxious. Nottingham was more than fifty miles away; they'd be on the road for over an hour after the raid, with every cop between Nottingham and Birmingham scouring the streets for them. A lengthy pursuit on unfamiliar roads would be tough work, even for an experienced getaway driver.

"I've asked Chapman for a replacement on the team, but the names he's come up with just aren't ready yet, so we're going to have to run one short for a while. In the meantime, we need to replace Wesbo's spot in the driver's seat, so I've decided…"

Mickey felt a nudge in his side. Eyes fixed on Deano, he waited for the decision.

"…Dougie, I'd like you to take over."

It was like a dagger through Mickey's heart. Dougie was a damn good driver, but he instinctively knew he was better. There was nothing else for it.

"Is there any reason why *I* can't be considered?" he stated calmly, his voice slightly quivering.

Deano paused before answering. "Thanks for volunteering mate. I just think Dougie's got a bit more experience. I've heard you know what you're doing, but you could probably do with a bit more practice, that's all."

He wasn't going to let it go that easily. "You're right, I *can* do the business behind the wheel. And I don't mean any disrespect to Dougie, 'cos I agree; he's fucking good. But nobody really knows who *is* the better driver, do they?"

"What are you suggesting, 'cos if it's a tag match you're after, you can forget it. We're never doing that again, not after what happened to Shags!"

"I don't blame you; we couldn't believe what we saw that night."

The moment the words left his mouth, the eyes of the room turned towards him.

"What do you mean, 'we couldn't believe what we saw'?" a gobsmacked Deano replied. "You're not telling me you were actually there are you?"

Mickey looked round the room; five sets of unblinking eyes stared back.

"We both were," he replied innocently. "We were out doing our nightly patrols and it all sort of…happened in front of us. What's the problem then?"

"The problem? The problem is we've never really known what happened; only what Hood told us. Why haven't you mentioned it before?"

"Well, none of you ever talk about it; we kind of thought it was taboo."

Deano slowly nodded his head. "I guess it has been; especially as we don't get to see Shags anymore. His mum blamed us for what went on that night – she moved out the area and took him with her. Anyway, tell us what happened and don't miss anything out."

Mickey took a deep breath and began. Reaching the disastrous conclusion, his pace increased.

"...and then as the Type-R dabbed its brakes, the Renault rushed towards him and whacked his back end. That was that; Shags had no chance. He lost control, left the road, and slammed straight into a wall!"

"And what did that wanker Hood do?" Ronnie asked in disbelief.

"Well to start with, he pulled up next to the wreckage. I thought he was going to get out and help."

Mickey paused, his eyes flicking to Danny.

"But he just sat there, engine revving. Then, as the people started to come out, he turned his lights off and floored it. We didn't see him again after that."

"So that twat just left him to die!" Ronnie erupted.

"Are any of us surprised?" Deano said angrily. "It's exactly as we suspected, and now we've got our proof!"

Taking to his feet, he turned the TV off and stood in front of the widescreen.

"We owe it to Shags to get our revenge. We've gotta put Hood and his boys out of business, and we'll start with this weekend! You're right mate," he said turning to Mickey. "We don't know who's the best, and you boys have earned the right to a fair shot. We'll sort it the old way; fastest lap around Woodlands Park decides it. You both happy with that?"

Mickey and Dougie nodded.

"We haven't got much time, so we'll do it Thursday night at nine; that'll give you both chance to get some practice in. This time there'll be no fuck ups, and guys...may the best man win!"

***

Having acquired a turbocharged Audi, Mickey soon became one with the car. By the time night fell on Thursday evening, he was ready; this was his one chance...and he wasn't going to blow it!

The car park he and Danny drove onto, was the same they'd overlooked from their den all those years ago. First to arrive, they parked in front of it, their RS4's xenons burning deep into its heart.

"Did you ever think we'd be sat here in our own knock-off?" Danny asked, staring into the undergrowth.

"I didn't think..." Mickey smiled at his mate, "...I knew!"

Half listening to the background music, he turned the lights off and waited in the darkness, his pulse beginning to quicken. It was time to concentrate; coming up, one lap around the park he'd walked so many times as a kid. Closing his eyes, he drove the course in his mind – imagining every twist, every turn, every place of danger.

Soon, a second car approached, giving the customary double flash. It was another Audi RS4, but quite different to the first. Bright blue with extra body kit, Dougie's ride looked every inch the brash counterpart to Mickey's discreet black version. Getting out, they began to admire each other's wheels.

"You might as well give up now; this beast's chipped to 600 bhp!" Dougie joked.

Dammit, Mickey kicked himself, why hadn't he thought to boost *his* car's power?

"Wouldn't matter if it had a thousand horses; it's all down to the driver's skill round here!" he laughed back, trying not to show his frustration. "I'd beat you if I had a Lada!"

By now Danny had wandered over to the blue Audi.

"Has it really got 600 horses?" he asked admiringly.

"Of course not, I'm just winding Mickey up…and it looks like he's having it a treat!"

"You bastard," Mickey grinned, faking a punch at his tormentor.

Dougie swayed leisurely to his side, before offering his hand forward. Mickey grasped it willingly.

"Good luck," Dougie nodded.

"And yourself mate, and as Deano said, 'may the best man win'!"

Seconds later, Deano turned up in a third car. Pulling up next to the two Audi's, he jumped out; mobile in one hand, a heavy black torch in the other.

"Right, we all know what we're here for," he said, addressing the group. "And the longer we're here, the more chance of being seen, so we'll get on with it straightaway. I'll quickly go over the rules as it's a long time since we did this."

Shining his torch towards the start line, he gave them the lowdown. "It's a standing start. I'll count down from five with my hand in front of the screen; so make sure there's no false starts. You'll be timed over one complete circuit of the park's perimeter, and to make sure you don't take any short cuts, your opposite number will sit next to you!"

"I'd better not go first then, or poor Mickey'll be too scared to drive afterwards," Dougie chuckled.

"In your dreams big mouth!"

"To keep it fair, we'll flick for it," Deano said reaching into his pocket for a coin. "Mickey, you're the new boy, you call."

"Heads," Mickey said as Deano flicked the coin up into the darkness.

"Heads it is," Deano declared, his torchlight picking out the silver. "Do you want to go first or second?"

"I'll take second; see what I need to beat," Mickey replied, his mind beginning to focus. This shit was real...he'd probably never get another shot.

"Right, let's get on with it," Deano continued. "Dougie, once you've done your circuit, get straight back here to swap over; I'll give you your time before Mickey starts his lap. Mickey, once you're done, drop Dougie off and we'll all get going. After the noise you pair'll be making, every cop in the neighbourhood will be flying towards us. Dump the motors in your garages, meet back at mine, and then I'll announce the winner, okay?"

Nothing more needed to be said. With a pat on the back from his mate, Mickey climbed into the passenger seat and strapped himself in. As they drove up to the wooden posts surrounding the perimeter track, Dougie paused while Ronnie removed a pair with his sledgehammer. In through the space, he brought his car to a halt on the start line.

Lined up on the car's offside, the posse watched and waited.

"Five seconds!" Deano announced, readying his iPhone's stopwatch.

On came the car's lights, illuminating the track before them. Launch control engaged, the engine note rose.

"Go!"

Shooting off along the perimeter track, the lap flew by at a furious pace. Dougie could handle a car alright, Mickey smiled, hanging on through yet another powerslide; he was going to have to drive a perfect lap to beat him.

No sooner had the rally stage begun, than Dougie was flinging the sporty Audi around the final corner. Burying the power towards the finish line, he flew past the posse, span the car on its handbrake, and blasted back onto the car park.

"Got to be fair to you mate, that was fucking impressive," Mickey said as they pulled up.

"Cheers, I was right on the ragged edge. If you can beat that...you deserve to win!"

Having jumped out of one car and into the next, they quickly made their way back to the start.

Deano poked his head through the door. "One minute, fifty-two. Top driving, a new record!"

"Yes!" Dougie hollered.

"Don't worry, he hasn't won yet. Don't forget, the old record was set a few years ago, before we had cars as quick as these. Mickey, you're still in with a chance."

Shutting the door behind him, Deano raised his open hand in front of the screen. Subconsciously, Mickey shut the world out; his eyes solely on the track ahead. Launch control set, first gear engaged, full beam on – ready to go!

Deano's voice faded away; Mickey's focus way beyond the fingers counting down in slow motion. As the final finger withdrew into Deano's palm, he released the footbrake, activating a four wheel launch up the track. On the paddles, he powered through the gears before throwing the Audi sideways into the first corner, its tyres hurling a wave of pebbles onto the grass. Balancing his car on the throttle, he squeezed gently until the track straightened out, then floored it away once more.

Increasingly feeling as one with his machine, the circuit passed by in a blur. Corner after corner flew by without difficulty...only one more to go, and then the home straight. Momentum maintained from the previous bend, he approached at 100mph. He knew the corner well; but in the dark, at this speed...he just hoped he'd judged it right.

However, the moment he stood on his brakes he knew he hadn't. Feeling the ABS's judder ride up his leg, he instinctively turned towards the corner.

Suddenly, the Audi's back-end slew to one side.

"Shit!" Dougie yelled, his eyes fixed on the rapidly approaching trees.

Sliding off the track, Mickey's eyes widened in horror...

25

Instantly wrenching his wheel into opposite lock, he only had one option, and instinctively…he took it. Flooring the gas with all his might, tyres sprayed pebbles in every direction as they desperately fought for grip.

Now half onto the grass, he hung on for dear life.

Wheels spinning furiously…they suddenly found traction. Biting deep into the mixed surface, the four-wheel-drive system hauled the RS4 back in to line. Keeping it planted, he hammered down the final straight and over the flying finish.

"Jeeez that was close, I honestly thought you'd over-cooked it!" Dougie said, releasing his grip on the seat.

"Nah, I had it all under control," Mickey smirked.

"Well, whether you meant it or not, it was still quality. See you back at Deano's, I'll have some tissues ready for you!"

"Yeah, yeah, yeah; you should be a comedian!"

As Dougie jumped out, an animated Danny leapt in. "That was the business mate, you looked fucking awesome!"

"Yeah, it went alright. Did you manage to sneak a look at the time?"

"You must be joking, Deano wouldn't let anybody near him. You're gonna have to wait 'til we get back to his place."

Excitedly discussing the flying laps, they hurried back to the garage. Mickey knew his lap had been quick, but had it been quick enough? Even his biased best mate struggled to choose between the two. He was right, they'd just have to wait for Deano's verdict.

With the air thick with sirens, they were the last to scurry back to the maisonette.

Deano was ready and waiting.

"I suppose you want to know the results?" he said, pulling a slip from his trouser pocket. "As I said earlier, Dougie set the lap record with an impressive time of one minute fifty-two. Mickey…" he said turning to face him, "…you also drove your nuts off. You completed the lap in one minute, fifty…"

As Deano paused, Mickey leant forward, his eyes straining to glimpse the time on the paper.

"…one! Mickey was faster by one second. Congratulations mate, you're officially the second driver!"

"Yes!" Mickey shrieked, punching the air in celebration just as he was jumped on by the equally ecstatic Danny.

Shaking his head, a smiling Dougie stood up, and offered his hand again.

"Well done mate," he said as they shook. "I'd be proud to be crewed up with you."

"So unless there's any objections, it's decided," Deano continued. "We'll use the two RS4's on the job, so make sure they're both ready; you know the score – full tanks, re-plated, spares in boots. Saturday night, be here by midnight, we're leaving at one, okay?"

Okay? Mickey grinned. Okay! Things just couldn't get any better!

***

Saturday night was soon upon them. Everybody was on time; nobody underestimated the challenge ahead. To get to Nottingham and back without being spotted, would take planning, skill…and luck.

"The reason we're making such a trek is because we're hitting the biggest designer warehouse in the country," Deano began. "As you would expect, it's gonna be tougher to get into than normal; they've got anti ram-raid posts around the outside, and industrial strength shutters covering the entrance. There's nothing we can't handle, we've just got to accept it'll take a little longer than normal. Ronnie, your angle grinders will make short work of the metal posts, and I'll rip the shutters off once Dougie's hooked them onto my tow bar."

Mickey committed every detail to memory; he couldn't afford to miss a thing.

"For this, more than any job, we *all* need to be clued up. It's off our patch, so we'll rely heavily on our navigators," Deano continued. "As ever, Ronnie will be mine; Mickey, you need to choose yours. As you know, Rushy has always done the job for Wesbo, but the choice is yours…who do you want it to be?"

Mickey went quiet for a moment. He knew exactly who he wanted sat next to him, the same person who always sat next to him; the friend he trusted with his life. But he had to tread carefully; Rushy was well respected.

"Rushy…" he replied turning towards him, "…you've always done a great job, and I've never known you make a mistake. However, I wouldn't be where I am without Danny. No offence intended, but my choice is Danny."

"No offence?" a puzzled Rushy responded. "Mate, I'd be kicking your ass if you'd made any other decision. He's your best mate, he won't let you down."

"That's settled then. Eccy will join you in your motor, the rest of the boys are with me. Normally, I'd be the lead car throughout, but as it's your first time, you can take the lead after the job. That way, if we do get the chase, I can keep them at bay for you; 'cos believe me, you're gonna have enough on your plate as it is!"

***

Parked up in the pitch-black side street, the raiders waited in silence; their faces dimly lit by dashboard lights. With his engine rumbling impatiently,

Mickey stared at the road ahead, his fingers drumming up and down on the wheel.

Right on time, the brake lights on Deano's Audi flashed twice; it was time to move.

Everything went as planned. Angle-grinders in hand, Ronnie made short work of the metal posts, while Dougie's chains ripped the shutters clean off the building. Once their sledgehammer had smashed through the glass, it was all too easy. Undisturbed, they dashed in and out, grabbing box after box, until the motors were filled to the brim. Alarm bells ringing, the moment their boots slammed shut, Mickey led them quickly away.

The raid may well have gone without a hitch, but their good fortune was about to run out. Three miles into their getaway, blue lights heading in the opposite direction drove past them at speed.

Mickey glanced in his mirror. The traffic car was bound to be rushing to the burglary, but would it clock their two motors? After all, they *were* travelling at the speed limit, minding their own business.

Who was he trying to kid? Two high-performance Audis, the only cars on the road, heading away from the ram-raid! There was only one result, and the police car's sudden brake lights confirmed his fears.

"Shit," he muttered under his breath. "We've been rumbled."

Danny remained glued to the sat-nav, maintaining a running commentary as the now fast-paced escape headed onto the country lanes.

Mickey's eyes flicked front and rear. Behind him Deano kept close, but further back, the hazy blue strobes refused to disappear. Was it his imagination, or were they getting closer? To the front, his full-beam lit the road up ahead; hedges and trees mere blurs to his side. On unfamiliar roads, in the darkness of night, he was driving by the seat of his pants.

Eccy sat silently in the rear. Danny only spoke to give directions. Five minutes flew by with no let-up in pace. But by now, there was no doubting the traffic car's ability; it had swallowed their lead and remained glued to their tail. With every mile that passed, Mickey could feel the net tightening, and there was still more than thirty to go. They needed to get rid of their pursuer, and quick!

But far from losing their hunter, they were about to gain another.

In the distance, Mickey spotted blue lights pulling up at a junction; the passenger jumping out as it stopped.

"He's got a box in his hand," Danny yelled. "He's gonna try and sting us!"

There was no way out. With a cop car behind and hedges to his sides; his only hope was to try to blast through.

With just two hundred metres to go, Mickey kept it floored; could the cop get it out and deploy it in time?

One hundred metres. The officer had the case open; his hands a flurry inside. Fifty. Out came the spike strip. Mickey's speedo read 120 and climbing. Ten. The cop turned and threw...

26

Spikes glistening in his headlights, the stinger disappeared below Mickey's bonnet; its front edge dipping towards the road surface.

Bang!

Striking the Audi's bumper, the stinger cannoned into the air, its deadly spines bursting outwards. Diving for cover, the officer rolled to safety as the Audis flew by unscathed.

"Fucking hell!" Danny shouted. "Well played mate, another second and we'd all have been history!"

Heart pounding, Mickey's eyes flicked back to the mirror. The first cop car hadn't budged, and now the second was racing up behind.

Three miles flashed by in a heartbeat; a junction loomed large in his headlights.

"At the end of the road, turn left and immediately right!" Danny called out.

Jumping onto the steaming brakes, Mickey set the car up, ready to slide to the left. Behind him, well before the junction, Deano suddenly came to a halt in the middle of the narrow lane, blocking their pursuers' path.

With a quick tug on his wheel, Mickey dived through the staggered crossroads. Pressing ahead, he drove as fast as he dared, until only darkness filled his mirrors once more.

"I think we've given them the slip," he said breathlessly, his focus unwavering.

"Well we're gonna have to keep it gunned mate, we're not out of the woods yet," Danny replied, briefly looking up from the sat-nav. "Every cop car in the world's gonna be after us, and by my reckoning we've still got twenty miles to go!"

Luckily for the fleeing raiders, communication between neighbouring forces was at best slow, and at worst, non-existent. Swallowing up the remaining miles, the flying Audi crossed force boundaries without interference, and they soon found themselves back on the Greet.

Car safely garaged, he darted the short distance home, his mind racing over the previous hour's events. It had been exhilarating for sure; the raid, the chase, the escape. But what had happened to Deano? Without him, he'd never have evaded capture. Had he sacrificed himself to save Mickey's skin, or had he managed to make his getaway? He desperately wanted to call to find out, but what if he was still being chased? Or worse still, what if he was in custody, and his phone was now in police hands?

A long sleepless night lay ahead.

***

With each passing day, Hood's crew became increasingly desperate. In contrast to Deano's posse who travelled far and wide to secure their bounty, their brutal crimes shifted closer and closer to home. Requiring little planning other than pre-meditated violence, their prey could just as easily be found passing through the nearby leafy suburbs. With a community up in arms, the clamour for action could no longer be ignored.

Behind his computer screen, Inspector Gladstone shook his head as yet another crime report landed. Flicking through the details, the office phone interrupted his concentration.

"Yes?"

"Hi Paul, it's Mr Moore's secretary here. Can you pop up and see him as a matter of urgency please?"

"I take it he still hasn't worked out how to dial my extension then?" Gladstone joked. "Yes, no problem, I'll be up shortly, I'm just slogging my way through these infernal reports."

"Thank you, he's expecting you right away."

Replacing the phone, he glared at it for a moment, murmuring, 'Well he can bloody wait!' under his breath. Straight back onto his computer, it was half-an-hour before he finally made his way upstairs.

"Ah Paul, good to see you at last," Chief Supt Moore beamed as he walked in. "Please take a seat."

"How can I help you?" Gladstone asked tiredly.

Mr Moore smiled. "Tell me, how's the sector work going?"

"As you well know, it's tedious and un-rewarding. Now please explain why you've summoned me, as I have countless reports to complete before some senior officer kicks my arse!"

"Come, come Paul," Mr Moore grinned, reclining in his leather chair. "We're not here to quarrel, I just thought you might wish to seize an opportunity that has arisen."

"And what opportunity would that be Clive?"

"It was heartening to see your interest in the car-jackings at our last meeting. I appreciate that we may have held different opinions at the time, but things have…moved on slightly since then."

"By 'moved on', you actually mean 'we're now being hammered' don't you? And let me guess, you've had your ass chewed off by the Chief!"

The sternness returned to Mr Moore's face, his insincere smile wiped clean away.

"Paul, I seriously hope you're not trying to lecture me with a torrent of 'I told you so's'. As you well know, there are many ways to build trust and confidence within our communities, but as long as we work constructively together, we will succeed."

"Listen, as far as I'm concerned, what's done is done. The important issue is what we're going to do now. So tell me: what *are* we going to do, and how do I fit into your plans?"

"That's very encouraging Paul, thank you. Well, I would certainly like to channel your passion and knowledge into eradicating the problem, to which end, I'd like you to establish a motivated team to stamp out these heinous crimes. I take it you'd be keen to rise to the challenge?"

"Providing I get the budget and manpower the Chief decreed, then I'd be more than happy to give it a bash."

"Good, I knew I could rely on you. Now I've got a few names in mind who are keen to assist. I thought Sergeant Jenkins, and PC's Foster, Padley..."

"Whoa!" Gladstone interrupted angrily. "I'm not having that bunch of wasters on my team. If you want the project to fail, use that shower of shit by all means; but you can get some other fool to lead them!"

"Come now Paul, I'm giving you an opportunity to get away from the mundane work you detest; you need to meet me halfway on this. I appreciate the names mentioned need some stimulation, but you're the ideal chap to inspire them."

"That's bollocks! If I can't choose my team, I'm not interested," and with that, Gladstone rose to leave.

Mr Moore exhaled loudly. "Alright, alright. Tell me who you have in mind and I'll see what I can do."

Re-taking his seat, the tall Inspector rattled off his choices.

"Okay, leave it with me. In the meantime, tie up your loose ends and be ready to start tomorrow."

***

Mickey hardly slept a wink; Deano's fate never far from his mind. Still fearful of calling his phone, he had to wait until the agreed afternoon meet-up to discover what had happened.

"Don't worry mate," Danny said, pushing on Deano's front door. "He's bound to have escaped; he's the best in the business!"

The empty living room was just as they'd left it twelve hours earlier. Curtains still drawn, even the empty drink cans still littered the floor. A feeling of dread began to creep through Mickey's veins; there was no sign of life, no sign of the posse's return.

"C'mon, let's check his room," he said hurrying into the dark corridor.

The bedroom door was shut. He put his ear to it and listened.

Nothing.

Bollocks. Surely he hadn't been caught; this was Deano, the legend. He tapped the wooden door with his knuckle. Still nothing.

Again he rapped, this time a little louder.

Barely audible, a drowsy grunt replied. Taking it for an invite, he entered the musty room.

A voice rose croakily from beneath the bedclothes. "Bloody hell guys, what time do you call this?"

"Sorry mate, but it's one o' clock as agreed. We were getting worried for you."

"Shit, I must have forgotten to set my alarm," Deano replied, rolling over. "Chapman's gonna kick my ass; I was supposed to let him know the results of our trip by midday. Are the others here yet?"

Almost as he finished, footsteps on the stairs delivered their answer.

"We'll leave you to get changed, then you've got to tell us what happened; we've been bricking it thinking you got caught!"

"Where's your faith guys?" Deano laughed. "Listen, I'll fill you in in a minute, but I've gotta speak to Chapman first. Do us a favour, get me a strong black coffee will you; I'm totally shagged."

Leaving Deano to make his call, the lads joined the others in the lounge. Hot drinks in hand, they were soon joined by their leader.

"Well?" Mickey said, the moment Deano sat down. "What the fuck happened to you?"

"Hey, I could ask you boys the same question. Did you have any problems?"

"Nah, we didn't see the filth after you pulled your little stunt. But what happened next...they were right on top of you?"

Sitting back in his armchair, Deano took a sip before replying. "Well they probably thought they'd got us covered. Let's face it, with two cars behind, they could split up if we did the same. But it was all pretty simple really; we just looked for where the road narrowed and came to a stop. There was no way they could pass, so we just sat there waiting for them to do something. Eventually, the passenger jumped out and ran towards us, but the moment he reached our doors, I pretended to blast off. Fair play to him, he sprinted back to his motor...only to see me pull up again! Poor old plod didn't know what the fuck to do! He just stood there in the darkness, door open, waiting for our next move. Sure enough, the sucker finally came running back over. Well of course, we did the same again; left him grasping nothing but thin air! We were pissing ourselves, it was just like the Keystone Cops!"

By now Mickey was practically crying with laughter.

"We could have continued all night, but we knew the chopper would've been scrambled, so it was time to fly ourselves. I won't lie, it wasn't easy; the coppers were all over us. With the clock running down, I took a risk I knew they wouldn't. We approached a massive junction at over 130, the 'Stop!' signs huge in our headlights…"

Mickey's eyes widened.

"…I kept my foot planted, took a deep breath and blasted through! The coppers behind didn't want to know; I could see their lights dipping straightaway. By the time they managed to get going, we'd disappeared, and we never saw them again!"

"To be fair, it's not often my arse twitches," Rushy said. "But when we went over that main road, it didn't so much twitch as explode!"

The laughter continued all afternoon, with everybody chipping in with their own stories, until as darkness drew in once more, it was time for the lads to head home. With no raids arranged for the coming week, they'd been tasked with acquiring cars.

Sauntering back, Danny mulled over their plans. "What do you fancy going for?" he asked.

"Not too bothered really, but the one for the weekend has got to be special, or have you forgotten what we told the girls?"

"Of course not, but what's gonna impress them the most?"

Mickey stopped dead in his tracks. "I think it's time to find out what Porsche can offer its biggest fans, and you know what…the faster, the better!"

***

Sat smugly in the country club's leather armchair, J.T. relaxed before an open log fire. Tapping his tumbler on the table, a well-dressed waiter scurried over to top it up.

"So do we keep things as they are, or is it time to step up our operations?" he asked his brother, dismissing the waiter with a flick of his fingers.

"Well, *Chapman* reckons they're working flat out at the moment," Johnny replied. "But then again, he would do wouldn't he!"

"True. And what about Porter? He is, how shall we say, a little less biased than Chapman."

Johnny laughed quietly to himself. "Well as you know, he's forever giving Chapman grief about the motors; reckons there's never enough coming in, despite the significant increases we've seen. The other side to our business is a little trickier to evaluate. Porter's reliant on customer orders, which on the lead up to Christmas has been pretty good, however, once we pass New Year, orders tend to fall away."

Taking a deep lungful from his Cuban cigar, J.T. tilted his head back and blew smoke towards the ornate ceiling. "And what's your take on things?"

"Somewhere between the two I guess. If burglaries *do* start to quieten down, the lads'll have more time to concentrate on motors. It's a win-win all round."

"You're probably right, we'll leave them be at the moment," J.T. said, eyeballing a fellow member who'd dared to look in his direction. "The other matter I had in mind was the amount we're paying these lads. Before we brought in the new system, they were more than happy with their wages; but if I'm not mistaken, we're now paying the winners practically double every month!"

"Actually, with their increase in productivity, they're pulling in more than double."

"Exactly! And of course, neither side actually knows how much the others have supplied every month!"

Slowly turning to face his brother, J.T. paused, a smirk beginning to form.

Johnny was on the same wavelength. "And if they don't know how much the other side's making, they'll have absolutely no idea if they're getting...short-changed."

"I'd prefer to call it 'adequately rewarded'!"

"Okay, so do you want me to raise it at our next general meeting?"

"I'm sure there'll be no need, after all, you're the one who looks after the books," J.T. winked. "You and I'll split the extra cash; it'll just be another of our little secrets."

27

Bearing the acronym 'C.A.T.S', the Carjacking And Theft Squad's office door remained locked to all but their elite team. Inside the cramped room, Gladstone addressed his sergeant and six constables. Hand selected, regarded as the best in their field, he'd fought hard to secure them. Traffic cops Ross Draycott and Nick Wilson knew the car thieves inside out, Strickers and 'Donkey' Darby were expert investigators, while Drewy's intimate local knowledge could prove invaluable. And if any target was daft enough to run; Gaz Williams's vicious sidekick, police dog Quincy, was more than ready to take on the challenge.

Completing the line-up, recently promoted Steve Hanson had a fearsome reputation as a thief-taker. Seated next to his Inspector, he faced their new team as Gladstone laid out their objectives.

"Gentlemen, I won't beat around the bush; you're here today because you deserve to be. You share my loathing for the scum who violate our community; they've had it far too easy for far too long. Their reign of terror is coming to an end – it's time to take back our streets!"

Sat on desks between computer screens, the team remained silent, their eyes fixed firmly on their boss.

"But first of all, let me put my cards on the table. Our task isn't going to be easy; we'll need absolute commitment if we're to bring them down. Expect long hours, shift changes, and rest days cancelled at the drop of a hat. I understand these conditions are tough; they have an effect on our family and friends," he said, looking at each officer in turn. "So please speak now if you're unable to continue…you're free to leave without any hard feelings."

Nobody moved a muscle.

"Good, that's exactly what I expected," he nodded. "Now let's get down to business."

Opening his notepad, Sergeant Hanson gave out the postings. Each duo was allocated a callsign and given the keys to a performance car, including the 'furry-exocet'; a BMW 330 with quick release dog cage in its rear.

"How the hell did you manage to get hold of this little beauty," Gaz beamed. "Central Traffic never let anyone near it!"

"Ssshhh," Hanson replied, raising a finger to his lips. "We haven't officially got it. Let's just say the gaffer called in a few favours!"

"Well however you managed it, you've done the business; our shits aren't gonna know what's hit them!"

"I presume you're referring to our 'customers' Gaz!" Hanson shook his head, joining in the team's laughter. "Okay guys, settle down, the gaffer wants to finish off with a few words."

"Thank you sergeant," Gladstone began, the room immediately quietening down. "For the past few years we've seen a steady increase in vehicle crime, but as you all know, in the last few months it's exploded. More worrying is the escalation in violence. Originally the offences were sporadic, mainly confined to our city's affluent areas, but more recently the spectre has spread far and wide, impacting on every single neighbourhood. Intell suggests the epicentre lies within our patch; it is therefore *our* responsibility to eradicate the problem. Our first challenge is to identify the offenders…but let me tell you right here and now, taking out the minnows would merely prove a disruption, others would soon take their place. No, these crimes bear the hallmarks of a highly organised criminal gang. My intention therefore, is to take down their entire network, and I'm not going to rest until we have their 'Mr Fucking Big' exactly where he should be…detained at 'Her Majesty's Pleasure'!"

***

"Evening lads. Nice wheels!" the Old Varsity bouncer winked, holding the doors wide open as Mickey and Danny approached.

"Cheers guys," Mickey smiled back. "Can you keep your eyes on it for us; there's some right thieving scum round here!"

Packed to the rafters again, the lads pushed their way through the throng, and sidled around to the bar.

Mickey spotted her straightaway. Sat gassing with friends around an iron table, she and Katie were lost in their own world. Perfect, time to get some 'dutch courage' down his neck!

He'd managed to get onto a second Bud before being noticed by her friends. Drink in hand, Lara turned slowly.

God she looked stunning. Tight Levi's rose to a loose white top, which as she and Katie sauntered over, showed off her navel's golden ring.

"You pair playing hard to get or something?" Lara smirked. "You don't visit, you don't text, you don't call…"

"Us?" Mickey replied, feigning offence. "And we've come all the way over here, thinking we'd give you a nice surprise. Still, if you want us to leave…"

Lara moved in close, her soft hair brushing against him.

"No, you can stay if you want," she said, kissing his cheek. "Especially if you've brought another beast with you!"

"I presume you're not talking about Danny!"

Lara smiled. "You know what I mean, funny guy."

"Well, you won't be disappointed. Let's just say it's another surprise!"

Chatting and laughing together, time quickly passed them by. Never far from her thoughts, Lara prodded and probed all evening, desperate to find out what he'd brought. But to no avail, he kept her in suspense until it was time to leave.

Shrieking with excitement, she squeezed Mickey's hand as they walked onto the car park. "Come on then, put us out of our misery; so which little beauty is yours?"

"Oh that'd be too easy! Let's play a game instead," he replied, pulling the fob from his pocket. "You walk up to the car you most want it to be, then I'll press the button. If you pick the right one, we'll give you a lift home. But if you get it wrong…you're walking back!"

"Yeah right. Like you'd let two little schoolgirls walk home on their own," she said, batting her eyelids.

"Well let's hope we don't have to find out then!"

It wasn't a difficult choice. Parked up against the fence amongst the usual student bangers, the blood red Porsche stood out like a sore thumb. Releasing his hand in an instant, she ran to the sports car, her fingers immediately reaching beneath the handle.

"If this *is* the one, you're in for one hell of a night!"

"Oh dear, looks like you're walking then!" he said, ambling over. "How would a poor boy like me, afford a posh car like this?"

"Come on, don't tease," she smiled up at him. "Just press the bloody button!"

Instantly, the indicators winked as one. Letting out a high-pitched squeal, she pulled Mickey close, pressing her lips to his.

He felt their softness, but tantalisingly she withdrew, mouthed 'Later', and flung the door wide open. While Danny and Katie squeezed into the tiny rear, Lara jumped into the front; their three grinning faces staring back at him.

"Well, what are you waiting for," she laughed. "You promised me a ride!"

Jumping into the driver's seat, as he fired the engine into life, Lara's hand moved across to his thigh. Off onto the streets he cruised, his occasional throttle blips receiving squeezes of approval from his admirer.

But having posed around the city centre for a while, Mickey's heart suddenly missed a beat. It may have been a good distance behind, but there was no mistaking the panda's intentions.

Without a word, he pulled out to overtake the car ahead. Accelerating hard, his turbocharged supercar rapidly reached 110, before quickly ducking left into a side road. The sudden change in driving hadn't gone unnoticed.

"Okay speed freak, smooth it out will you?" Lara frowned, gripping a little tighter.

Mickey checked his mirror again.

Shit, he didn't need this. The police car behind was on a mission, flying round the corner on two wheels.

"Is that the police?" Katie asked uneasily from the back.

Frantically, he racked his brains for a believable story. "Yeah, it's only a crappy old panda, it's probably on the way to a job," he said, flicking his eyes back to the mirror. "A quick blast and we'll soon be out of their way!"

"Well come on then," Lara smiled. "Let's see what it'll do!"

Swiftly out onto a wide dual carriageway, the 911's power kicked in. Leaving the blue strobes trailing in his wake, by the time he'd dodged off onto side streets, the panda was consigned to history.

"Mmm, you're not just a pretty face then," Lara admired. "So, where are you taking us now?"

"Well it'd be a shame not to get the most from the car; I've only got it for the weekend. How about we take in some country air?"

"You must have read my mind," Lara smiled. "Make sure it's dark and quiet, we wouldn't want to be disturbed now would we!"

***

The CATS team's desperate search for evidence began. To begin with they started in-house; interrogating stop-forms, intell systems, even their own colleagues. Suspects, accomplices, vehicles, addresses; every morsel was collected, every link checked out. With numerous targets identified, they needed to be whittled down. Who *were* the main offenders, what happened to their booty, and where the hell were they going to strike next!

His team off taking statements, Gladstone sat alone with his sergeant.

"There's no way I'm going to just put a sticking plaster on the problem," the Inspector declared. "We need long term solutions, not knee-jerk quick fixes. I therefore suggest, that once we've identified our initial targets, we sit tight; its pointless striking too soon. No, we need to watch them like hawks, see who they associate with, allow them to run free for a while. If we're to get to their bosses, we'll need evidence, and plenty of it. Now, as our Chief Super naively craves instant results, we might have to tell him the odd white lie to keep him happy. Are you okay with that Steve?"

"Fine by me gaffer, we all know what he's like!"

"Thanks, I know I can count on you. Of course, it's important we keep our team on side as well; they're likely to get a little dispirited if they don't start feeling collars."

"Believe me gaffer, as long as we keep them in-the-loop, they'll be more than happy."

"Excellent. Now let's get down to our plan of attack. Once we've identified our main offenders, we'll make sure uniform disrupt their movements; stop checks and searches every time they get spotted. That'll kill two birds with one stone. Firstly, it'll push them away from *our* patch; keeping figures down and our gaffer happy. But more importantly, it'll generate crucial intelligence towards future conspiracy charges."

"Sounds good to me, the lads'll enjoy getting in their faces," Hanson nodded. "And plain clothes, what do you suggest they get up to?"

"I want cameras outside our target's addresses. When do they come and go? Who with? How do they arrive and leave? I want to know everything about them, everything!" Gladstone demanded. "We need to re-visit every single previous victim; there may be some nuggets we missed first time around. Leave no stone unturned Steve; the smallest clues can lead to the biggest discoveries."

"Okay boss, I'll task the lads accordingly," Hanson replied, finishing his notes. "But there *is* still one source we've not tapped into yet, and it's probably the most important of all. I've yet to see any intelligence coming from within this group. If we're serious in taking out the ringleaders, we desperately need somebody on the inside."

"I agree wholeheartedly. However, in my entire career I've never known a group as tight as this. Months ago, I tasked our source-handlers to find a suitable target, but despite their best efforts, they came back empty handed. What we did find out, is that they're more scared of their own bosses than they are of us. It's a position that needs reversing, and I intend to do just that!"

28

Continued monthly losses meant Hood faced an increasing mutiny. With no teamwork, no trust, and no cash, they'd resorted to petty thieving to pay for their drugs. Struggling to keep control after yet another monthly drubbing, his meeting with Chapman was borne out of desperation; he needed help, and he needed it quick.

Tucked away inside an alcove at The Black Horse, he began to chew over his problems.

"It's fucking ridiculous! We're having motors away like there's no tomorrow, and yet Deano's fucking posse are still supposed to be stuffing us!" he ranted, scowling at his half empty glass. "How can that possibly be true? Somebody's gotta be making the figures up."

Chapman looked down at the crestfallen youth. Months of heroin abuse had taken its toll; his previous healthy glow replaced with a pasty gauntness.

"There's no cheating going on, you're simply not delivering enough," Chapman told him directly.

"Not enough!" Hood practically exploded. "We're working every waking hour, we're putting our lives on the line, and you tell me that's not enough?"

"I can and I will," Chapman replied, calmly taking another drink. "They're beating you because they've got their heads screwed on, and *you* clearly haven't."

"Why? What the fuck are they doing that we don't? I don't see *their* headlines in the papers. We're the ones taking the risks, and as far as I can see, they're doing fuck all!" he bellowed at the older man.

"Don't you *dare* raise your voice at me, you insignificant piece of shit!" Chapman replied furiously. "Have you even looked at yourself recently? You're so drugged out your mind, you can't even think straight. Do you think you're some kind of big man, just because you and your cronies are in the paper every day? Well do you?"

Hood shrugged.

"If you had any brains, you'd have worked out that not all publicity is good publicity. You're not the only one who reads the papers you know. You need to be more careful son; if you carry on the way you are, you'll end up in the birdhouse or the grave!"

"Okay, okay, I get what you're saying, but this system's tearing us apart. We just need to get a win; we're desperate for cash. Do me a favour will you," he said lowering his voice. "Tell me how they're doing it?"

"To be honest, I haven't asked any questions; it doesn't pay to in this game," Chapman replied nonchalantly. "No, you're gonna have to work it out for yourself."

"Well we're stuffed then, aren't we? We're working our balls off for nothing, so what's the fucking point?" Hood said, the anger returning to his voice. "You can tell J.T. to stuff it up his arse; we're better off working for ourselves!"

"I'll do you one favour and one favour only…I won't pass that last comment to J.T.," a stone faced Chapman replied, finishing his drink in a single swig. "I expect to see an improvement straightaway. If I don't, or I hear any more bollocks from you, your next meeting will be with Razor…and fucking good luck with that!"

***

Intelligence arriving into the CATS office took time to gather momentum. Information from all sources fed into the computer systems; analysts deciphered the results. Slowly but surely, patterns began to emerge – and so did the prime suspects. At last, it was time to take action, time for a more pro-active approach.

Now early spring, on a wet Monday morning, Gladstone addressed his keen team.

"First of all, I want to thank you for your patience. I appreciate you'd rather have been making arrests, but your hard work is about to bear fruit," he said, opening a buff coloured sealed envelope. Pulling out a thick wad of papers, he passed them to Hanson to hand out.

"Inwardly digest every name and every face before you," he said, writing their details on the whiteboard. "Some are already familiar to you, but a word of caution; they use violence on a daily basis and won't think twice about using it on you. Now take a look at the board while Steve gives you the low down."

As Gladstone stepped aside, the names displayed proved why he was the best in the business. Starting with the words, Seamus HOOD…he'd written down each and every one of his drug crazed crew.

***

Wearing his trademark dark suit and bright tie, J.T. was out patrolling his manor. Tinted windows firmly closed, his BMW's 'Bang and Olufsen' delivered a Mozart recital fit for a concert hall.

From between his thick fingers, a fat cigar stump polluted the inside; it's acrid smell filling his uncomfortable passenger's nostrils.

"Chapman my friend, we've been over this topic time and time again. The system's working, business is booming," J.T. stated, as he slowed towards red lights.

"You're right. We *have* enjoyed exceptional success...so far," Chapman replied. "But..."

"But what?" J.T. interrupted, bringing the car to a halt.

Chapman fidgeted in his leather seat.

"Well on the plus side, Deano's posse are surpassing all expectations. They seem to have a limitless supply of quality motors."

"And on the negative side?"

"On the negative side," Chapman paused. "Hood's boys are struggling."

"Struggling?"

"To be fair to them, they're obviously working hard; you've only got to read the newspapers to see that."

Without taking his eyes off the road, J.T. nodded his agreement.

"The problem is, they haven't earned any money for a few months now, and let's just say...they've fallen into expensive lifestyles."

"You mean they're hooked on gear," J.T. replied bluntly.

"In a nutshell, yes. And as we both know, the craving could make them careless. Without any money, they're going to look for it in other ways," Chapman said cautiously. "If they're out petty thieving, they're likely to get themselves banged up. I'm concerned their contribution could dwindle away to nothing if we keep the system in place."

Bombshell delivered, Chapman waited for the inevitable backlash.

But nothing came. Instead, J.T. drove off in silence; a silence that remained until they pulled up outside Johnny's rural retreat.

Grinding his stub into the ashtray, J.T. turned to face his henchman.

"I'll tell you what you're gonna do," he said through clenched teeth. "You're gonna go back to Hood and pass him a message. Tell him, I don't give a shit about their money problems; they earn it working for me, and me alone. Tell him, I'd better not see a reduction in supplies or I'm gonna think he's taking the piss. And finally you can tell him, that if I think he's taking the piss; he's fucking dead!"

Leaning forward, his head practically making contact with Chapman's, he added, "Do-I-make-myself-fucking-clear?"

Chapman nodded obediently.

"Good," J.T. said, releasing his seatbelt. "And let that be the last I hear of it."

***

Desperately hunting for prey, Hood and his crew were out prowling the city streets.

"Come on guys, how long's this gonna take?" Decca whined. "Just get on with it, we need to get back and score."

"Well you'll just have to fucking wait. If we're gonna do a hit, it's gotta be a good one," Hood bit back. "The only way we're gonna beat Deano's wankers is to target the rich. If it isn't top-end, I'm not interested!"

Decca scowled and sat back in his seat; his craving would have to wait…but not for long.

"Spin it round!" Hood suddenly called out, straining to look over his shoulder. "I think I've spotted today's winner!"

Pulling off a driveway behind them, a black Bentley drove off in the opposite direction.

"Nice one mate, there's a hundred grand's worth there!" Soldier grinned, swiftly turning their old Megane around.

Only a mile up the road, the luxury motor pulled up at red lights. Absorbed in his hands free chatter, the businessman failed to notice the two hooded youths sprinting towards him, baseball bats in hand.

Smash!

His window exploded, its splinters bursting inwards, peppering his face as he turned towards the blow. He'd barely had time to flinch before the first punch landed.

"Get out the fucking car!" Hood screamed, his weapon held aloft.

Almost paralysed with fear, the suit raised his arms helplessly, just as his nearside window received the same treatment. Reaching in, Decca unlocked the door, and knife in hand, leapt onto the passenger seat.

"Leave the fucking keys, and get the fuck out or I'll slice you up!" he yelled through his balaclava.

In sheer panic, the businessman fumbled at his seatbelt. The moment it released, Hood grabbed him by his collars, and dumped him on the tarmac. Jumping into the now vacant seat, Hood floored the gas, dodged round the car in front, and flew through the red lights at speed.

Soldier immediately set off behind, but his only path through the traffic was blocked by the injured man's body. Aiming directly at him he gunned the accelerator.

Wide-eyed, the victim desperately attempted to roll out of his way…

29

Parade for the CATS team was in their usual office at four in the afternoon. Nick Wilson was the last to arrive, cramming a crusty baguette in his mouth. His colleague's barracking was met with a casual shrug, as he took his seat on the remaining desk.

"Nice to see the pride in your appearance is as good as your time keeping ability," Sergeant Hanson shook his head. "With your permission, we'd like to make a start?"

Showering his teammates with crumbs, Wilson made an inaudible reply.

"Cheers Nick, you buffoon!" Draycott shook his head, wiping the debris from his trousers. "Any chance you could keep your food to yourself?"

Their entertainment was cut short by the office phone. Hanson answered, signalling for the others to quieten down.

Replacing the handset, he updated the team. "There's just been a car-jacking at knifepoint in Solihull town centre. They've taken a black Bentley, and the offender's descriptions are bang on our targets. We need to get out there before they stash it away."

"Anything from the victim?" Gaz piped up.

"Apparently, they tried to run him over, but he managed to roll clear. He's shaken, but nothing serious," the sergeant replied. "This lot are gonna end up killing somebody; we need to get them before they do. Oh and don't forget, there's a bottle of scotch for the first arrest!"

Most of the team didn't even hear his final words; they were already sprinting towards their cars, donning their stab-proofs as they ran. This was what they'd been waiting for; now it was time to get even.

***

In tandem with their old Megane, the Bentley rushed back towards the Greet. Their initial buzz over, the mood inside was far from victorious.

"Have a mooch round for any goodies," Hood instructed, slowing for traffic. "Chapman can have the car, but from now on, *we're* keeping any perks inside."

"Fucking right," Decca replied, clambering from seat to seat. "This car's gotta be worth fifty grand to him, and what are we likely to see from it – fuck all!"

"I've told him we can't go on like this, but he still thinks he can just treat us like shit. Well it's time we had something to show for our troubles!"

"Bingo!" Decca exclaimed. "There's an iPad behind your seat, and the dozy twat's left his mobile on charge!"

"Thank fuck for that; should be enough for a shitload of smack. Now let's get this back quickly, it's time for our afternoon fix."

***

"Yankee-Mike, Yankee-Mike to all units," the radio blared. "Be advised, MPAS-One has visual on the stolen Bentley in the Chelmsley Wood area. Any units who can make, please respond with call signs."

"Yes!" Gaz shouted excitedly, grabbing hold of the transmitter.

"Tango Charlie One-Six, show us making the last," he called up as Draycott launched the furry-exocet towards their target.

With the Midlands Police Air Service helicopter holding its position high above, the navigator calmly relayed movements to the ground crews below. Co-ordinated by Force Control, the CATS team began to encircle their targets.

"All units be warned," the radio crackled. "The Bentley's believed to be in company with a silver coloured Megane. Caution is advised when dealing with the offenders; a large knife and baseball bat were used during the theft."

"No surprise there then. Still, they'll need more than a knife to take on Quincy, won't they boy!" Gaz grinned.

"MPAS-One to all units," the navigator continued. "I can confirm, the Bentley is still in convoy with a silver Megane; it's approximately six car lengths behind."

Rushing along a side road ahead of their targets, Draycott slowed for the junction ahead. The two cars were moments away; they'd pass across their nose any second. "Quick, see if you can get the stinger out before they get to us!"

"We haven't got time mate," Gaz replied. "They're almost here!"

"Shit, you're right," Draycott said, raising his eyes to the skies. "Knock the lights off before they see us!"

Braking hard, they came to a hasty stop at the give way line, their heads immediately spinning to the right. A stream of traffic approached, and there nestled in the middle, their two targets drove leisurely by. Filtering in two cars back, Gaz updated the control room. With colleagues tucking in not far behind, it was now just a question of 'when', not 'if' the motors made off.

Another junction loomed. The Bentley signalled left, quickly followed by the Megane.

"Looks like it's time to play," Draycott smiled.

And he was right; no sooner had they turned, than the Bentley's tyres lit up the tarmac. Lights and sirens activated, the dog-rocket took up the chase.

Ploughing through the streets, the pace was unrelenting. With the chopper holding steady above, the ground units kept a safe distance behind. But the thieves were desperate to escape; taking increasingly dangerous risks as they blasted back to the Greet.

Inside the dog car, Quincy's barking was reaching a crescendo.

"They've gotta be our boys, they've circled the estate three times!" Gaz called out.

"They'll dump it in a minute," Draycott replied. "They know they can't shake us, they'll have to try it on foot."

"And we'll be up for the challenge," Gaz said, glancing over his shoulder. "Won't we boy!"

A few corners later, the cars split up. While Strickers peeled after the Megane, the dog-car kept close to the Bentley. On the straights it left them for dead, but the two-tonne limo's cornering wasn't a patch on the 330. Suddenly, it braked violently and dived down an access road.

"This is it. Get ready for the bail out!" Draycott shouted above the sirens.

Gaz was a step ahead; unfastening his seat belt with one hand, holding onto the door with the other.

Down the narrow track the black Bentley flew, throwing up dirt in its wake. Reaching the end, the sports limo slid to a halt; its two occupants sprinting off through the haze. Ducking down a path, they desperately attempted to make the most of their head start...but Gaz's hand was already on the cage release.

"Police! Stand still or I'll send the dog!" he screamed.

Whether they heard him or not, the fugitives showed no let-up in pace.

Cage door wrenched open, Gaz barely had time to apply a short lead before Quincy was off; dragging him through the settling smoke, its eyes fixed on the fleeing prey. Overhead, the helicopter blades drowned out another hollered warning. The youths were gaining ground, Gaz had to take action...he needed to release the hound.

No longer constrained by its lead; head down, ears pinned back, the land-shark flew across the uneven surface.

Unaware of the danger behind them, the two youths raced towards a tall fence. The first flung himself up and over, but his mate two seconds behind...was two seconds too late.

Leaping at the fence, he glanced over his shoulder just as Quincy launched into attack. The dog hit him hard; its fangs sinking deep into his thigh, as its momentum took them tumbling to the ground. Its grip released in the fall, Quincy instantly struck again – mauling on the youth's flailing arm.

"Quincy, leave him!" Gaz shouted, catching up with his dog.

But the hound paid no attention. Locked on, its head thrashed from side-to-side.

"Get it off!" the youth screamed, his face contorted in pain.

Re-attaching the lead, Gaz bellowed at his dog, yanking it back with all his might. Reluctantly, it released, but straining at its leash, remained snarling inches from the snivelling thief's head.

"One in custody, one still outstanding," Gaz confirmed on his radio as Draycott caught up. "You stay with this one, I'll go after the other," he said, as with one last snap at its victim, Quincy was off again.

Initially directed by the hovering chopper, they scaled the fence and sprinted across the backyards.

"We lost sight as he went into the next garden," the radio crackled in Gaz's ear. "Even the thermal camera can't penetrate the thick foliage. He's definitely in there – over to you!"

Hauling his dog over the fence first, Gaz dropped down into the undergrowth. Completely overgrown, the garden rose uphill towards derelict outbuildings, while leading down to the house, brambles and low branches strangled what remained of a path.

"Police with a dog," he shouted, clipping an extension lead on. "Come out or I'll send it in!"

But there was no reply, and no movement. Gaz paused, as if giving the offender a final chance; a chance he failed to take.

"Find him Quince!" Gaz commanded, and headed off towards the outbuildings. But with no signal from his dog, he turned to head back to the house.

Suddenly, Quincy's head jerked up from the ground. Nostrils flared, ears erect, it paused for a moment…before lunging forward, almost taking Gaz clean off his feet. Head down, it charged, only slowing when it reached a ramshackle shed at the side of the house.

The door appeared tightly shut, but his dog's snarls told Gaz all he needed to know. Again he shouted his warning, again he received no reply. Squeezing his fingers between door and frame, he slowly prized them apart…

30

The moment the light rushed in, a fearful voice cried out, "Okay, okay, keep it away from me!"

Quincy was desperate to get through though, thrusting his head between Gaz's legs as he attempted to step inside. In the far corner, a tarpaulin began to move. Arms raised high, a youth slowly rose to his feet.

"Get out, and get on the floor!" Gaz ordered, backing away from the shed. "Face down you little shit, and don't move, or the dog'll have you!"

Doing exactly as he was told, the youth threw himself to the ground, and placed his hands in the small of his back. Gaz's colleagues rushed in to cuff him; while tail wagging, his work complete, Quincy was led back to his cage.

"Now that's what I call a result," Draycott grinned, welcoming his partner back. "Two in custody, and the Bentley recovered without a scratch!"

Everything had gone perfectly to plan; but even *they* couldn't believe what they were about to discover.

***

Limping into the custody suite, the first prisoner was welcomed by Sergeant Hanson.

"Well, if it isn't our old friend Seamus Hood. Looks like you *bit* off more than you could *chew* today!"

"Piss off dickhead!" he hissed back. "Next time I see that dog, I'm gonna fucking kill it!"

"Now, now, there's no need to get angry with me. I'm just concerned for your welfare, like we all are here at Stechford."

Scowling, he hobbled up to the custody officer's counter, and leaning against it, took the weight off his injured leg.

"Get off my fucking desk!" a voice bellowed from behind. "Now stand up straight and put all your property on top."

Cursing to himself, Hood shuffled back slightly, and gingerly sifted through his pockets.

"Sergeant, we have reason to believe that he is an active user of Class A drugs. I therefore wish to conduct a full body search," Hanson requested.

"You must be fucking joking! There's no way you're doin' a strip search on me."

"I'll be the judge of that," the custody officer intervened. "And you'll be glad to know that I agree with the officer. Take him to the doctor's room lads…and let me give you some advice son," he said turning to face Hood directly. "I'm in charge of your custody here, and what I say goes! So don't piss me off or I'll make it extremely difficult for you, understand?"

"Go fuck yourself!" Hood spat back. "Just wait 'til my brief gets here, he'll fucking sort you out!"

But Jonas hadn't arrived yet, and Hood was forced to submit to the humiliating search. Carefully removing each item, he winced as the clothes brushed against his wounds.

"Ouch! Glad that wasn't my arm," Hanson grimaced at the bloody mess.

"Don't worry, Quincy's very particular in his tastes," Gaz replied, finishing the examination. "He only ever bites scum!"

"Satisfied?!"

"For now, yes," Hanson replied, the search failing to find any drugs. "But once you return from hospital, you've got some pretty tricky questions to answer."

"You'll get nothing from me. I didn't do anything, your dog mauled me for no reason."

"You'll have to do better than that Hood; didn't you see the chopper above – it's captured everything on camera. Now do try to make the most of hospital, 'cos believe me, by the time you return…we'll be more than ready for you!"

After slowly re-dressing, Hood was led back to the custody area, just as the handcuffed Decca arrived.

"What the fuck happened to you?" Decca asked open-mouthed.

"What does it look like…savaged by a fucking dog, that's what!"

Decca looked him up and down. "Well that'll teach you for not keeping up!"

"Yeah alright, thanks for your support – mate!" Hood scowled. "Anyway, where did you get nicked?"

"I was minding my own business having a kip in a shed, when this lot turned up!"

"Yeah, they're always picking on us…"

"Okay you pair, that's enough talking," Gaz interrupted. "Now move along Hood, you've got a long night ahead."

***

Inside their packed office, Gladstone began to brief his ecstatic team. Not only had they nabbed the pair in the Bentley, they'd also locked two up from the Megane.

With prisoners lodged in cells and solicitors notified, a race against time had begun. By law, the officers had twenty-four hours to bring charges; if not…they'd all be released.

"Well done chaps, you've done a damn fine job. But I warn you now, it's only just started."

Gladstone's solemn expression quietened the animated team.

"Yes, we've taken out four targets, and yes they appear banged to rights. But we're going to need a watertight case to take this anywhere near court. Algernon Jonas and his colleagues will be defending, so expect them to use every dirty trick in the book. Their first ploy will be to run the clock down. Hood's off to hospital for treatment, then he's entitled to eight hours rest, then they'll string out his consultation. So in reality, we'll be left with less than six hours to interview and get him charged! And that's just the first one; don't forget we've got three more in the traps!" he frowned, pausing to sip from his coffee.

"Our plan of attack is as follows," he continued. "Forensic teams are examining the vehicles as we speak, but results will take several weeks. Tonight, we *just* need to search addresses, seize clothing, download helicopter footage, visit the Bentley victim, write our own statements and prepare disclosure! Once we've completed everything, you can grab some sleep. But we can't take our eyes off the clock; we need to be back by six in the morning. So gents, let's get cracking; we haven't got a moment to waste!"

***

Despite Hood claiming to be of no fixed abode, surveillance on his home leading up to his arrest meant getting a search warrant was easy.

Gladstone himself led the search team at Hood's address, and with no response heard at the door, gave his nod to force entry.

Draycott stepped forward, iron 'Enforcer' in hand. Swinging it back, he slammed it into the wooden door, which in a cloud of splinters, practically burst off its hinges. 'Dragon Lamps' blazing, his colleagues surged forward, moving swiftly from room to room. Satisfied nobody was home, they returned to the lounge, ready for a meticulous search.

But they didn't have to look very far. As Hanson swung his beam across the room, the evidence was lit up for all to see. Gazing at the newspaper cuttings covering the far wall, he whistled quietly to himself. "My, my, they have been busy boys. Thank goodness they haven't got a brain cell between them!"

"Mmm, looks like we've hit the jackpot," Gladstone nodded. "Let's get photographic here asap."

"It's just a shame there's still nothing to identify their bosses," Hanson replied, poring over the clippings.

"Believe me Steve, we will," Gladstone smiled. "This is merely the beginning of their end."

***

In contrast to each prisoner's eight-hour sleep, the CATS team barely managed eight between them. Bleary eyed, they returned for their morning's briefing.

"After last night's discovery, do not be deceived that our job has become any easier," Gladstone began. "On the contrary, it's substantially increased our workload. However, it does provide us with an ideal opportunity to send these scum away for many, many years. Every victim on those walls needs re-interviewing – our offenders were too arrogant to cover their faces, so I'm confident we'll get some positive ID's. And hopefully, a few clearances should keep Mr Moore off our backs; you know how he's been whingeing lately!"

A few wry smiles surfaced on the tired faces.

Once Gladstone had wrapped up his briefing, the interview teams made towards the custody suite. As expected, Jonas arrived an hour late; his delay tactic parried by the comprehensive disclosure packs presented to him and his colleague. His next ploy, demanding Hood be granted immediate bail on medical grounds, was quickly rebuffed, and so, with no more cards to play, his clients were ready for interview.

One-by-one, they went through the motions, without a reply being given between them. With the clock running out, and no more tricks left to play, they were finally ready to be charged.

First up was Hood, with Gladstone in close attendance.

"Seamus Hood, you are charged with robbery, possession of an offensive weapon and dangerous driving," the custody sergeant began. "The officers in the case have requested that you be denied bail due to the serious nature of the offences, and the likelihood that you'll commit more. Mr Jonas, do you wish to make any objections on behalf of your client?"

"Of course I do. You will see from your records that Mr Hood has not come to your attention for over two years. He has never failed to attend court, he will be denying all charges, and may I remind you, at no time has he accepted any guilt in this matter. It is therefore completely inappropriate for him to be kept in custody; he is unquestionably entitled to conditional bail."

The custody officer looked down, studying the papers before him.

"Unfortunately Inspector, Mr Jonas is correct. You have provided insufficient grounds for me to deny his client bail."

Hood's head slowly turned to face the tall Inspector, his smug grin mouthing, 'Wanker'.

Ignoring him, the custody sergeant continued. "Do you have any further objections before I make my decision?"

His stern face softening to a dry smile, Gladstone looked Hood in the eye. "We have conducted a search at your home address and found considerable evidence linking you and your friends with a series of violent car thefts. You are therefore under arrest on suspicion of further robberies."

His smirk disappearing, Hood began to plead his innocence. "That's fucking bollocks, I haven't…"

But his eyes had returned to the counter, where one after another Gladstone was laying out a series of photographs.

Jonas and the custody sergeant examined them closely. Hood turned away.

"Do you still have any objections Mr Jonas?" Gladstone smiled.

Removing his specs, the wily old solicitor pursed his lips. "Not at this stage Inspector. However, I *would* like to know what you propose to do with regard to these *alleged* offences?"

"As you can imagine, we need to conduct extensive investigations; so it's likely to be a few weeks before we're ready to interview. Oh and before I forget, we also have video evidence from outside Hood's flat clearly showing your other three clients visiting him on a daily basis. I'm sure I don't need to explain the 'conspiracy' implications, so I hope there'll be no further objections to *them* being kept in custody?"

"Thank you for your disclosure Inspector," Jonas spat out. "I'll advise my clients accordingly."

***

Back in the CATS office, the room was buzzing.

A grinning Gladstone walked in carrying a large cardboard box. Placing it on the table, he opened the flaps.

"There's one each chaps," he said, lifting a large whisky bottle from inside. "Put it somewhere safe, then you're all to join me in the bar for a few drinks…and that's an order!"

A cheer went up from the team, as they delved inside for their reward.

"Well come on, what are you waiting for?" Gladstone said, leading the way out. "Let's make the most of round one; I have a feeling their bosses are gonna make the next ones rather more difficult!"

***

"Half a crew gone? You must be fucking joking!" J.T. exploded, throwing his Glenfiddich against the country club's panelled walls.

Remaining seated, Chapman looked at the floor, desperately avoiding eye contact as J.T. continued his rant. "Well at least Jonas is on the case; he'll soon have them out…won't he?"

"Err, I'm afraid," Chapman faltered. "It doesn't look like he will."

"And why the fuck not!" J.T. bellowed.

Around the room, a few audible 'tssks' accompanied the lowering of papers.

Reducing his volume, J.T continued through gritted teeth. "Well – why the fuck not?"

Before he could reply, a waiter scurried towards them, dustpan and brush in hand. Grateful for the pause, Chapman waited for the mess to be cleared before continuing.

"The information has come straight from Jonas's lips. All four were locked up last night after getting chased in a Bentley."

"Yes, yes, you've already told me that, I just don't understand why he can't get them bail. What's so different this time?"

"Unfortunately, our boys haven't been too…clever."

"Go on."

Again he paused, as the waiter returned with a fresh glass.

"It appears that the boys in blue have been keeping their eyes on Hood's place for some time now, and they conducted a search after the arrests."

Chapman swallowed hard. "From what I can gather…"

"Come on, come on, spit it out!"

"There were newspaper clippings of their previous jobs all over the walls."

J.T. remained rigid, the veins on his forehead almost ready to burst. Slowly, he leant forward.

"What the fuck were they thinking of!" he fumed. "How could anyone be that stupid?"

Squirming in his seat, Chapman remained silent.

"So tell me," J.T. continued, staring him in the eye. "When *will* they get out, 'cos so help me God, I'll be waiting outside when they do!"

"Well, Jonas can't be certain, but he's expecting the charges to stick, so…they're looking at a minimum of five years each."

"Chapman, are you trying to wind me up?"

"No, no of course not. I'm just passing the messages on."

"You'd better not be. Now piss off and get a meeting set up for tomorrow night; we need to sort our response straightaway."

Needing no further invitation, Chapman quickly scuttled off.

The moment he was out of earshot, J.T. turned to his brother, who'd sat silently throughout the exchange.

"I'm sure he took a fucking pleasure in telling me that. If he as much as mutters '*I told you so*' at the meeting, I'm gonna break the tosser in half!"

"He's the least of our worries," Johnny replied tersely. "Losing so many workers in one hit will make it extremely difficult to maintain business at its current level."

"Well they'll just have to work harder to make up for their brainless mates then!"

Johnny slowed sipped his whisky before replying.

"Maybe, maybe not. Perhaps we need to adopt a different approach; take a look at the bigger picture."

"Go on."

"Look, we shouldn't be surprised that the cops have begun to focus on our teams; we've been far too successful for far too long. With all the resources they have at their disposal, there's no way our lads can maintain their current productivity. The balance of power is strongly weighted against them; we need to reverse the equation."

"What exactly were you thinking of?" J.T. asked under his breath.

"I'm not sure yet. But let's just say we need to make a statement…one they'll never forget!"

31

At ten o' clock precisely, the three magistrates stepped onto the platform behind their panelled desk. Before them, the defence and prosecution stood and bowed.

On taking their seats, chains clattered as detention officers led four crestfallen youths up the steps leading into the wooden dock. Each offender sat handcuffed to a guard, until with heads bowed, they stood to confirm their names and addresses.

Formalities over, the prosecution went first. Focusing on the Bentley theft, the evidence was overwhelming; they were gunning for a remand in custody.

Next up, Jonas shuffled his papers, lowered his spectacles, and slowly rose to his feet.

"Your worships," he bowed. "I would respectfully request that you look beyond the crown's biased interpretation, and consider the *real* facts I'll put before you today. Yes, an innocent man was the victim of a particularly violent crime, and of course, we extend our sympathies to him. Nevertheless, the young men before you have at no time accepted any part in the robbery; it is simply a case of mistaken identity."

While Jonas continued to weave his deceitful web, Gladstone quietly entered the court, taking up his position next to the prosecutor.

"So why should you grant these innocent young men bail?" Jonas said, approaching his conclusion. "Firstly, they have never failed to appear at court. Secondly, the police have confirmed that each has a permanent address, and finally, a friend of theirs feels so strongly about their unfortunate situation, that he is prepared to put up a substantial surety to guarantee their future attendance."

Ending with a contrived smile and slight bow to the magistrates, the wily solicitor took a seat. But just as they rose to retire, the prosecutor interrupted proceedings.

"Your worships, please excuse my intrusion, but the officer in charge of the case has just arrived. I would be grateful if he'd be allowed to address you with reference to this matter."

"Of course," the head magistrate replied. "We would be interested to hear his thoughts."

Taking to his feet, Gladstone bowed and started his rebuttal.

"Without wishing to prejudice any future trial, I can inform you that for the past few months we have been gathering evidence against these defendants in connection with a particularly violent spate of robberies. Following the search at

Mr Hood's home address, we now have overwhelming proof that I anticipate will result in numerous charges for all those stood before you."

Pouring himself a water, Gladstone allowed his words to be digested.

"They are highly likely to receive lengthy sentences; sentences these young men would be keen to avoid. I have no doubt whatsoever that not only would they skip bail, but with nothing to lose, would wreak further widespread violence upon our communities!"

Outraged, Jonas leapt to his feet the moment Gladstone had finished. His voice shaking, he frantically attempted to refute Gladstone's arguments, but to no avail. Having retired to consider their judgement, the bench soon returned stern-faced.

"We are unanimous in our deliberations," the head magistrate began. "We have decided that due to the seriousness of the offences involved, it would be inappropriate to grant you bail. You are therefore all remanded in custody…take them down!"

***

The previous thirty-six hour's events ensured a sombre start to J.T.'s meeting. Fresh from his appointment with Jonas, Chapman kept them updated.

"They've all been sent to prison, and from what I can gather, we need to plan without them for many years to come."

"And I'll be waiting for them when they return!" Razor growled, punching his empty palm. "Bleedin' idiots!"

"Indeed," J.T. frowned at his meathead. "Now moving on…as I see it, this presents us with two problems to discuss this evening. First off, how do we ensure current supply levels are maintained? And secondly, the police are becoming a nuisance; it's time we sent them a message! So – who wants to go first?"

Initially nobody moved. Then, after a short silence, Porter spoke up. "Well the most obvious solution is to replace them man for man."

J.T. made no reply, merely turning to Chapman for his reaction.

"Look, you all know my thoughts. We've already promoted some of the lads too early, and the next group are nowhere near ready; they're just too inexperienced."

"Desperate times require desperate measures!" Porter snapped back.

"Maybe so, but how can we be sure of their loyalty? What would happen if they got caught and started squealing to the police? The consequences are not even worth contemplating."

"I have to say, I share Chapman's fears," Johnny spoke up. "We could be inviting trouble if we bring them on too quickly. No, we need to think of something else."

"Well we could leave them as are they are," J.T. suggested. "The four remaining fools would just have to make up for the others, 'cos let's face it, they're all as much to blame."

"I agree they deserve to pay for their mistakes," Chapman nodded. "However, if I'm completely honest…they're already at, if not beyond their limits; I'm not sure we can get any more out of them."

"You'd better not be implying this is my fault," J.T. bristled. "Or you'll be picking your teeth out the back of your throat! The system was fine; they fucked up 'cos they were stupid! Do I make myself clear?"

"Yes, yes, of course," Chapman cowered. "I'm not pointing the finger; I just don't think the lads who remain can cope on their own. We might need to explore other options before increasing their workload."

J.T.'s stare was unrelenting, his eyes narrowing as Chapman squirmed.

"So what *do* you suggest then?" he eventually enquired.

Visibly relieved to be given an olive branch, Chapman continued hesitantly. "Well…I kind of agree with Porter's 'desperate times require desperate measures' phrase. I can only see one realistic solution; it just might not be very popular."

"Go on, spit it out."

"Okay, okay. I think we need to consider…bringing the two groups together."

J.T. said nothing, his only movement the frown beginning to form.

"Before these arrests, the monthly results showed an increasing gulf between the teams. I've taken the liberty of speaking to Deano, and to be quite frank, they could increase production if they had more bodies. Yes, they'd have to put their rivalry to one side, but I just can't see any alternative. If we wish to maintain current supply levels, we need to give Deano more workers."

Digesting Chapman's speech, the room remained silent.

Finally J.T. broke the peace. "How certain are you that Deano can deliver?"

"I'm absolutely positive. Their system is so good that we can order the make, model and colour one day, and they'll have it delivered the next!"

"To be fair," Porter nodded. "Deano's been bang on the money."

"Okay, I hear what you're saying. Chapman – on your head be it," J.T. replied begrudgingly. "Unless there's any better ideas, we'll give it a go. If they've got any issues with it, tell them to contact Razor."

"Too fucking right!" his meathead grinned.

"I'll leave the payments down to Johnny to sort. Deano's posse can stay at their current rate, but until they prove their worth, Hood's halfwits can have just enough to get by."

Inputting the minutes, Johnny gave the briefest of nods, his eyes not moving up from the laptop.

"Right, now let's get onto the second subject – what are we gonna do about the filth? Johnny, perhaps you can explain."

Adjusting his glasses, his brother lifted his head up from the screen.

"I've *also* been speaking to Jonas. He believes that Hood's crew had been targeted for some time; suspicions I've confirmed with our contact at Stechford. While it would be reasonable to assume that they'll wind things down now that they've arrested the main offenders, nothing can be taken for granted."

"Porter, make sure our man on the inside receives some extra sweeteners," J.T. directed. "We'll need to keep one step ahead, just in case they start snooping in our direction."

"Our other problem is the bloody helicopter," Johnny continued. "From what Jonas tells me, it was the chopper's video that had them banged to rights."

"You're not wrong there," Chapman nodded. "Talking to the lads, it's the biggest problem they face. No matter what motor they're in, they can't get away from the flying pigs! Maybe we could choose targets closer to home; give the lads a chance to return before the chopper gets airborne?"

"No can do mate," Porter replied. "I've no issue with them nicking the motors locally, but the merchandise I get orders for, tend to come from specialist warehouses, and they can be anywhere in the country."

"I've got an idea," Razor piped up. "Why don't they stick to doing their jobs at night?"

"What are you babbling on about?" J.T. asked tiredly.

"Well it stands to reason, doesn't it? The chopper can see them during the day, but if they go out at night, it can't see where they're going, can it? And, and…" Razor continued on a roll, failing to clock the shaking heads around the room, "…even if it *could* see the lights on their cars, it wouldn't be able to see our boys run off into the darkness, now would it?"

"Have you ever heard of torches?" Porter asked sarcastically.

"Yeah, but they're too far away to see anything with a little torch!"

"True, but unfortunately they've got a humongous fucking torch attached to the bottom of their aircraft. It's as bright as the fucking moon!"

"Well, we could always shoot the moon thing then," Razor shrugged.

"Wait a minute," J.T. said, straightening himself in his seat. "What did you just say?"

"We could always shoot the moon."

"Razor," J.T. smiled. "That's the smartest thing you've ever said!"

"Thanks boss," Razor replied gleefully. "Do you want me to make the arrangements? My boys are pretty handy with a sawn-off!"

"I think you can rest your brain cells for now," J.T. laughed. "We're not *actually* going to shoot the chopper's light out, or we'd have every cop in the country after us! In any case, their thermal imaging could find our boys no matter what. No, what we need to figure out, is how we can destroy the helicopter; *that's* how we're gonna 'shoot the moon'!"

32

Lara's bedroom was unlike any Mickey had seen before. Clean, bright and tidy, he'd just started to make the most of her double bed when his mobile interrupted their fun.

He knew who it was; only one person had that ring-tone. Leaning over Lara, he fumbled to retrieve the phone from his jeans.

"Just leave it," she sighed. "They'll call you back, or leave a message if it's urgent."

And if it had been anybody else, he wouldn't have touched it; the timing couldn't have been any worse.

"Sorry babe, I've got to take it. It's an important client after some tasty motors," he said as Lara wrapped her arms around his shoulders. "I'll only be a minute, keep yourself warm."

"Okay blue-eyes – but be quick, I'm waiting," she smiled, sinking back beneath the sheets.

Pulling his phone out, Mickey went onto the landing to take the call. Straightaway he noticed the tension in Deano's voice.

"What's the matter mate?"

"We need an urgent meeting. Meet us at my place in half an hour."

"Yeah, no problems, I'll bring Danny. What's up?"

"Plenty! But I'll update you when you arrive," Deano said, ending the call.

Puzzled, Mickey looked at the blank screen. What on earth was going on; it wasn't like Deano to be so edgy. Returning to the bedroom, he leant over and gently kissed Lara's forehead.

"Everything okay?" she asked, looking up.

"Nothing I can't handle," he replied, picking up his discarded shirt. "But I'm afraid I've got to shoot."

"Oh come on Mickey, surely it can wait an hour; it's not often mum and dad are out. We've got the place to ourselves for once, and you know you can't resist me!" she teased, lifting the sheets invitingly.

"If only I could," he smiled, bringing his lips to hers. "But I've really got to go. I'll come and pick you up later, and don't worry, I'll make it up to you."

"You'd better," she winked. "Or you'll be looking for another girl!"

Quickly re-clothing, Mickey made his way downstairs, banging the lounge door as he left.

Danny's head popped out…just in time to see his mate heading towards the car.

"Bollocks," he muttered, nipping back inside. Moments later, he was out too; waving with one hand, slipping trainers on with the other.

Mickey was ready, engine running.

"Bloody hell mate," Danny exclaimed, slamming his door shut. "This had better be important, I was approaching fourth base!"

"Something's up with Deano," Mickey frowned.

"There was something *up* with me," Danny chuckled back.

"Ha, bloody ha! Seriously mate, something's not right. He wouldn't say what over the phone, but from the tone of his voice, I don't think it's good news."

Heading straight over to Deano's, they chatted the possibilities over. But as they were about to find out, their guesses were wide of the mark.

"Lads, I'll get straight down to business," Deano began. "I had a call from Chapman this afternoon. The good news is, we won't be seeing Hood and three of his boys for a few years, 'cos right now they're sitting in the cells with fuck all chance of bail!"

A stifled cheer rose briefly, before quickly dying to a whimper. All eyes remained fixed on their leader.

"The bad news, is that J.T.'s made a decision that's gonna piss us all off. To cut a long story short, Hood's four remaining players…are being sent over to join us."

"Fuck off!" Ronnie shouted. "We're not working with those tossers. It isn't our fault they got caught!"

Even Mickey joined in as the room erupted.

Vainly making damping down gestures, Deano attempted to make himself heard above the din.

"Give it a fucking rest boys," he shouted. "Do you think *I'm* over the moon about it, heh? I told Chapman exactly where he could stick his plans, but he made things very clear; it's happening whether we like it or not!"

Ronnie was still incensed. "They're out of order, we'd be better off going alone. We do all the work, we take all the risks, and they end up with most of the dough!"

"Good idea, Ron," Deano replied sarcastically. "Your memory not working too well? Remember what happened to Kenny Griffiths when he had J.T.'s Beemer away? Do you think he'd hesitate to do the same to us? Well, do you?"

"Probably not, but if we all told him bollocks, there'd be nobody left to do his dirty work!"

"If you really think that, then you're more stupid than Hood. J.T. would take great pleasure in taking us out one-by-one; you'd be running scared forever. Is that what you want?"

"No, of course not. It's just not fair. We didn't get any help when Hood's crew were the winners; *we* were left skint! We've had to work bloody hard to get to where we are, and now we're supposed to just hand over our secrets to his remaining idiots!"

On and on the argument continued, but in Mickey's mind it was pointless. J.T.'s order was final; they were going to have to work together. But how the hell was he going to work with Tommy? And with a meet up arranged for the following day…this was indeed bad news.

***

After a well-earned break, the CATS team returned in good spirits. Spread out on the rest room's soft armchairs, they chatted amongst themselves until their Inspector brought them to attention.

"First of all gentlemen, I would like to thank you for your fantastic work so far. Secondly, you're probably wondering what's been happening on your days off?"

Gladstone paused; the whole team sat and waited.

"Well for a start, you'll be delighted to know that all four offenders were remanded in custody," he smiled. "Furthermore, I held a case conference yesterday with CPS. Following positive ID's from witnesses, they are willing to authorise conspiracy to rob charges against all defendants. If we manage to secure convictions on that basis…they'll be off our streets for a minimum of *five* years!"

Taking a moment to allow the cheering to die down, he sipped his coffee before continuing.

"But let me be quite clear, we've only just scratched the surface. Our targets may not have uttered a word during their interviews, but they were a little more careless in their cells. Officers eavesdropped on their chatter, and as we suspected, they're just small cogs in a much much bigger machine. If we *are* to stop these crimes ever happening again, we have to completely dismantle their network. In short guys, we're not going to rest until we've brought their bosses to justice!"

On cue, Sergeant Hanson took over. "Currently, we have little information on the group's hierarchy, so we've come up with a controversial plan – and we need to keep Mr Moore in the dark. Despite the evidence we have against them, we've decided to let Hood's remaining boys run free for a while. There's no way they'll stop working; they need to feed their habits…so with a bit of luck, they'll lead us straight into the arms of their leaders."

***

Walking into the bowling alley the following day, Mickey's anger had hardly relented.

"If that dickhead starts getting lippy, I'm gonna punch his fucking lights out!"

"Only if *I* don't get to him first," Danny replied.

"Can you believe we've gotta tell him our secrets," Mickey grumbled making his way to the bar, and ordering their drinks. "All that hard work, just handed over on a fucking plate!"

"You with the lads in the corner?" the barman asked, returning with their cokes.

Glancing across, Mickey spotted the posse in a dark alcove. But they weren't alone; an older man he hadn't seen before was sat with the group. Deano gave him a nod.

"Yeah, we're with them."

"In that case, your drinks are already paid for," the barman said shuffling away.

"Cheers," Mickey replied, and went off to join the others.

"Pleased to meet you," the older man welcomed them. "I understand your team's success is mainly down to you pair."

Mickey wasn't quite sure what to say. Who was this man? He briefly shot a look at Deano.

"I'm sorry, very rude of me...I'm Chapman by the way," he said extending his hand. "As I was saying, you guys are doing a cracking job; J.T. himself has asked me to pass on his thanks."

Slightly nonplussed, Mickey shook his hand and took his seat next to Danny.

"Listen, I understand why you're all not happy," Chapman continued, addressing the group. "And rest assured, these changes are nothing to do with your excellent work. Unfortunately, J.T.'s made his mind up, so I'm gonna have to ask you to work with us on this."

"I've spoken to the boys," Deano replied. "They're not best pleased, but they'll do what needs to be done."

"Very wise," Chapman nodded. "You wouldn't want to end up like Hood and his mates. Let's just say J.T's arranged for a few friends to welcome them to prison life!"

If only Tommy had been with them, Mickey thought to himself; that would have wiped the stupid smirk off his face.

"Their fate has already been decided, the courts and J.T.'s friends will see to that," Chapman continued. "However, *your* fate is firmly in your own hands. So don't let us down, we won't accept any drops in performance."

Mickey's attention suddenly switched to the entrance doors. In strolled Tommy Burns, making a bee-line to the bar with his scruffily dressed mates. Looking up, Chapman shook his head at the barman, who simply turned and walked away. Tommy's shouts for him to return were immediately cut short.

"Get your arses over here," Chapman bellowed. "And keep your traps shut!"

Reluctantly, the group ambled over; Tommy's glare towards Mickey unflinching.

"What the fuck are you looking at, you prick!" Mickey reacted.

"You, ya dickhead."

Mickey was on his feet in a flash.

But Danny swiftly stepped in. "Chill out mate, he's not fucking worth it."

"Enough!" Chapman growled. "We're here to make a fresh start, not settle old scores. Now sit down, we need to get on with our business."

Pissed off for allowing Tommy to wind him up so quickly, Mickey slowly returned to his seat.

"Now listen carefully, 'cos I don't intend to repeat myself," Chapman continued. "Deano – it goes without saying, you'll be the man in charge. Keep an eye on them, but as long as they're bringing the motors in, you can let them go off on their own. However, when we need you all for a job, the new boys will become the third car."

Turning towards Tommy's boys, he eyeballed each in turn. "You will do exactly as Deano says. If I hear you've disobeyed orders in any way, you can expect an immediate visit from Razor. And let me assure you, he is bitterly disappointed he hasn't been allowed near you…yet!"

Despite the threat, it didn't take Tommy long to regain his arrogance. "And what about the payments, who's gonna pay us our dough?"

"It will be the same system as we've always operated. I'll give Deano the money, he'll distribute it how he sees fit."

"No way, you know he'll never give us our fair share. Why can't you pay us direct?!"

"*You* are in no position to tell *me* what to do. If you don't like it, you can fuck off!" Chapman fired back. "But you'd better pray the filth get to you before J.T. does!"

Scowling, Tommy slumped back in his seat.

"And that goes for the rest of your idiotic group; you're lucky you're being given another chance. So don't come here thinking you can dictate terms, 'cos it's not going to happen!"

Mickey sat back and smirked; old Chapman didn't seem so bad after all.

"It's time to put your suspicions behind you; you're part of a new team now," Chapman resumed, his tone mellowing. "They're going to teach you how to steal without violence; it's easier, and keeps you out of the shit. In fact, it's so much easier, the four of you will be expected to deliver as many motors as your whole group managed previously. I do not expect to be disappointed, understood?"

Again, his stare went deliberately from one to another, unmoving until each new recruit nodded their acceptance.

"Right, I'm going to leave you to it. Deano will run through everything you need to know. Oh, and before I forget, in return for your co-operation, we're arranging a pleasant surprise. Your most feared enemy is in for a shock…the police chopper's days are numbered!"

33

Inside the intelligence office at Stechford Police Station, a lunchtime case conference was about to begin. Countless mug shots shared the wall space with graphs mapping crime patterns, while blinds covered windows to keep out prying eyes.

"I have been asked by the Chief Constable herself to pass on congratulations to you and your team," Mr Moore said to his Inspector. "And she informs me that she'll be watching with interest when their time for sentencing arrives."

"Thank you," Gladstone replied, nodding his head from across the table.

"Not only have we succeeded in charging the offenders with conspiracy to commit robbery," his boss continued. "We have also experienced an incredible ninety percent drop in car-jackings across the force area. I think you will all agree, this is an amazing achievement and reflects positively on our division."

"More like, 'reflects positively on your career'," Gladstone muttered under his breath.

"I'm sorry Paul, I didn't quite catch that?"

"I said that we couldn't have done it without you sir!"

"You're too kind," Moore beamed. "I'm sure we'd all agree it's been a team effort, and I look forward to the fine work continuing."

Folders and iPads before them, officers from neighbouring forces presented their latest crime trends, and as the meeting progressed, a distinct pattern emerged: luxury cars were disappearing...fast.

DC Richards, the Worcestershire intelligence officer, was particularly vocal.

"We're getting hammered every...single...night. It's impossible to combat; they're striking over a vast area with no obvious pattern. But these boys are no amateurs; they're highly professional, skilfully using hi-tech equipment rather than stealing the keys. CCTV at a victim's home recently captured her Mercedes being stolen; the whole operation took less than a minute!" he said, shaking his head. "We suspect the offenders live somewhere within the Birmingham area, so any help you can give us would be gratefully accepted."

"So what makes you think that *our* villains are responsible?" Mr Moore replied indignantly. "As I've already explained, our main targets are languishing in the cells."

"Well...ANPR analysis suggest they generally head towards your area."

"That's hardly convincing. Look, I'm more than happy to help out if there's concrete evidence, but to be blunt, you need to provide me with more than just supposition."

"With respect sir, if I could assist," Gladstone cut in. "Although we've accounted for some of their main players, there's still plenty more at large. My team are carrying out surveillance on a few suspects as we speak, and without wishing to compromise the ongoing operation, it looks like they've teamed up with a larger group who appear to be involved in the wide-scale theft of luxury cars. I have reason to believe that DC Richards is correct; the majority are being stolen from the Worcestershire area."

By now, Moore's face had turned crimson. "Thank you for enlightening us Paul," he scowled. "Perhaps in the future you would kindly inform me first – that's what the chain-of-command's for!"

"Very well sir," Gladstone nodded. "Do forgive me, I was merely following your last '*do not disturb me unless you have results*' order."

With a glower, Moore moved the meeting quickly on to other matters. Following its conclusion, Gladstone and Richards retreated to the CAT's office.

"So what makes you think your boys are doing all our thefts then?"

Looking around the empty room, Gladstone closed the door behind him. "Listen, I'm trusting you on this; it's vital our discussion doesn't go any further...even old Moore's unaware of what I'm about to tell you."

"You have my word."

"Surveillance on our car-jackers showed them to be unprofessional, reckless, and hooked on drugs. Once we locked the first four up, our four remaining suspects went straight into hiding; something we were happy to allow. We quickly located them, and decided to let them run...hoping they would lead us to their bosses."

"Good plan. I can see why you kept Mr Moore in the dark."

"Quite," Gladstone replied, pausing as footsteps passed the office. "The results were surprising to say the least. Within weeks they'd joined up with another group we hadn't looked at before...only this group were completely different; they were far more professional. Straightaway, their habits changed dramatically. They suddenly became surveillance conscious, using techniques we'd normally expect from career criminals. But we knew they hadn't returned to robberies; the gaffer's right, we've practically had zero reported. So what were they up to? After all, they still needed cash for their drugs."

"I think I can see where this is going."

"Then we had an interesting breakthrough. By good fortune, one of our obs team was on his way into work when a sporty Jag passed him with two of our targets on board. PNC revealed they'd just stolen it from a village on your patch...without keys! Okay, we can identify the lads responsible, but the arrests will have to wait; we're focusing on the bigger fish."

"Very interesting," Richards nodded. "Looks like our hunch was right. So tell me, what's next; how long can you wait 'til you strike?"

"That's a damn good question. The answer probably depends on how long we can keep Mr Moore off our backs. For now, our static obs will continue. We have cameras on various target's houses, including the address which seems to be at the heart of their operations. It belongs to a well-known car thief called Deano. He's a hero amongst the local kids, they reckon he's the next Lewis Hamilton! Anyway, he's also well known to our boys; but we've always seen him as a petty criminal…a joyrider at best. My instinct tells me we've underestimated his abilities; he may well be the key to unlocking this group," Gladstone explained. "I have to say though, his team are good; they're impossible to follow covertly, their motors disappear into thin air, and we're still no closer to their bosses! It's only a matter of time though, I'm confident of that."

"Obviously we're suffering more than anybody. Is there anything we can do to help?"

"Information is the key. I'm desperate for the details of every keyless theft you've suffered over the past twelve months. I also need to know the moment a new one is reported, especially if a Tracker's fitted."

"I'll have to run it by my D.I., but I can't foresee any problems."

Continuing to formulate plans, it was a couple of hours before the meeting drew to a close. As DC Richards headed back to his rural force, Gladstone retired to the station bar.

As usual, the seating area was practically deserted; the only custom a few retired officers exchanging war-stories.

"Hello Paul," an ex-sergeant greeted him. "Haven't seen you down here in a while."

"Long stressful days, Fred. I hardly get the chance anymore…you remember what it was like."

"You're not wrong there. We didn't go home for two weeks solid during the riots!" he said, the other pensioners voicing their agreement.

"You old boys want a pint?" Gladstone offered.

Almost as one, they downed their drinks and brought their glasses down.

"Don't mind if we do," Fred replied, licking the froth from his moustache. Recently retired, he was a well-known character at the nick; his tall stories not quite matching his experiences in CID. An ever-increasing waistline reflected more accurately where he'd spent the majority of his career.

"So what keeps you here so late?" Fred continued, clinking his fresh glass to the Inspector's.

"The normal," Gladstone smiled. "Too much work, and too little time. Still, we're getting some cracking results."

"Oh yes, it's been all over the papers this week; sounds like your team did a fantastic job. Question is, did you manage to get them all? In my experience, there's always a few who squirm free from the net."

"You're not wrong there, but as we both know, they can't get away forever. They'll come again, mark my words."

Banter soon took over from police work; the good old days versus the new. As the night wore on, Fred and Gladstone were eventually the last to leave, and headed out to the car park together.

"So what do you think about this graffiti that's getting daubed everywhere?" Fred asked.

"I'm not really sure what you're talking about; what graffiti?"

"You know…the slogan that's all over the estates; it's everywhere!"

"To be honest, we're a little too busy to be interested in graffiti!" Gladstone chuckled. "I'd have thought you would be too! Are you sure you haven't had one too many?"

"Perhaps, but this is different. From what I can gather from the local kids, it's aimed directly at the police; they reckon something's about to go down."

"Okay, you're starting to get my attention now," Gladstone frowned, coming to a halt. "So tell me, this slogan…what on earth does it actually say?"

"'Shoot the moon', that's all, 'shoot the moon'."

34

Angered at having to give away their secrets to Tommy, the following weeks saw Mickey keeping his enemy as far away as possible. Left to do their work alone, he and Danny kept up their supplies; continually seeking out new manufacturers to challenge their skills…and impress the girls. All good things had to come to an end though, and the news he'd been dreading was about to be delivered.

"Sit down lads," Deano said, ushering them into his lounge. "I'll say the same to you as I've said to the others. We're going on a job tonight and we've been told to take the new boys with us."

"Bollocks," Mickey replied, his heart sinking. How on earth was he supposed to work alongside Tommy and his cronies? They didn't have a clue what they were doing, and there was no way he'd ever trust them! What the hell was J.T. thinking of? Their jobs were risky enough without letting a bunch of bagheads get involved!

"Listen, nobody's happy about it, but all the moaning in the world's not gonna change things. So let's stop whingeing, and just get on with it. Agreed?"

Begrudgingly, along with the others, Mickey nodded his head. Deano was right; they'd known this day was coming, they'd just have to work alongside Tommy whether they liked it or not.

At eight fifteen precisely, Ronnie went down to let the new boys in; their return greeted by a wall of silence.

"Sit yourselves down," Deano said, gesturing to the floor.

Shuffling in, the moment they took their places, Deano started the briefing.

"We've been given instructions to clear out a sports store; they've just taken a monster delivery of the new England kit," he explained.

Running through the plan in even greater detail than normal, all was going well…until he started to hand out the jobs.

"As usual, I'll be driving the lead car. Tommy, you're behind me with your crew, which leaves Mickey taking up the..."

"Whoa, not so fast. Why should we go in the middle!" Tommy exclaimed.

"Because I said so, that's why. If you don't like it, don't bother coming. But *you* can explain to Porter why we didn't return with the goods he was expecting."

"You're not listening! I never said we weren't coming," Tommy continued. "What I *am* saying, is I'm a better driver than Mickey, so I should be at the rear. If the cops get on our tail, I'm the only one who can sort them out."

"What the fuck are you trying to say?" Mickey reacted, unable to suppress his anger any longer.

Tommy turned to face his rival.

"I'm not *trying* to say anything, I'm just telling you how it is. I'm the better driver; you need me and Deano either side to protect you," he replied, taking to his feet.

Mickey rose to meet the threat, practically nose-to-nose with his enemy. Unflinching, he stared into Tommy's eyes, the years of hate ready to explode.

Neither spoke, neither moved a muscle.

"That's enough!" Deano shouted, his earlier calmness disappearing. "Tommy, you'll do exactly what I fucking say. Mickey's at the back because he's the best driver I've ever worked with. If you've got a problem with that, you know where the door is!"

Tommy stood defiant.

"And if you don't sit down right now, I'll fucking kick you out myself; understand!"

For a moment, Tommy remained motionless…but as Deano went to stand up, he shot a final sneer towards Mickey, and returned to his place on the floor.

"Good," Deano said, sitting back down. "Now perhaps we can return to the plans for tonight!"

***

"No officer with experience on the streets believes in coincidences, so I'm not going to start right now," Gladstone stewed, pacing around the crowded office. "Our cameras outside Deano's captured every one of our targets turning up for a meeting last night. Then, only half an hour after they left, fifty grand's worth of England kit was stolen in a ram-raid! Thirty minutes later, and guess what, Deano and Tommy are seen skulking back to their homes. Now I don't know about you lot, but that's too many coincidences for me!"

Remaining quiet, the CATS team waited for more. Gladstone didn't disappoint.

"These stills," he said, sticking eleven photos to the offender's wall. "Were taken outside Deano's when they left to go out to the job. Call me cynical, but I reckon the video from the store might give us some interesting results. Okay, they're bound to be wearing balaclavas to cover their faces, but I'd be mightily surprised if we don't see a match with their clothing!"

Taking a step to one side, he paused while his team studied the photos.

"Now, although our targets have become well known to us over the past couple of weeks, we also know they have precious few convictions. Is this because they're new to the business, or as the evidence would increasingly suggest, that they're good at what they…"

Suddenly, the office door burst open. Sergeant Hanson strode in and thrust an envelope into his gaffer's hands.

"Thanks Steve," Gladstone said opening the flap. "I take it these are the stills from the ram-raid?"

"Hot off the press boss. I think you'll find they make interesting viewing."

Pulling out the A4 photographs, his officers huddled around.

One-by-one, he stuck them below the eleven suspects.

"Well would you believe it; another coincidence!" he said sarcastically. "Okay, so it looks like some of them have changed their outer clothing, but there's no mistaking the footwear; our raiding party have exactly the same as the eleven leaving Deano's house! Maybe not enough for CPS to run a trial, but more than enough to confirm our suspicions. These boys are in even deeper than we'd given them credit for…it's time for us to turn up the heat!"

***

Having parked his Mercedes on double yellows outside Starbucks, Porter placed his fake disabled badge in the windscreen, and walked inside. Near to the window, behind a wooden table, J.T. and his brother sat reading their papers.

"Sit yourself down," J.T. instructed without looking up. "I see you're still using the old disabled ploy."

"Saves being bothered by the rozzers; I can't believe everybody doesn't do it!" he joked, taking his seat.

"Can't say I've ever been bothered by tickets. I always leave them to Jonas to sort out; he's never lost one yet!" J.T. laughed back, as a waitress brought over their orders.

Drinks in hand, the talk quickly turned to the reason for their meeting.

"So what's the news from our contact then?" J.T. asked

"Not as good as it could be I'm afraid."

"What do you mean?"

Porter took a sip before replying.

"Well he doesn't know the full story, 'cos the man in charge, a bloke called Gladstone, is playing his cards close to his chest."

"Gladstone heh. Now that *is* interesting; Paul and I go back a long way," J.T. mused. "I'm surprised he's still in the job."

"Apparently, the only people in the know are the ones on the operation itself. My contact's given me the snippets he's heard, but the rest is pure guesswork."

"So what exactly *does* he think is going on?"

"Look, if you already know Mr Gladstone, you'll be aware of his reputation. By all accounts, once he's got his teeth into something, he'll never let it go."

"You're not wrong there," J.T. said ruefully.

"Anyway, *he's* heading the operation, which probably accounts for why our bunch of idiots ended up in prison. My contact believes they're still working on the case…as if there's some unfinished business to attend to. He thinks

Gladstone has stumbled onto something that's making him dig deeper. Whether that means he's after our boys, or somebody else, he really doesn't know for sure. Either way, we need to be careful nothing leads back to us."

"How the hell could it?" J.T. said angrily, his mood changing in an instant. "None of the boys would be stupid enough to talk…would they Porter?"

"Of course not," he replied defensively. "I just think we need to be on our guard, that's all."

"Perhaps a little distraction is needed," Johnny said in a low voice. "We could simply kill two birds with one stone. When we successfully shoot the moon, it'll make our lads work a little easier, while giving old Gladstone something more important to think about."

"Sounds good to me," J.T. replied. "But have you worked out *how* yet?"

"Well, I think I've formulated a plan; it just needs some fine tuning. Perhaps I could discuss it with you…later?"

The subtle hint wasn't lost on J.T.

"Okay Porter, keep pumping our contact; the more you can find out the better. Now if you don't mind, Johnny and I have some business to attend to."

Porter looked down at his half-eaten bun and barely touched coffee. Lifting the napkin from his lap, he slowly placed it on the table, and stood up.

"Keep me informed Porter, and don't tell another soul, understand?"

While Porter scuttled back to his Merc, the brothers watched on from their window seats before continuing.

"So what exactly *is* your plan then?" J.T. asked.

"It's pretty obvious really. The helicopter only spends ten per cent of its time in the air, the rest is spent on the ground. We'll simply acquire a heavy truck, drive it straight through the airport's barriers, and the rest as they say…will become history!"

A smile spread out across J.T.'s face.

"That my little brother, is the best idea you've ever had. I bet Gladstone's already wondering what the hell all the graffiti's about; well it's time he found out…it's time for revenge!"

35

Despite Mickey's concerns, the first ram-raid had gone surprisingly well; even the unusually subdued Tommy Burns had followed his instructions to the letter. Following its success, the group had managed to settle into an uneasy relationship: keeping their distance during the week, working together at weekends, with every smash-and-grab passing without incident.

Now gathered together again, the group awaited instructions for their next job. But tonight, something wasn't quite right; Mickey couldn't help but notice the change in his leader's tone.

"Pay attention guys, 'cos our next job's gonna be the toughest one yet," Deano began as the room fell silent. "We're hitting an upmarket store in Leicester that's about to start selling watches. But as you might guess, it's none of your cheap crap; these beauties are Rolex, Breitling and the like…worth up to thirty grand each!"

Mickey took in a deep breath. Thirty grand a watch was big money, even by his standards. A decent haul would outstrip anything they'd done before.

"Porter assures me that if things go to plan, our haul could be worth in excess of half a million pounds! But, and there's a big but here…it's not going to be easy. First of all, being a department store, it's got six floors and the watches are on the second. Once we're in, it'll take time to get to them, and just as long to get back to the cars. Secondly, the front doors are shuttered at night, and security patrol the inside. If that wasn't enough, once we've done the job, we've got to make our way back from Leicester, with every cop in the Midlands after us!"

Mickey's mind flicked back to his first raid in Nottingham. Leicester was a similar distance; at least fifty miles of unfamiliar roads to cover.

"To start with, we need the right motors for the job," Deano continued. "We know the cop's latest Beemers are quick, so whatever we choose will need to be quicker. As it's watches we're after, there's no issue about boot space – it's all about performance. We'll meet here Sunday night at ten to go over the details; in the meantime Ronnie and I will visit the store. Guys, I won't lie to you, it's going to be risky; it's crucial we work as a team. Any questions so far?"

There were many questions in Mickey's mind, but none that needed airing right now. He waited until he and Danny were walking home before opening up.

"I've got a bad feeling about this job," he confided. "It's got trouble written all over it, and we both know who's likely to cause it!"

"C'mon mate, you've gotta let it go. They've done alright so far, we've just gotta accept that they're here to stay."

"I know, I know, I just hope you're right, 'cos there's something eating away at me that I can't explain…and it always surfaces when Tommy's around."

"Don't worry, we'll be fine, and anyway," Danny replied, his eyes widening. "What are we going to use on the job? I fancy another 911, in fact, why settle for a Porsche when you can have a Ferrari!"

Slowly, Danny's infectious enthusiasm won through; a smile gradually returning to Mickey's face. "Can you imagine turning up in a bright red Ferrari; Tommy would be jealous as hell! Mind you, I'm not sure Deano would be too impressed; after all, we are supposed to be keeping under the radar!" he laughed. "No, we need something subtle, four wheel drive and blistering quick. Which car ticks all those boxes; something that's served us so well in the past?"

Without a moment's hesitation, Danny beamed back the answer. "Audi RS4 of course. There's nothing on the road that'll touch it!"

***

And it didn't take the lads long to find.

The following evening, having sat patiently watching the rush hour flow by, a blood red RS4 eventually trundled past, the congestion making it all too easy for them to follow unnoticed behind. Continuing onto the motorway system, it made its way to a small village outside Worcester, where the oblivious owner tucked it safely away for the night...or so he thought.

***

Inside the deserted CATS office, Sergeant Hanson was ploughing through reports when a call from DC Richard's broke his concentration.

"Ah, my favourite intelligence officer," Hanson laughed quietly to himself. "Thanks for sending me the European paperwork mountain, you'll be glad to know it's still doing my head in!"

"My pleasure. And guess what, there's more on the way after the last couple of nights!" Richards joked back. "However, I might have some good news for you at last. In this morning's early hours, we had a red Audi RS4 stolen from Pershore. Once again it bears all the hallmarks of your boys, but interestingly it's fitted with a Tracker, and the signal's been activated."

"Interesting indeed," Hanson smiled. "And forensics, did you manage to get anything from the scene?"

"You're joking aren't you, you know what this team are like! And there's no CCTV at the victim's address either, so it's all down to you guys to solve!"

"That's fine, leave it with us; let's just hope this is the breakthrough we've been after."

The moment he finished the call, Hanson was on to his team. Within the hour, they'd all rushed in, eager to make the most of their lead.

"I don't need to tell you how important this information could be," Gladstone enthused. "Three high performance cars were taken last night, only 24 hours after a meeting at Deano's where all of our targets were present. My hunch is that they've been taken for a specific purpose; they're planning something big. To get a step ahead, we need to track the Audi down, install a camera, and watch it round the clock. So let's not waste any more time; the clock's ticking, let's get out there and find it!"

Using a well-rehearsed system, the team set to work straightaway. From outside their station, the unmarked cars drove off in opposite directions, before turning to criss-cross the city. Able to locate a Tracker's signal from up to three miles away, the car's receiver units constantly scanned the airwaves. It wasn't long before the first alert sounded.

"Bingo," Gaz shouted, looking at the code on his screen. "It's got to be our beauty."

While he updated the control room, Draycott brought their car to a halt and studied the display. The screen was split into two sections: vertical lights on the left showed how close they were, while a circle of lights on the right guided them in the right direction.

The control centre were soon back in touch.

"Yankee Mike to all units. Tracker confirm the reply code relates to an outstanding stolen red Audi RS4 taken overnight from Pershore."

"One-Six received," Gaz replied. "Can you ask them to boost the signal?"

Working in tandem, the two cars drove in ever decreasing circles towards the wealthy Firs estate. Turning into a dead end, only apartment blocks stood before them.

"The signal's coming from our left, we've got eight out of ten bars," Gaz said flicking his eyes up from the screen. "Try that little access drive."

Gravel crunching under fat tyres, they rolled alongside a line of garages towards the apartment block's car park. Two vehicles sat all alone in the parking bays, but neither were the red Audi they were looking for.

"Bollocks, I thought we'd turn the corner and it'd be there!" Gaz exclaimed, the lights on his Tracker rising to nine bars. "Still, it's got to be in one of the garages...but which one?!"

Moving carefully along the line, they waited for the signal to reach its ten bar peak. Then, to make sure, they edged past it, immediately triggering a light to drop out.

"Right, it's definitely in 28," Draycott confirmed, reversing back into position. "Thank God this system's so good."

"Maybe so, but I won't be happy until I see it with my own eyes."

"No can do mate," Draycott replied, turning the car round and driving off. "Imagine if we were spotted going in? And do you remember the intell we had about them marking the garages? We just can't take the risk; this is the best lead we've ever had on these boys!"

"Yeah, yeah, you're right. I'd just hate to think we were wasting our time, that's all."

"You and me both. We're just going to have to place our trust in the Tracker; it's never let us down before, and I'm sure it's not going to today."

Even as they made their way back to Stechford, colleagues from technical support were hurrying over to the garages. Swiftly installing a camera outside, a live-link to the station was in place within the hour.

"Good work fellas," Gladstone smiled, shutting the door behind him. "You'll be glad to know I've managed to persuade Mr Moore to let the Audi run. He's made it clear it's on my head, so let's make sure we get it back in one piece, or the owner's going to be asking some pretty searching questions!"

"Okay, so here's the plan," Hanson took over. "We're gonna watch the screen around the clock; I'll give you the rota in a minute. When our targets return, no matter what the time, we expect everybody to get here immediately."

"And when it moves…are we just going to let it drive off?" PC Wilson asked.

"Well, we need to remain flexible; we'll have to react to what's happening," Gladstone replied. "I suspect it's to be used on a job, so ideally we'd like to catch them in the act. But of course, that all depends where it goes down. If it *is* too far away, we'll get them on the way back – when the spoils are still in the car. My plan is to prove that they're career criminals, and not just petty thieves."

"Are we *really* gonna let them run free boss?" Gaz frowned.

"To a degree, yes. It's a pity the car's tracking system doesn't have GPS, or we'd be able to follow them every step of the way. However, as we've already found out, it's extremely accurate, and Air Ops assure me they'll pick it up from over ten miles away," he replied. "Now, are there any more questions before I go off to the management meeting?"

"Just changing the subject slightly," DC Darby said. "Have you heard about the slogan that's getting daubed everywhere; you know the '*shoot the moon*' thing?"

"Well I'm aware it could be related to the police, but that's about as much as I know. Why, do you think there's a relevance to what we're up to?"

"Sorry boss, I'm as much in the dark as you are. What I *do* know is that it's everywhere; walls, shops, phone boxes, everywhere! You've always told us not to believe in coincidences, so for me it's just too big a 'coincidence' that just as we start locking their boys up, this graffiti appears."

"Sounds like they're trying to goad us then, doesn't it? Perhaps the people who run these teams don't like the attention they're receiving. Oh well, they're going to dislike us even more when we take their next team out. And after that…we're coming for **them**!"

36

Anxious all week, Mickey's mind was struggling to focus on anything other than the big job. But the team were depending on him; he had to put his fears to one side. And so, as Deano began the briefing, he listened in carefully; he couldn't afford to put a foot wrong tonight.

"We'll all make our way separately to the meeting point. I've written down the postcodes and route, so make sure you update your sat-navs," Deano said, handing out copies to the navigators.

"It's a church car park, only half a mile from our target. From there, we'll travel together, and pull up outside in our line of three. If everything goes to plan, we'll leave in the same order, and stay together until we return to the Greet. Any questions so far?"

Mickey tensed, expecting Tommy to object. But for once, he kept his peace.

"I'll be in a Nissan GT-R, Mickey's gone for an RS4. What have you got Tommy?"

"There's only one car for this job, and I've bagged it! A BMW M3, as black as the night, and this one's been seriously chipped," he said smugly, giving Mickey a less than subtle sneer.

"Excellent," Deano nodded, picking up a large pad. "Now let's get on with the plan."

Placing it on the floor, he folded the cover sheet over to reveal a hand drawn layout of the building.

"This is the ground level," he explained, circling the sketch with his pen. "It's designed to keep people like us out...so here's how we're gonna get in!"

Shoulder-to-shoulder, the posse gathered around their leader as he carefully ran over the attack. After explaining how they'd break in, he turned the page over to reveal the second floor.

"Don't get taken in by the watches in the display cabinets – they're imitations. The real ones are in the store room here," he said, marking its position on the map.

"Its door is kept permanently locked, but our contact informs us it's flimsy. Ronnie, one good kick should be enough. When you're inside, go to the cabinet on the back wall. It'll have been left unlocked, and has all the real watches inside. Ronnie, Danny, Eccy; fill your bags asap, then get out as quick as you can – the other boys will be hot on your heels."

"And what exactly *are* my boys doing while yours are grabbing the glory?" Tommy asked indignantly.

"The job I thought they'd enjoy most...dealing with security!"

"What do you mean?"

"Look, there's at least two guards inside, but we've no idea where they'll be. I suggest Alf and Nozza keep a lookout on the ground floor, while Max keeps watch on the second. Rushy and Dougie will also be helping out; they'll be on the first…"

"So my lads can't be trusted," Tommy interrupted. "Is that what you're saying?"

"Trust? That's something *you've* yet to earn," Deano replied angrily. "Have you any idea how much time and money has gone into this job?"

Tommy shrugged.

"How do you think we know so much about the store? Do you really think I'm going to put all that hard work at risk…well, do you?! We just need you to do what you're told. So are you in, or are you out?"

"Of course we're in," Tommy spat back. "My lads know exactly what they're doing."

"Good. And while we're at it, it's about time your boys signed up to how *we* work. We're not a bunch of thugs, so I don't want any violence. Security are just a couple of old guys on minimum wage; they'll probably shit themselves when they see masked raiders coming in. Just act aggressive, herd them into a corner, and stay with them until we're all out. Let me repeat, '**no violence**', okay!"

***

Despite watching their screen around the clock, the CATS team had witnessed five days pass by without a hint of movement at the garages. Tonight, stuck with the graveyard shift, Strickers wearily zoomed in and out to keep himself awake. The endless coffees were taking their effect though; a toilet break was needed.

Pulling his chair back, he yawned, stood up, and took one last look at the screen. But just as he started to turn away…three dark figures emerged from the shadows. The movement stopped him in his tracks.

Wearing caps, and scarves to cover their faces, they strode towards garage 28.

Back in his seat, Strickers swiftly re-focused the lens, just as the tallest youth pulled out a mobile, and kneeling down, shone it at the base of the doors. Taking a key from his pocket, the youth swiftly removed the padlock.

Strickers kept his eyes glued to the screen, and grabbing the office phone, frantically dialled Gladstone's number.

"Boss, it's Strickers," he said excitedly. "We've got action at the garage – three youths are opening the doors as we speak."

"Okay," the Inspector's croaky voice replied. "Keep talking, tell me what's happening."

"The taller youth's gone into the garage, the others are outside keeping dog," he commentated. "Headlights are on, something's driving out...standby, standby...yes, I can confirm, it *is* our red Audi!"

"Right, time is of the essence. You know what to do, I'll see you in half an hour."

No sooner had the line gone dead, than Strickers began calling the team. While they made their way into work, he was onto surrounding divisions, neighbouring forces, and finally the area's helicopter.

Their response was in full swing, but the Audi was out on the loose...could they *really* get it tracked down in time?

***

Bleary eyed but wide-awake, the CATS team quickly streamed in. Desperate to identify the offenders, they replayed the Audi's departure, but it was impossible; their face coverings and new trainers thwarting even the keenest of eyes.

"Gentlemen, thanks for coming in at this ungodly hour," Gladstone said, striding into the office. "As I said before, we need to remain flexible throughout tonight's operation. They could be anywhere right now; they may even be doing the job as we speak! For the time being, we're at our control room's mercy; if they're on the ball, we should be able to respond in time. In the meantime, Strickers, can you and Donkey get to the garage in case our boys return unexpectedly. Everybody else, get out and start hunting. With a bit of luck, we'll know the direction they're returning from long before they reach us. But until then, we need to cover every possibility. Okay, good luck guys; it's time for action."

***

Dark clouds concealed a full moon overhead, as sticking to the speed limits, Mickey followed Danny's directions through 'A' roads and country lanes. His car was perfect, like a natural extension to his body; flowing through the bends, surging with every accelerator squeeze, breezing over dips and crests. And yet, he struggled to enjoy the drive; his mind fast forwarding to the raid, and the potential pitfalls ahead.

An hour later, they arrived at the church. Deano's sky blue GT-R was already waiting, its aggressive front grills barely visible in the shadows. Mickey reversed in tight, lowering his window to chat. Soon joined by Tommy's black BMW growling onto the car park, everybody got out and huddled around the GT-R's bonnet. For the final time, Deano went over the plans, and then, as the church bell struck three...face coverings went on, engines fired into life.

One behind the other, they rolled towards their target. Undisturbed, they abandoned their motors outside the store's vast frontage, and flinging their doors open, began the attack. Deano was first out, angle grinder in hand, sprinting towards the shutters. No sooner had he sheared their locks off, than Tommy thrust them upwards.

Adrenaline firing through his body, Mickey grabbed the sledgehammer from the GT-R's boot and rushed towards his accomplices. Without breaking step, he swung the heavy tool forward and slammed it into the exposed front doors. The toughened glass exploded on impact, but even as the splinters showered down, his team were on the move; rushing past him and into the store.

Hurrying back to the GT-R, Mickey dumped his sledgehammer, and raced to the door of his Audi. Heart pounding, he scanned in every direction. Other than Deano and Tommy doing the same, there were no other signs of life. Hovering his hand over the horn, he watched and waited; there was little he could do to help them now.

Inside the store, Ronnie's group had managed to sprint to the stockroom unchallenged. But moments later, down on the ground floor, Tommy's sidekicks intercepted two security guards struggling to respond. Without warning, the thugs launched into attack, clubbing the uniformed men over their heads. Not content with knocking them to the ground, the pumped-up raiders continued their assault, raining blow after blow on their defenceless bodies.

Even above the sirens, Rushy and Dougie overheard the disturbance. Charging down the escalator, they yelled for the onslaught to stop, but whether they were heard or not, the violence continued regardless. Leaping off the bottom steps, they dived onto Tommy's boys, sending everybody sprawling to the floor. All four jumped back to their feet; two intent on more violence…two determined to stop it.

Oblivious to the commotion inside, Mickey stood in his doorwell, staring at the smashed entrance. "Come on, come on," he muttered to himself, glancing down at his watch…the seconds were ticking by.

Having booted the storeroom door off with a single kick, Ronnie's team ran straight to the cabinet in the corner. Just as they'd been told, its door was unlocked; its booty all ready to plunder. Rapidly stuffing the watches into their holdalls, they quickly turned and fled. Retracing their steps to the front entrance, they bolted down two escalators, rushed past their mates' stand-off, and escaped through the smashed glass doors.

Eccy was the first to Mickey's car, flinging his bag across the back seat as he dived in closely behind. Hot on his heels, Danny practically skidded across the bonnet on route to his door. The moment it closed, Mickey released launch control, sending his Audi hurtling off down the narrow city streets. Back in his element, he breathed a sigh of relief. Everything seemed to have gone to plan;

both the posse and the stash were out safely. All they needed to do now, was to avoid the police...

37

'*Incoming call – Gladstone*' flashed up on the traffic car's screen; the shrill ring disturbing Draycott's painstaking hunt.

"Guys, it's all systems go," the gaffer's voice announced over the hands-free. "There's just been a ram raid in Leicester; three vehicles involved and they're heading our way. Make towards the M42, we'll try to intercept them on the force boundary. A word of warning though, they're carrying tools and aren't afraid to use them. Right, I've got to update the control room, good luck!"

"Yes!" Gaz hollered, activating the blues and twos. "We're finally gonna get 'em!"

Racing out to the city's limits, the CATS team headed for their pre-arranged strategic locations. And it wasn't long before the helicopter passed the message they'd all been waiting for.

"MPAS-One to all units. Be advised, we've picked up Tracker code 'Foxtrot One Five Zulu Zulu' coming from the direction of Leicester. This relates to a stolen red Audi RS4. Will keep you informed with any further updates."

"Sounds like the gaffer's hunch was right," Draycott grinned, pulling the car to a halt near Coleshill.

"Yeah, he's got the fabled sixth sense people talk about; no wonder he's nicked so many villains over the years."

"Maybe so, but even *he* doesn't have a clue about the 'shoot the moon' graffiti. Have you seen it recently…it's going up quicker than the council can take it down!"

"So what's your take on it?"

"I haven't got a clue mate. It's obviously aimed at us, although how the hell they managed to daub it on our front office the other night I'll never know…cheeky bastards! Perhaps they reckon we've got more chance of shooting the moon, than we have of catching them!"

"Well if that *is* the case, they're gonna get a nasty surprise tonight then!" Gaz replied, his words almost drowned out by another transmission.

"MPAS-One to all units. Be advised, we are currently approaching Nuneaton; signal is increasing in strength, and moving steadily towards us."

"Nuneaton? They're not that far away mate. And by my reckoning, if they're not using the motorway, *we're* in the prime position!" Gaz smiled, the excitement in his voice picked up by his dog. "Alright, alright, calm down," he said, tickling Quincy's neck through the holes in its cage. "It'll be time to play in a minute."

"MPAS-One to control. We now have visual on three fast moving vehicles approaching 'Over Whitacre' on the B4114. I can confirm, the stolen Audi is at the rear."

"All received MPAS-One," the control room replied. "Can you pass details of the other two cars?"

"Affirmative – lead vehicle is a blue Nissan GT-R, the second a black BMW."

"All units be advised, reference the last transmission, these vehicles are believed responsible for a burglary in the last half hour in Leicester. Extreme caution is to be used; they are thought to be carrying weapons and have seriously injured two security guards at the scene," the controller continued. "Tango Charlie One Six, can you confirm you're at Coleshill, junction with the B4114?"

"Yes, affirmative," Gaz replied.

"MPAS-One, take talk through with your ground unit."

Maintaining commentary from the air, the chopper continued to follow high above. With half a mile to go, and the targets racing headlong into their trap, the air observer handed over to his ground based colleagues.

"Tango Charlie One Six to control. I can confirm we have multiple headlights approaching," Gaz updated calmly.

Draycott pulled back on the paddleshift. "This is it mate; it's time to catch the bad guys!"

***

Inside the Audi, Mickey had started to relax. The unfamiliar route along dark rural roads had flown by without difficulty, and now in the distance, streetlights finally approached.

"It's all down to you now," Danny said, turning the sat-nav off. "We're just about back on home turf."

Still third in line, Mickey started to brake on his approach to the roundabout. Masked by the cars in front, he was the last to see it…a liveried BMW sat ready and waiting.

"Bollocks, a bloody 330," he said as they passed in procession.

"Shouldn't be a problem for this little beauty!" Danny nervously laughed back.

Flicking his eyes to the mirror, Mickey cursed. The traffic car had swung in behind, its lights and sirens already blazing. But the roads were dry, he knew them like the back of his hand, and his car had stacks more power. It should be relatively easy…as long as Tommy did what he'd been told.

Sure enough, the raider's performance advantage soon took effect; quickly extending a decent lead over the cops. However, as they hurtled ever closer to home, Deano's GT-R was suddenly lit up like a beacon.

"Where the fuck's it coming from?" Mickey called out.

"Behind us!" Eccy shouted, craning his head to look up through the rear screen. "It must have been following us!"

"Okay, okay, let's keep calm; we know what to do," Mickey replied, his adrenalin burst disappearing. "We need to split up…it's each to their own from now on!"

Deano was on the same wavelength. On reaching the next roundabout, he flung his steering to the right and briefly tugged on the handbrake, sending his car into a controlled powerslide. Straightening its nose, he planted the gas, launching his motor past Mickey and away.

To his front, Tommy blasted straight ahead. Good, good, Mickey thought to himself; that left one remaining exit. With Tommy out of his way, it should be relatively easy…as long as the helicopter went after the others!

In a wide arc, he slid around the island, and gunned it. He just needed to stay calm now; the Greet's relative safety was only five miles away.

He glanced in the mirror once more. "Okay guys, the 330's trying to come after us, but he's a long way behind," he called out. "The chopper's nowhere to be seen, see if either of you can spot it?"

But before his mates even had chance to answer, the road in front turned to daylight.

"Shit!" Danny yelled out. "Now what?"

"We'll stick to our plans," Mickey replied calmly. "Okay, we can't outrun the chopper, but we can easily outrun the cops. We'll head towards the tower blocks and disappear inside. Eccy, make the call to Simon; he should be ready and waiting in Birbeck House."

"Already on the case mate," Eccy said, mobile in hand. "He'll have the doors open the moment we arrive."

There were no other options. Mickey knew he could handle the BMW's behind, but the helicopter was a completely different matter. With the floodlight dancing ahead of his path, his mind drifted back to Chapman's promise to deal with the chopper…why hadn't he sorted it sooner!

The pursuit continued to thunder through the city streets. With few other road users to hamper his progress, Mickey guided his Audi missile towards home. Leaving the original traffic car and subsequent pursuers in his wake, only the telltale beam of light remained…escaping into the tower block should be a breeze.

But something was troubling him. As the roads flashed by, his mind kept returning to the same question; how *had* the helicopter known where they were? If there'd been a Tracker on one of the cars, the cops would have had plenty of time to find it during the week. But he knew they hadn't been near the garages; even Tommy would have spotted the disturbed pebbles. Of course, it was possible they'd been grassed on. After all, hadn't Deano mentioned that somebody from the store was in on the job? Still, the questions would have to wait; he needed to concentrate on their escape…his mates were counting on him.

Tearing through the dark streets, Mickey's eyes flicked back to his mirror. The chasing pack were now miles behind, if only he could get rid of the chopper. Appearing to circle ever lower, its brilliant light continued to flood through his windscreen, blinding him with every revolution.

Only half a mile to go; he just had to keep focused, they'd soon be home and dry.

The empty road was dead straight ahead, with green lights shining brightly in the distance. He briefly glanced down at the speedo; 110 and climbing. There was no need to slow, he'd just bury the throttle, and feel the horses kick in. Eating up the tarmac, his turbocharged Audi raced towards the intersection, and then suddenly he spotted it…

Right at the edge of his peripheral vision, there was movement; rapid movement!

In an instant he reacted. Lifting his foot off the gas, his head spun to face the danger. Blazing headlights on a collision course charged towards him. What the fuck were they doing; *their* lights were on red!

Ignoring the screams rising from his friend's mouths, he yanked on the wheel, and plunged his brake pedal down. Instantly, the Audi's bonnet nose-dived towards the tarmac; its stability systems struggling to remain in control.

But the black blur was almost upon him.

Almost in slow-motion, it began to cross his path; its alloys disappearing beneath his dipping bonnet, its four terrified occupants twisting in their seats towards him.

Clinging onto his steering wheel, he braced himself for impact…

38

But nothing happened.

Somehow the black bullet flew past.

For Mickey though, his problems had only just started. Although his steering jerk had managed to deliver a crucial change in path, it had also sent his big saloon hurtling towards the kerb. In an instant, he threw the steering back in the opposite direction, but like a pendulum, the vehicle's tail whipped round...now he too was merely a passenger.

Striking the kerb at ninety-degrees, the two nearside wheels sheared off; barely slowing his car's passage across the pavement. Hands still in opposite lock, Mickey stared wide-eyed over his shoulder; they were heading straight for a solid oak tree...and there was nothing he could do to stop it.

As his Audi slid onto grass towards certain destruction, self-preservation took over. Releasing the steering, he drew his legs upwards, and curled his arms over his head.

The collision was devastating, the old oak shuddering as his Audi disintegrated on impact. The exploding debris initially shrouded the car from view, but as the smoke slowly dispersed, the sheer extent of its destruction was revealed.

Wrapped around the tree's thick trunk, the wreckage was barely recognisable; its flowing lines now twisted and deformed.

And inside the Audi's remains...nothing. No sounds, no movement; nothing.

But eventually, little by little, Mickey's eyelids started to lift; his eyes straining to focus on the carnage.

Through the missing windscreen, a blue haze in the smoke.

In front of him a crumpled dashboard, a spent airbag sagging from the wheel.

Nothing made sense. Was he dreaming – trapped in a nightmare?

Gradually, other senses began to return. Pungent fumes filled his nose, wailing sirens pierced his ears, and the throbbing pain...was everywhere.

And then, from deep within, a memory rose to the surface...Danny!

Slowly, carefully, he rolled his head to the left; his vision struggling to focus on the harrowing sight. Seat crushed to almost nothing, his life-long friend was almost on top of him; his chin resting limply on chest.

Eyes widening, Mickey's pain raced to the surface. "Danny! Danny! Danny!" he screamed.

But Danny couldn't hear his calls...Danny's short life was over.

***

Out of sight, but constantly racing to keep in touch, the furry-exocet had been desperately following the chopper's directions, when the emergency message was passed.

"All units, all units, make the junction of Meadway at Mackadown Lane; the Audi's had a major RTC," the anxious navigator broadcast. "Control, we need fire and ambo asap!"

"Bollocks!" Gaz yelled out. "What the fuck have they done?"

Draycott made no reply, his foot still planted on the gas. Rounding the next kink in the road, all became suddenly clear. Despite the quarter mile straight to the lights, there was no mistaking the scene of destruction; a cloud of dirt was settling...wisps of smoke rising.

Sliding to a halt alongside the carnage, the smoke's source was obvious; its tendrils rising from beneath what remained of the bonnet.

"Fuck me, they're gonna fry!" Gaz exclaimed.

"Come on, we've gotta put it out!" Draycott shouted, flinging his door open. "You get the extinguisher, I'll grab the crowbar."

Ignoring Quincy's frantic baying, they grabbed their tools and sprinted to the wreckage.

First to the car, Draycott immediately set to work; prizing away at the mangled bonnet. "Hurry up Gaz, they're a right mess in there," he yelled. "We might already be too late, but we've got to give the poor buggers a chance!"

A fiery blast sent him swiftly jumping backwards.

"Careful mate," Gaz hollered, shielding his eyes from the flames. "This thing's about to blow!"

"If it does, those lads are history. Try the doors, see if you can drag 'em out."

The obvious door was the driver's; the others twisted beyond recognition. Gaz grabbed the handle and yanked...but it was jammed solid, and reaching in through the smashed window, the inner one gave the same result.

Inside the wreckage, two youths were sat upright in the front; their motionless bodies held in place by their belts. Heads a matter of inches apart, they faced each other, as if arranged in death by an outside hand.

And then...a groan.

But which one?

Gaz quickly clambered in through the window. The driver was alive...breathing...just.

"This one's still with us!" he shouted to Draycott. "And I think there's one in the back. I'm gonna try and get through to him."

"Get 'em out, as quick as you can! This thing's stuck," Draycott called back, continuing to wrench away at the bonnet. "I can't budge it!"

"Mate, I've got no chance! The driver's wedged between his seat and the wheel; his legs are going nowhere!"

While Draycott continued to struggle at the front, Gaz crawled further in. Sure enough, crushed into the rear footwell, a third youth was barely conscious; his occasional groans the only clue to his position.

But by now the heat was building quickly. The only barrier between engine bay and occupants had been breached; the first flames now licking through the holes in the bulkhead.

Ducking down, Gaz grabbed at the handle beneath the driver's seat. But no matter how hard he pulled, it wouldn't budge. In a final act of desperation, he hauled on the driver's body, but apart from a barely audible gurgle, there was no reaction. The body was jammed, the heat overpowering – he had to get out, and quick.

To the front, Draycott shielded his eyes, desperately diving in and out, as time and again he was forced back by the heat. Finally, the bonnet gave way; sending flames flaring up as fresh oxygen fed the blaze.

Grabbing the extinguisher, Draycott aimed its nozzle at the inferno. Blast after blast engulfed the flames…but it made little impression. The fire had taken hold; there was nothing more he could do to stop it.

Throwing the spent extinguisher on the floor, he rushed to the driver's door, just as the next units arrived.

By now Gaz was struggling; the heat and smoke rapidly sapping his strength.

"Grab my arm," Draycott shouted, reaching in through the window.

Gratefully, Gaz grasped his colleague's forearm; their combined force just about pulling him clear.

"Jesus that was close," Gaz panted, practically collapsing onto the grass. "Get the lads over here, they've got to get that fucking fire out!"

Rushing with extinguishers to help, their colleagues quickly took over; emptying canister after canister until finally the flames were under control. Soon joined by firefighters and medics, the rescue operation passed to the experts; the cops more than happy to take a back seat at last.

***

In and out of consciousness, Mickey's mind flashed from one nightmare to another:

A fire crackling, his flesh burning. Was this really hell? He deserved it after all…didn't he?

Calm voices in his ear, a jab in his leg; peace flowing through his veins.

Strong hands lifting him clear, laying him down, taking him away.

Inside an ambo, strapped to a stretcher, a cop's arms pinning him down.

White hospital sheets, machines round his bed, doctors by his side.

A horrifying image looming larger and larger; an image he couldn't free from his mind. Staring at the blood-covered face, his mouth began to form the word 'Danny' over and over again.

His voice gaining in volume, the medical team's discussion swiftly broke off.

"Quickly sister, increase the sedation before he comes to!" the consultant ordered.

But Mickey's eyes were already wide open; darting wildly from side-to-side. Muscles tensing, veins bulging, he suddenly sat upright, screaming, "Danny! Danny! Danny!"

"Now Sister! Before he arrests!"

His dose dialled up to the max, drugs rushed into his rigid body, but couldn't reach their target in time.

With his senses shutting down once more, only the medics could hear the high-pitched monotone alarm to his side. Even as they scrambled to attach defib paddles to his bare chest, Mickey's tunnel of light was slowly constricting. For a moment though, it paused, settling on childhood memories with Danny, and then...

And then the light went out.

39

The following day, with the door firmly closed behind, Gladstone addressed his troops.

"Yesterday's events are without doubt a tragic loss of life. We may be on different sides, but I'm sure you'll all agree, we are united in our sympathy for the deceased's family. Personally speaking, I'm devastated. And I'm not too proud to admit that I've spent the last twenty-four hours questioning my own decisions," he said solemnly.

"But the conclusion I've reached is categorical. Nobody in this room is responsible for the collision," he stated. "In fact, it is only due to *your* bravery that the loss of life wasn't greater. No, the blame lies entirely with the two drivers involved. We cannot and will not accept responsibility for their dangerous driving. Our city streets are not the backdrop to 'Grand Theft Auto'; when collisions occur, real people get hurt!"

Pacing round the room, Gladstone continued uninterrupted.

"For the past twenty-four hours, I've had to fend off an angry Chief Superintendent. He's had his ass chewed off by the Chief Constable, and he's demanding I close down our department. For the moment, I've pacified him with the promise of big results, but believe me, he's in no mood to be patient!"

The angry Inspector abruptly came to a stop. "Let me be quite clear about this – it's not *us* who have blood on our hands; it's the despicable men who send these lads out to do their dirty work. And the one thing these tragic events *have* achieved, is to strengthen our resolve…we're *never* going to rest until we bring them to justice!"

***

But for the medical team's rapid intervention, Mickey would have remained asleep forever. Three times they 'shocked' his battered body, three times it fell limply to the mattress. Finally, on the fourth attempt, his heart responded weakly; its faint pulse enough for the staff to work with. The days that followed were touch and go; his vital organs maintained by machines, kept alive for his or another's use.

Harrowing nightmares filled his unnatural coma, the drugs deepening the macabre images in his mind. Occasional flirts with consciousness were swiftly dealt with by the nurses; his heart too weak to cope with the real world. But as the days passed by, one by one, the medical machines withdrew their help; his body slowly coming to terms with its return to normality.

His strength gradually returning, the sedation steadily dwindled, until finally, his eyelids lifted open.

"It's okay Mickey," a voice said softly at his side. "You're safe, you're gonna be just fine."

Where am I, he thought, rolling his head towards the voice.

Brightness struck his retinas, his eyes squinting until the room gradually came into focus.

"You're in Heartlands Hospital," the nurse's voice continued. "You're a proper fighter Mickey, now just relax; you need to conserve your strength."

Confusion flowed through his mind. Why was he in hospital? How long had he been there? Where was Danny? An icy fear took hold. Something was wrong; what had happened to his friend? Desperately, he strived to remember: green lights, a black flash…heading towards a tree.

Mustering the strength to open his mouth, he croaked out the one word that mattered.

"Danny?!"

"All in good time, Mickey," the nurse smiled back, as his eyelids closed again. "You'll need to be a lot stronger before we go there."

***

Despite the days that had passed, J.T. was still on the warpath. While the Power Firm remained rooted to their seats, he paced around his lounge, his veins struggling to contain his charging blood.

"Wait 'til I get my hands on the little shit; he's gonna wish he'd joined his mate on the slab!" he ranted. "Out of all the jobs to fuck up on…he chooses this one! Nearly half a million fucking pounds he's cost me. I should have known he'd let me down; his dad always did – it runs in the fucking family!"

Still shaking with rage, J.T. stopped to refill his glass.

Taking the pause as an opportunity, Porter vainly attempted to offer a glimmer of hope. "Okay, we may have lost Mickey's share, but at least Deano returned with his bag-full. Those watches alone are worth some serious cash."

"I've already been through this with Johnny. With the dough we've paid out to the insiders, they'll only just cover our costs. And anyway, that's not the point; this was supposed to be our biggest earner ever! Not only have I lost a small fortune, I've also lost another three workers, and to cap it all, old Gladstone's gonna be gloating like he's won the fucking lottery. Jonas had better get Mickey some bail, 'cos when he gets out, I'm gonna rip his fucking head off!"

"Leave him to me Boss," Razor shouted, jumping to his feet. "I'll sort the little bastard out!"

"Don't worry my friend, we'll all get a piece of him; I'm gonna make damn sure of that," J.T. replied. "But first, I need to tear a strip off their leader.

Chapman, arrange for a meet up with Deano this afternoon; his boys owe me some payback."

"Will do, he's expecting the call."

"Good, so he should be. I'll speak to Jonas myself; he needs to know *his* neck's on the line if Mickey doesn't get bail. In the meantime, we need to sort that bloody helicopter out. Johnny, you can join me this afternoon; it's time for Deano to shoot the fucking moon! Gladstone's about to see who's *really* in charge around here!"

***

Sat on the drive-thru's car park, Deano glanced nervously at his watch. Five o' clock Chapman had ordered; they were already fifteen minutes late. However, there was nothing he could do but sit and wait; he was in deep enough shit as it was. Half an hour later, J.T.'s black BMW finally rolled through the entrance, and ignoring Deano's frantic headlight flashes, drove to the opposite corner instead.

Straightaway, Deano jumped out and hurried over to his boss. Seeing Johnny in the front passenger seat, he waited at the door, until eventually the tinted window descended.

J.T.'s big head leant across. "Get in!" he ordered.

Deano did exactly as he was told; the motor moving off the moment his arse touched the seat.

"Johnny's gonna do the talking," J.T. continued, picking his way off the car park. "'Cos if I do, I'm likely to lose my temper, and I don't want to lose another of my workers, now do I!"

"No, boss."

"Right answer. Now listen carefully to what my brother has to tell you."

Adjusting his position on the soft leather, Deano leant forward.

"As you may have gathered, we're not very happy with what happened the other night. You and your team have lost us a great deal of money. This is not acceptable; we need to redress the losses."

"I'm really sorry," Deano replied quietly. "You're right, we messed up."

"Fucking right you did!" J.T. snapped back.

"As I said," Johnny continued unfazed. "It is down to you to redress the losses. You will begin by doubling the car supply."

Taking in a deep breath, Deano sat back in his seat.

"Look, I respect what you're saying, and we'll definitely do our best," he stammered. "But we're really up against it at the moment. We've lost three of our best lads, and their replacements have only just started their training. We'll do our damndest, we'll work flat out, but with three less…it just might not be possible."

Suddenly, J.T. stood on his brakes, the car screeching to a halt. Flicking his seatbelt off with one hand, he turned and grasped Deano's throat with the other.

"Don't you dare tell me it's not fucking possible," he bellowed, tightening his grip. "You *will* deliver what I order, or I'll break every bone in your fucking body – got it?"

Eyes bulging, unable to speak, Deano could only nod his reply.

"Good," J.T. glared, slowly releasing the pressure. "I'm glad we understand each other, 'cos we've got another little job for you to do, and this one had better go to plan!"

By now, the irate driver behind had had enough. Blasting his horn, he gestured out of his window.

J.T. flicked his eyes to the mirror, just in time to clock the two fingered salute.

"Judgement Time for dickhead!" he snarled, leaping from his seat.

Five strides later and he was at the driver's door. Throwing it open, he unleashed his fury; punch after punch hammering home.

Leaving his victim spark out in his seat, J.T. returned to his car. "Now don't wind me up any more," he barked, pulling away sharply. "Or *you'll* be getting the same!"

Nobody, least of all Deano, said a word; the drive continuing in stony silence.

Avoiding J.T.'s occasional scowls in the mirror, Deano pressed himself up against his door, until eventually, Johnny re-started the conversation.

"Chapman will contact you shortly; he has a list of cars to acquire. In the meantime, you'll crack on with the job my brother mentioned earlier; it should prove mutually beneficial. We understand that our old friend Inspector Gladstone has been behind our recent difficulties, so it's time to give him a taste of his own medicine – it's time to 'shoot the moon'."

"No problems," Deano answered quickly. "We'll do whatever you want us to do."

"Good," said J.T., turning to look over his shoulder. "That's the smartest thing you've said today."

***

His eyes slowly opening, Mickey began to take in his surroundings. Monitoring equipment beeped constantly in the background, while to his side, a drip hung loosely on a frame; its tube feeding into his forearm. With no staff in sight, the only other person awake was sat up in the bed opposite.

"Excuse me mate," he croaked. "Where are we?"

Lowering his paper, the middle-aged man looked over his glasses.

"Heartlands Hospital. You're in the high dependency ward. How are you feeling?"

"A bit groggy to be honest. Do you know how long I've been here?" Mickey asked, slowly hauling himself to an upright position.

"Best part of a week mate. You've been out for the count for most of it."

Mickey rubbed his eyes, his thoughts quickly returning to the accident.

"Did anyone else come in at the same time?" he asked anxiously. "A couple of lads my age?"

"I really don't know mate, you'll have to ask the nurses. Just press the red button hanging on the side of your bed; somebody'll soon come out to see you."

Turning to his side, Mickey located the lead and pressed. Within seconds, a smartly dressed sister scurried in.

"Mr Wilding, I see you've come round at last. And you've obviously worked out what the button is for; you press it, and we come running. It is however, for emergencies only; we're not here to wait upon your every whim. Do I make myself clear?" she asked bluntly.

"Er, yeah, I understand," he replied hoarsely.

"Good, now how can I help you?"

"My friends...there were two others in the car when I...when I had the accident. I've gotta know, can you tell me...are they okay?"

"I'm sorry; I'm really not in a position to give you that information. But I will make some enquires for you. Now are you in any pain or discomfort?"

"I'm, I'm okay," he winced, adjusting his position. "I just need to know how my friends are."

"Listen, it's no good worrying about anybody else for the moment," she said frankly, turning to go. "We need to make sure that *you* get better first."

Mickey groaned with disappointment. All he could think about was the blood covered face of his friend. Hour after hour, he lay in despair; every doctor and every nurse giving the same non-committal response. Finally, at three in the afternoon, two uniformed officers walked into the ward, and marched straight to the side of his bed. Without a word, they pulled the curtains round, and removing their caps, sat down.

"Mickey, I'm Inspector Gladstone and this is PC Draycott. We're the officers investigating Monday morning's events. We're not here to interview you, we're just here to introduce ourselves and answer any questions you might have."

Heart pounding, he asked the question.

"I really don't care what happens to me, you can throw away the key if you like. I just need to know; tell me...please...did my mate Danny pull through?"

"It's not good news I'm afraid," Gladstone responded solemnly.

"What do you mean 'it's not good news'? He's got to be okay, he's got to be!" Mickey replied, his voice breaking with emotion.

His head bowing slowly downwards, Gladstone passed the words Mickey had been dreading all day. "I regret to inform you, that despite the medics' best efforts, they couldn't save him. I'm sorry Mickey, Danny is dead."

Mickey stayed perfectly still, his body unable to move. Danny couldn't possibly be dead; this was his childhood friend, the one person who'd always been there for him…they *must* be mistaken, they just must! His stare unwavering, it remained firmly fixed on the Inspector.

Gradually, as he lifted his head, Gladstone's eyes met Mickey's gaze. "We're really sorry, we understand how difficult this must be for you."

In that very moment, Mickey felt his world collapse. Turning to bury his face deep in the pillow, an emotional wave thundered through his fragile mind. Memories flooded in; their lives, their laughs, their loves. How could it all be over; how could there be life after this? Why couldn't *he* have died instead – after all, the collision was all his fault…wasn't it? Danny and Eccy had trusted him with their lives, and he'd failed them.

Eccy…shit… Eccy?!

Quickly lifting his head, he wiped his eyes on his arm.

"What about Eccy? Don't tell me he's dead as well?"

"No," Gladstone said, shaking his head. "He's broken his leg quite badly, and his body's as battered as yours. But he'll recover, he'll be just fine. He's currently on the next ward along; I'm sure they'll allow you to see him shortly."

The officer's final words passed over him; his mind returning to Danny, to guilt, to shame. As his voice screamed out, and his body became rigid, staff rushed swiftly to his side; dialling in the sedatives…returning him once more to the mercy of his nightmares.

***

"So what do you think?" Gladstone asked as they walked off the ward.

"It's not often I say this, but you've gotta feel for the kid," Draycott replied.

"What do you mean?"

"Well, in my experience, all they normally care about is themselves. But Mickey's different; that reaction was genuine. He really *was* more concerned about his mates than himself."

"He's got some tough times ahead then; we'll probably be the least of his worries," Gladstone mused. "However, in time…he could be exactly what we've been looking for."

40

As Mickey's injuries began to heal, two uniformed officers were posted to the ward's exit; a situation he was more than happy to live with. There was no way he could face seeing the posse just yet, and what on earth was he going to say to Lara? He'd managed to persuade his mum to tell her he was 'away on business', but he'd have to face her at some point. And worse still, what about Katie? She didn't even have a clue that her boyfriend was dead!

The guilt felt too much to bear, but still his memory couldn't, or wouldn't, clear the haze. What exactly *had* happened? How had he lost control? Was there anybody else involved? He desperately needed answers – he had to face the truth, no matter how painful it might be.

Lowering himself into the wheelchair at his bedside, he pushed the wheels forward, and taking in a deep breath, carefully edged round the ward.

The officer standing guard wasn't impressed. "Where do you think you're going?" he demanded.

"Please...I know what you must think about me, but I've just got to see my mate. I promise I'll only be a few minutes, please let me through...please!"

The officer looked down at his distraught face...and took pity.

"Alright son," he nodded, taking hold of the handles. "I guess it won't do any harm," and pushing Mickey through to the next ward, brought him to rest next to his sleeping friend.

Remaining at Eccy's bedside, Mickey watched, and patiently waited. Time and again he winced as he looked at his mate's injuries: the leg lying rigid inside a metal frame, the jagged gash stitched up on his forehead.

It was only as the afternoon drew to a close, that his friend began to awake.

Tears rolling from his eyes, Mickey whispered just loud enough for him to hear. "Eccy...it's Mickey."

His head slowly turning towards the voice, his mate's eyelids began to open.

"I really fucked up," Mickey sobbed. "I'm so sorry."

"What are you on about?" Eccy replied, his eyes opening a little wider.

"Danny's dead," Mickey said, burying his face in his hands. "I killed Danny, and I nearly killed you."

Bent over in the wheelchair, his whole body shook, the distress proving too much to bear.

"Heh? Mate, you've got it all wrong," Eccy replied slowly. "You didn't kill Danny – you saved my life. What the fuck do you think happened?"

Gradually, Mickey raised his head, his reddened eyes still streaming with tears.

"I don't know...most of it's a blur," he stuttered. "There's only bits I remember: the raid in Leicester, traffic cops at a roundabout, splitting up to head home. But then it all gets a bit hazy. All I can see are bright lights dancing in front of me, a green light in the distance, and then nothing...nothing until...until...Danny."

As the disturbing image took over, Mickey's eyes dropped to the floor once more.

"You can't remember why we crashed?!" Eccy asked in amazement, adjusting his position to directly face his friend.

"No – I just know I must've fucked up."

"Like I said, *you're* not to blame. You didn't fuck up; it was that wanker Tommy!" Eccy said angrily.

"What are you talking about? We split up, raced off in different directions; we didn't see Tommy again."

"Oh yes we fucking did! Mate, I'll never forget what happened; it's etched on my mind forever!"

"Really?" Mickey replied doubtfully, pushing his chair closer to the bed. "So what exactly *did* happen?"

"Well for a start, you're bang on about the bright light. After we split up, the helicopter was practically on top of us. Before long, we were racing along the Meadway, approaching Mackadown Lane on green; and again you're right, they were definitely green, 'cos I was watching from between the seats. Just as we reached the junction, that wanker came out of nowhere; he tried to blast through on red! Somehow, you threw the car sideways, and we missed him by a whisker. From then on...you had no chance."

Looking up, Mickey's eyes locked onto his mate's.

"Listen," Eccy continued, meeting his gaze. "If it wasn't for your reactions, we'd have smashed into Tommy, and every single one of us would be dead!"

A frown broke out across Mickey's forehead; the words triggering a faint memory...the flash of black, four faces frozen in fear.

A rage started to build.

"I'm gonna fucking kill him," he seethed. "If it's the last thing I do; I'm gonna fucking kill him."

***

With his intensive treatment over, it was soon time for Mickey to swap his medical bed for a police one. Having said his goodbyes to Eccy, he felt strangely relieved to be led away in handcuffs; for the sake of his sanity, he needed to face up to his problems.

Inside the squad car, Mickey sat back and watched Draycott pick his way through the rush hour traffic. Was it really only a year ago that he'd arrested him after the Golf chase? So much had happened since then; so many exciting adventures. But what had been the point; what had it all led to? If only he could turn back the clock, he'd swap it all in a heartbeat, just to have Danny back beside him.

Having battled through the gridlock, roller shutters clattered behind them as they entered the rear compound. Mickey shuffled off his seat, inhaled the fresh air for one final time…and walked in to face his fate.

The custody block's hustle and bustle was in stark contrast with the hospital's relative peace. Having queued for an eternity to get booked in, the formalities were eventually completed, and Draycott led him away to a cell.

"Want one?" the officer offered, pulling a pack of twenty from his pocket.

"Err…yeah," Mickey replied, gratefully accepting the offer. "Thanks."

"Listen, we're not here to crucify you; we know you're going through hell," Draycott said offering a lighter's flame. "Yes, we need to deal with what's happened, but we're also here to offer you support."

Mickey leant forward and cupped his hands around the flame.

"So is there anything we can help you with; anything you need?"

"You mean, you scratch my back and I'll scratch yours," Mickey chuckled. "Sorry, I'm really not into grassing."

"I'm not suggesting you are Mickey. I'm just saying that there's probably stuff we can help you with at the moment, that's all. Look, have a think about it, I'm not going to hassle you," the officer said, turning to leave. "But you know where I am if you need me."

Alone, hunched over on his wooden bench, Mickey inhaled deep drag after deep drag. Help? Damn right he needed help, but where on earth should he start? According to his mum, Lara and Katie still didn't have a clue what'd happened; so how the hell was he going to tell them? Then there was Tommy – if he'd told the posse a pack of lies, were they all getting ready to lynch him? And on top of everything, his mate's funeral was next week; no matter how much it hurt, he had to be there…he just had to. For all those reasons and more, he desperately needed to get out, but how? There was no way the cops'd give him bail, and there was no way he'd grass to get his freedom.

Pulling the foul smelling blanket over his shivering body, he closed his eyes and curled into a ball; a disturbed night's sleep lay ahead.

***

Thanks to Mickey's stay in hospital, the CATS team's preparations had been meticulous. Frame by frame, they'd studied mountains of footage; from the stashed Audi's collection, to the raid at Rackhams, to the final moments on heli-telly. The evidence was overwhelming, their disclosure folders crammed full with statements and reports…all awaiting Jonas's impending arrival.

"Mickey's had all night to stew on things. Do you think he's ready to talk?" Gladstone asked.

"Somehow, I doubt it," Hanson replied. "I reckon the phrase 'thick as thieves' was based on this group. Once Jonas gets hold of them, they never tell us a thing!"

"You're probably right, but as I've said before, Mickey's a little different," Draycott spoke up. "And don't forget, right now he's vulnerable; very vulnerable. While he's grieving, we just might find a way in."

"Let's hope so, 'cos although Mickey and Eccy are banged to rights, we've got nothing more than circumstantial evidence on the others," Gladstone frowned. "And if we haven't got enough to take Mickey's little team down, we sure as hell haven't got enough to take out the real bosses! Something needs to change, and right now…Mickey's our only hope."

41

Jonas's consultation lasted well over two hours. Statement by statement, he led Mickey through the evidence; every account dissected, every response agreed.

"They won't disclose footage from their various cameras yet, so make sure you say nothing when they do," the solicitor instructed. "We both know they've got enough to charge you already; all we can do is minimise your role, so don't go shouting your mouth off, okay?"

"Look, I really don't care what they charge me with," Mickey replied. "I've just *got* to get bail; there's things I need to sort on the outside before they send me down – I owe it to Danny."

"Bail?" Jonas laughed. "I'd be careful what you wish for."

"What do you mean?"

"My instructions are very clear young man. Of course I'm here to represent you, but my main concern is to *ensure* you get bail. J.T. wishes to speak to you personally, and he won't get the opportunity if you're locked away for the next five years, now will he?"

"Heh? What does he want to speak to me about?"

"You are either very stupid or extremely naïve. He has lost nearly half-a-million-pounds worth of watches, and unsurprisingly…he's none too pleased. Personally, I'd be more worried about what *he's* got planned for you, than what the police have. In fact, if I was you I'd be praying I *didn't* get bail," Jonas snapped.

Mickey's anger rose straight to the surface.

"Well guess what – you're not me! Do you think I give a shit about the bloody watches? I want bail so I can get to Danny's funeral, to sort things out with the people who loved him, and to tell my mates the truth!"

"I may be here for your legal advice, but let me give you a reality check. If you do get out, I wouldn't go shouting your mouth off to J.T., or I can guarantee we'll be attending *your* funeral as well. Now let's get back to the matter in hand. Our interests are aligned; we both want bail. The only way to get it, is to minimise your involvement. Oh, and make sure you only implicate the other two in your car; you don't know anybody else involved, understood!"

Daring not to speak for fear his rage might boil over, Mickey merely nodded his head. Staring at Jonas's wizened features, he wondered what his motives really were. Whose interests was he serving? Was he telling the truth about J.T., or merely putting the frighteners on him? The questions just added to the confusion in his mind. He needed someone to turn to, someone to confide in; but the only person he really trusted was gone, and would never be there for him again.

The interview room seemed much smaller than he remembered. A large screen covered one wall, while two pairs of chairs faced each other across a table covered in papers. Using a remote, Inspector Gladstone brought the screen to life, while Draycott read out the legal introductions.

"Mickey, I'd like you to explain your movements during the early hours of Monday the seventh please?" the officer began.

Jonas butted in before Mickey had chance to reply. "I have advised my client to make no comment until he has seen the content of your video recordings."

"Our pleasure," Gladstone smiled.

With a click, a familiar scene filled the screen...garage number 28.

Mickey gasped. Their operation had been doomed from the start! Wide-eyed, he watched as Danny came into view, opened the garage doors, and stood guard as he drove the car out.

Tears welled up, and as Danny jumped into the passenger seat, he couldn't bear to watch any longer.

"On behalf of my client, I'd like this interview suspended. He's in no fit state to continue!"

Ignoring Jonas, Draycott spoke directly to his client. "I know it's upsetting Mickey, but we really need to speak to you about this footage. We can stop for a while if you want, but it'll only delay things; we'll have to return to the same questions at some point."

Mickey wiped his eyes with his sleeve. "I'm okay," he said quietly. "Let's get it over and done with."

"Thank you. Now can you tell me, who were the lads at the garage?"

As agreed with Jonas, Mickey began to answer the officer's questions, only admitting what was impossible to deny. Yes, he, Danny and Eccy had taken the car from the garage, and yes he knew they were off to do a burglary in Leicester. But how the car came to be in the garage, and who else was involved in the job; he simply didn't have a clue. All instructions had been received by mobile phone, but unfortunately, he'd thrown the pay-as-you-go sim into the scenery on the way to the job.

Moving on, the officers turned to the burglary itself. External footage showed the posse arriving, thrusting the shutters up, and shattering the glass with a sledgehammer. Instantly, as the raiders rushed in, the view changed to inside the ground floor.

The picture quality was excellent. Mickey could see the fear etched in the guards' faces as they confronted the masked thieves, but then...what the hell were they doing? Dumbstruck, he watched Tommy's boys lay into the guards.

Even above the alarm, the audio picked out the old men's screams. Blood curdling blows continued to rain down on their helpless bodies, until Rushy and Dougie charged down to intervene. Draycott paused the recording.

"I'm sure you'll agree, the sickening attack we've just witnessed was completely unprovoked," he said sternly.

"I object," Jonas interrupted. "The coverage clearly shows that my client did not enter the building; he was stood *outside* throughout the attack. He is therefore in no position to answer any questions relating to what happened *inside!*"

"I do have a tongue in my mouth; I can speak for myself you know," Mickey responded angrily, glancing at his brief. "Listen, the two who did that are a fucking disgrace; those security guys were just doing their job. I had no idea there'd been trouble inside; it's the first I've heard of it."

Turning from the screen, he looked Gladstone in the eye. "Can you tell me, are the guards okay?"

"Well…one suffered a fractured skull, while the other chap's got two broken arms for his trouble. I wouldn't say they're okay, but they'll live," the Inspector informed him. "But I'm sure that if you really *are* appalled by your mate's actions, you'll be more than happy to pass me their details – won't you?"

Letting out a deep sigh, Mickey sat back in his chair.

"They're no mates of mine, but you know I can't do that," he said shaking his head. "They're bang out of order, but I can't grass; it's more than my life's worth."

"Why, who are you scared of Mickey. Who's pulling your strings?" the Inspector probed.

Mickey looked across to Jonas, who fired a 'don't-even-think-about-it' scowl back.

"No-one," he replied through gritted teeth. "I just work for myself."

"But if that is the case, why is it 'more than your life's worth'? Tell me Mickey, who *are* you really scared of – who?"

"Mr Gladstone," Jonas interrupted again. "Can I remind you that we've just witnessed two thugs commit an act of horrific violence. I would think it's quite obvious who my client is scared of…isn't that right Mickey?"

"Yes," Mickey hissed back.

With Gladstone and Jonas continuing to lock horns, the hours passed slowly by; question, objection, question, objection – neither side gaining an advantage, neither side giving an inch. But eventually, even they needed a break.

Relieved to be out of the stuffy room, Mickey took a stroll into the exercise yard; hot chocolate and cigarette in hand. However, following close behind, Jonas wasn't in the mood for relaxing.

"What the hell do you think you were doing in there?"

"What do you mean? It's supposed to be *my* interview isn't it?" Mickey replied irritably.

"It may be your interview, but you're not the one paying for my services, remember? I'm here to make sure you don't drop yourself or anyone else in the shit, and right now you're not making my job very easy!"

"Yeah, you've made it quite clear you don't give a fuck about me. All you're interested in is protecting our bosses."

"Don't be so bloody ungrateful!" Jonas spat back. "Just make sure you do as I say, or you'll regret it!"

Turning away from his brief, Mickey was furious. Wasn't Jonas supposed to be there to help him? He didn't seem to care about anyone but J.T. What about the poor security guys, what about Eccy...what about Danny! Downing the remains of his hot drink, he flicked the fag end away, and turned, ready to face his demons. Next up was coverage from the helicopter, and the end to his disastrous pursuit.

Back inside the interview room, he soon realised just how hopeless their escape had been. The chopper had been following them for miles; no wonder the traffic cops had been ready and waiting. The room now in complete silence, his eyes remained fixed on the screen as the critical moments approached.

"Subject vehicle approaching junction with Mackadown Lane at speed. Lights are currently green in his favour," a voice broadcast above the sound of rotor blades. "Control, be advised, there's a black vehicle approaching from the right. They appear to be on a collision course."

Mesmerised, the world around Mickey disappeared; his focus solely on the calamitous events unfolding before him.

"Neither vehicle appears to be slowing...if they don't back off now, they're going to...shit!"

Abruptly, the commentary cut off just as Mickey's RS4 slew sideways, missing the BMW's rear by a whisker. Tommy's motor disappeared in a streak off the screen, leaving the Audi momentarily fighting to regain control, before mounting the offside pavement and...

"I don't think we need to see any more," Draycott said solemnly, freezing the picture just prior to impact. "However, I *would* like to ask you for your thoughts?"

Mickey swallowed hard, struggling to retain his composure.

"Look, I admit I was doing well in excess of the speed limits; I just wanted to get back to my manor. But, you have to believe me, I would never put my mates' lives at risk. You saw for yourself, my lights were on green; there was nothing I could do."

Draycott nodded his head, a movement echoed by his Inspector.

"We do believe you Mickey. However, the person driving the BMW was happy to take risks, wasn't he?"

"I object. My client is here to answer questions about his own actions, not those of others," Jonas barked.

"You're right," Mickey replied. "He didn't give a shit. *He's* the one who killed Danny."

"So tell us Mickey, who was driving it?"

Jonas could stand no more, slamming his folder onto the table.

"My client has already made things quite clear. Apart from those already identified, he doesn't know any other person involved, and even if he did, he'd be unable to assist you due to fearing for his own safety…and quite rightly too!"

"Mickey, I'll ask you again. Can you tell us who was driving the BMW?"

"I'm sorry. I'd really like to, but I can't…I just can't," Mickey muttered, his head slowly wilting downwards.

As far as Mickey was concerned, the interview was over; he'd seen all he needed to see, and said all he needed to say. Paying no attention to the arguments around him, his mind replayed the final moments time and time again. Eccy was right; there *was* only one person to blame. Right now, he had no idea how, but one thing was for certain…he wasn't going to let Tommy get away with it.

With nothing more to be gleaned, the officers wrapped up the interview and returned to the custody desk. While Jonas scuttled off to complete his papers in a separate room, Mickey gladly went for another leg stretch in the exercise yard.

"You don't seem too happy with your brief," Draycott said, joining him outside.

"He's a prick. He doesn't give a shit about me," Mickey replied accepting another cigarette.

"Yeah, you're probably right, but you know what, he's no different to the rest. All they're really bothered about is making a stack of cash."

"Yep, I'm beginning to see it's all about the money," Mickey nodded. "I guess it's the same for you guys!"

"On our wages? You must be joking," Draycott laughed back.

"So what do you do it for then…the sociable hours?"

"Yeah, you've got us sussed. We work every hour God sends, get physically and verbally abused, and still everybody hates us!" the officer smiled. "Yep, it's a wonderful job; fancy swapping places?!"

His eyebrows raised in reply, Mickey took in a deep drag. "So seriously, what do you do it for?"

"Well you know what, we're actually not that different to you boys. In fact, there's a few officers here who'd be doing exactly the same as you if they weren't doing our job."

"What do you mean?"

"It's quite simple really. Think of the buzz *you* get on a job; how the adrenaline shoots through your veins when you're chased, and the highs you feel when you get away. Am I right?"

"Yeah, of course, but I don't see how that's the same as your job."

"At any time on any day, we can suddenly get that excitement; that kick, that thrill of the chase. And like you boys, we work as a team. Can you imagine how we felt when we took Hood and his pals down…they're gonna be off the streets for years!"

Unwittingly, Mickey's head nodded slightly, his mind mulling over Draycott's words. Maybe there were some similarities, but it didn't change the fact that it was the police who were his enemy…weren't they?"

"So you see Mickey, in many ways, we're actually quite alike. And you and I certainly share the same view about the events we just witnessed."

Mickey's brow furrowed. "What do you mean?"

"The attack inside the store – I believe you. You were just as pissed off as we were. Correct?"

"You're damn right. We'd agreed threats only; no violence."

"And the driver of the BMW? Again, I totally agree with you; *he's* the one to blame for Danny's death. But what I can't understand, is why you won't tell us who they are; I mean, you don't owe them anything do you?"

"I wish I could," Mickey replied honestly. "But they really would kill me; you have no idea what they're like."

"I don't get it Mickey. From what I can see, you don't seem to be scared of the lads in the Beemer, or even the thugs in the store."

"Scared of those dickheads? No fucking chance," he replied angrily. "It's them who should be scared of me!"

"So who then? I guess it's somebody higher?"

"You said it," Mickey replied, crushing his cigarette butt underfoot.

"Listen," the officer continued, offering a fresh fag. "I asked you last night if there was anything we could do for you. Did you think of anything?"

Taking the cigarette to his lips, Mickey weighed up his next move. He knew exactly what he wanted, but there was no chance…was there? And even if they did help him out, they'd be bound to want something in return. Still, it was worth finding out; what was the worst that could happen?

"Seriously…I'm desperate for bail," he said, looking Draycott in the eye. "I need to speak to Danny's girlfriend; she doesn't know what's happened yet. And

I've got to get to Danny's funeral, I've just got to. After that, you can throw away the key as far as I'm concerned."

Draycott took in a deep breath. "I won't lie to you, that's not going to be easy. If we *were* to wangle you bail, we'd certainly need some back scratching."

"Look, I've already told you I can't grass. Not only would I be a dead man walking, but I couldn't let the posse down; they're like my family."

"I hear what you're saying Mickey, but maybe there's some middle ground; a way that suits us both?"

A puzzled look spread across his face. "What's that then?"

"Well, it's obvious this wasn't your first job, you're far too professional for that."

Mickey slowly nodded his head; he knew exactly what the officer was hinting at. "You want me to give you some TIC's?"

"If you *were* willing to have some offences taken into consideration, we might just be able to strike a deal."

The decision was easy. He was bound to be given a long stretch for his part in the burglary; a few TIC's would make no difference whatsoever.

"Okay, you give me bail, I'll give you TIC's."

"I'll be honest with you, bail wouldn't be without its conditions. You'd have to sign on at the police station every day, and keep to a strict curfew which we'd be checking regularly."

"That's fine," Mickey replied, shrugging his shoulders. "I'll be going nowhere...absolutely nowhere."

***

Charged and bailed within the hour, Mickey shoved his property in a bag and walked free. Alone, he left the station and turned towards home.

From their office above, Gladstone and Draycott watched him hurry away.

"How did it go?" the gaffer asked.

"He's not ready to talk to us yet," Draycott answered. "But you were right; he's pissed off with some of his team, he's pissed off with his bosses, and now he's pissed off with old Jonas! How much more it'll take, I really don't know...I just hope he lives long enough to find out!"

42

"That was Jonas on the blower," J.T. said, chucking his mobile on the table. "He reckons Mickey was a cheeky little shit throughout, and damn lucky to get bail!"

Pacing past his brother, he stared out of the lounge window. "So the question is; what are we going to do with him?"

Johnny continued typing away, his shoulders shrugged in reply.

"One thing's for sure, I need to teach him a lesson. Nobody, and I mean nobody, fucks up like that and gets away with it! And then he has the nerve to get cocky with the solicitor *I'm* paying for!"

Marching back to his seat, he snatched his phone back up.

"What are you doing?" Johnny enquired, without raising his head.

"I'm gonna get rid of the problem!"

"Do you really think that's wise?"

"Of course it is. I'm down half a million pounds, and *still* he disrespects me in front of the law!" J.T. spat out, scrolling through to Razor's number. "He and his mates need to be taught a lesson."

"Whilst I'd agree he needs to be shown the error of his ways, it's actually in *all* our interests to keep him alive."

"How do you mean?"

Folding his laptop down, Johnny turned to face his brother.

"The bottom line is, he's still a valuable asset. He and Danny revolutionised how Deano's posse operate, and we're the ones who've benefited the most. Yeah, he fucked up on this job, but there'll be plenty more in the future. He's going to be under no illusion that he owes you...massively."

"I hear what you're saying, but he can't get away with it; my reputation's on the line."

"We also need to consider, that for the time being we're at least one worker down, with no suitable replacements on the horizon. To bring inexperienced boys in would be a massive risk, and let's face it, we don't need any more jobs messed up, now do we?"

Remaining on his feet, J.T. digested his brother's words before replying.

"Yeah, I guess you're right. Okay, for the time being I'll let him live, but rest assured...he's gonna wish I hadn't!"

***

Walking home, Mickey tried to collect his thoughts. It was obvious who he needed to speak to first; but how on earth was he going to explain everything to her? There was no way he could dress things up; the truth was, he was a thief, and Danny had died as a result – the sooner she knew the facts the better. But he'd have to return home before he could speak to her; his police scrubs stunk, and the cops had seized his phone. He just hoped his mother wasn't in; he had enough on his plate already.

Making as little noise as possible, he slipped into the hallway, and crept into his bedroom. Good, it was exactly as he'd left it; his spare mobile charged and ready to go. Dumping his dirty clothes on the floor, he threw on some clean ones, and slipping his mobile into a pocket, turned to leave.

But his visit hadn't gone unnoticed.

"Oh Mickey, what did I do wrong," his mother sobbed, wrapping her arms around him. "I've always tried to stop you going the same way as your father, but I failed you son, I failed you."

"Don't be silly mum, you've done nothing wrong," he whispered in her ear. "Everything's down to me, I'm the one who's messed up."

Tears smudged mascara as they rolled down his mother's face. He looked into her searching eyes, but this wasn't the time for explanations; he had darker demons to face right now. Pulling her close, he waited patiently for her shaking to slow.

"Mum, I've got to go," he sighed, softly kissing her head. "I need to see Lara, it's time she knew the truth."

"Okay son, I understand," she nodded, slowly releasing her grip. "But whatever happens...I'll be here for you when you get back."

Grabbing some cash on the way out, he headed off on his longest journey.

Memories were everywhere as he walked: the stinger on Broad Lane, the Mercedes on The Square, the jump on Alwold Road. And finally there was Woodlands Park; the den, the Fiesta, the race around the perimeter. It had all been so exciting, sharing adventure after adventure with his best mate...yet it all seemed so meaningless now.

Next to the den, he sat in the warm sunshine, scrolling through his menu to 'L'. Fingers trembling, he touched the screen and awaited her reply.

"Hello?"

Straightaway his stomach tightened.

"Hello, who is it?"

"Lara– it's me," he whispered, barely able to speak.

"Oh right, you've decided to ring me at last have you? I've been worried sick about you. Where the hell have you been?"

"Lara, we need to talk."

"Bloody right we do. Katie and I are well pissed off with you pair!"

His eyelids squeezing shut, he brought his hand up to cover his face.

"Mickey?" Lara asked, her tone changing as he struggled to talk. "Are you alright?"

"Yeah…yeah," he choked out. "I just need to see you…straight away."

"Err…okay. Where do you want to meet up?"

"Can you…can you get to the little park at the end of your road?"

Slowly and quietly, Lara made her reply. "You're not going to…dump me are you?"

Mickey swallowed hard, desperately holding back his emotion. "Lara, I love you more than you could ever imagine," he said, the tears flowing down his cheek. "I'll be there in fifteen minutes."

Wiping away the wetness, he stood up, taking one last look at their den. He imagined crawling into its core with Danny, lying side-by-side, sharing a joke and a fag. If only he could return to those innocent times, if only he could change the past, if only he hadn't…

He quickly turned away. Now wasn't the time; he had to get to Lara.

Head down, he hurried to their meeting, desperately working out what to say; but before he knew it, he was opening the low metal gate at the private park's entrance. After walking down the loose-stone path, he took a seat on their familiar wooden bench. Shoulders hunched, he stared blankly at the ground.

Before long, the gate's creak disturbed his dark thoughts. Looking up, for one joyful moment he couldn't help but mirror her infectious smile as she bounded over. Rising to meet her, he flung his arms out wide. Her tight squeeze drew a sharp breath, but the pain could be ignored; this was a moment to savour…it was likely to be his last.

"I've missed you blue-eyes," Lara smiled, cuddling up to him on the bench. "You really worried me on the phone; you sounded so…distant."

Lowering his head, Mickey's eyes returned to the ground.

"Okay, what's going on?" Lara frowned. "You're making me nervous."

"Lara," Mickey said raising his head. "I've got something to tell you that's going to change your world."

"What are you talking about? Have you been taking something?" she asked anxiously. "You know I don't like drugs, they're for losers and…"

"Danny's dead," Mickey cut in bluntly.

Lara stared open mouthed.

"You are joking aren't you? Please tell me you're joking?"

"I wish I could, but it's the truth – he's dead," Mickey choked. "We'll never see him again."

He watched the warmth drain from her face; the joyous smile gradually replaced by disbelief. Neither spoke, the only sound the soft breeze in the leaves above.

Finally, regaining her composure, Lara's trembling voice spoke up. "How? How did it happen?"

No matter how many times he'd rehearsed the reply, he knew he was no more ready right now. All he did know, was that she deserved to know the truth; so that was exactly what he was going to tell her.

"Please don't hate me, I'm hurting enough already."

"Don't be silly Mickey, I don't hate you," Lara replied, wiping a tear from his eye. "I love you more than anything in the world."

Taking her soft hand to his, he began.

"We've been lying to you and Katie ever since we met you. My father doesn't own a car dealership; he's been in prison most of my life."

"What are you talking about?" she stammered. "I don't understand."

"We've been living a lie. All those flash cars; they didn't belong to me, my dad, or anyone else I know. I stole them Lara – I'm nothing more than a thief."

Motionless, Lara's stare remained steady.

"We were on the way back from a job…another car from our group nearly hit us," he spluttered. "I tried to avoid them, but I lost control. We hit a tree on Danny's side…he didn't have a chance."

The moment he finished, he felt her hand slowly slide from between his. Folding her arms, her stare narrowed, the only movement a slight shaking of her head.

"Talk to me Lara," Mickey pleaded. "I love you, I never meant to hurt you; I just wanted to impress you."

"How dare you!" she said, her voice trembling as it grew in volume. "Our whole relationship has been a sham. Maybe the nice cars *were* impressive, but it was you I wanted; at least the person I thought you were! How can you have done this to us!" she erupted. "I thought I loved you too, but clearly I made a mistake. All along, the person I thought I loved didn't really exist – you make me sick!"

Taking to her feet, she looked down at Mickey's forlorn face. "You drove us around in stolen fucking cars! Oh yes, it all makes sense now; that night, driving off from the police in the Porsche. You'd have been happy to kill me in a chase too, wouldn't you Mickey!"

"Lara, you have to believe me," he implored. "I wouldn't ever hurt you, you mean everything to me."

"'Wouldn't ever hurt me'? That's just another lie, isn't it? Well let me tell you straight Mickey Wilding, if that really is your name; don't ever come near me again…just leave me alone!" she screamed. "Leave me alone!"

Her body shaking with every sob, Lara turned to go.

Rising to follow, he called out from behind. "Lara, what about Katie? I owe it to Danny – she needs to be told the truth."

His words stopped her dead in her tracks. On the spot, she turned to face him directly.

"Don't you dare go anywhere near Katie; you've already caused us enough pain!" she spat out. "We never want to see you again Mickey – never!"

With that, she turned her back on him…and walked out of his life.

***

Dusk was falling by the time he left the bench. Lost in his pain, he'd paid no attention to the time, until an ambulance's siren jogged an important memory: his curfew, he'd forgotten about his bloody curfew! If he was spotted on the streets outside his permitted hours, he'd be back in custody with zero chance of bail. Jumping to his feet, he pulled his hoodie over his head, and rushed through the alleyways home.

Exhausted, he kicked off his trainers, and slumped down onto the sofa.

"So how did it go luv?" his mother asked, walking in with a coffee.

Mickey shook his head.

"I'm so sorry son. Maybe she just needs some time to herself; time to think things over."

"No, she's made it quite clear that she hates me. I've lost Danny and now I've lost Lara – what the hell did I do to deserve all this shit!"

Sitting down beside him, she put her arm around his shoulders, and pulled him close. "Don't worry luv, things will sort themselves out, they always do."

Time passed slowly by as TV soaps played in the background. But Mickey's mind was far away; struggling to focus on anything other than Danny and Lara. And what did he have left…the posse? Was that really what he wanted when his sentence was up…a return to thieving? And anyway, what was the point without Danny by his side?

Suddenly, a loud knock at the door interrupted his torment.

"Who the hell can that be?" his mother asked, getting up.

"If it's anybody for me; I'm not here, you haven't seen me," he said in a low voice. He couldn't even face seeing his mates just yet, and after what Jonas had said at the station, he *definitely* didn't want to meet J.T.'s henchmen.

Remaining on the sofa, he listened to the muffled voices. Moments later, two sets of feet approached down the hallway; one distinctly heavier than his mum's. Heart in mouth, he looked up as the door opened…

43

"Hello Mickey, good to see you're at home."

For the first time in his life, he was actually pleased to see the police.

"I told him you weren't here son, but he said you were on a curfew; that you'd go straight to prison if I didn't let him check!"

"Don't worry mum, this is PC Draycott, he's been alright with me; they're not all tossers down Stechford you know."

"Mickey! Don't be so rude," his mother scolded.

"It's okay Mrs Wilding, he's probably right. I'm afraid there's idiots in every job," the officer said raising his eyebrows. "Mickey, although I'm here for your curfew check, I could also do with having a quick chat. Is there somewhere we can speak in private? No disrespect intended Mrs Wilding," he added.

"Don't worry about me; I need to sort a few things in the bedroom. I'll leave you in peace."

As his mum left the room, Mickey motioned for the officer to sit down.

"So what's this about then?" he asked. "You only saw me a few hours ago."

"I did, but the station's back yard isn't the best place to talk is it? And let's face it, walls have ears!" the officer smiled. "I'll be straight with you; we need to speak about where we go from here."

"I'm not sure I'm with you; it's pretty obvious where I'm going from here."

"Maybe, maybe not. Mickey, you strike me as being different to the offenders I normally deal with. You're intelligent, focused, and most importantly, you genuinely care for others – you could have a meaningful future."

"Future, what future? For the next five years I'll be sitting in a cell thinking about how I lost my girlfriend and killed my best mate, all in one fell swoop. And when I get out, what's my future going to be like then? I'll be mid-twenties, without a qualification to my name, and the only skill I'll possess is how to steal people's motors! Don't get me wrong, nobody else is to blame; I chose my path and now I'm paying the price."

"You *have* chosen your path, and yes, so far Mickey you've not made the best choices. But although you probably can't see it at the moment, you're still young, you've got many good years ahead. Think of your future as like a kite in the sky; right now, you've still got hold of the strings, but the fiercer the winds blow, the stronger you'll have to hold on, or you're right…the kite'll fly away. Your future is in *your* hands, and your hands alone."

Mickey sat back. What exactly did Draycott mean? What were the winds he was talking about – Lara, the posse, J.T.? And in any case, how could he make choices from inside a prison cell?

"Listen, have a think about what I've said to you. Maybe the time's coming to consider yourself for a change. Do the people who don't give a damn about you and Danny really deserve your loyalty?"

Taking a small business card from his top pocket, the officer offered it to Mickey.

"We have a team whose job is to gather intelligence while keeping their sources completely anonymous. I know it goes against everything you've ever known, but someday you might need some help holding onto those strings. If you do, give me a call."

With that, Draycott stood up and replaced his cap. "Sometimes Mickey, everything isn't quite as it seems…it's up to you to find the truth."

The truth – what was the truth? Who *could* he really trust?

"Get some rest Mickey," Draycott said, making towards the door. "You're gonna need it."

***

Following the officer's visit, Mickey spent the entire weekend plunged in darkness, holed up in his bedroom. With misery consuming every waking moment, he contemplated the easy way out. Lying on his bed, time and again his eyes were drawn to the light cord hanging invitingly over his head. It seemed so easy; in a few seconds he could be free from his pain forever.

But as the two days crept by, the clouds in his mind started to clear. Although his self-loathing remained, something else was building inside; something far more powerful…something called revenge! Why give Tommy the pleasure of taking his own life, when he could make *him* pay instead. How though; that was now the question.

After a broken night's sleep, Mickey awoke feeling queasy. It was Monday morning, today was the day; the day he said goodbye to his friend. Bent over, bile rising in his throat, he stumbled into the bathroom and retched down the toilet.

"Come on son, it'll be alright," his mother sighed, fastening her dressing gown as she walked in to join him. "I know you're going through hell, but after today it'll all start to get better," she said massaging his shoulders. "Funerals aren't just about goodbyes, they're also about remembering the good times, and by the sounds of it, you pair had *too many* of them!"

Managing a weak smile, Mickey lifted his head.

"I'm gonna put the kettle on. Go and get yourself cleaned up; you never know who might be there."

Gingerly, he stood up and stared at his reflection. He looked awful. He hadn't shaved for a week, his hair was a mess, and dark circles surrounded his eyes. Jeez, what must Lara have thought when he saw her; he looked like he'd been dragged through the jungle. He couldn't let the others see him like this. It was time to stop feeling sorry for himself; today of all days he needed to be strong.

Bath run, he lay in the warm water, his tension drifting slowly away. By the time he'd washed, shaved, and gelled his hair, he felt refreshed; ready for what lay ahead. Why *should* he turn up with his head stooped; Danny's death wasn't his fault. No, he was going there with his head held high; it's what Danny would have wanted. Dressed in his Dad's dark suit and black tie, he hugged his mum and left.

It was a warm summer morning; blue skies with an occasional white cloud floating by. Lost in his own world, Mickey walked along wondering how the posse would react to him. Had they spoken to Eccy yet and learned the truth, or had Tommy brainwashed them with a pack of lies? They'd all be at the funeral, but today wasn't the day for payback; he still hadn't worked out when that'd happen yet. How he wished Danny was with him; he'd have known what to do. Again and again he returned to the same question: why on earth had he swerved to avoid Tommy's Beemer? If he'd have just hit it, Danny might still be alive, and they'd be going to Tommy's funeral instead!

Deep in thought, he failed to notice the blacked out BMW cruise silently up behind. Its passenger window slowly descending, Chapman's voice took him completely by surprise.

"Hey...Mickey. Don't you want to talk to us?"

Shit! Keep walking Mickey, keep walking, he told himself; he definitely didn't need this today.

"Err...yeah...of course I do," he stammered. "Any chance we can chat later...it's just...I've got to be somewhere important right now."

"As it happens, we've got to be somewhere important too. Jump in and we'll give you a lift."

Looking into the car he could see Chapman was dressed smartly. But without the customary black tie, he certainly wasn't on the way to a funeral. Although he didn't recognise the burly driver, he knew the Beemer well; Deano had warned him never to go near it – it belonged to one of their bosses.

"Err...thanks for the offer, but I really could do with clearing my head," Mickey mumbled, quickening his pace. "It's a bit messed up at the moment."

He knew he was in trouble. What was it Jonas had said at the station? That he should be 'more worried about what J.T.'s got planned for you!' Bollocks, this had to be J.T.'s car...he needed to get away, and quickly.

"Come on Mickey, jump in the back; we'll be at the cemetery in no time," Chapman smiled.

"Seriously, thank you, I'll be fine," Mickey replied, desperately planning his escape route. "It'll do me good to get some fresh air."

Suddenly, the driver's left hand yanked a pistol from his waistband.

"Get in the fucking car now, or I'll blow your head from your fucking shoulders!" he bellowed, bringing the car to a sudden halt.

Eyes fixed on the black barrel, Mickey froze. What the hell was he going to do now?

44

There really was only one option; he couldn't outrun a bullet. Pulling open the rear door, he climbed into the back of the car.

"Now shut the fucking door!"

With the pistol still trained on him, Mickey did exactly as was told.

Only as he drove off, and the central locking activated, did the driver tuck his pistol away.

Furtively, Mickey scanned around; sizing up his options for escape.

But there were none; a stocky bald-headed meathead was sat next to him, and he looked like he was ready to kill. Not daring to make eye contact, he focused on the blank screen in the headrest instead.

Turning to face him, Chapman was the first to talk. "Mickey, it's probably best I introduce you to my friends. Sitting next to you is a pleasant chap called Razor, although let me assure you, you'll find it in your interests not to piss him off. And your chauffeur this morning is J.T; I guess you've already learnt not to upset him!"

So it *was* J.T.; the head of The Power Firm, the man in control of his life. Of all the days to meet him, why did it have to be today? Nothing good could come from this; this was no chance meeting...he was in deep shit.

"So Wilding, why do *you* think we've picked you up today?" J.T. asked, his eyes fixed on the road ahead.

"Err...I don't know," he replied meekly. "Chapman said you were going somewhere important, so I guess we're going to the funeral?"

"Funeral, the fucking funeral!" J.T. exploded. "Why would *I* be going to the fucking funeral? I don't give a shit about Danny; he's a fucking failure, just like you are!"

As if on cue, Razor lashed out with his fist. Taken completely by surprise, Mickey's head slammed backwards, the thug's gold sovereigns ripping open his freshly shaved cheeks.

"No Mickey, we're not going to your mate's fucking funeral, but we could be off to yours!" J.T. continued to bawl. "You didn't think you could lose me half a million pounds and expect to get away with it did you!"

Mickey didn't dare to reply; whatever he said he knew would be wrong. Instead, he brought a hand up to wipe away the blood.

Wrong decision.

Turning square on, Razor swung his fist once more.

"Answer the fucking question!" the meathead screamed, his face practically connecting with Mickey's.

Semi-conscious, his face contorted in pain, all Mickey could croak was a, "No sir," in reply.

"Good, so you *can* learn quickly after all," J.T. nodded. "Now then, you're probably feeling rather sorry for yourself at the moment; am I right?"

Not knowing what he wanted to hear, Mickey grunted a response.

"And so you should be!" J.T. roared. "First of all, you've killed one of *my* workers. Now, while he's just another number to me, he's a number who needs replacing."

Despite the pain, Mickey felt his anger steadily building. So all along they'd merely been pawns; nothing more than numbers to the men who controlled them? All the rewards, all the praise – all to keep them sweet. Danny had given his life for these men...for what? Sluggishly, he raised his head and stared at J.T., the hatred filling his eyes.

J.T. glanced in his mirror. "Is there something you want to say to me?"

Oh yes, there was plenty he wanted to say, but right now he knew better than to sign his own death warrant. A slow shake of his head would have to do.

"Secondly," J.T. continued. "You've put another worker in hospital, and by the time you go to prison, I'll be three down. Have you any idea the problems that causes me?"

Again, Mickey slowly shook his head; a reply met by another crunching blow to the face.

"Answer the fucking question!"

Having blacked out the moment the strike landed, Razor's roar fell on deaf ears.

"Alright, he's had enough for the moment," J.T. instructed. "You can complete your work later."

"Okay boss – these kids just can't take it like real men."

"And don't forget, we need him to drive at the end of the week, so don't finish him off...yet."

In and out of consciousness, Mickey struggled to make sense of the journey. City streets, motorways, country lanes passed him by, until eventually the road started rising. It felt like they were climbing a mountain, but it couldn't be could it; they couldn't be that far from home?

Finally pulling onto a deserted car park at its peak, Razor and Chapman manhandled Mickey's body out, and laid him on the bonnet.

Head pounding, eyes stinging, Mickey could hardly feel the pulp where his nose had once been. And where the hell was he? Wiping his eyes to clear the smeared blood, they slowly regained their focus. He'd awoken from his nightmares, only to be confronted by their reality – the same three men stood around him; their intentions abundantly clear. He raised himself to his elbows.

"Thirdly, and most importantly," J.T. continued. "By my reckoning you owe me half a million pounds. Now the question is; how the hell are you gonna repay me?"

From behind his back, Razor pulled out a crowbar, and rhythmically slapping it into his hand, began to approach.

Despite the pain, Mickey remembered the punishment for not replying.

"I...I don't know," he grunted, spitting thick blood onto the dusty floor.

"*You* may not know," J.T. responded. "But *I* have a few ideas. You do want to repay me, don't you?"

With metal striking flesh filling his ears, Mickey couldn't blurt his reply out quick enough.

"Of course...of course...I'll do whatever you want."

"Now that's more like it," J.T. smiled. "It's funny really; your dad let me down once, and just like you, had to be shown the error of his ways. He was never the brightest I'm afraid; always getting caught, always doing time. Yes, you and your dad are very alike."

Mickey sat himself up, his strength gradually returning. His tormentors stood in a semi-circle around him: J.T. in the middle, his henchmen either side.

"Let's face it Mickey, it'll take you your whole life to repay me, so that's exactly the deal I'm offering. You'll work for me forever, and if I see fit to reward you at any time, you'll consider it as a gift, not a wage. From this day on...I own you!" J.T. snarled. "Of course, you could choose your alternative."

Razor took a step closer, the tapping speed increasing.

"So Mickey, do you wish to accept my generous offer?"

Razor's maniacal grin told him everything he needed to know. This was no idle threat; the thug was ready to kill.

"Yes, yes...whatever you want," he choked out.

"Excellent," J.T. smiled. "In that case, I have a little job already lined up for you. *You're* going to destroy the police helicopter; Deano will fill you in with the details. Following that, you will of course be going on the run from the police; after all, you're no use to me rotting in jail, are you?"

"No," Mickey murmured, his head drooping down.

No sooner had he answered than he doubled up; Razor's sledgehammer to the stomach almost cutting him in half.

"Speak up when you're spoken to!" the thug roared down his ears.

Raising his head, Mickey replied with what little breath remained. "I said I'll do whatever you want."

"Good," Razor grinned. "And make sure you keep it that way."

Stepping forward, J.T grabbed Mickey's collars, raising his bloody face to meet his own. "Well it looks like you've missed your mate's funeral after all. Never mind, he was an insignificant piece of shit anyway...wasn't he?"

Despite the pain searing through his body, despite his dulled senses urging survival – he'd rather die than betray his friend.

"Wasn't he!" J.T. bellowed.

Without a word, Mickey lowered his head, and awaited the inevitable punishment.

Razor didn't disappoint; his metal bar instantly slamming against Mickey's legs. Almost as he fell to the ground, Razor drove his knee upward, its impact with Mickey's jaw sending him sprawling in an unconsciousness heap. Now lifeless on the ground, he neither saw nor felt the brutal assault that followed.

Seemingly taking pleasure from his work, Razor unleashed blow after blow, until finally, J.T. calmly tapped him on the shoulder.

"Alright Razor, he's had enough now; it's time for us to go."

"Okay boss, if you say so," Razor sulked, directing a final kick at Mickey's defenceless body.

Without as much as a second glance at the motionless rags on the ground, the men returned to their car and drove off. If Mickey was lucky, somebody would come across him in time, if not...

***

After a short service at the old chapel, mourners followed Danny's coffin into the cemetery grounds. Snaking along narrow paths, they made their way towards the freshly hewn earth alongside his mother's grave.

For somebody as young as Danny, the turnout was relatively small, with only a few relatives mixing with the youngsters turning up to pay their respects. One group stood together; solemnly lined up as the coffin was slowly lowered. Heads bowed, tears rolling freely down cheeks, the original posse stood to attention while the minister read out the last rites. On the grave's opposite side, Tommy and his cronies shuffled and fidgeted, their dry eyes darting from one to another.

The service complete, Deano and his friends bowed as one. Turning to leave, they parted as two figures in dark shades approached from behind.

Supported by her friend, the smaller girl knelt down, carefully scooping dry soil into her pale hand. Tears streaming, she gently sprinkled the earth.

"Goodbye babe," she whispered. "I just want you to know, I forgive you – I'll love you forever."

Steadying her friend, Lara passed her a red rose. With a kiss to its bloom, Katie lowered it to the grave and released. Finally, her slender frame trembling, she turned, and with Lara as her guide, walked slowly away.

Hanging back from the other mourners, Deano waited for the girls to catch up.

"Please forgive me," he said politely. "But I couldn't help hearing you at the graveside. Danny and Mickey were private kinda guys; they hadn't spoken about…" Deano paused, struggling to find the right words. "…well, if I'd known, I'd have been in touch straight away. I just want you to know how sorry we are; he was an amazing guy, we're all gonna miss him terribly."

"Thank you," Lara replied quietly, her tearful friend still shaking on her arm.

"If there's anything we can do for you, we're more than happy to help," Deano offered.

Lara gently shook her head. In silence, they continued to amble towards the black cab parked at the exit; its engine rattling to life as they approached.

Opening the side door, Deano guided the girls inside. But as he went to close it, Lara leant forward. "You mentioned Mickey earlier; do you know where he is? I was expecting him to be here."

"You're right, he should have been. He and Danny were like brothers; he would've given anything to be here today, anything."

"I saw him Friday evening, but I'm afraid things didn't go too well; I really upset him," Lara frowned. "You don't think he'd have…harmed himself do you?"

"Mickey? No way, he's one tough kid. No, something's happened to him, and I intend to find out just what."

"Look, if I give you my number, can you call me when you find him. After the way I treated him Friday, I don't think he'll want to talk to me, but I'd just like to know he's okay."

"Of course I will. I'm Deano by the way. Who should I ask for when I call?"

"It's Lara, and my friend's Katie. Call me any time, day or night; I probably won't sleep until I've heard he's alright."

"Rest assured, I won't be sleeping until I've found him either. I'll call you the moment I do."

"Thank you," she replied closing the door behind.

Watching the taxi drive away, Deano slowly shook his head. "I'll call you alright; I just hope it's not to invite you to another funeral."

45

Mickey carefully took his first conscious breath; gasping as broken ribs prevented him from inhaling too deeply. Gradually lifting his battered head, his eyes slowly regained their focus.

Where the hell was he? It just looked like a desolate car park in the middle of nowhere.

After sitting up, he paused to gather his thoughts. His suit was plastered in blood and dirt...shit, he was wearing a suit – he was supposed to be at the funeral! His eyes darted to his left wrist; maybe he could still make it in time. Another groan. His watch had gone, and so, as he searched his pockets, had his wallet and phone. Groggily, he made it to his feet, and once the world had stopped spinning, began to hobble towards the exit.

Battered, bruised, and alone, he came to a halt. How had it come to this? He'd lost everything: his best friend, his love, his dignity. And now, having missed his mate's funeral, he was stranded with no money, no phone, and no idea where he was.

"Why?!" he shouted out, dropping down to his knees.

What had it all been for? They'd been used all along by ungrateful thugs who'd treated them like shit! What more could they take from him; there was nothing left he could lose.

So consumed in self-pity, he didn't notice the small car trundling up the hill. Pulling up alongside him, the driver and passenger approached.

"Are you okay young man?" the lady asked, kneeling down to his side.

Struggling to keep his composure, Mickey screwed his eyes shut. Head stooped, he slowly nodded.

"Well you don't look it to me," her husband said emphatically. "Now let's get you in the car and take you to hospital."

Placing his arm beneath Mickey's, he helped him to his feet.

Too exhausted to argue, Mickey shuffled onto the front passenger seat. Wincing with every bump as they left the car park, he stared blankly into the distance; his rescuers chatter merely background noise to the troubles in his mind.

"I said, 'What happened to you up there?' You look like you've been beaten to a pulp," the man asked again, a little louder.

"Don't be so nosey Harold, he doesn't have to tell you if he doesn't want to," his wife replied indignantly.

Their raised voices stirred Mickey from his thoughts. "It's alright, you deserve an explanation," he flinched. "I upset the wrong people – they taught me a lesson."

"The bastards!"

"Mind your language Harold, there's no need for that!"

Glancing across at Mickey, her husband raised his eyebrows.

"You can't let them get away with it; you could have ended up dead! I hope you're going to speak to the police," the lady continued.

"What good will that do?" Harold replied tersely. "Look what happened to us; they never got anybody for *that*, did they?"

"Well it wasn't easy was it? The robbers who nicked our car had their faces covered; how were the police supposed to know who they were? At least this young man knows who did it."

Mickey's ears pricked up. "What happened to you then?"

"Oh, we don't want to burden you with our problems, you've got enough of your own," Harold replied politely.

"No, really. I'm interested, what happened?"

"Oh well, we've got a few minutes before we get to the hospital," he continued. "I'm sure you've heard a lot worse, and by the looks of things, you've been on the receiving end yourself. We were lucky I suppose."

"Come on Harold, get on with it, we haven't got all day," his wife nagged from the back.

"Alright, alright, keep your wig on," he scoffed back. "It was a few months ago. We didn't always have a little Fiesta you know; we used to have a top of the range Lexus. I bought it as a present to myself when I retired, but we only had it for six months. Oh, it was such a perfect motor; we used to think we were royalty riding around in our posh car, didn't we love?"

"We certainly did. Lord and Lady Muck we called ourselves; all the neighbours were jealous."

"Anyway, we were at the supermarket, just loading some shopping in the boot when I turned to put the trolley away. Next thing I knew, four hoodlums came running over. One of them put a knife to Mavis's throat, while another one grabbed me, drew his fist back, and yelled, 'Throw me the keys, throw me the keys!'. Well, I don't mind admitting I was terrified, so I just chucked him the keys. He didn't even thank me; just shoved me out of the way while the knifeman pushed Mavis to the floor. Before I knew it, they'd jumped into the car and zoomed off, missing poor Mavis by inches. They could have killed her!" he said angrily.

Mickey kept quiet; he knew exactly who'd done the attack.

"It's alright for those young thugs; they just drive away with their spoils – they have no idea the damage they leave behind. Mavis has never been the same since; she's permanently on medication and she's still too scared to go out on her own. I'm surprised the shock didn't kill her!"

"Did you ever see your car again?" Mickey asked, already guessing the answer.

"No, it disappeared off the face of the earth; 'stolen to order' the police said. Yes the insurance coughed up, but a lot less than I paid for it. Not that it mattered; I'll never have a posh car again. I'd rather have this little Fiesta any day."

Mulling over the old man's story, Mickey began to think about his own victims. He'd never really paid them any attention; after all, it was only their insurance companies who really lost out...wasn't it? Yet here were two real victims. They weren't rich; just hard working decent people, who now lived in fear of thieves like him.

But still he was puzzled. "You've been through all that, and yet you still stopped to help me. Why? I might have been acting; I could've robbed you again."

"I don't really know," Harold replied. "I guess we're from a different generation; we're just too trusting I suppose. You looked like you needed help, so that's exactly what we gave you."

Mickey still didn't get it. Why had strangers taken risks to help him, yet the people *he'd* risked his life for, beat him to a pulp and left him for dead? Everything he'd ever known was falling apart. Who *were* the bad guys, who could he trust, who genuinely wanted to help?

***

Razor had done his job well. X-rays revealed several broken ribs, a patchwork of deep bruising, but nothing that wouldn't heal. Although the staff insisted he remain overnight for observations, Mickey had other plans. Self-release forms signed, he gingerly limped free again.

Thanks to Harold, the change in his pocket paid for the buses he needed to drop him by the cemetery gates. Hobbling through the avenue of trees, he headed towards the chapel-of-rest. But finding it all locked up and nobody in sight, he sat on its stone steps, wondering where on earth he should start; the grounds were so vast – Danny could be anywhere.

But while he gathered his thoughts and his strength, a voice from his side disturbed him.

"Can I help you mate?" the man asked.

Turning slowly, Mickey looked up to see a man in overalls approaching.

"I'm looking for my friend's grave," Mickey winced. "He was buried here earlier today."

"Sorry chief, I'm closing up for the night. If you pop back tomorrow, I'm sure the vicar will help you out."

Mickey swallowed hard. "Please, it's really important to me...I need to see him right now. I promise I won't stay long."

Looking him up and down, the groundsman slowly nodded.

"Looks like you've had enough trouble for today," he smiled. "Come on, let's get you to your mate."

Supporting Mickey's arm, he slowly guided him to the graveside.

"Take as long as you want. Don't tell anyone, but there's a hole in the fence at the end of this path," he winked. "I'm really sorry for your loss mate; I know exactly how it feels. But remember this, it might feel like the end of the world right now, but things do, and will get better; I promise."

Looking down toward the soft earth, Mickey gazed at the flowers, and at the flattened turf to their side. Closing his eyes, he imagined the scene hours earlier, as Danny had been lowered into the ground.

He'd spent his whole life with Danny, but now...now he'd missed his ending; he'd failed his friend again.

Kneeling down to read the tributes, one card stood out; it must have been handwritten by Deano. Attached to a bunch of white lilies, it simply read; *'Brother, I miss you. Mickey'*.

Using his bloodied sleeve, he wiped the tears from his cheek. "Oh Danny, why?" he whispered, his voice cracking with emotion. "I can't cope with this alone; I need you more than ever. Come back Danny...please?!"

Sobbing uncontrollably, he lowered his head to the ground.

Consumed in grief, alone in despair; the hours passed by as he lay next to his fallen friend.

But as the bird's melodies welcomed dusk's arrival, the dark clouds in his mind slowly shifted. Danny might not be with him anymore, but he knew exactly what he'd have wanted him to do. Eventually rising to his feet, he bowed his head above the disturbed earth.

"Stay close to me brother," he said, his eyes narrowing. "I'm gonna make them pay!"

46

Returning home, Mickey went straight to his bedroom. Closing the curtains, he turned the light off and lay in the darkness; his face buried deep in the pillow. His body needed sleep to heal, but his mind refused to help; revolving instead around the events that had brought him to this. The posse, the Power Firm, the police: who were his friends, and who were his enemies? Everything seemed turned on its head…except Tommy!

A gentle knock at the door disturbed his thoughts. He ignored it, he didn't want to talk to his mother just yet; she'd only fuss over his injuries. Turning up the sides of his pillow, he blocked out the sound.

The door opened quietly; a figure walked towards him.

Feeling the side of his bed sag, Mickey didn't move…hoping his mum would get the message.

But this certainly wasn't his mother.

Soft hands touched his neck, then tenderly massaged his shoulders. Dropping the sides of his pillow, Mickey turned to face his visitor. Aqua-blue eyes greeted his own.

"What…what are you doing here?" he blurted out.

Gently cupping her hands beneath his wounded head, Lara cried softly. "Oh babe, what have they done to you?"

Mickey looked away, shaking his head slowly in reply. Opening her arms, she pulled him close to her chest.

He couldn't quite take it in. Despite every lie, every deceit, she was here for him; but how?

"I'm so sorry Mickey," she cried, wiping away her tears. "I should have been there for you."

"Don't be silly, there's nothing you need to be sorry for," he said, pulling her closer. "It's me who needs to be sorry."

As one, they lay together, face to face, gently drying the other's eyes.

He could have stayed there forever; nothing would have been more perfect than falling asleep in her arms…but he was puzzled; the questions in his mind refusing to disappear.

"I still don't get it; how on earth did you know I was here?"

"I met a friend of yours at the funeral," she began.

"You went to Danny's funeral?" he said, completely taken aback.

"Yes," she replied quietly. "After you dropped your bombshell, I went to tell Katie; she made me see things in a different light. I won't lie, she's devastated. But she'd been so in love with him, that all she cared about was Danny; not the secret life he'd led. She was desperate to go to the funeral – she needed to tell him she forgave him."

"So you went with her?"

"I did. And the one person I wanted to see…wasn't there. I wanted to talk to you Mickey. I *also* wanted to tell you that I forgive you; that I'd help you get through this."

Pausing for a moment, Lara pulled out another tissue. "I was worried sick when I couldn't see you there; I knew you'd never have missed it. I needed to talk to someone, but I didn't know who. Then one of your friends approached me; he said his name was Deano."

Mickey nodded. "He's one of the few people I can trust right now."

"He was worried for you. He said he'd find you, and call me when he did. I heard from him an hour ago; he's been searching for you all day with no joy. He gave me your address and suggested I wait for you here. Seems, I'm not the only one who cares for you," Lara said staring deep into his eyes. "Anyway, enough about my day. Tell me what's happened to you?"

He closed his eyes, and considered his choices. Should he tell her everything? After all, she deserved to know the truth. But he loved her dearly; she needed protecting, not putting in danger. What was the right thing to do?

"You need to understand, these are evil people. If they find out I've been talking, they'll kill me, and they'll come after you."

"Mickey, I'm not scared, I'm here to help you. We can get through this, as long as we do it together," she replied, stroking his bruised forehead.

There was nothing else for it; he had to tell her everything. Letting out a sigh, he began. From childhood excitement watching performing cars, to climbing the ladder of crime. Leaving no stone unturned, he ended with J.T. and The Power Firm; the men who ruled by fear.

Open mouthed, Lara's head shook as he talked through his beating on the car park.

"So all he cared about was the bloody watches!" she said angrily.

"Yep, and he couldn't give a shit about Danny!"

Revelations over, they lay in silence. Had he gone too far, had he told her too much? Hugging her tightly, he prayed she'd stay; he couldn't face losing her again.

Finally, she spoke up. "So what are you going to do then?"

"Right now, I really don't know; I still haven't had chance to get my head straight."

"Well one thing's for certain, you can't keep working for J.T; he doesn't give a damn about you!"

She was right. He'd always looked up to J.T.; the powerful boss watching their backs. He remembered the hushed tones in the playground whenever his name was mentioned, the rewards he'd given them, the respect everyone showed them 'cos they were his boys. But today he'd had a wake-up call of the most violent kind – J.T. was no more than an evil tyrant. Now he'd seen the truth, he despised him and everything he stood for. Why *should* he show him any loyalty? The person who really deserved it, was lying here in his arms.

"You're right; I don't owe him anything. I'd rather he kills me, than work for him again."

"There's only one choice you can make then," Lara sighed. "You need to go to the police, and tell them everything."

"I wish it was as easy as that," he replied. "It'll be my word against his, and he's got the best lawyers around. Nothing would stick; he'd get straight out and come looking for me…and we both know how that'd end up!"

What other options were there? There was no way he could take on J.T. and his cronies; that'd be suicidal. There *was* one way out though…

"We could always get our stuff together and move far away?"

"Oh Mickey," Lara smiled, stroking his hair. "It's a lovely thought, but it really wouldn't solve anything. We'd have no money, nowhere to stay and we'd spend our lives looking over our shoulders. That's no way to live is it? Anyway, I think I know you better than that; you're a fighter, you don't run from your problems."

"Yeah, you're right; we've gotta find a way to bring him down," Mickey nodded. "The question is…how?"

Lying quietly in each other's arms, the day's traumas slowly receded away. Despite the battering he'd taken, he slept deeply for the first night in weeks. No longer burdened by the lies, the future now seemed a little clearer; Lara was his future, the fightback had begun.

***

Their late morning lie in was eventually disturbed by Lara's mobile. Drowsy-eyed, she peered at the screen.

"It's Deano," she said, handing it over. "I'm sure he'll be pleased to hear your voice."

Putting the phone to his ear, Mickey greeted his friend. There was so much to catch up on, but right now wasn't the time. For the moment they kept things brief: there was to be a meeting that night at Deano's, Mickey was expected to be there.

"Are you going to go?" Lara asked.

"I haven't got a choice. Until we come up with a plan, I'll have to do exactly what I'm told."

"I guess so – but what if you get caught by the police again?"

Mickey stared blankly at the ceiling. "I really don't know," he shrugged. "I'm in deep enough shit as it is."

"What do you mean? Do you think they'll send you to prison?"

"I don't think they'll have much choice; they'll see me as a professional car thief who's partly responsible for Danny's death. If I'm lucky, as it'd be my first time inside, I'd probably only get a couple of…years."

The moment the words left his mouth, the significance hit home. They'd only just got back together, and now he'd have to face losing her all over again.

Entwined together, they lay in silence once more.

Eventually, Lara spoke first. "I understand why you can't tell the police what's happened, but maybe you could help them find out for themselves?"

"What do you mean?"

"Well, if they knew what J.T. was planning, they could easily catch him in the act. He'd never need to know it had come from you."

"It's a good idea, but I never know what he's up to. We just get our orders, and do the jobs. He leads a completely separate life to us; he never gets his hands dirty."

While he spoke, Draycott's words came back into focus. Despite J.T.'s hurricane, he was still alive; still holding the kite strings tight. And now the very person he was holding on for, was stood squarely next to him, gripping the strings just as tightly.

"There is somebody I could talk to," he pondered. "Maybe it's time to give him a call."

***

Later that evening, Mickey was the first to arrive at Deano's.

"Bloody hell!" Deano winced. "*They* didn't mess about, did they?"

"What do you mean?"

"Don't worry mate, I know you didn't get them from the accident. Chapman's filled me in with what happened yesterday," Deano said handing him a coke. "That's why you're here before the others; I wanted to have a chat with you first."

Feeling a little uneasy, Mickey took a seat and opened his can.

So why did Deano want to talk to him? And how were the others going to react; had they fallen for Tommy's lies? The empty room wasn't helping.

Sat on the edge of his seat, Deano started the conversation. "It's difficult to know where to begin. Have you had chance to speak to the others yet?"

"No. As you can see, the only people I did meet decided to re-arrange my face!"

"Well for what it's worth, Chapman and I have had a blazing row over what they did. If it wasn't for Razor lurking in the background, I'd have knocked the bastard's lights out! It wouldn't have done me any good, but I'd have felt a whole lot better!"

"Thanks," Mickey smiled. "And what about the others, do *they* know what happened?" he added cautiously.

"No, and it's probably best they don't. The less they know; the better."

"Yeah, I'm sure you're right; J.T.'s in no mood for loose lips."

Deano took a long swig before continuing. "So I bet you want to know what's been going on since the accident don't you?"

"Well I guess I haven't been 'Mr Popular' have I?"

"Far from it mate, far from it," Deano re-assured. "When Eccy came out of hospital, he made sure everybody knew the truth; Tommy's been keeping his head down ever since. Our boys want to have it out with Tommy's crew, but J.T.'s made it very clear that we've got to work together, no matter what!"

"Even after the last fuck up?"

"Even after the last fuck up. If you ask me, J.T. and his Power Firm are starting to lose the plot."

"So what are we going to do? We can't let Tommy get away with it," Mickey frowned. "He's just gonna be laughing at us!"

"We haven't got much choice have we? It's the same old story I'm afraid; we do as we're told or we end up in hospital. Don't worry, their time will come mate, and I'll be right beside you when it does."

Foraging inside his pocket, Deano leant over and handed Mickey a new mobile.

Turning it on, he glanced at the screen; a picture from happier times – he and Danny sat on the bonnet of their Porsche.

"Anyway you sly old fox," Deano chuckled. "I met two darlings at the funeral. How the hell did an ugly git like you pull tasty ladies like that!"

For the first time that day, a smile broke out on Mickey's face. Sitting back, he began to explain; from their chance initial meeting to her surprise re-appearance at home.

"You're a lucky man," Deano grinned.

"Haven't *you* got a girl then?"

"Nah, I never seem to keep hold of them. I've been caught in the thieving game all my life; there's never been anyone who'd put up with it. No surprise really," he laughed quietly to himself.

"Well have you ever thought about going straight? I mean, there must come a point when you've had enough of the aggro."

Deano shifted in his seat. "I'm in the same position as you mate," he replied, looking directly into Mickey's eyes. "J.T. owns me. If I ever left; he'd kill me!"

Mickey flinched at the phrase.

"I take it you know what J.T. said to me then?"

"Yep, exactly the same as he said to me ten years ago when *I* messed a job up. He thinks you're his property now – just like I am!" Deano replied angrily.

"Haven't you ever done anything about it?" Mickey asked, amazed.

"Yeah, it's all I thought about to start with, but they made sure I knew exactly what would happen if I did; my first hospital visit saw to that. I'm not proud to say it, but my whole adult life's been spent as their slave, 'cos I've been too scared to do anything about it!"

Taken aback by Deano's admission, Mickey listened in astonishment; Deano held the same hatred for J.T. as he did! But there was no way he could tell him about his own plans, no matter how much he trusted him. It was something he'd have to do alone…and hopefully he'd set Deano free.

Footsteps on the stairs ended their private chat. One-by-one the group entered, with each of the remaining posse making a bee line to welcome Mickey, while Tommy's boys made sure they steered clear.

Wasting no time on formalities, Deano launched straight into the reason for their meeting.

"What we aim to do this Friday night is going to change the face of all future operations. Chapman has given us the green light to 'shoot the moon'…we're finally gonna destroy the police helicopter."

Once the cheer died down, Deano continued with the plan.

"It's pretty simple really. First of all, we need to steal a heavy wagon and hide it near the airport. Then, on Friday night, we'll pick it up, smash through the perimeter barriers, and ram it straight into the chopper. Add a Molotov into the cockpit, and we're rid of our greatest threat. Any thoughts?"

With such an obvious plan, Mickey wondered why they hadn't done it before. What use had all this 'shoot the moon' goading been? If they'd destroyed it weeks ago, they'd never have fouled up the biggest job to date, and Danny would still be alive!

No doubt J.T. was behind this, and just like everything else about him, it stunk! Boy, he was going to enjoy bringing him down…it was time to make the call.

47

Pulled tightly around to hide his face, Mickey's hoodie pointed down into the taxi's footwell. Heart pounding, he fought the desire to tell his driver to turn back. He was about to betray everything he'd ever stood for; his friends, his bosses…himself. Not daring to glimpse at the outside world, he willed the journey to end. Would he be spotted, was he being followed – it felt like J.T.'s eyes were everywhere.

His taxi was slowing; almost down to a crawl as its wheels passed over speedbumps. He must have reached the leisure centre, and looking down at his watch, he was bang on time.

"Go round the back mate," he instructed, peering out at the car park. Normally, he'd be looking for an expensive motor and watching out for the cops; but today, he prayed they were ready and waiting.

To his experienced eye, one car stood out from the rest. Parked in the furthermost corner, a dark grey Civic sat alone in the tree shadows. A headlight wink confirmed his hunch.

Pulling up just short, he paid his fare, and holding his hood in position, quickly scurried over.

"Hi Mickey, glad you could make it," Draycott said, as he clambered into the rear. "If it's okay with you, we'll get going straight away; I'm sure we're all keen to avoid prying eyes!"

Mickey nodded, lying himself down on the seats.

"This is Smudger by the way," Draycott continued, gesturing to the front passenger as he headed off the car park. "He's the source handler I told you about."

Remaining hidden from view, Mickey barely heard the officer's chatter; his mind too busy running over what he was about to do. Through the city streets and out into the countryside they drove, until after a while, he felt the surface change beneath the tyres.

"You can sit up now if you want," Draycott suggested.

Slowly, he rose from his seat. They were travelling down a dirt track with thick shrubbery either side.

"Where on earth…?"

"We're in a forest, five miles north of the city. The only things likely to disturb us round here are the wildlife, so don't worry, you're completely safe."

Thank fuck for that, Mickey thought. Anybody, literally anybody, could be on J.T.'s payroll. Lowering his hood, he glanced around as the car came to a halt in a small clearing.

"So – what did you want to talk to us about?" Draycott asked, turning to face Mickey for the first time. "Geez! What the hell happened to you!"

"I guess I pissed off the wrong people," he replied candidly. "Only, *they've* pissed the wrong person off this time!"

The officers remained quiet; Mickey was in full flow.

"What you said to me the other night…you were right. Danny and I have spent our lives working for scum; people who don't give a shit about us. They're the ones who did this to me!"

"Sounds like you've got every reason to be angry with them," Draycott replied sympathetically. "But how do you want us to help you?"

"They're evil, they've got to be stopped; *they* need to taste justice themselves for a change. I've got to be honest with you though; I only get told what *my* team are planning. I never get to hear what the bosses are up to, so I'm not too sure how I can help."

Draycott looked across at his colleague; his glance met back with a smile.

"Mickey, just the fact that you're here right now, tells me a lot about you," Smudger spoke up. "I've worked the streets for many years; I've seen how gangsters rule by reputation and fear. They rely on people like you to keep them rich. Am I right?"

Mickey nodded his reply.

"It's a pretty good system, 'cos everybody's too scared to grass, and without that information we never get close to them. We're not foolish Mickey, we've got a good idea who they are and where they live. We watch them, we follow them, but they have a habit of keeping their hands clean. We'd love to topple their little pyramid and take out their 'Mister Big', but the only way we'll ever manage it, is to get someone on the inside," he concluded, fixing his eyes on Mickey's.

"But like I told you, the only time I got close to them, they beat me within an inch of my life. I just don't think I know enough to help you."

"You'd be surprised how much you can assist us Mickey," Draycott continued. "I've spoken to my gaffer, and he's willing to help you…if you're willing to help us."

"What do you mean?"

"First of all, let me tell you what we can offer. As you know, you're up for some serious charges, and under normal circumstances…you'd be looking at two to five years. If you *were* to help us get the main players, we'd negotiate a deal with CPS, which would probably mean your sentence getting suspended. Instead of being inside for a few years, you could be out enjoying life with Lara."

A frown broke out across Mickey's brow. Last time he'd spoken to Draycott, he'd just returned from being dumped.

As if he was reading his mind, the officer continued. "It's alright Mickey, you're being straight with us, so I'll be straight with you. We've been watching your place from the moment you were released; we'd be failing in our job if we didn't. We saw an attractive girl turn up at your house on the night of the funeral; we just put two and two together."

Bollocks, they had cameras outside his home…no wonder they'd been happy to grant him bail!

"Yeah, that was Lara alright. She's been a star; I don't think I'd be here if it wasn't for her."

"You're a lucky man, she's a beautiful girl. I'm sure you wouldn't want to spend the next few years without her, would you?"

"Of course not."

"Well, remember what I said to you last time. You've been used and abused all your life; you owe them nothing. It's time to look after yourself for a change."

"As I say, I want to help, I just don't know as much as you think."

"Well we believe you do, you just don't realise it," Smudger continued. "But let me tell you what else we can do. We can set you up with a fresh start in life: a new home, in a new area, with a new identity. You and Lara would never have to live in fear again. Consider your alternatives Mickey, 'cos let's face it, they're pretty bleak. You'd go to jail for a few years and come out no different than before. No qualifications combined with a prison record would make you unemployable, so guess what, you'd end up resorting to thieving for the rest of your life. And let's be honest, there's no way Lara's gonna stay with a criminal is she? So basically the ball's in your court; you can do as much as you can to help us, or you're free to walk away and we'll forget this meeting ever took place."

"No, I came here today to do the right thing," Mickey replied resolutely. "I just want some guarantees first."

"Go on."

"You have to remember that some of the gang are my mates. They're good people, just stuck in the same position as me. I need some assurances that they'll be looked after."

Draycott exhaled deeply. "I'd need to run it by my gaffer, but to be honest Mickey, I'd be surprised if he agreed; we can only do a deal with those who try to help us. We're all bound by the law; everybody has to face the consequences of their actions. I take it all's not well in your team?"

"It used to be tight," Mickey nodded. "We'd do anything for each other, but now…well let's just say we've got some right wankers in the group."

"Let me guess, the wankers are the ones who beat the security guards up, and made off in the Beemer?"

"Bingo."

"Is there any way you can isolate them from the others?"

"No chance. Now our numbers have reduced, we all have to work together."

"Okay, I'll have a chat with the boss, but I really can't make any promises. In the meantime, I could plead your case better if you gave me something to go back with. Is there anything planned that we need to know about?"

Mickey took a deep breath. His whole life he'd been taught to hate snitches, but as the words came out, he felt relieved of their burden.

"We're doing a job on Friday," he started. "It's to do with all that 'shoot the moon' graffiti?"

"Go on," Draycott replied, leaning towards him.

Settling back in his seat, Mickey began to explain the daring plan: from the wagon theft, to the firebomb, and everything in between.

"That's it, that's everything I know," he said, looking from one officer to the other. "I'm trusting you now; you've got to do everything you can to keep my mates out of it."

"Well, what you've just told us will certainly help; I'm sure my gaffer'll be chuffed. We'll put together our own plans, and in the meantime, give Smudger a call on Friday with the final details," Draycott replied. "But before we finish…you've mentioned your bosses and how you'd like them to face justice. However, you've yet to tell us much about them. Can you help us out; do you know who they are?"

"Oh yes, I know who the bastards are alright," Mickey scowled. "They call themselves 'The Power Firm', and they've all got different jobs. A bloke called Chapman looks after us, while Razor's the heavy who hands out the beatings. There's some others I don't know, but the man behind it all drives around in a private-plated black Beemer. He goes by the name of J.T., and he thinks he's fucking invincible!"

"That young Mickey is exactly what we needed," Draycott grinned. "And believe me; he's not as invincible as he thinks!"

***

After dropping Mickey off safely, the officers hurried back to their nick.

"You two look pleased with yourselves," Gladstone remarked, as their beaming faces entered the office. "I presume your meeting was successful?"

"You could say that," Draycott replied. "I think we've just witnessed the biggest breakthrough yet on the so called 'Power Firm'. This could be the beginning of their end!"

Replacing his mug on the table, Gladstone motioned to Hanson to lock the door behind. "That's quite a profound claim. Perhaps you could fill me in with the details."

"The bottom line is, his bosses have pushed him over the edge. Remember the injuries we spotted on the surveillance cameras? They were a punishment for not getting the watches back safely. He's willing to help us regardless of the packages we can offer him. His motivation is simple; he wants to bring his leaders to justice."

"Now that is positive," the Inspector smiled. "'Justice' is normally associated with our side of the fence. Do you really think we can trust him?"

"It's impossible to say for certain. He's been to hell and back over the last couple of weeks, his head's all over the place, and right now he's hurting badly. Yes, there's a danger he could change his allegiance once more, but you know what, somehow I doubt it. Not only did his best mate die, but they beat him up and made him miss the funeral! I don't get the feeling he's in a rush to forgive them!"

"Good, good," Gladstone nodded. "They've ruled by fear for far too long. Perhaps they've chosen the wrong individual this time; let's hope he's got the resolve to see things through. So tell me, what did he have to say for himself?"

"Well, he was refreshingly honest, and eager to help. However, he did seek assurances that we'd look after some friends within his group, so to speak."

"I hope you told him that wouldn't be possible?" Gladstone frowned.

"Of course," Draycott laughed quietly. "He maybe a little naïve, but he *is* prepared to help us out. Just being within that group gives him access to info that *we* can only dream of; we need to make the most of it!"

"I agree entirely, but before we start to task him, he needs to prove he's trustworthy. We need specific information to act upon."

Pulling scribbled notes from his pocket, Draycott laid them on the table. "This is why we're grinning like Cheshire cats!" he smiled. "How long have we been trying to find out what the 'shoot the moon' graffiti's been all about?"

"Too long," Hanson tutted.

"Well, according to Mickey…they're about to destroy our helicopter!"

Gladstone drew in a deep breath. Worth in excess of three million pounds, it was irreplaceable. Without it, the force would be left utterly exposed.

"How on earth do they expect to succeed in such a bold attack? They surely don't intend to shoot it out of the sky…do they?" he asked dumbfounded.

"No," Draycott chuckled knowingly. "They may well have access to weapons, but a surface-to-air missile is still a few years off!"

"Well how *do* they plan to do it then?"

"It's surprisingly simple really. They've recognised the helicopter is at its most vulnerable when it's sat on the ground…so they plan to smash into it with a wagon, torch it, then drive off into the sunset!"

"Surely there must be security: gates, barriers, fences etc?" Hanson retorted.

"Only one set of gates," the Inspector mused thoughtfully. "And they'd cave in the moment the vehicle hit them."

"Exactly," Draycott replied.

Nobody spoke.

Deep in thought, Gladstone tapped his lips with his forefinger. Finally, he broke the silence.

"Chaps, you were right to be so pleased with yourselves," he nodded. "If they'd succeeded with their audacious plan, our ability to fight crime would have been decimated, our police service humiliated, and our criminals…triumphant. If the plan is true, and from what you're telling me I have no reason to doubt it, then it would have been the single most important blow our force, and perhaps any force, has ever suffered. We need to act, and act quickly. I'll contact the Chief Constable to get the wheels in motion. In the meantime, we need to update air ops, and get a firearms unit down there asap. Steve, can you brief our team; I want round the clock obs on all of our targets, starting now! Do you all understand?"

No words needed to be spoken. The solemn stares said it all.

"It goes without saying; everything we've just discussed is top secret. If our enemy were to get wind of our plans, it'd undoubtedly mean a death warrant for Mickey. We need to make sure we protect him…he's one of us now."

48

Within fifteen minutes of calling his Chief Constable, Gladstone found himself in her office; delivering a full briefing to her staff.

"And how credible is your source Mr Gladstone?" she asked as he finished.

"Although he is untested Ma'am, I'm confident he's telling us the truth. As you know, we've been wondering for some time about the 'shoot the moon' graffiti, and now, thanks to our source, it would appear we've discovered the meaning just in time."

"Indeed, the consequences of such an attack are staggering," she replied angrily. "*I* will deal with this personally. Inspector Khan," she said turning to her staff officer. "Cancel my remaining appointments, and have my driver ready to leave in five minutes. We're going straight to the airport; let's hope the defences aren't as useless as our criminals believe!"

Unannounced, their arrival was met with panic and surprise; the Air Op's Inspector stumbling to field his superior's interrogation.

"Perhaps I can take you on a tour of our facilities to allay your concerns ma'am?" he stammered.

"Yes Mr Williams, do that," the Chief glowered. "And I sincerely hope I'm not disappointed!"

Leading the way, the Inspector began by pointing out his first line of defence – a plastic arm rising and falling at the entrance to the car park.

"To gain entry you need the appropriate swipecard," he explained. "In order to have one issued, you have to pass rigorous security checks."

"That thing's not strong enough to stop a pedal bike Inspector!" the Chief bellowed. "I hope there's more substantial protection ahead! Lead on."

At the car park's edge, the party walked up to a wire-mesh perimeter fence, in the middle of which, a gate secured by a small padlock prevented access onto the airfield itself.

"I hope you are joking Mr Williams…is this it?" she said open-mouthed.

"While I can understand your concerns," the Inspector explained. "We are unable to construct a more substantial barrier as this is the emergency route for rescue vehicles; they require rapid access twenty-four hours a day."

Walking through the opened gate, they looked towards the Heli-Pad. For a hundred metres, a narrow tarmac strip cut a swathe through freshly cut grass, ending at the motionless, and utterly exposed helicopter.

The Chief shook her head from side to side.

"So," she said, turning to the Air Ops Inspector. "How *are* we going to protect it? Mr Williams, I placed you in charge here; give me a solution!"

His face flushing, he stuttered his reply. "As I said ma'am, it's very difficult to create a stronger defence; the airport's health and safety regulations don't allow anything that prevents unrestricted access for fire and rescue."

"Dammit man!" the Chief exploded. "I didn't ask for what we couldn't do. I asked for solutions...for what we *can* do! Just how long have you been down here?"

"Three years, ma'am."

"Three years! For three years you've overlooked your primary responsibility. How is it that our criminals have discovered the abject lack of protection, yet you appear to be completely naive? You're a disgrace Inspector! Now, can *anybody* suggest a practical solution?"

"If we take what Mr Williams has said to be true ma'am, then we need to look at the problem from another angle," Gladstone spoke up. "Follow me if you will."

With that, he and the Chief strolled along the tarmac towards the helicopter, the others following a few paces behind. At the track's end lay a large tarmac square, in the centre of which was a white circle bearing the letter 'H'. Perched on the 'H', the helicopter sat ready for action.

As he reached the Heli-Pad, Gladstone turned to look back at the perimeter gate.

"I don't believe the solution lies with the outer security over which we have little control, but actually within this perfect square of tarmac," he stated confidently. "History provides the answer. When our ancestors were attacked, they didn't stay in their fields to fight; they retired to their castles, keeping the raiders at bay from within their fortress."

"That's absurd, Mr Gladstone," Inspector Williams blustered. "We can't just build fortifications around it. It would take months, you'd need planning permission..."

"I think *I* can see where he's coming from," the Chief interrupted. "Please continue with your proposal Paul."

"It's quite simple really. First of all, we dig a deep trench around the outside, then we use temporary concrete blocks to create a low, solid barrier surrounding the tarmac's edge. Combining these features will effectively make any vehicle based attack doomed to failure."

"Absolutely," the Chief replied. "Can I confirm we're expecting the strike to be on Friday?"

"Yes ma'am, but we'd be unwise not to prepare for it earlier."

"I wholeheartedly agree. Inspector Khan, start the preparations immediately. No matter what it costs, I expect our defences to be in place without delay. Keep me updated with the developments, and oh…you can tell HR to begin the recruitment process for Mr William's position; it has just become vacant!"

***

As demanded, progress was rapid. While an armed guard provided cover, contractors toiled through the night. Heavyweight diggers carved deep channels, and with the concrete barriers soon lowered into position, work was completed within twenty-four hours. Secure within its protection; the helicopter was safe – the cops were ready for the attack.

***

Mickey watched Chapman with disdain. There he was, sat in Deano's normal armchair, his stern expression receiving the posse's undivided attention.

"First of all, we need to discuss who's doing what," Chapman began. "The less people involved the better, so you're only gonna take two cars. I want two in each motor and one to drive the wagon."

"But we *all* want to be in on this one; it's the biggest job yet!" Tommy protested.

"When I said 'discuss', I may not have made myself clear. Our discussion is a one-way affair. I discuss with you, you keep your trap shut, understand!"

Looking down at the floor, Tommy scowled but kept silent.

"Right then. Deano, elect the crews, the rest can leave straightaway!"

"Ronnie's alongside me. Mickey, you'll come with us to pick up the wagon. Tommy, you'll take Nozza with you."

"Okay. You've heard what he's had to say," Chapman instructed, walking over to the lounge door. "The rest of you can get out…now!"

Heads bowed, the others left under Chapman's dismissive gaze. Slamming the door behind him, he sat back down and continued.

"You boys have got sloppy, mistakes have been made; it's time you became more disciplined," he declared. "Now listen carefully, 'cos this is our final meeting before tonight's mission. Deano, we believe the filth have got cameras on your place, so instead of meeting up here, you'll find a suitable spot near the airport."

While the remaining heads nodded, Mickey's stomach churned. It was as if Chapman was one step ahead of the cops: he knew they were under surveillance, and he'd restricted those in the know. Had he been tipped off about a grass within their group? Shit, what if one of the coppers was bent? If J.T. already knew what Mickey was up to…he was as good as a dead man walking.

"For the battering ram, Deano's nicked a fully loaded skip wagon, which he assures me will demolish everything in its path. He's also sorted his getaway car, so the only motor not accounted for is yours Tommy. I take it you're ready for action?"

"Of course," Tommy replied with a broad grin. "Brand new Maserati Quattroporte, nicked directly from the showroom. The fools were kind enough to leave the keys on display; it'll do the job nicely thank you!"

"Good," Chapman continued. "Now pay attention, Deano's gonna fill you in with the finer details."

Mickey's heart thudded against his chest. He was in too deep now; he had to follow things through to their end. One thought did calm him slightly though: if J.T. really did suspect him, why was he being given the most important job? No, he couldn't know yet, and until he did, Mickey was going to do everything in his power to take him down. So as Deano spoke, he sucked up every last piece of information; as did his new mobile…recording all the proof the police needed.

***

With Mickey unable to give the stolen skip's exact location, the CATS team spent several hours combing the local area before finding it. Technical support swiftly followed, discreetly positioning a camera on a nearby telegraph pole.

The find was the final confirmation needed to prove Mickey's information was reliable. Following its discovery, the excited team gathered back at base, waiting for their battle plan to be revealed.

"I won't waste time with pleasantries," Gladstone announced, walking into the office. "We have an important job to do, so let's get straight down to business."

Remaining standing, he took his place at the front of the room.

"We believe the attack will go ahead tonight as planned. At half past ten the offenders will drive straight to Kelvin Close where they'll collect the skip wagon. They're in two cars; a black Jaguar XF-R, and a silver Maserati saloon; needless to say, both vehicles are stolen. Our informant will initially travel in the Jag, but will then take control of the skip lorry. I must emphasise, that for his own protection, he is completely unaware of how we are acting on his information. Once they've confirmed the helicopter's on the ground, they'll make their way to the airport and smash through the gates. As you know, their intention is to head straight for the chopper and ram it into oblivion. Of course…" Gladstone said, raising an eyebrow, "…we're not going to let that happen, are we?"

"We will however, allow all three vehicles to enter Airport Way," he continued, pointing out the access road on a map. "After they break through the outer barrier, Sergeant Hanson and I will drive in behind, lights and sirens blazing. This should attract the attention of the Maserati, which we are told will peel off as a decoy. By now, Drewy will have set up at the exit to Airport Way, blocking all the traffic from the right. Having been forced to turn left, the Maserati will head straight towards Strickers, who will be waiting up the road with a stinger. The dog car will then take over the chase...so I hope Quincy's hungry Gaz!"

"I've deliberately not fed him for days boss!"

"We're not committing everybody to the Maserati though. After he's sent it towards the stinger, Drewy will hold position, and take up pursuit of the Jag when it eventually emerges. Any questions so far?"

"I take it you want us to sting the Jag as well then?" Strickers asked.

"Aaah, I'm glad you raised that point. As you all appreciate, Mickey is our only opportunity to get to the bosses; tonight shows just how important he is. After consultation with the Chief herself, we have agreed that he's too valuable to lose at this stage – the Jag will be allowed to get away."

Around the room, sharp intakes of breath greeted the revelation.

"Now while I know this may not sit comfortably with some, I am convinced the end justifies the means. Right now, we're building evidence against the leaders; but the truth is, even after this job, there's only enough to nail Chapman. We need more, and the only person who can help us will be sat in the back of the Jag. Now, does anybody have any objections?"

Unblinking, to a man they shook their heads.

"Good," Gladstone nodded. "Obviously, we have to remain flexible. If they do something unexpected, we'll have to act as we see fit. Remember, tonight's primary objective is to prevent the helicopter getting damaged; after that...everything's a bonus!"

***

Mickey trudged towards the meet, his mind fretting over the call he'd made to Smudger. He'd told the officer everything he knew, but in return had received very little: no hint at the police response, no guarantees to look after his friends. Was he really doing the right thing? How could he lead his mates into a trap; they'd defended him, supported him...trusted him! Lost in his thoughts, he almost collided with Ronnie in the garage block shadows.

"Careful mate," Ronnie said stepping to one side. "Are you on a different planet tonight?"

"Sorry mate, I can't get the job out my mind; I've just gotta get it bang on."

"Listen, don't give it a second thought; it's the easiest one yet. We'll be in and out in two minutes flat, you'll see."

"Yeah, I'm sure you're right. It's just after what happened last time..."

"Mate, I understand. But don't forget, we'll be with you all the way. We're here to look after each other, remember?"

His words were like a dagger to the heart. There was still time to pull out; he could warn them of the trap! But if he did, they'd...

Deano's arrival interrupted his panic. Calmly nodding his greeting, he led them to the lock-up, and jumped inside the Jag. Out into the open, he paused just long enough for Mickey to close the doors behind, before leisurely driving away.

While Deano chatted over the daring strike, Mickey focused on his own plans. He would have to do exactly as Chapman had demanded; anything else would be suicidal. But, after the police had sprung their trap, he'd be free to do as he wanted, and that meant doing his damndest to help his mates get away.

Mind made up, his attention returned to his friend's conversation.

"I guess the filth'll soon know what the graffiti's been about," Deano smiled.

"Well it's got all the local kids talking; they've been scrawling it everywhere without a clue why! *You* must know who came up with it?" Ronnie smirked.

"Chapman spread the word, but I'm pretty sure it came from J.T."

"Why's that then?" Mickey frowned.

"Well from what I can gather, it was originally just meant to wind the local cops up. But then it turned into something more personal; something to do with an old score he wanted settling," Deano replied, glancing in the mirror. "There's a gaffer called Gladstone down at Stechford nick; it was his team who sent Hood and his pals down the steps. Apparently, he's also the one who sent J.T. to prison. J.T.'s never forgiven him...I guess this is his way of getting even."

Interesting, Mickey thought to himself; Gladstone and J.T. had history, and plenty of it. No wonder they were so keen to take each other down!

Before long, they turned off the main roads and headed into an industrial area's back streets. Parked practically in darkness outside a ramshackle scrap yard, the skip-wagon was perfectly hidden in plain sight...unlike the gleaming Maserati behind.

The moment Deano pulled up, Mickey jumped out, and headed towards the lorry. Ignoring the guard dogs barking to his side, he climbed into the cab, inserted a screwdriver, and turned. As the diesel engine chugged to life, he glanced around the cockpit. Just as Deano had promised, it was all pretty straightforward; three pedals, a gearstick, and muck...plenty of muck!

Inside the Jag, Ronnie checked his aircraft tracking app for the final time. The chopper was on the tarmac...it was time to shoot the moon!

49

What a heap of shit, Mickey cursed, accelerating as quickly as his heavy lorry could manage; which was little more than a low speed trundle. Ahead, he could see Ronnie furtively checking over his shoulder, while behind, the Maserati was so close it was practically pushing him forward. Tommy's irate face loomed large in his wing mirror. Mickey smiled…little did he know what was coming his way!

Lumbering out onto the dual carriageway, his eyes scanned everywhere; would the police go for a strike on the way to the job? It didn't look like it; the roads were empty, apart from an occasional vehicle passing their sluggish convoy. Only half a mile to go, even at these speeds they'd arrive in less than a minute.

Nearly there, and yet he felt so very different to normal. Where was the adrenaline bursting through his veins? Tonight all he felt was sick, sick to the pit of his stomach.

Into Airport Way and still no sign of cops; the whole area was deserted. It was just another job, he told himself, his heart beginning to pound at last; if he dealt with it like any other, he'd be fine.

As the Jag pulled to one side, he spotted his first target in the distance. Pressing his gas pedal to the floor, his wagon gradually picked up speed, passing his mates and taking the lead. Still no sign of the police; surely they weren't going to let him reach the chopper!

By now, his momentum was building. Nothing could stop him slamming through the first obstacle, and it didn't; the flimsy plastic arm disintegrating on impact. Unhindered, he thundered onward. A brief glance in his mirrors confirmed everything was going as planned: Deano was tucked in behind, while Tommy had pulled up at the barrier.

Ploughing ahead through the floodlit car park, he lined up the gates at its edge. Foot still planted on the accelerator, he braced himself for the collision. But despite their solid appearance, they were no match for his heavy wagon; the impact sending them flying off their hinges and into the airfield's darkness. Careering unchecked towards the Heli-Pad, a smile broke out at last…perhaps under different circumstances this would have been bloody good fun!

But where the hell were the cops?!

Ahead, its blades drooping, the helicopter sat silhouetted against the bright terminal buildings in the distance. It all seemed too easy. His metal juggernaut was picking up speed, there was only fifty metres to go – the chopper was a sitting duck!

And then…his heart stopped.

From a distance they'd not been visible; their low height merging with the Heli-Pad's tarmac. But now, as he closed in on his target, his elevated position brought the concrete barricade sharply into focus. Was that it; was that all the police had planned? With his wagon's weight and speed, the barriers might slow him slightly, but there was no way they'd stop him taking out the helicopter…surely they had something else up their sleeves?

Speeding ever closer, he desperately considered his options: rush on regardless, or abandon the mission and dive into the Jag. But there really was only one choice; one way to avoid suspicion, one way to avoid J.T.'s wrath. With the gas pedal floored, he changed up a gear…he was going to go straight through the barriers!

A quick yank to check his seatbelt, and he was ready for the hit. But now, almost on top of the barricade, he suddenly spotted the extra defence. Practically invisible in the darkness; a deep ditch surrounded the landing pad. His eyes reacted in an instant, searching for a break in its path. But there was nothing; there was no way out. Despite the speed he'd gathered, it'd be impossible to hurdle; it was almost as wide as a car! Shit, he had to do something, and quick!

Slamming his foot onto the brake pedal, the wheels locked instantly. But the sudden weight transfer unsettled the wagon's heavy load; its fully-laden skip swinging ominously towards the cab. Side-to-side, Mickey slung the huge wheel, desperately fighting for control. But his actions were futile; the deep channel was almost upon him. Eyes fixed on the inevitable impact; he failed to spot the black helmets popping up on the landing pad's opposite side – their barrels trained squarely on his vehicle.

There was nothing more he could do. At the last possible moment he released the wheel, lifted his foot from the brake, and curled himself up in a ball.

Front end plunging downwards, the deep pit swallowed his cab whole. But as its heavy skip shot forward, the lorry's rear end kicked skywards, the momentum enough to slowly pitch the whole wagon over…before crashing back to earth upside down.

Fortunately for Mickey, he'd blacked out on impact. Left dangling by his seatbelt, his protective cab had disintegrated around him, slamming his limp body one way then the other before finally coming to rest.

Sliding their Jag to a halt, his friends were out and running even before the carnage had ended. Dodging the falling debris, they raced towards the upturned cab. Deano was the first to jump into the deep channel, his hands wrenching the buckled door open almost as he landed.

Mickey wasn't moving.

"I'll take his weight," he shouted, taking hold of the limp body. "You get his belt off!"

Squeezing into the remaining space, Ronnie reached up to click the release, and grabbed hold of Mickey's legs. Carefully, they lowered him to the cab roof.

"Is he still with us?" Ronnie asked, as Deano checked for his breathing.

"Just," he nodded quickly. "But we need to get him out of here…now!"

Between them, they hauled him clear, and laid him on the Jag's rear seat. While Ronnie jumped in beside Mickey, Deano flicked the car into gear and floored it; the fat tyres wheel-spinning away across the tarmac. Blasting back through the missing gates, he was at the car park's exit within seconds.

"Fucking great," he shouted out. "Tommy's decided to bottle it; he's nowhere to be seen!"

But Deano was about to grasp the reason for Tommy's absence. Racing away from the car park, he spotted blue strobes in the distance.

"I don't believe it," he gasped. "The cops are waiting for us!"

"How the fuck did they know we were coming!" Ronnie shouted, his arms cradling Mickey's bloody head.

With the exit from Airport Way blocked to his right, Deano flung the Jag into a powerslide across the police car's nose, and accelerated away through the gears.

Mickey groaned as he began to come to; the pain from his battered body overwhelming. Blood flowed freely from his forehead; stinging his eyes, filling his mouth with its sickly sweet taste. Slowly, carefully, he pushed himself up.

"How you feeling," Ronnie asked.

"Pretty shit; I feel like I've been hit by a sledgehammer."

"More like a skip!" Deano called over his shoulder, barely lifting off the accelerator as he passed an unmarked police car; its occupants scrambling back in through its doors.

Still groggy, Mickey wiped his eyes and tried to focus.

"Where are we?" he asked.

"You haven't been out for long mate; we've only just left the airport," Deano replied. "But take a look behind; we've already got two cops on our tail!"

His latest collision fresh in his mind, Mickey eased a seat belt over his bruised shoulder. Normally he'd be checking all around, reporting on their pursuers…but right now, all he could do was sit back and close his eyes; the last place he wanted to be was in the middle of another fucking pursuit.

The chase was unrelenting. Racing through the city streets, their hunters remained unshakeable behind. Finally, even with his eyes closed, Mickey recognised where he was; the familiar bumps on Alwold Road's service drive…the scene of his first arrest!

"Wake up sleepyhead; get ready to brace!" Deano shouted, guiding his Jag over the rough surface.

Looking up, Mickey was grateful there wasn't a squad car waiting for them this time, just the raised earth 'jump' he'd used so many times before.

As they turned towards the ramp, he ducked his head down, and grasped the grab handle with all his strength – this was going to hurt!

He felt the tyres bite into the hard earth, then nothing; just weightlessness as it flew over the five-foot incline….before landing heavily, crushing his injured back once more.

Ignoring Mickey's screams, Deano instantly re-applied the power, pulling the car back into line as he blasted along the dirt track and away.

"Quick, we've bought ourselves a little time, but they'll soon surround the area," Deano called out, sliding the Jag to a halt. "We'll help you get back to your place Mickey, but then we'll have to do one, okay?"

Dazed and confused, he weakly nodded his reply. Gingerly, he attempted to drag himself out, but it was hopeless; he'd barely moved before he slumped back onto his seat.

Diving straight in, Deano quickly pulled him out. Taking an arm each over their shoulders, he and Ronnie hauled him along, his toes dragging limply across the ground as they approached the main road. Sirens were everywhere, but the street was clear; Mickey's maisonette only seconds away.

Before they'd even had chance to knock, Lara was at the door, hurrying them inside.

"What the hell happened?" she asked angrily.

"Sorry, we honestly haven't got time right now; we've gotta get going," Deano replied, laying Mickey on the bed. "Bell me later, let me know he's okay," and together with Ronnie rushed out before she could ask any more.

***

Gladstone's smile said it all. Returning from the custody suite, he strolled into the CATS office, his fist clenched in triumph.

"Nice work chaps; it couldn't have gone better if I'd planned it myself!"

Other than Sergeant Hanson, he was the last to return. Though it had been two hours since the action had finished, an excited buzz still filled the small room. He was right to be happy; everything had gone precisely to plan. As predicted, Tommy's Maserati had fled straight into their trap; its shredded tyres leaving them stranded nearby. Unwisely attempting to outrun Quincy, Tommy had been ripped to pieces, while Nozza had taken the only sensible option; standing perfectly still, his arms in the air, surrendering to the cops on the spot.

Meanwhile, Deano's 'airtime' over the Alwold Road jump had provided the perfect excuse for his pursuers to give up without raising suspicion.

"Thanks for all your hard work chaps, I hope you're as delighted as I am. For the first time ever, we actually managed to get a step ahead. We've sent a clear message that *we're* in control around here. However, while we celebrate tonight, we can't become complacent. Our enemy may well be licking their wounds, but I expect them to…no, I'm *relying* on them to come out fighting. And when they do, we'll be ready; one step ahead again, ready to bring their leaders to justice!"

Impromptu applause broke out, cut short almost immediately by Hanson entering the room, his arms frantically gesturing for them to calm down.

"I've just finished speaking with the firearms team dug in around the helicopter," he began. "From what they could see, the ditch did its job a little too well; the wagon flipped over on impact. Mickey's mates in the Jag were seen to drag his body out, before driving off at speed. In short, they have real concerns he may not have survived the impact."

"Nah, he may have been hurt, but he's certainly not dead," Wilson spoke up. "He must have come round not long after they'd left the airport, 'cos I definitely saw him sit up during the chase."

"Well that's certainly good to hear, he's a brave lad," Gladstone replied. "Last night's success is entirely down to him; we'll need to make contact in the morning."

"There was one small hiccup in our plan though," Hanson continued. "Debris from the impact exploded everywhere. Unfortunately some landed on the helicopter, so it's been grounded while they inspect for damage. First impressions are good; it looks like there's just cosmetic scratches and the like, however a full inspection will have to wait until daylight."

Almost as Hanson finished his sentence, Strickers answered the office phone. "It's the Chief sir," he said handing it to Gladstone. "She'd like to speak to you."

The whole room hushed down, and waited for the update.

"The Chief just wanted to pass on her congratulations, and thanks you for your hard work tonight," he smiled. "She re-iterates my view, that we must ready ourselves for the backlash. J.T and his henchmen will be furious; they'll be desperate to find the mole in their midst. For Mickey's sake…let's just pray they never do!"

50

Ignoring his mobile's piercing ring, J.T. pulled his duvet ever tighter over his head.

But still it rang.

With a groan, he rolled over and squinted at the screen.

"What the fuck do you want?" he answered. "It's the middle of the pissin' night!"

"Erm, it's not good news I'm afraid," Chapman's voice trembled. "Shoot the moon failed."

J.T. sat up, rocking slowly backwards and forwards, his anger steadily building.

"J.T.?" Chapman asked, the silence deafening. "Are you still there?"

"Of course I'm still fucking here! I'm just working out whose legs I'm gonna break. Do you wanna be the first?"

Barely pausing for breath, J.T. continued his rant. "How the fuck could it have failed? It was fool-proof; all they had to do was ram the bloody thing! Spit it out Chapman, what the fuck happened?"

"Well I don't know the full details yet, but from what I can gather from Deano, they drove into a trap; the police were waiting for them."

J.T.'s hand tightened around his mobile.

"Well we both know what that means," he seethed. "Some little shit's been opening their mouth to the wrong people haven't they! Get the boys round my place for ten and make sure Deano's there. Somebody's gonna pay for this...with their fucking life!"

***

Sat fidgeting next to Chapman, Deano remained silent. So too were the rest of the Power Firm as they awaited their leader's wrath. Now 10:15, he was late – ominously late.

Heavy feet thundered down the stairs. The lounge door burst open; J.T. was ready to explode.

"This is fucking war!" he raged. "Nobody crosses me and gets away with it. Deano, tell me exactly what happened...and don't leave anything out, or so help me God, you'll be the first to pay!"

Taking in a deep breath, Deano began; his audience hanging on to every word. In detail, he ran through the night's events, finishing off with the news that Tommy and Nozza had been arrested.

"Jonas is planning to get them bail when they're up in court tomorrow," Deano concluded. "They're gonna plead ignorance to the whole helicopter plot; he reckons he can cast enough doubt to swing it."

"Well let's hope he does, 'cos I need to speak to every one of your little fuckers to get to the bottom of this!" J.T. raged. "And while we're on the subject," he said, leaning towards Deano. "Tell me, why do *you* think it all went wrong?"

Swallowing hard, Deano stuttered his reply. "Boss, you've got to understand, there was nothing we could do…the cops were waiting for us!"

"Of course they were fucking waiting for you; that's bleeding obvious!" J.T. screamed. "The question is; *why* were they waiting for you?"

Visibly ducking to avoid J.T.'s roar, Deano desperately gathered his thoughts.

"They were waiting for us…'cos they knew we were coming," he stammered. "Either they'd worked out what the graffiti was all about, or…they were tipped off."

"Exactly," J.T. replied, calming slightly. "So the next question is; if somebody *did* tip them off…who the hell was it? Who'd be stupid enough to take *me* on!"

"Honestly boss, I don't know. If I even had the slightest suspicion I'd tell you – you know I would. But the truth is, I haven't got a clue."

"And at this stage, nor have I; but rest assured I will," he bristled. "And when I do, I guarantee the coppers will *never* hear from him again!"

"I can help you there boss," Razor piped up. "Remember the last guy who grassed on us? Before he had his little…accident, we sewed his lips together. I can get my skewer ready again if you want?"

"Thank you, I know I can always rely on your support," J.T. smiled at his henchman. "Now, I'm expecting the same from the rest of you, so get out there and do some digging. Speak to every contact and every source; I want a name, and I want it *now*!"

Taking their cue, the group nodded and rose to leave. All apart from Deano…J.T.'s hand on his shoulder saw to that.

"And as for your lot, if they're not locked up, I expect to see them today; one an hour, every hour, starting at two o' clock, okay?"

"Of course boss, I'll sort it straight away. The only one who might struggle is Mickey Wilding. I haven't had chance to speak to him yet, but from the state he was in last night, it wouldn't surprise me if he's back in a hospital bed."

"Let me make myself perfectly clear. Unless he's dead, he will see me today as requested. Do you understand what I'm saying?" J.T. spat out, leaning even closer.

"Yes, yes. He'll be there," Deano replied, backing ever deeper into his seat.

"Good, and you can let them know that Razor'll be joining me. As you can see, he's chomping at the bit to help, and let's just say his lie detection test won't be as pleasant as Jeremy Kyle's!"

***

Inside Stechford's custody suite, the atmosphere was just as intense. While Jonas briefed his clients, the CATS team formulated their plans. Once both sides were ready, Tommy's interview began.

"I wish to read out a pre-prepared statement on behalf of my client," Jonas interrupted, the moment the officers completed their introductions. "It is signed by Mr Burns, and as is his right, he has chosen not to answer any further questions, as it provides a comprehensive account of his actions."

Opening his briefcase, Jonas pulled out the statement, adjusted his half-moon spectacles and began to read aloud. Half-truth, half-deceit, it described how Tommy and Nozza had sneaked in to take the Maserati from a showroom before taking it for a joyride. Despite dumping it the same day, the car was never recovered, so they decided to take it for another blast later in the week. While they were out, they spotted some youngsters in a sporty looking Jaguar being followed by a skip wagon. Out of curiosity, they trailed the two vehicles until they reached the airport grounds. However, when they saw the wagon smash through the barriers, they panicked and turned around, at which point the police arrived.

True to Jonas's opening statement, Tommy refused to answer any further questions, remaining cross armed and grinning throughout. With Nozza's interview following exactly the same format, the frustrated officers returned to their colleagues.

"What a load of fucking bollocks!" DC Darby swore, slamming the door behind.

"Maybe so, but how are we going to prove any different?" Strickers replied.

"Indeed...Jonas is a cunning old opponent," Gladstone mused. "He's covered exactly what he knows we can prove: CCTV from the showroom, their convoy to the airport, and the high speed pursuit away."

"There's no way his story will get past a jury, but it might just be enough to sneak bail," DC Darby shook his head. "The only real way we can disprove it, is for Mickey to stand up and give evidence. We couldn't make him do that...could we?"

"Not while I have breath in my body!" an indignant Gladstone replied. "He's put his life on the line for us; we will *not* let him down. Don't lose sight of the bigger picture guys; Tommy and Nozza are insignificant compared to J.T. and his cronies. They are our real targets – Mickey is still the key."

Gladstone paused for a moment, as if waiting for a response.

None came.

"No, we'll go with what we've got for the moment," he concluded. "We'll just have to let the courts decide."

***

Considering the battering his body had taken, Mickey slept surprisingly well; nature's self-healing kicking in. In contrast, Lara hadn't slept a wink; her night spent removing glass slivers, bathing lacerations, and tending to his every wound.

It was late morning before his peaceful slumber came to an end; his mobile's jingle saw to that.

Slowly coming round, he squinted, and fumbled his hand towards the sound.

"Morning sleepyhead," Lara sighed as his hand met hers. "Just ignore it; I'm sure they'll ring back. Anyway blue-eyes, how're you feeling?"

Opening his eyes a little wider, he gazed at her smiling face. "Things could be a lot worse."

Carefully, he shifted position, reaching out for his bloodied jeans.

"It was Deano," he croaked, looking at the missed number. "I'd better get back to him; it all kicked off last night."

Before he could face the call, Mickey trudged off to freshen up; but even a splash of water couldn't alter the image staring back in the mirror. Open wounds, bruising, swelling; how could Lara even bear to look at him! Painkillers; they were the only answer for the moment…just a pity they'd do nothing for his looks!

Returning to the bedroom, he picked up his phone.

"Deano, it's Mickey, you guys okay?"

"All good mate. We managed to avoid the cops, which is more than can be said about Tommy and Nozza!"

"Go on," he replied, a smile breaking out on his battered face.

"Right now they're sweating it out at Stechford nick; seems they weren't as good as they thought!"

"Oh well, can't say I'm too bothered."

"Yeah they're no great loss," Deano continued. "But as you can imagine, J.T.'s done his fucking nut. He thinks we were set up; he's out for revenge!"

Mickey shuddered. Had J.T. sussed him already?

"Any ideas who grassed?" he asked casually.

"I haven't got a clue, and to be fair, he could just be pissin' in the wind. What I do know, is that he's taken it personally; I've never seen him so angry. Don't shoot the messenger, but one-by-one, we've been ordered to pay him a visit…today!"

"Today?" Mickey recoiled. "I'm fucked mate. I should be in hospital, not pandering to his fucking ego!"

"I'll put you down for eight o' clock then. You'll be the last in, so hopefully he should've calmed down a bit by then."

"Cheers," Mickey huffed. "I can't wait!" and tossed the phone back onto his bed.

"Today's the day of reckoning then," he said, turning to Lara. "I just hope the police have kept their side of the bargain, or this'll be the last you ever see of me!"

***

Eight o' clock on the dot, Mickey rapped on J.T.'s front door; the strength of his knock belying his feeling inside. Heavy footfall approached, before Razor's squat frame filled the doorway.

"Next!" he barked, sweeping his arm to one side.

Guided into the lounge, Mickey cautiously looked around. Soft leather sofas, fine art and chandeliers contrasted a bare wooden stool in its centre…it wasn't difficult to work out where *he* was supposed to sit!

Taking up a seat opposite, Razor's stare bore deep into Mickey's evasive eyes. In silence they awaited J.T.'s arrival.

Whisky tumbler in hand, he eventually strolled in; a disdainful sneer breaking out the moment his eyes landed on Mickey.

"So who the fuck do we have here then?"

"A piece of shit we should have got rid of last time!" Razor roared, jumping to his feet. "I blame myself boss; if I'd done the right thing, he couldn't have fucked up…again!" he screamed, heaving Mickey to his feet.

"It's okay Razor, you can put him down for now. You can see he's a little…delicate at the moment, but I'm sure he understands the importance of telling me the truth," J.T. directed, gesturing for his henchman to return to his seat. "Don't you Mickey?"

"Yes, I understand," Mickey replied, memories of his previous meeting fresh in his mind.

"Good, then let's get on with it," J.T. continued. "Things didn't quite go according to plan last night; the question in my mind is why? Why, after all the careful preparation did it all go so spectacularly wrong? There is of course only one answer; somebody must have loose lips. So tell me Mickey, have you got loose lips – are you the grass?"

As if to emphasise the question, Razor rose from his seat and walked behind Mickey's stool.

What did they already know? Had the cops dropped him in it? Had they worked it out for themselves? He only had one option available. He had to lie; lie as convincingly as possible.

"No, I'd never squeal on my mates. All I've done for the past week is stay at home. You can see the state of me; I've just been trying to rest."

"And what about your girlfriend...Lara isn't it? You told her our plans didn't you? She couldn't wait to snitch, could she?"

"Yeah, you fuckin' dickhead," Razor screamed down his ear. "You've been telling her our little secrets. She's a whore; she's gone and grassed on you!"

Shit, they knew about Lara! If they suspected him, *she* was in deep trouble too!

"No, I've never told her anything. Yes she's been looking after me, 'cos I keep getting myself injured; but you have to believe me..." he pleaded, looking from one aggressor to the other, "...she hasn't got a clue."

"Do you think I'm fucking stupid?" J.T. scowled. "Every time you return home, you look like you've done ten rounds with Tyson! She'd have wanted to know exactly what's been happening; you told her didn't you?"

"Yeah, you lying little shit!" Razor screamed, the force of his slap practically knocking Mickey from the stool.

His head ringing, Mickey desperately attempted to collect his thoughts. In suspecting Lara, J.T. couldn't possibly know the truth; he was clearly guessing. However, his error of judgement was more dangerous than the truth. Somehow, he needed to throw them off the scent.

"You're definitely not stupid J.T., and nor is Lara. She's a bright girl from a posh family; there's no way she'd stay with scum like me if she knew the truth."

Swilling the ice cubes in his tumbler, J.T. mulled over Mickey's reply.

"Mmm, I suppose there is some truth in that. My contacts have told me all about her posh gaff, and her doting daddy."

"Lucky son, lucky," Razor whispered into Mickey's ear.

"Which brings me back to you again. I mean, you're probably not very happy with us, are you? First of all your mate dies, and then you get a beating for your troubles. So was that your motive Mickey – revenge? Or did they offer you a little bung, and promise to drop your charges?"

"J.T., you have to believe me, it's never crossed my mind; me and the boys owe everything to you. As far as I'm concerned, whoever grassed deserves everything that's coming to them," Mickey spluttered. "After my last beating, do you think I'd risk getting more? I promised to do whatever you wanted, and that's exactly what I did last night. Look at me boss...I nearly died for you!"

"We fucking wish you had!" Razor bellowed, his heavy backhand this time succeeding in knocking Mickey clean off his seat.

"Okay Razor, that'll do for the moment," J.T. nodded, as Mickey struggled back to the stool. "I've already spoken to Deano, and to be fair, he tells me you gave it your best shot, so at this stage...I'll have to believe you. You're right to show me your loyalty Mickey, but if I even suspect you're lying, you'll be swimming in concrete, understand!"

With J.T. appearing to have swallowed his story, and Razor having returned to his seat, Mickey relaxed a little. He knew he wasn't out of danger yet though, he needed to keep his guard up; J.T. still hadn't finished.

"So if it's not down to you or your girlfriend, who do *you* think's been spilling the beans?"

"To be honest, I'm not really sure. But you're right, the cops knew everything. We drove straight into their trap; somebody definitely tipped them off."

"Fucking right they did. One of your so-called posse tried to pass it off as a coincidence earlier; he certainly left here a little wiser."

"And a little sorer!" Razor chuckled.

"There must be someone you're suspicious of Mickey. Who don't you trust?"

Apart from them knowing all about Lara, their questions so far had been much as he'd expected. Having prepared his answers before he arrived, this was another he'd been waiting for.

"You know I don't trust Tommy or his mates, but I really don't think he'd grass. All he cares about is money, and I'm sure the police wouldn't pay him as much as he gets from you."

"Are you saying he'd sell out if the price was right?"

With the seed of doubt planted, Mickey backed off. "No, no, I'm sure he wouldn't. After all, he was the one who got arrested last night wasn't he?"

"Maybe so," J.T. frowned. "But he's got some fucking questions to answer when he gets out. In the meantime, have a long hard think about what we've chatted about. If you hear anything, you report directly to me. Now piss off and await your next instructions."

Rising to leave, Mickey began to follow Razor to the door.

"Oh, and Mickey," J.T. called after him. "If I find out you've lied to me in any way...I *will* kill you!"

51

It was nearly dark by the time the CATS team finally completed their court papers.

"Thanks for all your hard work guys," Gladstone said, signing off the file. "We've certainly won the battle, however we've still to win the war. Right now J.T. and his men will be licking their wounds; we need to be ready for their backlash."

"We'll be ready gaffer, and so will our secret weapon," Draycott winked.

"Yes, he's certainly done us proud; which reminds me, did you manage to get hold of him?"

"Not yet. I've left him a message to make contact when it's safe."

"Okay, let me know when he does," Gladstone nodded, putting his pen away. "Right, well I think we've all earned some downtime, so if anybody fancies a drink...the first round's on me!"

Needing no further invitation, the team headed straight to the station bar. By the time their gaffer joined them, they were already finishing their first pint.

"Thanks for the drink boss," Gaz called out from the back of the room. "We've told the barman to put them on your tab!"

As Gladstone looked over, the group raised their glasses as one.

With a smile on his face, Gladstone shook his head and paid the bill, before joining them on the upholstered red benches. His team in high spirits, the evening passed quickly; their latest success never far from their chatter.

But gradually the group thinned out, until by eleven o' clock, other than Fred ploughing his money into the fruit machine, only Hanson and Darby remained in the bar. Now sat facing each other on high stools, they continued to chat about their boss.

"You've got to hand it to him; old Gladstone's done the business again," Hanson slurred.

"Yep, he's called everything right so far; he's got the infamous copper's sixth sense!"

"True," Hanson said, his voice lowering. "But just think where we'd be without our little helper."

"Examining a wreck at the airport, that's where!"

"Geez, the shits would have had a field day," Hanson continued. "They'd have taken control of the streets until we replaced it...and when would that have been?"

"God knows! A new chopper costs millions."

"And with *our* budget cuts, we'd probably never see one again!"

"Yep, young Mickey's been a godsend; without him we wouldn't have had a chance."

"So what do you think's gonna happen next?" Hanson asked, paying for another round.

"Like the gaffer says, J.T.'s gonna come out fighting...and when he does, we'll be ready to take him down!"

"Well I just hope you're right mate, 'cos I've got a bad feeling J.T. will have something up his sleeve. He may be a nutter, but he's a cunning bastard; that's why he's ruled the streets for so long. Mark my words, we underestimate him at our peril...let's hope Gladstone's as good as we think."

***

Sat in front of his TV with Lara, Mickey's mind chewed over the past twenty-four hours. Although they'd been a complete nightmare, in reality, they could have turned out far worse. Yes, he'd taken another battering; but Tommy was banged up, the plot had failed dismally, and J.T. still didn't know a thing! The only real issue was Lara; he'd promised to tell her everything, but he couldn't, could he? What would she do if she knew J.T. was watching *her*...watching her family? He desperately needed to protect her, but how?

He needed time to think; now wasn't the time to make rash decisions. Glancing at his mobile, he noticed a missed call, and the answerphone icon flashing. Slightly puzzled by the number, he put it to his ear, and listened to the coded message. "*Hello Mr. Wilding, your doctor's appointment needs changing. Can you call back straightaway.*"

Message deleted, he typed in a number from memory.

"Hi Mickey, thanks for getting back to me," Draycott answered. "How're you feeling? From what I understand, you took another pummelling last night."

"Yeah, I went a right ball of snot. I guessed you'd stop me somehow, but I wasn't expecting a bloody ditch!"

"Sorry about that. You knew we couldn't give you the heads up; you needed to act naturally, or you'd have given the game away."

"No, I'm fine with it. And anyway, it saved my life this afternoon."

"What do you mean?"

"J.T.'s had us all over to his place; one an hour, every hour. He's on the warpath, trying to find out who grassed. He did the questioning, while Razor softened us up a little."

"So how did you get on? I take it you held your nerve, or we wouldn't be talking right now!"

"Yeah, they gave me a few slaps, but nothing too bad really. They've probably done the same to everybody else."

Lara nuzzled closer. This wasn't the time to talk about J.T.'s interest in *her*; he'd have to wait until he and Draycott were on their own before discussing *that* little problem.

"Deano went in before me," he continued. "He told them I'd been knocked out giving it my best shot, that there was no way I could have known what was happening. I think he swayed it for me; I'm pretty sure I'm not their number one suspect at the moment. Anyway, tell me, what's happened to Tommy and Nozza?"

"Charged and kept in custody. Unfortunately, your friend Jonas reckons the courts will bail them. To be honest, if the magistrates do fall for his bullshit, they'll be back out in the morning I'm afraid. I take it they'll get a similar reception from J.T.?"

"I don't think he'll be quite as friendly," Mickey smiled. "I may have dropped a subtle hint that Tommy's the grass!"

"Oh dear, it couldn't happen to a nicer guy. I'm kinda hoping he gets bail now!" Draycott laughed down the phone. "Talking of J.T., do you have anything more for us?"

"Not much, he's too busy trying to find out who grassed. The only snippet I did hear was about your boss; apparently he's the one who sent J.T. to prison – he's been holding a grudge ever since."

"That's interesting."

"Now I've been to his house, I can tell you where he lives if you want…although, I guess you've already worked that one out?"

"Yeah," Draycott replied. "You could say we made it a priority after your previous info. And from what you've just said, he's dropped another clanger; we'll now have video evidence of who his associates are. We've rattled him Mickey – the net's slowly closing in."

"Good," Mickey grinned. "I hope it fucking strangles him!"

***

Desperately seeking a name, Porter had spent the day travelling far and wide. But with midnight approaching, he was returning home empty handed. Nobody he'd spoken to had even heard about the daring plan, let alone who had spilled the beans. J.T. was *not* going to be impressed.

Electric gates swinging open on command, his big Mercedes rolled onto his gravel drive. Placing it in park, he was about to turn off, when his hands-free rang again.

'*Unknown number*' came up on the screen.

"This had better be important," he muttered, before accepting the call. "Yes?!"

"Porter? I've got some news for you," the voice broadcast from his speakers.

"Who is it? Your number's not coming up."

"It's Fred, I'm on a payphone."

"Ahh yes; Fred. Good to hear from you, what have you got for me?"

"The little snitch you're after…is it still five grand for his name?"

"Of course Fred, I've never let you down before have I?" Porter answered calmly. "Mutual trust is important in business; so tell me, who *is* the grass?"

"Well…I've just overheard a couple of the lads chatting in the bar; they've been working on your case," the retired cop stammered nervously.

"Go on, I'm all ears."

"They said 'young Mickey's been a godsend', if that makes any sense."

"That makes perfect sense Fred, perfect sense," Porter smirked. "Your money'll be through your letter-box by the time you wake up."

Ending the call abruptly, he touched a stored number on his screen.

"J.T., it's Porter. I've found him…I've found the dead man walking!"

52

"No surprises I'm afraid," Gladstone said, striding into the office. "Another bunch of lefty, liberal, limp-wristed do-gooders on the bench. Bail's been granted, with just *one* pathetic condition: they've got to report to the police station daily."

"That'll teach them!" Hanson replied sarcastically.

"Tell me about it; not even a night-time curfew. I sometimes wonder why we even bother locking them up when all those naïve fools do is let them back out. No wonder we struggle to keep a lid on crime!"

"Don't worry boss, it's not all bad news; I had a chat with Mickey last night," Draycott piped up. "Fortunately he's not badly injured, and he's passed me a few little nuggets."

"Go on."

"Apparently J.T.'s vengeance is aimed squarely at you boss. You convicted him many years ago, and he's been holding a grudge ever since. I guess your renewed interest in his activities have sent him over the edge!"

"Well, well, he's taken things personally has he?" the Inspector laughed. "To be honest, I hadn't given it a second thought."

"So what was the score boss; his conviction just says GBH."

"You'll be surprised to know, he thought he was above the law back in those days as well. He was convicted for a machete attack on a gangland rival, and to be honest, I'm surprised he's not to come to our attention since. It looks like we've underestimated him; he's intelligent, well protected and extremely violent. To take him down again, we'll need good, solid, evidence."

"He may be bright, but the pressure's getting to him. Yesterday afternoon, everybody had to go to his house for questioning…"

"All in front of our cameras?" the Inspector interrupted.

"Exactly! The lads are reviewing the footage as we speak," Hanson added, popping an aspirin into his water.

"Heavy night was it?"

"Yeah, it's all Donkey's fault," Hanson replied. "He made me stay to the end."

"Oh well, at least you both made it back this morning; we've got stacks of work to do."

"So what's the plan then boss?"

"Well for a start, we need to get a warrant to search J.T.'s house; I reckon it'll be a goldmine. But as I was just saying, the only way we'll get one is to gather evidence, and plenty of it! Yesterday's footage helps, but it won't be enough on its own."

"Well he's bound to send his boys out to work again soon," Hanson said, gulping down his headache cure. "He'll want to show us he still means business, especially now it's become personal."

"And we'll be waiting for them when they do…Mickey'll see to that," Gladstone replied, a grin beginning to form. "And those two half-wits released today will bounce straight back into custody. I'm sure the magistrates won't be so tolerant next time; especially as they'll be stood alongside their ringleaders!"

***

By mid-afternoon, J.T.'s trusted team were back in his lounge; their leader on the rampage.

"Friday night was nothing more than a complete and utter balls up! Gladstone and his merry men have been out celebrating…at *our* fucking expense! And now we all know why," he seethed. "Mickey fucking Wilding!"

"The lying bastard! He told me it wasn't him," Razor frowned, clenching his spade like fists. "Wait 'til I get my hands on his scrawny little neck."

"All in good time Razor," J.T. replied. "But for now, we need to be careful. If he's in plod's pocket, they could be watching his every move. No, we need to get rid of the problem without the finger pointing at us!"

Rising from his armchair, he began to pace the room.

"Why don't we get the Bulawayo Boys to sort him out?" Porter suggested. "We could conveniently be on CCTV at the country club, while they're out doing the job?"

"Yeah, that's probably the easiest option, but our reputation's on the line here. No, Mickey's *our* problem…*we're* gonna sort it!"

"How about the classic double-cross," Johnny spoke up from behind his desk.

"What did you have in mind?"

"It's quite simple really. We still have an ace up our sleeves: the cops are blissfully unaware that Mickey's cover's been blown," Johnny continued, barely looking up from his laptop. "We'll arrange another raid, knowing full well that Mickey'll spill the beans. His police friends will rub their hands together with glee; after all, he's earned their trust now hasn't he? They're bound to commit every resource to our intended target; it would potentially give them enough evidence to take our boys off the streets for years. However, while the lads are on their way to the ambush, we'll spring a trap of our own."

Johnny paused for a moment, taking time to remove his glasses.

"Go on," his brother encouraged.

"Porter will call Deano with a change of plan…some bogus premises needing to be hit on the other side of the city, where guess what; we'll be awaiting their arrival. While the city's crimefighters are sat waiting for the raid that's never gonna happen, we'll have all the time in the world to deal with *our* little problem!"

"Brilliant!" J.T. grinned. "Oh I'd love to see Gladstone's pompous face when he realises the informant he's supposed to be protecting is missing, presumed dead. He'll be retired on the spot; his reputation ruined – perfect! Now unless anybody's got a better idea, I suggest we get to work."

***

It didn't take Porter long to find the targets. A huge electrical warehouse on the city's outskirts had previously been earmarked for a hit. It'd make the perfect decoy for now; the genuine attack would have to wait another few weeks. The posse's true destination lay fifteen miles away, in a disused industrial area; ideal for the plans J.T. had in mind.

His inspection complete, Porter sat on his Merc's bonnet, and facetimed his boss.

"Are you sure we won't be overlooked," J.T. frowned at his phone.

"You might find the odd rat hanging around, but other than that…" Porter grinned, scanning the area with his mobile, "…you can see for yourself, nobody will even hear him scream!"

"Good. Get hold of Chapman and fill him in with the details. It goes without saying, no-one, and I mean no-one outside the Power Firm gets to know our plans; no other fucker can be trusted!"

***

Sat chatting to his mates in Deano's lounge, Mickey's stomach churned; he'd betrayed them once, and would undoubtedly have to do it again. But he had to act as he always did; nobody could suspect a thing.

His mood wasn't helped by the rigid stare from across the floor. Every time he looked up, he was met by the same insolent glare. Eventually he'd had enough.

"What the fuck are you looking at?"

"Your ugly mug," Tommy scowled back. "You look like a fucking freak!"

"Difference is, mine will heal. What's your excuse?"

"Alright, alright, cut it out you two," Deano interrupted. "We've got enough on our plate already."

"Yeah, and we all know why, don't we?" Tommy sneered.

"What the fuck are you on about? If you've got something to say…say it!"

"I don't need to say anything. Your actions have done all the talking haven't they?"

"What do you mean by that?"

"Well you're the one who's fucked up both times; first off you killed your mate, and the next…you couldn't even hit the target!" Tommy goaded.

His anger rising, Mickey glanced to his side. An empty bottle, that'd do; that'd re-arrange his face nicely. His hand twitched in anticipation.

No, he couldn't...not yet. Tommy's hot air was exactly that; there were better ways to get his revenge. He needed to stay patient; there wasn't long to go, Tommy would soon get his justice.

"You're pathetic Tommy," he eventually replied, his calm voice hiding the anger inside. "We all know who really killed Danny don't we? Oh, and unless you've forgotten...you were the only muppets to get caught the other night!"

"Only because somebody grassed on us, and we all know who that was don't we?"

"Of course, it must have been me, mustn't it?" Mickey mocked. "I mean, I'm the one who nearly got killed; that's exactly what a grass would do, wouldn't he? Perhaps if we *are* looking for the grass, we should start by asking how *you* managed to get bail so quickly? Anybody else would've been locked up and had the key thrown away; but no, not you pair. You get caught trying to destroy the police helicopter, and yet you're straight out with only one poxy bail condition!"

Rising to his feet, his face cherry red, Tommy struggled to contain his fury.

"Fucking come here and say that!" he screamed.

"Enough!" Deano shouted, stepping in front of Tommy. "Nobody knows who grassed, if in fact anybody grassed at all! Let's face it, the fucking graffiti gave them enough clues. Right now, we've gotta put everything behind us; we need to work together, not against each other, alright?"

Begrudgingly, with a final glare at his tormentor, Tommy slowly sat down.

"Good, now let's get on with our next job," Deano said, returning to his seat. "Chapman's keen for us to get straight back to business. He's identified an electrical wholesalers on a business park in Sutton; apparently it's crammed full of iPads. As you might expect, security there is hi-tech, however...he's arranged for a power cut to strike on Friday night, just as we arrive!"

Bit of a shame really, Mickey considered, this was just the sort of job he used to love; a daring night-time raid with the prospect of decent rewards.

"We need three motors," Deano continued. "Tommy, I want you and your boys to get your hands on a hefty 4x4 with enough grunt to ram straight through the shutters. Mickey, you'll take Rushy and Dougie, while I'll take the others."

Mickey looked round the room. So Deano still trusted him with the wheel, and nobody, not even Tommy had raised a murmur.

"Okay, now listen in carefully. Despite the help we'll get from the power cut, I've been warned that the job is far from easy. It's on a brand new business park, so it's been designed with security in mind. For a start, there's a guard hut with a barrier at the entrance. There's no other way in, so we'll have to ram through it in the 4x4, and then blast straight on to our target. I'm assured that the security guard will stay at his post and call the police, so by my reckoning we've got five minutes maximum to get out before the cops arrive. Although the power cut should take out the CCTV, keep your faces covered just in case."

There'll be no need for CCTV, Mickey thought to himself, the police will be ready and waiting; if only he could tip his mates off first. Or maybe, just maybe, Gladstone could find a way for them to escape again.

"If we're to clean the warehouse out, we're gonna have to work as a team," Deano continued, the room deadly silent. "Tommy, as soon as you reach the warehouse, drop your boys off, then reverse as hard as you can through the shutters. There's only flimsy doors behind, so you should be able to punch straight through. The stock we're after is stacked against the back wall; grab as many as you can and fill the cars up. After that, it's every man for himself; get your asses back to the garages asap. Any questions?"

"What about the layout of the business park?" Tommy asked. "How am I supposed to know where the warehouse is once I've gone through the barriers?"

"Chapman assures me it's dead simple; it's the big place at the end of the drive. Apparently, you can't miss it!"

***

Deep in thought, Mickey walked home in the dark. It had to be his last job; there was no way he could go through this again. Was he really doing the right thing? To grass on J.T. meant grassing on his mates. To give evidence against J.T meant starting a new life – away from his friends, his family, his roots. But what was the alternative; a life as J.T.'s slave?

He thought about Danny; how his life had been taken by Tommy, and how J.T. hadn't given a toss. What would Danny want him to do; roll over and become J.T.'s puppy?!

No chance, and anyway, he was in too deep now; he'd have to see it through whatever…thank god J.T. didn't have a clue who'd grassed.

53

And see it through he did. Decision made, he arranged for a meeting the following day.

Pulling his hoodie tight, he jumped off the bus in Bromsgrove; a small market town ten miles from home. Just as Draycott had described, a slight hill rose to the churchyard opposite, where, in the stone wall's recess, the officer sat on a wooden bench together with Smudger.

"It's good to see you Mickey," Draycott smiled. "Do you want a seat, or would you rather take a walk round the grounds."

"Here'll do fine," he replied, taking his place on the end.

"Crikey, you alright mate?" Draycott asked. "You're looking worse than ever!"

"I'm okay," Mickey shrugged, keeping his head lowered. "It's just the bruising coming out."

"Well you need to be careful, Lara won't want to be seen dead with a Quasimodo!"

Mickey laughed quietly to himself. "Yeah, it's been so long since I was normal, she can't remember what I really look like."

Hands shoved deep into his hoodie's side pockets he looked out at the peaceful view. Sitting on a small rise, the church grounds fell slowly downhill to a small brook winding its way through the valley. In the foreground, gravestones jutted out at strange angles, while in the distance, locals milled around the busy marketplace, oblivious to his watchful eye.

"So," Draycott said, breaking the silence. "You mentioned on the phone last night that you've got something for us?"

"Yeah, there's a job I need to tell you about," he said taking out his mobile. "We're hitting a warehouse on Friday – it's all here, every word."

"You managed to record the meeting again?"

"Yeah, but I can't say I'm too proud of myself," he said, slowly shaking his head. "Look, I know you can't make any promises, but Deano's as much a victim as I am. And the other boys; they're not bad lads…"

"Mickey, I need to stop you there. They're no longer your responsibility; you need to think about yourself from now on."

"What do you mean?"

"Well, we managed to avoid arresting them on the last job; partly to respect your wishes, but also to keep your group intact – it suited all our needs," Draycott said looking him in the eye. "It's unlikely we'll do the same again."

"So what *will* happen to them?"

"Quite simply, the choice is theirs. If they're willing to help put J.T. and his cronies away, then we'll cut them a deal."

"And if they don't?"

"Mickey, you need to understand, that when you commit crimes, you create victims: those victims deserve justice. If your friends are unwilling to help us catch their bosses, then they'll have to suffer the consequences."

For a moment, Mickey looked to the floor as he mulled over the officer's words. He remembered Harold and Mavis helping him when he needed it most; how their lives had been devastated by Shark's appalling attack.

Slowly, he lifted his head. "I know you're right," he said, turning to face Draycott once more. "It just doesn't sit very well, that's all."

"Look, the decisions you're making aren't meant to be easy. No matter what happens Friday night, your life's going to change forever."

"And what is going to happen, are you gonna lock J.T. and his mates up at the same time?"

"Well I'll have to talk to my boss about the exact details, but I would imagine so. From that point onwards, I guess we'll be left with two possible outcomes. Either we'll have enough to send J.T. and the Power Firm away...or they'll worm their way out of it and live to fight another day."

"But what about *my* evidence," Mickey frowned. "Surely that'll be enough?"

"Maybe, maybe not; it's why we need Deano and the others to support you. Although *we* know you're telling the truth, the courts will take a lot more convincing. Jonas will attempt to discredit you because of your previous links; he'll say you're just out for revenge."

"That isn't fucking fair!"

"The whole system isn't fair. You've experienced it for yourself; it's biased towards the offenders – victims come a very poor second."

"Are you telling me I'm putting my life on the line for nothing?!"

"No, not at all. All I'm saying is, we'll need more than just *your* evidence to secure convictions. And believe me, we're working flat out to do that."

"And if they don't get convicted?"

"You'll have succeeded in smashing a huge hole in their network. They'll know we're watching their every move; 'cos we'll know who they are, where they live, and what they're up to. In fact, in order for them to continue, they'd probably have to move out of the area, if not the country. So you see, no matter what the outcome is, *you'll* have sealed their fate."

Mickey looked over the graveyard and down towards the town. He'd been certain J.T. would go to prison after everything he'd done; how the hell could he get away with it? And if he did, what then? How could he and Lara ever be safe again? Shit...Lara!

"But if they don't get sent down, we all know who they'll be coming after don't we? And it's not just about me anymore; they'll be gunning for Lara as well."

This time it was Draycott's turn to frown. "Okay Mickey, something's obviously happened. What haven't you told us yet? What makes you think she's in danger?"

Letting out a sigh, Mickey shook his head and began, carefully leading them through the meeting at J.T.'s.

"Look, it's one thing them coming after me, but I can't risk Lara getting hurt. She's got nothing to do with all this shit, you've gotta make sure she is safe!"

"Listen, we'll do everything in our power to protect you and Lara. We promised you a new life, and that's exactly what we've arranged," Smudger explained. "You and Lara will soon have new identities and your very own place in the country."

"Really?"

"Really. The Chief's signed it off herself," Draycott confirmed. "It's nothing more than we owe you Mickey. You've done an amazing job so far; you've brought J.T. and the Power Firm to their knees...and now it's time to finish them off."

"And I will, I just have to be certain that Lara's protected," Mickey said, his eyes meeting the officer's. "Can *you* give me your word you will?"

Draycott returned the gaze. "You have my word Mickey. I'll personally make sure of it."

"Thank you," Mickey replied quietly. "I'm trusting you; I know what J.T.'s like."

"We also know what he's like. He's an evil man who'd think nothing of taking the life of anybody who crosses him; that's why we want to put him away. We'll keep her safe, I won't let you down."

Mickey kept his stare. Could they really guarantee her safety? Who really was in control round here; was it J.T. or Inspector Gladstone? Yes he trusted Draycott, but what about the other cops; did they really give a shit about him or Lara? Then again, what choice did he have; he definitely couldn't trust J.T.!

"Okay," he eventually nodded. "But please...please don't let me down."

"We won't Mickey, we won't."

"I came here to do the right thing," he said swiping open his phone's menu and selecting send. "And that's exactly what I'm gonna do."

Draycott's phone chimed. "I take it that's the recording?"

"Yep, it's all down to you guys now...I'm trusting you with our lives."

54

With this being his final job, Mickey was keen to go out in style. One car he'd always fancied, but never driven, was an Aston Martin DB9. An overnight visit to the countryside soon put that right; his fishing-rod through a letterbox easily hooking keys to the racing green supercar. Once safely tucked away, a quick call to Draycott filled him in with the details.

***

Having listened in to Mickey's secret recording, and been updated with the Aston's theft, the CATS team were ready to plan their response.

"There's a saying in the police called the six 'P's: Proper Preparation Prevents Piss Poor Performance!" Gladstone said, beginning the briefing. "And I intend for us to be as prepared as we've ever been for anything."

His team made no reply for none was needed. For months now, they'd worked long hard hours, and now their original goal was finally in sight; the complete annihilation of The Power Firm.

Thanks to Mickey, the past few days had seen an acceleration in their workload. Having watched the key players around the clock, the cobweb of contacts had unravelled. Now, with less than thirty-six hours to go, as Gladstone continued to address their team, Hanson laid out dossiers detailing the complete framework of J.T.'s organisation.

"Gentlemen, take these profiles away and study them carefully. We'll reconvene tomorrow night at six for a final briefing, but for now, I intend to run through our plan of attack. So listen in, and respond accordingly," he said, removing a laser pointer from his top pocket.

Directing it at the whiteboard behind, he continued. "Our primary objective is to secure sufficient evidence to bring J.T.'s empire crumbling to the ground. To facilitate this, there will be two distinct elements to the operation. Firstly, there's our tactical response to the burglary, and secondly, the simultaneous execution of search warrants."

Pausing, his red beam settled on J.T's mugshot.

"I'll be leading the warrants teams," Hanson announced. "We're hitting seven addresses at exactly the same time: the five Power Firm bosses, together with Tommy's and Deano's. We're gonna need plenty of help, which brings me nicely onto the Operational Support Unit. We've been given seven specialist search teams to help execute the warrants, while all their remaining officers will be ready for action at the business park."

Knowing smiles broke out around the room. Hand-picked, the OSU officer's reputation was well deserved. Although their search skills would be useful, their main role lay with public order, with hooligans…with violence. They'd be praying for J.T. and Razor to respond with aggression, because for once, the thugs had no chance.

"Any targets at the addresses will be arrested and brought back here," Hanson continued. "I'll be the only member of our team going with the OSU; the rest will be with the gaffer – to where the real action is. Any questions?"

With no reply, he handed back to Gladstone.

"As Steve says, we'll be ready and waiting at the business park. Near to the entrance, I've arranged for an HGV to be parked up, as if waiting for a morning delivery. As soon as the raiders strike the warehouse, the HGV'll move forward and completely block the entrance. There's no other way out; there *is* no escape. With the trap sprung, I anticipate they'll abandon their cars and take their chances on foot. Hidden away in the HGV's rear, our OSU colleagues will be ready for the foot-chases, while you guys will be spread around the grounds to sweep up any stragglers. I've also made the helicopter aware, as it's likely to get manic with so many offenders on their toes."

"I take it we're going to allow them to complete the burglary?" Strickers enquired.

"Yes we are. We've concluded it's the safest option. Until the HGV is properly in position, we just can't prevent their escape. But when they abandon their motors; we'll strike!"

"How about Mickey, is he getting locked up too?"

"Yes," Gladstone replied. "And I'll happily explain why. Firstly, the OSU officers don't know anything about him, and it's important that that remains the case. Secondly, he's an offender; it's up to CPS to offer no evidence. And finally, while his group remain unaware, they may still pass him some info we can use."

"And how are we keeping in contact with Mickey?" Gaz piped up. "Is he gonna be wearing a wire?"

"No, it's just too risky for him. He'll text Draycott on his way to the car, but from then on...we're in the dark until they land. They're a professional outfit, so we're expecting them to arrive dead on midnight as planned!"

Wrapping the meeting up, Gladstone soon sent his team back to work. If they really were to take J.T. down, their efforts needed stepping up once more.

And to their delight, later that evening, the cameras opposite J.T.'s looked like they'd struck the final nail in his coffin. With the entire Power Firm turning up for a meeting, it appeared as though Mickey's info was sound; something big was about to happen...if only they'd had a camera inside.

55

The following day, at eighteen hundred hours precisely, the final police briefings began. Unaware of the operation they were about to take part in, eight OSU serials were in attendance.

While his sergeant took charge of the search teams in the conference room, Gladstone addressed the officers attending the raid. Speaking in the cramped CATS office, he finished off by emphasising the importance of their task ahead.

"For many years these gangsters have ridden roughshod over our neighbourhoods. For many months we've strived to bring them to justice. Well tonight we intend do just that, and destroy their empire forever!"

***

Lying in Lara's arms, Mickey's eyes remained fixed on his clock. Looking down at her sleepy head, he prayed these wouldn't be their last moments together. She'd changed his world; she was the reason he wanted a future. Maybe, just maybe, when tonight's job was over…they finally could have one.

The hands on the clock seemed to increase in pace as the time to leave drew ever nearer. Rising to go, he tried not to disturb her, but her arms tightened their grip as he moved. Moist eyes looked up at him, her mouth about to speak.

With a smile, he gently put a finger to her lips.

"Don't worry," he whispered. "I'll be okay; I'll be back before you know it, I promise."

Closing the door behind him, he hurried down the stairs and into the alleyway outside. Rushy and Dougie were already there; deft nods their only greeting as they fell into step alongside. Hands thrust deep inside pockets, Mickey's fingertips sealed their fate as they walked. In a well-rehearsed sequence, his finger swipes unlocked the phone, opened a pre-written text, and sent it straight to Draycott.

***

Their cars left in nearby side streets, Gladstone led his team onto the Business Park.

While he nestled down amongst discarded boxes opposite the target, his officers quickly spread out. Within seconds, the HGV pulled into position near the front entrance; its curtain sides concealing the OSU cargo.

The trap was set, and as Draycott's screen lit up with, *'Coming to the party?'* it looked like it was about to be sprung.

***

Relaxing at home, J.T. had been receiving his own updates. While operatic arias flowed from Bang and Olufsen speakers, the periodic phone calls confirmed everything he needed to know.

Porter started the ball rolling, passing on snippets from Fred who'd been tasked to hang around the station. No less than eight OSU vans were parked up in Stechford's backyard he reported; the officers all in meetings inside.

As the night wore on, the picture steadily built up, until with midnight fast approaching, a final call sealed Mickey's fate. From his tenth floor flat, less than a mile from the target premises, J.T.'s contact had a perfect view through his binoculars.

"Okay, there's about eight men in dark clothing approaching the security hut," he relayed. "One's gone inside, the others are spreading out across the estate."

"Good, good," J.T. smiled. "Keep it coming."

"There's a lorry pulling up by the front entrance. Hmm...that *is* strange. It's immediately come to a stop, and the driver's pulling the curtains around his cab. I've lost sight of the others; it looks like they've hidden themselves away."

"That'll do nicely," J.T. grinned, ending the call. "Hook, line and bloody sinker!"

Johnny briefly looked up from his laptop. "Excellent, our little grass isn't going to know what's hit him!"

"Yep, it's all coming together nicely," J.T. said, his eyelids closing to Nessun Dorma's opening bars. "We're just about ready for Judgement Time!"

***

Maybe it was the relief that his ordeal was coming to an end that kept Mickey calm as he drove. While his mates remained quiet, mentally preparing themselves for their upcoming adrenaline rush; his own thoughts were altogether different. What did the cops have planned for them this time? Would they allow him a chink of light to evade capture: they'd done it before, would they do it again? One thing was for sure, it'd feel good to have one last blast through the streets, particularly in the DB9.

"Take the next left," Rushy said, disturbing Mickey's thoughts. "The car park's round the back of the office block."

Mickey followed Rushy's directions, and having extinguished the Aston's lights, pulled up next to Deano's red Tesla. Lowering his smoked glass window, he looked across at Ronnie.

"Any problems?" Ronnie asked, nodding his greeting.

"No, none at all. But tell me, what the hell are you doing in an *electric* car?"

"Cheeky bastard!" Ronnie joked back. "Have you ever been in one of these? It's like shit off a shovel, especially when you press the '*Insane*' button!"

"Fuck off, you're having me on."

"Honestly mate, it's right here on the digital console! When you press it...fuck me does this thing go!"

But their light-hearted banter was soon interrupted by an unlit black Range Rover driving towards them.

"Aye, aye, here's trouble," Ronnie said, nodding in its direction.

Hmm, little do you know what's coming *your* way, Mickey smirked as his enemy drew alongside.

With everybody present, they gathered round the Tesla, listening to Deano's final instructions.

"We're leaving at five to," he said. "If we stick to the speed limits, we should get there bang on midnight."

Mickey looked at his watch – ten to twelve. His nerves began to rise.

"Tommy, when we arrive don't slow; just accelerate hard through the barriers. We'll be following close…" Suddenly, his words were cut short by his mobile's piercing ring. Pulling it from his pocket, he glanced at the screen and frowned.

"Porter?" he answered, walking a few steps away. "Is everything okay?"

Mickey strained to listen in. Why on earth was Porter calling?

"Yeah, just one minute," Deano continued, and jumping into his car, shut the door behind.

Subtly, Mickey tried to look in. Deano was chatting away, and having flicked the interior light on, had grabbed a pen and paper from the glove compartment. Mickey's heart began to race; what the fuck was going on?

He didn't have to wait long to find out, and when he did, he felt his world implode.

"That was Porter," Deano confirmed, emerging from the car. "There's been a change of plan!"

56

'*A change of plan*'? There couldn't be a change of plan; the police were ready and waiting!

Mickey's heart was slamming against his chest; his stomach churning as fear instantly replaced his relative calm. Legs like jelly, he quickly took a seat on the bonnet. What on earth could he do? He couldn't question the changes; that'd only fuel Tommy's suspicions. But if he did nothing about it…the cops'd think *he'd* sold them out.

"Listen in," Deano said, summoning everybody back round. "Porter's had a tip off that needs immediate action; we'll return to this one next week. He's just been given the nod where there's a monster stash of cigarettes being stored; the only problem is, they're going out to the wholesalers tomorrow, so it has to be hit tonight."

"What the fuck's he playing at?" Rushy complained. "Does he really want another botched job?"

"You know the rules; whether we like it or not, we just do as we're told. Porter's been assured that there's no security there, and from what he's telling me, it's so out of the way it should be a simple in-and-out job."

"All the same," Rushy replied. "Changing plans at short notice is just asking for trouble!"

"Listen, I don't like it either, but we've got no choice. The fags are in a disused factory unit on the other side of the city. He's told me to get a move on, so I suggest that's exactly what we do!"

Mickey remained silent. Deano was right, they really didn't have a choice. Nothing he could say was going to change things, he'd just have to do what he was told.

"I've put the directions in the sat-nav, so follow me," Deano continued. "The plan's the same as this one; once Tommy's smashed through the shutters, the rest of us'll grab as many cartons as possible. Porter reckons we've got at least ten minutes before the police arrive, so we should be able to fill the cars to the brim."

With that, Deano turned to go. There was to be no further discussion; they were off.

Almost in a trance, Mickey followed Deano's lead. Taking second on the road, he drove automatically, desperately attempting to make sense of the turn in events. He silently swore to himself; he'd come so close to taking down his enemies! But with everything now out of his control, he needed to stay calm, stay alert; be ready for whatever came next.

"Are you okay?" Rushy frowned, as Mickey took in yet another deep breath.

"Yeah, I just don't like surprises being sprung; we've had enough of those recently."

"You're not wrong there mate. At least this job should be a breeze; it sounds like it's in the middle of nowhere!"

He hardly heard his mate's reply; his mind chewing over the change in events. Were they a coincidence or had J.T. planned them all along? If he had, the cops had seriously underestimated him.

A wry smile started to form; J.T. was a cunning bastard – the cigarette warehouse would be a walk in the park. And maybe a successful raid wasn't such a bad thing. After all, if he did what he was told, it'd show where his loyalty lay. But what about the next job; would J.T. try the same trick? And as for the cops; how could they ever trust him again?

Driving on autopilot behind Deano's tail-lights, every possibility led back to the same conclusion; he daren't do anything stupid, he had to go through with the raid.

***

With his brother sat alongside, J.T. reversed slowly off his drive. Making his final preparations on the move, he grinned as everything continued to fall neatly into place. Deano's boys were on their way; the Power Firm would be ready to greet them.

Before long, derelict buildings bounded the empty streets. It was exactly as he'd planned; the only witnesses would be those inside his cars, and with what he had in mind, that's just how he wanted it to stay.

Heading onto an abandoned factory estate, he drove between wire-mesh gates hanging loosely from their mountings, before heading up a weed strewn concrete drive.

"Perfect," he said, bringing his car to a halt in the deserted courtyard at its end. "Nobody'll find us here."

***

Meanwhile, the CATS team watched and waited. Gladstone looked down at his watch, the luminous arms standing out in the darkness.

Midnight. Nothing moved. The silence was deafening.

Five minutes passed; something was wrong.

Fumbling inside his pocket, he took out his mobile. Draycott answered on the first ring.

"Has Mickey been in touch?" Gladstone asked anxiously.

"No, I haven't heard a thing since the text."

Gladstone cursed to himself. "I've got a feeling we've been duped. These boys are professional, they stick to their plans; if they say they're going to hit at midnight – they hit at midnight!"

"You're right, something's up. They were only five minutes away when Mickey text, they should easily have been here by now."

"Okay, we'll give it until quarter past, then we'll re-assess."

Call ended, everybody held position…but still nothing moved; it was time to take action.

Emerging from his hideaway, Gladstone hurried over to Draycott at the rear of the building.

"Right, I need some straight talking. Either they've been diverted on route, or Mickey's been lying to us," Gladstone stated bluntly. "So tell me; could he be double-crossing us?"

"Well if he is, then he's the best actor I've ever seen. Trust me boss, he wouldn't have done this on purpose."

"Which leaves us with two alternatives…" the Inspector began, his reply cut short by his vibrating phone.

"Hello, Gladstone speaking," he answered.

The call lasted no more than thirty seconds; the Inspector's frown said it all.

"That was Hanson. They've executed the warrants; not one of their targets was at home. I guess that leaves us with just *one* alternative. The question is, how do we get to Mickey before he's history?"

***

In his battered black Cadillac, Razor was the last to arrive. Turning into the courtyard, he slid to a halt behind the three cars already parked nose-to-tail.

"Glad you could make it!" J.T. announced sarcastically.

"Wouldn't miss it for the world boss," he grinned.

"Good, now pin your ears back, 'cos we haven't got much time."

Huddling a little closer in the darkness, they listened carefully to their leader's lowered voice.

"Porter's just been in contact with Deano; they're already well on their way. Right now, young Mickey's too stupid to know what's going on, however, the moment they pull onto this wasteland, even *he's* going to smell a rat! Razor, that's where you come in."

"Good. I'm gonna tear him limb from fucking limb!"

"And you will my good friend…but not quite straightaway. For now, I want you waiting down the road, and make sure you're out of sight. Once they're through the gates, follow them in, and whatever happens, don't let the Aston leave. Do whatever you need to do to stop it, okay?"

"You can rely on me boss. Black beauty and I have never failed yet," he said, glancing at his car. "They make these into coffin carriers you know!"

"Hearses, Razor, hearses," J.T. exhaled loudly. "But don't forget, you're not to kill him straight away, okay?"

"Okay boss, not straight away."

"Chapman, you go with Razor; you know what his memory's like," J.T. instructed. "And chaps, let me just remind you, we're not here to fuck about tonight; we're here to set an example. Mickey tried to take us down – he failed. Tonight he pays with his life!"

57

Fifteen miles separated the city's two targets. Keeping to the speed limits, Mickey's convoy received little attention; the roads passing him by as he tried to make sense of his situation. Turning off the main road, he headed onto unfamiliar streets, travelling from one run-down estate to the next.

Through his smoked-glass windows, he checked out the passing scenery. Moonlight occasionally broke through dark clouds, illuminating dark abandoned streets; their windows covered in graffiti strewn boarding. To his front, Deano's Tesla indicated left, before turning into yet another deserted side road; just crumbling buildings, no sign of life.

Except one...and Mickey missed it.

Squeezed up an entry between empty houses, Razor's black Cadillac sat ready to pounce. As the convoy passed by, lights extinguished, it slowly rolled out from its hiding place.

Looking ahead of the Tesla's headlights, Mickey stared into the gloom. Housing disappeared from their sides, the road surface changing from tarmac to concrete as it headed towards ramshackle gates. Ambling through, Mickey's stomach tightened.

It just didn't add up; he instinctively knew something was wrong.

"Fucking strange place to have a cigarette warehouse," Rushy frowned. "Do you think Deano's lost his way?"

"Nah, he's still moving, we must be in the right place," Dougie replied. "I guess it's good security; nobody would have a clue what's hidden up here!"

Ignoring their chatter, Mickey tried to make sense of it all. Why on earth would a major company set up in this dump? And in all the time he'd been working for the posse, they'd never been to a place like this. Looking around, he frantically searched for clues.

The gates they'd passed through; why weren't they padlocked? The concrete road; it hadn't been driven on for years. And where were the signs; surely there would be *some* directions to the business?

As each second went by, the reason became increasingly obvious – the cigarette warehouse didn't exist.

So what were they really here for; what *was* he driving into?

***

The same question was running through Gladstone's mind. Returning to the HGV, he slid its curtain side open and joined the officers inside.

"For those of you not aware, tonight's operation was based on information from a source within the raiding party. Our last contact with him was an hour ago, when he confirmed that their three cars were heading towards us as planned. It's now clear they're not coming; our source must have been compromised. We are indebted to this young man; he has been instrumental in our attempts to bring down a criminal empire. Right now, as a result of his courage, he's staring death in the face, so guys…I need you to find him before it's too late!"

"We'll do whatever you want gaffer," the OSU sergeant replied. "You've got eight serials at your disposal; use us as you see fit."

"Thank you. Now first things first. PC Draycott, contact the helicopter; we need them up and looking for the three car convoy. 'E' serial, make your way back to Stechford and get fully kitted up; if we manage to locate these people, I'm expecting it to turn nasty. My team; scour the city, check out all the likely haunts. Although these guys could be anywhere, my hunch tells me they won't have strayed far; they'll want to scurry home as soon as their night's work is done. Time's against us gents; let's get out there!"

***

Straining his eyes in the dark, Mickey desperately searched for more clues. Another abandoned building loomed closer; the driveway swinging left behind it. A quick mirror check revealed nothing, just Tommy's blazing headlights uncomfortably close behind. Was Tommy in on this he wondered? Come to think of it, was everybody in on it? Wrestling to keep his fears under control, he dropped a gear and turned the corner.

As his headlights swung round, his suspicions became reality; three parked cars sat waiting in a line.

His heart froze. The lead car was unmistakeable; the same dark saloon he'd been forced into before Danny's funeral. Shit!! J.T. was here and he wasn't alone.

There could only be one reason why J.T. was here…and it wasn't to help them on the job. He was here to deliver payback, and the knife ripping through Mickey's stomach told him he knew exactly who to.

Fuck, fuck, fuck! Why hadn't he read the signs earlier? The last minute change of plans, the journey across the city, a wasteland in the middle of nowhere. Like a fool, he'd driven straight into their trap. He had to get out, and fast!

But where could he go to escape?

In front, the Tesla had reached the end of the makeshift cul-de-sac. Behind him Tommy was…shit, what was that racing up alongside? Lights out, a black Cadillac was almost on top of him. Where the hell had it come from, and what the fuck was Chapman doing in the passenger seat? It was all the confirmation he needed.

Practically at the barricade's mouth, his options were running out rapidly. With a factory wall to his left, and the speeding Caddy to his right; they were forcing him into their dead end. Only one option remained…take out the Caddy!

Decision made, he tugged the wheel sharply to the right, but for once Razor was one step ahead; Mickey's hesitation costing him dear.

In the moment before Mickey had made his move, the henchman had steered slightly away, before smashing his battering ram into the Aston's front corner.

As Mickey's wheel buckled on impact, airbags exploded, leaving him surrounded in cushions and smoke. Blinded and disorientated, he was oblivious to the Cadillac's continued momentum, which, maintaining its contact, slammed his stricken supercar straight into the factory wall.

With the impact resonating in his ears, it took a moment for his senses to return; his eyes struggling to make out the hazy movement outside in the smoke.

"What the fuck's happening?" Rushy shouted, struggling to release his seatbelt.

Paying no attention to his mate, Mickey jammed his thumb down on the starter button.

Nothing. The car was dead; he was stranded!

Survival instincts kicking back in, he threw off his seatbelt, and turned to grab the handle…only to see Razor's hefty frame hurdling the Cadillac's bonnet. With its bumper wedged against Mickey's door, the meathead was on top of him in a flash, his fist pulled back to deliver its first blow.

Helpless, Mickey dived down just as the punch burst his window. Showered in glass, he didn't have chance to see the open hand that followed.

Powerful fingers clamped round his throat, lifting him clean out of his seat. Releasing a strangled scream, he brought his hands up to Razor's wrist, but it was futile; the meathead merely reached in with his other hand, hauled him clear of the wreckage, and slammed him onto the concrete below.

Winded, struggling to gather his thoughts, he just lay there, waiting for whatever came next.

Razor beckoned him to get up with one hand; the other ready in a fist should he be foolish enough to do so.

Car doors opened. Heavy footsteps headed in his direction; the Range Rover's full beam grotesquely lighting up the advancing mob.

Taking one step forward, J.T. cleared his throat and spat in Mickey's face.

"Get his phone!" he ordered.

Instantly, Razor dropped to his knees and frisked his victim. Mobile in hand, he stood up and handed it to his boss. With a sneer, J.T. removed the sim and placed it on his tongue. Chewing slowly, he dropped the mobile to the concrete and crushed it underfoot.

"That'll confuse your friends," he grinned, spitting the sim's remains in Mickey's face.

Turning to the crowd, he continued to mock. "We are gathered here today...to deal with the grass within our midst. Fortunately, we've got all the time in the world, as he's conveniently sent his police friends to the other side of the city. Even as we speak, they'll be scratching their heads wondering why you lot haven't turned up for the iPads! What a shame they won't be coming to your rescue tonight Mickey, 'cos tonight you're all on your own. You've cost me a fucking fortune...and now you're gonna pay!"

58

While the OSU rushed to get changed, the CATS team sped onto the streets. Assisted by the scrambled chopper, they trawled every darkened back street, explored every dingy corner.

With his sergeant committed searching The Power Firm's homes, Gladstone was out leading from the front; controlling operations from his unmarked car. Again and again, his units called in with negative updates. He needed a positive lead; time was leaking away, and in the end his frustration gave way.

"Victor One to control, where's my update on the victim's phone? Surely our comms team have tracked it by now!"

"I'm afraid they're struggling to locate it sir; they believe it's been compromised," the control room replied. "They're trying cell site analysis, but it's gonna take some time, and it still won't locate the target precisely."

Exasperated, Gladstone stared angrily at his handset. His worst fears had been confirmed. 'Compromised' meant one thing and one thing only: Mickey's phone had been destroyed – he was completely at J.T.'s mercy.

"Victor One, that's received," Gladstone huffed. "And what about air support, have *they* got anything for us?"

"Negative sir," the air observer replied above the rotor noise. "It's a quiet night out there. Rest assured, if there *were* three cars together on the move, we'd spot them. The only thing we've picked up so far is a Tracker signal, but that'll have to wait until later."

Gladstone shook his head and continued along the side street, his eyes searching for clues; something, anything of interest. Suddenly, he stopped the car, his finger straight back onto transmit.

"Victor One to control. That Tracker signal; have you checked out what it relates to?"

"Negative Victor One. Your job has had primacy. Would you like us to contact Tracker?"

"Yes, as a matter of urgency please. Update me the moment you get a reply."

Parked up, the Inspector remained motionless. It was a long shot, but could it be the break they were after?

Two minutes later, his loudspeakers gave him the answer.

"The signal relates to a black Range Rover Sport, stolen in the last forty-eight hours from a residential address in Solihull."

Before the controller had even finished her transmission, Gladstone was on his mobile to Draycott.

"Ross, it's the gaffer. I know Mickey's driving a DB9, but did he say what the others were in?"

"No, he was going to find out tonight. All he *did* know was that Tommy's car would be used for ramming; that he'd been told to get a 4x4 of some sort."

"Well you know how I feel about coincidences…that Range Rover's gotta be Tommy's motor! And let's face it, right now we've got nothing else to go on. If we can find that car, I'll bet we can find Mickey!"

Cutting the conversation short, he was straight back onto control.

"Victor One, we believe the Range Rover may well be in the raider's party. Do we know whether the Tracker's got GPS or is it the basic system?"

"Sorry Victor-One," the controller replied. "It's radiowave only; we'll get them to boost the signal."

'Dammit' Gladstone cursed under his breath; GPS could've pinpointed the Range Rover precisely. "Okay," he transmitted. "Instruct the helicopter to start tracking immediately."

His order was unnecessary; the aircrew already a step ahead. From their elevated position, the Tracker's radio waves were like a homing beacon.

"MPAS-One to all ground units," the navigator's voice broadcast. "Be advised, we still have the signal…it's pointing to the south of the city."

Turning their motors as one, the CATS team hit the gas; the race against time had begun.

***

Mickey had no way out. Surrounded by heavies, in the middle of nowhere, he lay on the ground awaiting their next move. He knew his situation was helpless; the cops would be stranded miles away still wondering if he'd betrayed them.

"So you thought you could trick me, you pathetic little shit," J.T. seethed as he walked around Mickey's prostrate body. "You even had the balls to come into my home and bullshit me straight to my face! Nobody, but nobody, crosses *me* and gets away with it. Well now it's Judgement Time, and I'm the fucking Judge!"

Mickey kept quiet, not daring to provoke him any further.

"What's the matter; too scared to talk? I'm not surprised after all the talking you've been doing. Only…you've been talking to the wrong people haven't you? Or do you still have the cheek to deny it?"

What was the point in lying now, Mickey thought as J.T's verbal onslaught continued. However he'd managed it, it was clear J.T. had discovered the truth. And why should he deny it anyway? This was the man who'd threatened his girlfriend and scorned his best friend's death.

The anger started to build inside. He may well be going to die here, but why give J.T. the satisfaction of seeing him scared?

"You don't deny it then!" J.T. snarled. "You're actually admitting that you grassed on your mates! Well come on then, tell us how much the coppers are paying you – was it really worth your while?"

Continuing to pace round his prey, J.T.'s glare narrowed. The others looked on in silence.

"And to think you tried to put the finger on Tommy!"

"You fucking wanker!" Tommy reacted, stepping forward and booting Mickey in the chest.

Razor's thick arm shot out, yanking Tommy back before he could do any more.

"Yes Tommy, I didn't think you'd be too pleased with that," J.T. grinned. "Now, how would you like to do your friend some real damage?"

"I'd love to; he's no fucking friend of mine!"

"I thought as much," J.T. nodded. "If you look in my boot, you'll find something to help…soften him up a little."

"It'll be a pleasure!" Tommy replied, striding off to the Beemer.

While Razor ushered the group back, Mickey rose to his feet. Keeping his back to the building line, he furtively looked around. The crowd were spread out in front of him; there was no possible way to escape.

Or perhaps there *was* one?

Not only were the Range Rover's lights on, but the engine was running – the keys had to be in the car! Maybe, just maybe, he could break through the crowd and use it to getaway. He combed the sea of faces; was there a weakness, a sympathetic nod?

Not a chance, and to be fair, he couldn't blame them. They hadn't felt the pain of Danny's death, they couldn't see how J.T. had used them, and even if they did, they'd be too scared to turn against him.

As if second guessing his plan, Razor stepped a little closer; a broad grin etched across his leathery face. Mickey had no choice; escape was impossible, all he had left was his pride. If he was going down, he'd go down fighting, and by the looks of it…at least he'd get the chance to take his enemy out first.

Strolling towards him, Tommy was slapping a baseball bat into the palm of his hand. He walked into the makeshift ring, and goading Mickey forward, raised his weapon high in the air.

"Man, this has been a long time coming," he grinned. "I'm gonna enjoy every fucking moment!"

***

Although the helicopter's signal was strong, low clouds meant it was impossible to find the Range Rover's precise location; they needed ground units for that, and they were still over ten miles away.

Blasting through the city streets, the atmosphere inside Draycott's car was tense; the officers impatiently waiting for their car's Tracker unit to grab hold of the signal.

"MPAS-One to all units," their radio broadcast. "Signal strength is gradually increasing as we head south. Direction is constant; suggests target is stationary."

"Thank fuck for the helicopter! Our bloody kit's useless; when the hell's it gonna lock on?" Gaz complained.

"It will, we've just got to get close enough, that's all."

"Maybe so, but time's running out. And let's face it, the Tracker's our only hope; without it, we're fucked!"

"Keep the faith mate," Draycott replied, his eyes checking the empty Tracker screen for the umpteenth time. "We'll get to him in time. We have to…I promised him."

Meanwhile, their boss remained in constant touch with the controllers. Fearing Mickey was about to be murdered in cold blood, he'd summoned every firearms unit to assist. Now, with the entire police arsenal committed to him, he too drove like a man possessed, heading their rush to the south.

But with only a general area to head for, precious time was seeping away. They needed a break, and they needed it quick.

***

The first strike was exactly as Mickey expected.

From its lofty position, Tommy suddenly swung his weapon in a deadly arc towards Mickey's head. Any contact would've split his skull in two, but with a deft step back, he avoided the blow by inches. His opponent briefly off balance, Mickey shot forward, and with every ounce of strength unleashed a punch to his kidneys. The blow practically knocked Tommy off his feet, but his grip on the bat held firm. Incensed, he turned to attack once more.

Baying for blood, the crowd cheered Tommy on; but Mickey paid no attention – his focus was on Tommy, and Tommy alone. He'd always known this moment would come, and now, as he stared into the eyes of his life-long enemy, images of Danny flashed through his mind; laughing, crying…dying. Before him was the tosser who'd stolen Danny's life. If Danny was watching over him right now, he'd want him to show no mercy; and that's exactly what he intended to do.

Like wrestlers in a ring, the pair circled each other, waiting for their opponent's next move.

Tommy struck first. Lunging forward, he feinted a repeat of his previous attack. But as Mickey stepped back again, he changed direction mid-strike, and smashed the bat down on his leg.

Roaring out in pain, Mickey barely managed to duck in time, as the next swing narrowly missed taking his head off. Though his leg was on fire, there was no time to rest; Tommy was coming in for the kill, launching another scythe at his head. All Mickey could do was fling himself backwards, but in avoiding the strike, he tumbled to the ground…and Tommy was on him in an instant.

Silhouetted by the headlights, his enemy stood over him; wooden club raised high above his head.

"Prepare to die!" Tommy screamed, and slammed the weapon down.

59

"Got it!" Gaz shouted triumphantly, pressing their Tracker's lock-on button. "Just as the chopper said; it's definitely pointing south, so come on…step on it!"

"Mate, I'm giving it everything I've got!" Draycott huffed glancing down at the speedo, its needle racing past 100. "You do your job, and I'll do…"

"Alright, alright, keep your hair on, I'm just winding you up!" Gaz chuckled, grabbing the radio to update control.

"Well let's just hope the gaffer's hunch is right, 'cos right now we're putting all our faith on the Range Rover being Tommy's car."

"It will be," Gaz replied confidently. "The gaffer's never been wrong before. The real question is whether we can find it in time, 'cos if not…Mickey's dead!"

***

Though stinging from the blow to his thigh, Mickey's thirst for life and revenge remained strong. As the baseball bat crashed towards his skull, he instinctively flung himself to one side.

Tommy couldn't adjust quickly enough. Having slammed his club down with such force, it smashed into the concrete, ricocheted out of his hands, and landed a few feet away. Instantly, he lunged for the weapon…but Mickey had spotted his chance.

Grabbing hold of Tommy legs, he brought him tumbling to the ground alongside.

Mickey didn't dare let go. Having managed to even things up, now it was time to attack. Clamping Tommy's legs with one arm, he threw a punch at his groin with the other.

But Tommy was having none of it; his wild thrashing enough to free a leg, which kicked out at Mickey's face. Rolling away to avoid the strike, Mickey released his grip, and jumped back onto his feet.

Tommy was up too, rushing straight towards the baseball bat. But Mickey was just as quick; grabbing hold of him before he reached it. Toe to toe, they grappled like wrestlers, each struggling to gain an advantage…something more than brawn was needed.

Pushing against his enemy with all his strength, Mickey suddenly relaxed; the unexpected movement upsetting Tommy's balance. As he stumbled forward, Mickey dropped to one knee, and drove his shoulder upwards.

Perfectly timed, the strike practically ruptured his opponent's stomach. Doubled up in pain, straining to breathe, Tommy was briefly defenceless. Spotting his chance, Mickey slammed his elbow down.

What little breath remained in Tommy's lungs disappeared in an instant; the blow sending him crashing to the concrete. Gasping for air, he rolled onto his back, his contorted face searching skywards.

Mickey's eyes widened; it was too good an opportunity to miss...and he didn't.

Raising his foot, he drove his heel down.

Blood sprayed across the ground as Tommy's nose exploded; his screams quieting the baying crowd. But Mickey was far from finished; his mind all consumed with revenge.

His face a bloody pulp, Tommy began to rise. Struggling to get to his feet, he merely presented an even easier target. Mickey grabbed the back of Tommy's head, yanking it up just long enough for his enemy to register the grin spreading across his face. And then, plunging it downwards, drove his knee up to meet it.

The impact was shuddering, instantly laying Tommy out cold. As his limp body dropped to the floor, Mickey briefly stepped back. Blanking out the crowd around him, he knew exactly what he needed to do: if he was going to die here tonight, he might as well take Tommy with him. Slowly, he walked over to the baseball bat, and taking hold of it, turned towards his fallen rival.

But this was J.T.'s show, and it wasn't going to plan. A deft nod to Razor, and Mickey felt the meathead's vice-like grip close around his fingers. Prising the bat away, Razor muttered in Mickey's ear. "Go on son, give me an excuse; try and take it off me!"

The interruption brought Mickey back to reality. He'd been about to take a life; how the hell had it come to this? For a brief moment he'd felt power beyond anything he'd experienced before. It had been exhilarating...perhaps too exhilarating.

Pushing Mickey forward, Razor took a wild swing, the bat missing his head by a whisker. Unflinching, Mickey didn't even break step; he wasn't going to give them the pleasure of seeing him afraid. And anyway, he smiled to himself, even if they *were* about to kill him, at least he'd finally put Tommy in his place.

"Very impressive," J.T. announced, stepping towards him. "It's a pity you chose the wrong side; you could have been a real asset. Shame we'll never know now."

Remaining perfectly still as J.T. circled him, Mickey glanced up at the sky. Was that the far-off rumble of an engine?

If it was, it came and went all too quickly.

"I hear you and Danny were electronic wizards; the brains behind the thefts," J.T. continued, as Johnny passed him a small device. "So you'll have no difficulty telling me what this piece of kit does, will you?"

Mickey shrugged his shoulders. It just looked like an old mobile phone with an aerial.

"Well let me help you," J.T. smirked. "You're not the only gadget expert round here. My brother found this sneaky device on the internet and thought it might come in handy. It's called a 'sniffer'; it sniffs out tracking devices. And guess what…while you've been fucking around with Tommy, it's only gone and found a trace on the Range Rover. Now I expect your friends in blue to be doing everything in their power to rescue their little nark, and as we already know that they can't follow your phone anymore, I'm guessing they might follow the Tracker? Unfortunately for you, Johnny's got another piece of kit that'll stop them in their tracks…so to speak."

While J.T. chuckled at his own joke, Mickey's eyes turned towards the black box in Johnny's hands. It was about the size of an iPad, with various red lights flashing below the aerials on top.

"Take a look at this, 'cos it really is quite clever. The moment I press this button, every signal within fifty metres gets jammed: Trackers, mobiles…everything!" J.T. grinned activating the jammer. "So let me make things quite clear; you're on your own, in the middle of nowhere, and there's no way that anyone can find you!"

Though his situation was increasingly helpless, Mickey's head remained high; his eyes following his former leader's every move.

"But before we finish here," J.T. continued. "I think you owe us an explanation. And don't even think about lying, 'cos Razor's still unhappy with you bullshitting him last time around!"

"Fucking right," Razor replied, taking a step closer. "I'm so looking forward to this!"

Reaching inside his jacket, J.T. pulled out his black pistol. "And once Razor's had enough of you…*I'm* gonna finish you off!"

***

Hovering high above the city, the chopper continued to peer between clouds at the streets below. Beneath it, dog units, firearms and traffic swarmed south; their chase against time gaining pace.

"We must be within a few miles of it now," Gaz said excitedly, staring at his Tracker's screen. "The bars are starting to rise."

"Yep, and I think the helicopter's right; the signal's constant – it must be stationary."

Suddenly, their screen went blank.

"What the fuck?" Gaz exclaimed. "It's gone!"

"Don't worry," Draycott replied, accelerating their car forward. "It'll be back, we've probably just hit a blackspot."

But his optimism was cut short by the clamour on the radio. Everybody's signal had disappeared; now they were searching blind.

***

"Come now, Mickey," J.T. said quietly. "You're normally more than happy to talk. All we want to know, is why you grassed on the very people who've looked after you for so many years. It's not too difficult a question is it?"

Despite everything, Mickey felt surprisingly calm. He knew he was going to die here, so why shouldn't he be true to himself…he'd got nothing to lose anymore.

Yes he'd been sucked into a life of crime, and yes it had excited him; given him a way out. But when he'd finally grasped the truth, he'd attempted to make amends; he'd tried to do the right thing. No matter what happened tonight, he knew The Power Firm would never be the same again, and that was all down to him.

"Yeah I grassed on you, and I'm happy I did," Mickey spat out. "All you've ever done is use *us* to do *your* dirty work!"

As the final word left his mouth, Razor's sledgehammer punch smashed into the side of his head, knocking him clean off his feet.

"Get up, get up, you little shit!" Razor bellowed. "Don't you dare talk to the boss like that, or I'll break every bone in your fucking body!"

"Alright Razor, you can leave him be for the moment," J.T. instructed, before turning back to Mickey.

"Brave words from somebody in such a hopeless position. As I said before, you could have proved quite useful to us, mind you…you're no use as a driver are you? I mean, fancy killing your best mate! He trusted you Mickey, and *you* let him down!" he goaded, poking a finger in Mickey's chest. "I guess we should have sussed you out sooner; if you didn't give a shit about Danny, why would you give a shit about us?"

"You know damn well why Danny died," Mickey bit back. "Jonas watched the footage; I'm sure he's told you the truth. As everybody here knows: Tommy jumped the red, *he* killed Danny – *you're* just full of shit!"

Razor glanced at his boss, his clenched fist ready for action again. J.T. raised a finger, pausing the violent response.

"Of course, I nearly forgot. Your police friends buttered you up nicely didn't they; holding your hand, telling you you weren't to blame. Well where are they now? Look around you Mickey, do you see them rushing to help?" he smiled, looking up at the sky. "No, they couldn't give a shit. You were just a pathetic little pawn in their game. Don't you see; they just used you to get to me! Only problem is Mickey, I'm always one step ahead of you and your new friends!"

His empty words only served to swell Mickey's rage. Staring his despised leader in the eye, he longed to launch an attack, to gouge those eyes from their sockets…but it was futile. Not only would Razor take him down the moment he moved, but the pistol in J.T.'s hand had slowly moved higher. Now it was trained squarely on his head.

"So, any words of apology for your old friends? Surely they deserve something? I mean, they trusted you with their lives, and you betrayed them!"

For a moment, Mickey paused. He owed so much to Deano and the original posse; they'd guided him through the ranks, treated him as their own, been there for him when he lost Danny. Of course he regretted deceiving them, but there was no way he could expect them to understand; they only knew one code, and he'd broken it. Still, he had nothing to lose; they deserved to know the truth.

"You're right, I hate you, and your fucking Power Firm. And I couldn't give a shit about Tommy and his mates either. But," he said turning to the posse. "Whether you believe it or not, I've always tried to keep you out of trouble. You boys meant everything to Danny, and you *still* mean everything to me. After Danny's death, everything became clearer; we're just puppets being used by that wanker to line his own pockets. All he cares about is money; he doesn't give a shit about us!"

Razor couldn't hold back any longer. Taking a step forward, he buried his fist into Mickey's face, sending him sprawling across the floor. Deano edged forward, as if to help Mickey to his feet, but a glower from J.T. halted him in his stride.

Broken teeth mixed with the warm blood flowing into Mickey's mouth. But despite the pain, there was no way he was going to stay down. Shaking his head, he dragged himself back to his feet. With the blow still ringing in his ears, he swayed a little, raised his head, and glared deep into his enemy's eyes.

J.T. clapped slowly. "How heroic," he mocked. "Do you really think your friends are gonna be impressed by that little speech? You don't get it do you? I'm not the only one who's enjoyed the money we've made; you've all been handsomely paid, and you *love* it! Look at your designer clothes, your iPhones, the cash in your pockets to impress the birds. Do you think you'd have anything without me?" he barked, turning to the rest of the group, "Well do you?!"

Nobody dared to speak.

"Of course you wouldn't!" he scoffed, his gaze falling from one to another. "You'd all be bagheads on the street, thieving scraps to feed your addiction. Without me, you'd be nothing!"

Returning to Mickey, he thrust the pistol into the side of his head. "So can you now see what a fool you've been? Even your friends detest you; they'll all be happy to see you dead. They may have *pretended* to feel sorry for you after the crash, but underneath they were thinking exactly the same as me…they couldn't give a fuck about Danny; you'd lost them the biggest pay-out in history!"

"You're wrong!" Mickey screamed. "We're not like you at all. You only rule 'cos everybody's too scared to tell you how it is!"

Somewhere in the distance, he heard the low hum again.

J.T.'s head twitched. Looking up, he scanned the cloudy sky.

"Turn the fucking headlights off," he ordered as the noise grew steadily louder.

Mickey also searched the heavens, willing for the aircraft to break cover. Had they somehow managed to find him? Was he to get a last minute reprieve?

But the occasional breaks in the cloud revealed nothing. And as the engine's rumble drifted away, he resigned himself to his fate once more.

"Right, I've had enough of this charade," J.T. sneered. "It's Judgement Time!"

60

"Bollocks!" Gladstone yelled out in frustration. What the hell had happened to the Tracker signal? Parked up, he stared pleadingly at the blank screen...but nothing changed; the track was dead.

There was only one conclusion: J.T. must have located the Tracker.

He had to think quickly. Surely there must be another way to find Mickey, to get to J.T....before the inevitable.

Ignoring the incessant radio chatter, he weighed up his options. Randomly trawling the streets wasn't the answer; they were looking for a needle in a haystack. But if they couldn't track the cars, and they couldn't track Mickey's phone, what *was* there left to follow?

Suddenly, he grabbed his mobile and shortcut to Hanson's number.

"Steve, you still at J.T.'s pad?"

"I am boss, I'm afraid we're gonna be here some time."

"Good, that's exactly where I want you. I desperately need a phone number; J.T.'s preferably, but Johnny's will do nicely. They're bound to be using pay-as-you-go sims so they can change numbers with impunity. Search the bins Steve; find the packaging."

"We're already a step ahead boss. The OSU boys retrieved a discarded wrapping a few minutes ago. You got a pen and paper handy?"

"Fire away," Gladstone beamed. "Hopefully our boys have a scored a colossal own goal!"

Number taken, he was straight onto DC Richards, and quickly brought him up to speed.

"...so I'm asking for a little favour. I need a trace on the phone, and I need it now," he requested. "I know it can't be done legally in the time we have available, but I also know you have the contacts to do it. *I'll* take full responsibility should there be any fallout. So can you help us out; Mickey's life depends upon it!"

"Of course I can gaffer. Leave it with me, I'll get straight back to you."

With all radio transmissions recorded, Gladstone had to phone round his team with the revised plan: they'd follow the phone's GPS – it should take them direct to J.T.!

Unfortunately, DC Richards' return call ended all hopes.

"Gaffer, it's bad news I'm afraid. The phone's been in use all day alright, but it vanished off the map ten minutes ago. Last cell site was in the south of Birmingham. After that...well it's anybody's guess."

Gladstone slumped back in his seat. Was that their last hope gone? J.T. seemed to have all the answers. How on earth had he known about their operation? Only his CATS team knew all the details, and he trusted every damn one of them.

And now, not only had the Tracker disappeared, but every mobile signal had vanished into the same black hole. There was only one conclusion: J.T. was using a jammer – they were pissing in the bleeding wind.

Unless…

***

"And guess what?" J.T. grinned. "I find you guilty…not only of screwing your mates over, but more importantly, of screwing *me* over! There is only one sentence," he continued, passing the pistol to his henchman. "Razor…you know what to do."

Mickey was in no mood to plead for his life. Instead, he just stared straight ahead; his eyes fixed on J.T.'s sneer as he waited for his life to end.

"Bye, bye, you little wanker!" Razor grinned, raising the barrel to Mickey's temple.

But just as the safety catch flicked off…Deano charged forward.

Launching himself at Razor, the speed and surprise sent the pair tumbling to the ground…and the pistol sliding off across the concrete.

Mickey spotted his opportunity, the pistol no more than six feet away. Diving headfirst, he threw his battered body towards it, but with the gun coming to rest at Porter's feet, his final lunge was in vain.

Almost as his fingers grasped the cold metal, Porter simply kicked the weapon to one side. Stranded on the ground, he could only watch in despair as Chapman stooped down, and took his final hope of survival away.

Deano was in just as much trouble. Having fallen to the concrete, he desperately attempted to get up, but a powerful kick from Razor swiftly sent him crashing back down.

Despite his hefty frame, the meathead was surprisingly quick to his feet, reeling off a barrage of blows. Soon Deano's face resembled the same bloody pulp as the mate he'd just tried to save.

"Enough!" an enraged J.T. shouted. "Leave the fuckers to me! I'll finish them both off myself!"

His two bloody challengers lying practically at his feet, he snatched the pistol from Chapman's grasp, and waved his henchmen aside.

"Two bullets for you pair, leaves another four spare," he spat out, levelling his gun on the remaining posse. "So come on…who else wants their name on one?!"

***

A smile broke out on Gladstone's face. There was still *one* piece of technology he hadn't considered yet; technology even J.T. couldn't influence.

"Inspector Gladstone to control, get somebody on the ANPR system now. Feed in the Range Rover's details together with the Power Firm's cars. I want to know where they've been, where they were headed, and most importantly, where was their last activation!"

The pursuers paused and waited; their gaffer's plan simple but effective. With comprehensive ANPR coverage throughout the city, each vehicle's journey could be easily plotted. They might not be able to pinpoint their prey, but they'd quickly narrow the search area down, and with a slice of good fortune...

"Control to all units. ANPR analysis shows all vehicles converging to the same final activation – the A38 at Longbridge. The Range Rover was in convoy with an Aston Martin and a Tesla. It triggered the camera ten minutes after the Power Firm's vehicles. There have been no activations since."

Even before the transmission had finished, every unit was on the move; the hunt well and truly back on!

Gunning his own motor, Gladstone commanded as he drove. "Control, check out mapping. I need to know what's in the nearby area. My best guess is that they'll be tucked away somewhere quiet; far from prying eyes. Find me the obvious locations, and quick!"

The first crews were in Longbridge within minutes, but still they were searching blind. Every square mile would took time; something they didn't have on their side.

But then came the message they'd been waiting for.

"Mapping shows the district is densely covered in domestic housing, with an expanse of factory units to the west. The only log we've had from the area this evening was ten minutes ago; a report of noises coming from the old buildings off Furnace End. It's a routine call, we've not resourced it yet, but it just might be connected."

Connected or not connected, it was the team's only option. Charging as one towards Furnace End, they raced through the deserted backstreets. In a line, the unmarked cars rushed between ramshackle gates and onto broken concrete...

***

J.T.'s challenge was met with silence.

Deano's forlorn attempt to save Mickey was over; no-one else dared to join in.

Seeing his friend starting to come to, Mickey shuffled closer. Deano looked in a bad way; his eyes swollen almost to the point of closure. Putting an arm around him, Mickey carefully helped him sit up.

"What did you do that for?" he said, slowly shaking his head. "I didn't deserve your help; I let you down."

"No, you did the right thing," Deano grimaced. "It's what *I* should have done a long time ago, I just didn't have the balls."

"Shut the fuck up you pair of treacherous wankers!" J.T. screamed. "Get on your fucking feet, or so help me God, I'll shoot you like the fucking animals you are!"

He may have been hurt, but Mickey certainly wasn't broken; pride still pumped through his veins.

"Come on mate," he said quietly, helping Deano to his feet. "Let's go out with our heads held high."

Wavering on the point of collapse, Deano lifted his head. Shoulder to shoulder, they stood together; eyes fixed on their executioner.

Standing a matter of feet away, J.T. raised his weapon…and took aim.

61

Mickey's stare didn't waver. This was it then; it was all to end here.

But suddenly, the ground shook beneath his feet; the air filled with a thunderous noise.

Rising above the building line, a helicopter's nose soared into view; its brilliant white beam flickering over their heads.

Instinctively, Mickey grabbed Deano's jacket and dived for cover. Drowned out by the engine's roar, he wasn't even aware of the 'crack' from J.T.'s pistol. From point blank range, it had been impossible to miss.

But miss he had; the unexpected movements catching him briefly off-guard.

Barely above their heads, the chopper whipped up a dust-storm, while its 'night-sun' bathed the area in daylight. Beneath it, confusion reigned; the mob darting off in every direction.

Having hit the ground, adrenaline fuelled Mickey's dash for survival. Rolling away from J.T., he jumped to his feet and fled for cover. Dragging Deano with him, the pair dived behind the Range Rover as the next shots hit the dirt beside them.

Crouched behind the engine block, Mickey peered over the bonnet, and watched the action unfold.

"Put down your weapon!" the loudspeaker repeatedly commanded.

But J.T. was far from beaten. Pistol in outstretched hand, he aimed skywards as he sprinted towards his motor. Muzzle flash after muzzle flash sent the chopper climbing higher; briefly returning the area to darkness.

Having made it to his Beemer, J.T. dived into the driver's seat, his brother only seconds behind. No sooner had the doors shut, than the lights blazed into life, and smoke billowed up from the tyres.

But the moment it moved, headlights suddenly appeared from behind, as one after another, five plain cars screeched around the corner.

Standing a little higher, Mickey continued to watch open-mouthed. J.T. was surrounded: there was no way he'd just give up...would he?

He should have known better.

Spinning his car round, J.T. gunned it towards the only chink of light.

Spread out as they approached, the cops had left the smallest of gaps between the outermost car and the building line. Surely there wasn't enough room; J.T.'s desperate manoeuvre relied on the approaching Audi to bottle it.

And to Mickey's amazement, it appeared to do just that...suddenly swerving away from the charging Beemer. Seizing on the weakness, J.T. dived to the left and rushed into the surrendered space. Sparks burst skywards as his nearside scraped against the brickwork, but just as it appeared as though he'd squeeze through, the armoured police Audi deftly flicked back to the right.

Smashing straight into J.T.'s front corner, it slammed him into the factory wall.

No sooner had the BMW come to a shuddering halt, than the Audi's doors burst open. Clad all in black, two figures leapt out, and using their doors as cover, levelled their weapons on the steaming wreck.

Squad car after squad car rushed in, lining up to encircle their prey. While above them all, now hovering lower, the helicopter's blazing floodlight lit up the final showdown.

For a time nothing happened.

Ignoring the officer's bellowed commands, J.T. didn't move; his gaze remaining dead straight ahead.

Then slowly, his door opened, his arm extending it to its full width. Gun in hand, he waited, motionless.

As the chopper's beam focused in on his car, the commands from his side increased.

Gradually, his head turned towards them.

Pistol drawn, his face distorted with rage, he suddenly leapt from his seat and attacked.

But before he'd even taken his first step, the officers let rip; their hail of lead instantly hurling him backwards.

For a moment everyone paused.

J.T. was motionless; his buckled legs on the ground, his upper body laid out on the seat.

Further movement from inside the car sparked the firearms team back into life; their orders repeated to the figure clambering over J.T towards them. Clearly not wanting to make the same mistake as his brother, Johnny slowly climbed out, his hands outstretched and empty. Clasping them behind his head, he carefully walked out into the open. Obeying the officer's commands, he lowered himself to the floor: legs spread, hands in the small of his back.

Beginning to rise, the helicopter broadened its beam.

Cautiously, the firearms team began to edge out from behind their vehicles. Weapons trained, using a long shield as cover, two officers shuffled towards the Beemer.

Pausing at the rear door, their torches carefully searched its inside.

And then the atmosphere changed. Lowering their guns, an officer passed the 'ok' signal... followed quickly by a 'thumbs down'.

While they attended to J.T., others dealt rapidly with Johnny; frisking him, securing his hands with plastic cuffs, then hauling him away to their cars.

The main action over, Mickey's focus turned to the factory yard's entrance. Motor after motor continued to join the already substantial blockade. Nothing could get out; a metal wall had rolled in.

And now, all around him, the group who'd minutes earlier been baying for his blood, stood motionless; their arms slowly rising as weapons turned their attention on them. Only one person was daft enough to make a run for it; however Razor's charge for freedom ended abruptly as a police dog scythed him down. Thrashing one way then the other, the hound's jaws practically ripped him to pieces; the assault only ending when, with a smile on his face, the handler finally hauled it off.

To start with, Mickey didn't dare to move. Armed cops were everywhere: leading prisoners away at gunpoint, sweeping the perimeter boundary…approaching him and Deano.

All of a sudden, the masked officers dropped to a crouch; their guns trained directly on him.

He couldn't hear a word they were shouting above the chopper's rotors, but their message was crystal clear.

Slowly raising his arms in the air, he emerged from behind his cover.

Silhouetted by the chopper's intense beam, two tall figures walked past the firearms team towards him.

Mickey squinted at the light. The men were almost upon him before he recognised the one at the front.

"You can put your arms down now," Draycott said calmly.

"I'm sorry," Mickey exclaimed, his voice full of guilt. "You've got to believe me, I didn't double-cross you; *they* set me up!"

"It's not you who should be sorry Mickey, it's us," Draycott's colleague said, his body now close enough to block out the dazzling light. "I'm Inspector Gladstone, and as the person in charge of this botched operation, I can only offer you my utmost apology. We're the ones who let *you* down – I'm just relieved that we got to you in time."

"But how did you find me? Nobody knew we were here."

"All in good time Mickey. But for now, I guess you'd like to get yourself cleaned up?"

Before he'd even had chance to reply, officers rushed up from behind and grabbed at Deano's arms.

"Whoa!" Mickey called out. "He's done nothing wrong; *he's* just saved my life!"

With a quick gesture of his head, Gladstone moved his officers away.

A wry smile broke out on Draycott's face. "I take it you've also got some stories to tell!"

"You could say that," he smiled, winking at his mate.

"So did you see what happened to J.T.?" Draycott asked.

"Most of it," Mickey replied. "Is he dead?"

"Still breathing was the last I heard. Touch and go whether he'll make it."

"And even if he does, he's going nowhere quickly," Gladstone added. "While we've been chasing after you boys, other officers have been searching his home. Apparently it was a goldmine! They found Johnny's laptop beneath the floorboards, and it appears to document every transaction the Power Firm have ever made…including significant sums to a certain retired CID officer!"

Draycott raised his eyebrows; this was clearly news to him.

"My officers are putting his door in as we speak," Gladstone continued. "Rest assured, there'll be no special treatment; there's nothing we hate more than a bent cop!"

"Anyway Mickey, our boys have sorted the jammer," Draycott smiled, handing over his mobile. "So shouldn't you be letting someone know you're okay?"

"Shit, yes!" Mickey exclaimed, taking hold of the officer's phone.

To his surprise, it was already dialling, with Lara's name displayed on the screen. Taking it to his ear, he heard her answer straightaway.

"Where's Mickey, what's happened to him?" her anxious voice called out. "You promised you'd look after him!"

Mickey paused for a moment, struggling to hold back his tears.

"Lara…it's me," he choked. "It's over; they got him. Everything's gonna be okay."

Epilogue

Sitting on his patio in the late summer sun, Harry looked out to the meadows beyond. Life was good; their little cottage lay well off the beaten track, his new job paid the bills, and his gorgeous girlfriend was approaching with a refill.

"Hey blue-eyes," Charlotte smiled. "What are you up to?"

"Just chillin' out," Harry replied, taking the cold beer from her. "It's good to be able to relax at last."

"Well you deserve it," she said draping her arms around him. "You've been through enough recently."

"And by the looks of it, it was all worthwhile," Harry smiled opening his iPad's cover. "Take a look at this; it's literally just hit the papers."

Leaning over his shoulder, she read the headline story:

'Brutal Birmingham gang leader sent down for life'

The notorious head of a criminal gang known as 'The Power Firm' has been sentenced at Birmingham Crown Court today for his leading role in conspiring to commit robberies. Eleven other gang members were sentenced to a total of 99 years for their respective parts.

Judge John Price singled out Carl Pritchard, known locally as 'J.T.', as being the 'criminal director' of a 'violent, determined and professional organisation' that wreaked havoc throughout the Midlands. Pritchard, 52, was also found guilty of attempted murder, and was duly sentenced to life in prison.

Judge Price also condemned Thomas Burns, 19, for his 'utter contempt and disregard for his victims', and sentenced him to 14 years for causing death by dangerous driving.

Three defendants were given 2 year suspended sentences after they elected to assist the prosecution case, while Frederick Jones, 55, a retired police officer, was given 8 years, after the court heard how he'd abused his position to pass on confidential information to the criminal gang.

Outside the courts, Inspector Paul Gladstone from Stechford's Crime Team said, "This investigation saw us target a prolific criminal network, who for many years believed they were above the law. From the outset, we were determined to bring the ringleaders to justice; only then could our communities be protected from harm."

"I would like to endorse the judge's commendations for our officer's hard work and dedication, and in particular, to those young men who bravely gave evidence against their previous leaders. Without them, these vicious gangsters would still be walking the streets."

"Well, well, well," Charlotte grinned. "Looks like J.T.'s received his own 'Judgement Time' at last!"

"Yep, justice well and truly served! Just a shame I didn't get chance to see Tommy's face when *he* was sentenced; now that would have been a picture!"

"So what now – are you ever gonna get back in contact with Deano?"

"I'd love to babe, I really would. But we both know the score; we've been given a new start, we've just gotta leave our old life behind. Our safety, our future…our baby's future," he smiled, rubbing her tummy. "Depends upon it. The past is the past; it's time to move on."

***

Inside his prison cell, a rap on the cell door disturbed J.T.'s slumber.

"What do you want?" he growled, as the inmate shuffled into the room.

"The order you placed," the man mumbled, taking out a small parcel. "It's arrived."

J.T. sat up and snatched it from his hands. "About fucking time too, now piss off!"

"Now, now, don't take it out on him," Johnny said, swinging his legs over the top bunk. "He's just doing his best."

"That's as maybe. But the sooner we get on with our business the better," J.T. replied unwrapping the package. "And looking at this little beauty, we're just about ready to start."

With a simple swipe, the screen lit up, and he quickly typed in a number.

"Sean, it's J.T." he began. "I need you to do me a favour…"

Printed in Great Britain
by Amazon